CHAPTER ONE

Gossip is the hot brew that warms an icy heart. Koyam and Taki could always count on the mouthwatering taste of gossip to fire them up on the bitingly cold Andean mornings. The promise of chitchat made these two elderly street vendors suck their shriveled fingers with anticipation of the succulent details coming their way. But they were no mere chattering birds: they saw themselves as honorable listeners who never passed the tattling down the grapevine without a good reason or acted maliciously on hearsay.

Gossip simply provided tasty tidbits they could mull over while they sold their homemade souvenirs to the foreign tourists wandering Cusco's frigid Plaza de Armas. For the last three years, ever since Machu Picchu was added to the list of the Seven Wonders of the World, foreigners had descended like ravenous locusts, hungry to check yet another "Third World" Eden off their bucket list of exotic vacations.

On any other morning, these old friends would have sat on the cobblestones of the plaza, adjusting their voluminous black skirts, chewing and regurgitating each savory morsel the same way their llamas leisurely grazed on the distant hills. But not today. Today, they didn't even have the stomach to ridicule the *gringo* tourists pacing erratically in the Plaza de Armas, jittery after drinking too many cups of brewed, coca leaf tea, shouting into their cell phones. The word they'd overheard outside the Internet café on this frosty January morning was bitter and poisonous, poker-hot. It singed Koyam's heart, and inflamed her with a searing rage.

"Rodrigo! Did the *gringa* just say—Rodrigo?" she hissed, strangling the corners of her old alpaca shawl.

"Indeed, she did," said Taki. "But the youngest *gringa* said Rod. Perhaps they are speaking about a different man."

"If it is Rodrigo, they are not talking about a human being— they're talking about a monstrosity—"

"Calm down, Koyam, you always overreact. Let's get a little closer to the *gringas* and listen to what they're saying."

"We can get as close as flies in quinoa stew, but we're still not going to understand all the *gringa* chatter," Koyam retorted.

"We understand a lot more than they think we do." A mischievous grin lit up Taki's wrinkled bronze face. "How do you think we haggle and pester them into buying our souvenirs?"

Koyam didn't answer. She stared across the plaza towards the twin bell towers of the cathedral, silently invoking the sacred mountain beyond: Huanacauri. She didn't dare utter the name Rodrigo, not even as she begged her ancestors to curse this beast for eternity. She thought he had left Cusco for good, but if he was back, Koyam would be forced to retaliate.

Her lips were clamped, her mouth tight as the stone walls her Inca ancestors built in their sacred city. All these centuries later, it was impossible to wedge even a credit card between those stones. She and Taki loved to watch the tourists try, laughing whenever they broke their funny money; it was their very own street-clown show. Koyam didn't care if the credit cards were ruined. She and Taki only dealt in cash.

But today Koyam wasn't laughing. She sealed her lips so her prayers could not be observed by anyone else in the plaza. Her great-grandchildren often scolded her for openly talking about the ancient ways: the old beliefs in *huacas*, the sacred places and objects so revered by their ancestors. They forbade her to mention the supernatural being who feasted on sacrifices on top of Anahuarqui Mountain. They admonished her as if she were the village idiot, and not their seventy-year-old matriarch who still helped support the family. She felt sorry for them. Not only had they lost respect, they were forgetting the ancient ways. It would be their loss not to have Anahuarqui on their side.

Koyam tried to remind them of the words of Manco Capac, their emperor from centuries ago: "Do not forget us, your ancestors. Adore and cherish what we hold dear. The deities, the sun and moon, speak to us. Don't forget your ancestors who are all around you, watching everything that you do. Honor them. Respect them or they will—"

She never got to finish the rest of Manco's speech, made hundreds of years ago at nearby Ollantaytambo. Once her great-grandchildren had accomplished the purpose of their visit—to lecture Koyam, as usual—they fled to their next appointment. They all wanted to be perceived as young and modern professionals, working diligently in the tourist-related industries that had blossomed in Cusco in the last decade.

Every once in a while Koyam's sweet-talking great-granddaughters stopped by the plaza, saying they just wanted to chat with her and Taki before meeting up with a tour group outside the cathedral. They liked to remind Koyam that she should be happy they were living in such an advanced and technologically superior era. Taki knew what they really wanted: to shame their great-grandmother into silence, to stifle what they saw as her antiquated mumbo-jumbo about mummies and sacrifice and the afterlife. They didn't want her to feed tourists any pseudo-mystical gruel like the bogus shamans who set up shop in the shadowy outskirts of the plaza, offering the tourists a temporary high, and lots of nonsensical talk about the cosmos and harmony.

Those imposters—and their promises of an Inca paradise —seemed to attract lost souls from the four corners of the universe. Taki felt sorry for such down-and-outers, their pasty pale faces sagging with internal agony. They gazed at her as if they had just encountered their promised Mother Earth, their personal Pachamama. Taki, always compassionate, would bless them in Quechua, just as she did her own great-grandchildren.

"How can it hurt? Don't they deserve a drop of compassion?" she would ask when Koyam frowned at her.

Koyam didn't want these losers hanging around, siphoning more and more energy from Taki's goodwill, like their incessant hits from their druggie pipes. A Quechua blessing realigned the energy force of nature; it balanced one's relationship with all life forms, and was meant to augur abundant beginnings and appropriate endings—in the same way that planting potatoes in September and freeze-drying them on July nights made natural sense. Koyam believed Taki's blessings should be reserved for those who respected the spirits of the mountains and the life force in rocks, lakes and jagged peaks. Not these gaunt foreigners with less life force than a firefly. Koyam shooed them away with a swift slap of her hands; in the same manner she got rid of filthy cockroaches.

Koyam finished her silent supplication, pulling her multi-colored shawl tight around her stout shoulders.

"These types of *gringas*," Taki was saying, "the ones who are no longer university students, but who still travel in groups—they all have one thing in common: they complain non-stop! They gripe about this and they grumble about that. Let's get closer to them, so we can hear whether they're whining about Rodrigo."

Taki began gathering up the souvenirs she sold, placing a bundle of woven friendship bracelets with vibrant patterns on top of the alpaca hand puppets and the larger textile handbags. She tucked the handbags at the bottom of her bundle, and decided she wouldn't bring them out again today. Their intricate geometric patterns and vibrant colors represented the woven stories her ancestors had passed down to her, and the symbolism of each design weighed heavy in her heart. How could she explain to all these persnickety women tourists that the red zigzag of the bracelet weave represented the labyrinth at the Qenqo Temple, where the dead were embalmed and blood sacrifices performed in the holy chambers? All this would do is to send the nosier ones in search of the temple's ruins. Taki would rather not reveal the secrets of its carved tunnels and sacrifices to anyone.

Sometimes Taki just pretended not to understand the tourists' loud and slow-paced questions. "Caan yoouu tell me about the motif in this bright blue bag? Is this a real cocaaa baaag? Do yoouu still chew coca leaves? Caan I seee your teeeth? How much for the cocaaa baaag with the long red fringe? No, no, no, that's tooo muuch."

They always thought everything was too much. Money seemed to be the measure by which they judged everything. Taki could hear them as they walked around the plaza. "I booked this vacation online and used my points to upgrade my flight. Oh, and I also got a 30% discount on the hotel. I charged it all to my credit card, so I'll have to work extra-long hours to pay it off. So far, this vacation isn't worth all the money I spent, how about you?"

Taki wasn't up to haggling today. She had to save her energy to deal with Koyam's torrential storm of anger. Taki knew, without a shadow of a doubt, that the *gringas* were talking about the odious Rodrigo.

She lugged her bundles deep into the colonial arcade surrounding the plaza. Thankfully, there weren't that many tourists about today, so she didn't have to worry about the police shooing her away. Anyway, Taki knew how to charm her way around these young cops—she'd known most of them since they were babies—and some of the police seemed almost proud of the elderly vendors, in awe of their defiant pride. Taki and Koyam always dressed with care in their traditional voluminous black skirts and rainbow-colored shawls, their decorated red hats worn at a jaunty angle. Whenever they encountered a bossy police officer, they pointed to the large rainbow flag waving in the plaza. Just as the rainbow's colors represented the Inca Empire, Taki and Koyam were living relics who belonged in the plaza. End of conversation.

The door of the Internet café was open, as usual, and Taki peered in. The four *gringas* were still there. She plopped down on the ground, spreading out her bundles, and Koyam joined her. They rearranged their souvenirs, trying to hear what the four American women were saying.

At first all they heard was the clicking of the keyboards. Koyam sighed with impatience.

"Let them finish their online words," Taki murmured. "Every day they have to chitchat with all their friends back in the United States, bragging about their travels. Once their friends log off, they'll start their loud talking again."

"Online? Log off? How do you know these things?"

"This is the way my great-grandchildren talk. You have to learn these things. Here, try this: If you agree with someone, instead of giving them a pat on the back or a nod of the head, you have to punch your fist to their fist. Come on, try it!" Taki held up her fist, laughing at the sight of Koyam's horrified expression.

"The only thing I want to do with my fist," said Koyam, "is to put a jagged rock in it and clobber Rodrigo."

Taki sighed and shook her head.

"Throw the bitterness out of your heart," she urged Koyam. "You always think the worst of people. You have to learn to take things in stride and—"

"I haven't done it in sixty-eight years!" interrupted Koyam. "Why should I start now?"

"What do you mean, sixty-eight? We're both seventy. Don't tell me you're going senile."

"Shh!" hissed Koyam. Inside, Taki realized, the clatter of typing had stopped. "The *gringas* are talking again. What are they saying?"

CHAPTER TWO

It took Taki a couple of minutes to make sense of the raging river of English words. Koyam sat poker-faced, letting the words wash over her.

"They bark louder than yellow-tailed woolly monkeys in heat," Koyam said. "What are they complaining about now?"

The voice that rattled their ears the most belonged to a pretty, small blonde, whose hair color did indeed look like the yellow underside of an Andean woolly monkey tail. The other young women still sat at their computers, but this one restlessly paced to and fro around the small café, just like the woolly monkey leaps from one tree limb to the next. Every eye was on her—and Taki could see that she loved it.

"I'm so over this trip and it hasn't even started," she was squawking. "I mean, how can the tour guide not show up to meet and greet us? So rude! Before leaving Newps I emailed him and texted him, I even Skyped him. He was totally chill, and he spoke perfect English—he's half-American, from Boston or something. And by the way ladies, he's totally hot. *Smoking* hot. Like that South American polo player in all the magazine ads: tall, dark and handsome. I mean, not that I'm here to hook up with anyone. I mean, this is a girls' trip, right?"

"Wrong—so very wrong on so many levels!" one of the other women snapped, frowning at Yellow Tail. "This is an eco-tour for adventurous professional women physically fit enough to meet the challenges of a five-day hike."

The blonde strutted up to her.

"Listen up, girlfriend," she said. "No one is more fit than me, OK? Wait a minute—is it 'more fit than me' or 'more fit than I'? Whatever. I'm super fit, and I challenge you to keep up with me on the Incan trail. O.K. Hilary?"

Taki strained to see what was happening, half-leaning into the open door. She smiled at the manager sweetly, yet with a glint of defiance in her eyes. The locals preferred that the street vendors accost the tourists in the plaza and not in their establishments. But Taki's weather-beaten face was a harbinger of good and evil and the manager ignored her presence. The woman named Hilary cleared her throat and stood up, towering over the little blonde.

"Let me delineate the facts for you, Tiffany," she said. She wore her brown hair in a no-nonsense short hairstyle. "A—the proper words are 'than I' and 'Inca trail.' Really, I thought it was only Ivy League alums on this trip. B—Each one of us had to guarantee that we were in top-notch physical condition, so you are *not* the only one in shape here. And C—A major objective of this trip is to abandon our online dating addiction by harnessing the energy of the mountain *apu*—"

"Apoo? Apoo this, Hilary." Tiffany pointed to the ceiling with her middle finger. Even Koyam, who couldn't understand half of what the *gringas* were saying, knew what that gesture meant. "I'm not addicted to online dating, bitch—I just want to hike this effin' Incan trail. So get off my nuts. Gawd, your attitude and this frickin' altitude suck balls. I need a skinny latté—now."

She stomped towards the door, almost trampling Taki on her way out.

Hilary stood hands-on-hips, staring down the other two women in their group.

"Thanks so much for interjecting your thoughts on this matter," she said to them. "Have you got anything to say now about what we should do with the fiasco-at-hand? Gabriela? Mercy?"

Taki recognized the one named Gabriela: she'd sold her a hand-woven bag yesterday. She was a beautiful woman, with very white teeth. Her hair was inky black with corkscrew curls, and yesterday in the plaza she kept smoothing it with one hand, wrinkling her nose at the wind.

"I guess Tiffany's gesture says it all," the dark-haired young woman said. "We are royally screwed if Rodrigo doesn't show up. We can't walk the Inca trail without a guide. What do you think, Mercy?"

Koyam growled at the mention of Rodrigo, but Taki elbowed her and said, "Shhh—wait."

The fourth woman, who was tall and slim, her skin a creamy alabaster, adjusted her sunglasses on her long and elegant nose. Taki had no idea why she was wearing big dark glasses on such an overcast day.

"If this Rodrigo guy doesn't show up by tomorrow morning," she said, "we could email him demanding a refund and threatening legal action when we get home. Rodrigo insisted we pay in advance. The whole thing could be a scam."

At every mention of Rodrigo's name, Koyam flinched—again.

"Or we could hire another local guide," Mercy continued.

"But that might be dicey," Hilary said. "There are only so many hiking passes for the Inca Trail. The rangers, or whatever they're called, may say there are none left for this week."

"True," said Mercy. "And anyway, I'm not sure that everyone can afford to pay again for yet another all-inclusive package. I know Sandra is on a really tight budget."

"I hope she's feeling better," Gabriela said. "She's really finding it hard to adjust to this altitude. We should go back to the hotel to check on her."

"There's one other option," Mercy told them, drumming her fingers on the table. "We could all part ways here in Cusco. Each of us will go her own way and do whatever she wants."

Gabriela looked aghast at this suggestion.

"Mercy, we came on this trip together! I'll go along with whatever you can figure out for us, okay?" She stood up, pushing her chair back, and walked to the door. "Gosh, I can't believe I misjudged Rodrigo."

This time when Rodrigo's name was mentioned, Koyam elbowed Taki so dramatically it caught Gabriela's attention. Gabriela stared quizzically down at Koyam, but before she had the chance to ask any questions, quick-witted Koyam flung an armload of friendship bracelets on the ground.

"Missus, you buy," she said, with her biggest grin. "Very pretty. Very cheap. You buy."

"No, thank you." Gabriela took a step back and looked uncomfortable. "They're very pretty, but … I already bought my bag from you, remember?" Taki kept her head down, hiding her smile. Obviously, all street vendors looked the same to the tourists…and vice-versa.

Koyam pretended not to understand. With one hand she gathered up the bracelets; with the other she rubbed her neck, moaning in fake pain.

"You nice happy lady," she told Gabriela. "You buy three—
I make you a good price."

She moaned again for good measure.

"Come on, Gabby—let's go," Hilary said. The other young
women were at the door now, looking past Taki and Koyam
towards the windy plaza.

"We can shop later," Hilary said, her tone impatient. "Right
now we have to find that idiot Tiff, wake Sandra up—"

"Could we have a drink first?" pleaded Gabriela. "I want to
go to that cute place on the corner."

"OK. A drink, and then we sort out this Rodrigo problem."

Feeling the stab of the beast's name once again, Koyam
dropped her head. She scooped up the unwanted bracelets
and stuffed them back in her bundle. She and Taki huddled
together, as though they were sheltering from a storm, and
watched the *gringas* walk away.

"So the beast swindled them," Koyam muttered to Taki:
that much she'd understood. "He said he would come but he
hasn't. Let's just hope that monster never dares to show his face
here again."

To the proprietor's irritation, the three young American women
picked a table far from the large front windows, and they didn't
seem particularly appreciative when he brought over a free
round of Pisco Sours. This was the drink he always gave away:
they were sweet enough for the women tourists to drink, plus he
could make Pisco Sours with the cheapest ingredients. Once in
a while, this seemingly magnanimous gesture had the added
benefit of a bit of heavy petting with the inebriated *gringas*.

He knew just when to invite them upstairs to see the intricately carved balcony reserved for this lecherous purpose.

This trio of women barely stopped talking long enough to thank him, and he walked away, tapping the damp tray and shaking his head.

"Just what we need," said Hilary. "Another creepy waiter in our lives. Right, Gab? Look at the way he's staring at us. Yuk! By the way, I've been meaning to tell you, I love your online dating blog. I thought I was the only who met jerk after jerk online, until I started following your blog. Which, by the way, is exquisitely mordant satire."

Gabby smiled ruefully. "Thanks. Yes, I'm the lucky one who's met every hellish guy."

"So all the stories are really true?" Hilary asked, wincing when she took a sip of her Pisco Sour.

Gabby nodded. "All of them. I have the worst first dates ever. Like the obese guy who took one look at me and said, 'I thought you said you were in shape!' And then there was the bald psycho who kept on texting and threatening me for months after our botched coffee meeting. He kept saying I'd misled him when I told him that I graduated from Brown and not Harvard. He was in his 40s and he was still wearing this tattered twenty-year-old crimson sweatshirt with a disgusting stained letter H. Ugh! Let's toast to never subjecting ourselves to online dating again."

"Cheers!" Hilary clinked her glass against Gabby's.

"*Salud*," said Mercy.

"*Salud*," said Gabby, and Hilary looked perplexed.

"So, how come you two don't speak English with an accent?" Hilary asked. "You're Hispanic—I mean, Latinas, right? Your last names are real tongue twisters. You know, all my Latina friends at Harvard spoke English with an accent, and it was charming."

Mercy took a big gulp of the sugary drink to stop herself from snapping Hilary's head off. She'd already heard enough from Hilary to know the kind of pseudo-liberal viper she was dealing with. Maybe she could manipulate the inane Tiffany to set this bitch straight. Mercy liked to change her attack tactics, strategizing a plan of action while she worked out at the gym. Attacks by proxy satisfied her immensely. She could manipulate one fool and defeat another in one fell swoop. There were plenty of ways to cut Hilary down to size.

"That's probably because your friends were from Puerto Rico or other points in Latin America," Gabby was patiently explaining. "Mercedes and I are third-generation Californians. We speak English like every other American."

This made Mercy even more irritated. She was mad at Gabby for meekly justifying her heritage, and mad at Hilary for not having learned a damn thing at Harvard. Mercy, on the other hand, had learned that facing a tough competitor always made her a better athlete. She knew how to decimate the online bullshitters who posted things like "Tall white athlete wants to meet woman with the same qualities." They met her, all right, and they liked her—a lot. Until she challenged them to a game of tennis in 104-degree heat in Indian Wells, a long-distance bike ride on a rainy day, or an afternoon of sailing on the choppy waters off Dana Point, followed by a post-workout night of continuous humping.

She savored tightening her powerful muscular legs around her dates' exhausted heads as they tried to satisfy her with their dried tongues. When the Chads and Dougs and Keiths were wasted and couldn't satisfy her sexual urges, when they made excuses for their drooping appendage and self-disappointment, Mercy told them she would have to change her online dating profile: "Sorry, Bill or Kevin or Brent, but your tall whiteness is not satisfying me at all. I'll have to go back to my roots and only date macho Latinos." Mercy always relished the split second when she could see them trying to reconcile her height, gray-blue eyes, and fair skin with her comment about her "roots." That was her instant of winning a gold medal, her record-break-ing moment in revenge Olympics. These sons-of-bitches—or their daddies and grand-daddies—had screwed over her father and grandfathers for being "too Mexican" in their own California, a state that had been part of Mexico and home to her family for over 120 years. They had gotten in the way of her father's progress, always blocking his bids for small construction projects. They stuck out their big, greedy white hands and yanked his beating heart out.

When Mercy was admitted to Harvard, her tough dad cried like a child. He sold his house and worked several jobs to pay for all her private coaches and for her tuition, room and board, plus expenses. His daughter was not going to wipe tables at Elliot House, or pass up on trips to New York City or to Europe during spring break. She would have money to shop on Newbury Street and to eat at the quirky restaurants in Cambridge. She was his princess and he would treat her like a princess, even if it killed him. He didn't live long enough to see her walk up and receive her diploma.

When her dad died, Mercy didn't think her heart would ever be whole again. Her friends might call her Mercy, but she was really Mercedes del Rosario Hidalgo Fuentes, and this self—her true self—craved to avenge the demise of her defeated father. She responded to every tall white athlete on the online dating sites, and they scurried to meet Mercy Hidal, J.D. Mercy humbled every single one of them, made them feel not quite man enough, and squashed them to the ground like *cucarachas.*

"Earth calling Mercedes!" Gabby was tapping her on the shoulder. "Would you mind landing back in Cusco?"

"Sorry, I spaced out. It must be the altitude and these awful drinks. So, are we still trashing the a-holes we met online?"

Hilary chuckled. "Just one more story—it's my *pièce de résistance*. I'd been corresponding with this guy who sounded great. He was exactly my age, thirty-nine. He'd married his college sweetheart but they'd been divorced for eight years and they had no kids. He was this evolved engineer, and we had great conversations about environmental politics and the Green movement. So far, so good, right?"

Mercy tried to smile, but this guy sounded beyond boring. Almost as boring as Hilary.

"He wasn't a great looker, but hey, I'm not a beauty like you two. So we go camping to Yosemite, because naturally we both love the outdoors and wild life. We hadn't had sex at that point, so I was expecting a wild time in nature, right? You know what happens? This freak brings out two furry animal costumes. A fox for me and a bear for him."

Gabby burst out laughing, and Mercy couldn't help joining in.

"Well, how was the sex?" she asked.

"What sex?" Hilary wasn't laughing. "I freaked out. And then he pulled out all sorts of huge molded-plastic penises. Animal penises! When he showed me Moby's Dick—that was the final straw."

Gabby was choking on her Pisco Sour. Mercy thumped her on the back.

"So what did you *do*?" Gabby said.

"I pulled out my pepper spray and threatened to use it on him," Hilary said. "He retreated like a bunny rabbit."

"Please, you have to let me use this story on my blog," pleaded Gabby.

"Maybe. But wait, here's the kicker. Even after that fiasco, the next day I went back to the same site and started searching all over again for the perfect Mr. Tree-hugger. It's an addiction. I can't help myself. Obviously, I've come to the Andes to get cured. Haven't we all?"

"It's OK." Gabby reached out to take Hilary's hand, but Hilary blushed and pulled away.

"I don't want to sound pathetic," she said defensively. "I have a major position in a Big Five consulting firm. I have an Ivy League education."

"We all do," Mercy said. Women like Hilary drove her crazy. "Even Tiffany, apparently."

"It's just that I'm open to the whole notion of health tourism," Hilary went on, as though Mercy hadn't spoken.

Gabby looked puzzled. "Health tourism? You mean going to spas?"

"Some people call it mystic tourism," Hilary explained. "What I mean is, I'm receptive to the spirituality of ancient cultures. I hope to have a séance with a shaman who—"

"I think you have your New Age hocus-pocus all mixed-up," Mercy interrupted. She drained her Pisco Sour and wagged a hand at the proprietor to order another round. "Didn't you take any anthropology classes as a freshman? They don't have séances here. Andean ritual specialists are called *misayoq* and what they generally perform is a *pago* or *despacho*. These are offerings by a *misayoq* to the mountain gods. Since you don't believe in mountain spirits, it's not going to cure you of anything."

"Not even online dating," Gabby chimed in, with a sympathetic grin at Hilary.

"Online dating isn't a sickness," Mercy went on. "Actually, I see it more as an athletic competition, where the fittest win."

Gabby smiled adoringly. "Isn't Mercy's mind just amazing?"

"I don't know what you mean by, 'the fittest win.' Win what?" Hilary was frowning, clutching her sweating glass. "I guess I made some wrong assumptions about this tour group. I thought we all signed up for this trek as a way to overcome our incessant online search for our perfect match. I'm not ashamed to admit that I'm addicted to online dating. I want this hike on the mystical Inca trail to open my eyes and my heart. I want to be integrated with nature, without ego. All this talk about being the fittest, and being a winner; I don't get it."

The proprietor arrived with a second round of drinks, but Mercy couldn't listen to Hilary and her nonsense for another second. She slapped some money down on the table and stood up.

"You guys keep drinking," she said. "I'm going to go find our mystical tour guide."

Mercy stalked out before Hilary had the chance to say another word.

"Don't mind Mercy," Gabby told her. "She has the mind of a fierce warrior. It's always eat or be eaten with her. How else could she have climbed to the top of the legal world? But anyway, I agree with you. I really should give up on the online dating scene."

"Scene?" Hilary snorted. "Isn't a 'scene' a place where exciting and innovative activities take place? Surely you don't regard you and your pathetic computer screen as part of a sizzling happening scene, do you? If that's the case, you need a therapist and not a *misayoq*."

Gabby picked up her second drink, wishing she'd walked out when Mercy did.

"Better yet," Hilary continued, "stick to your satirical blog. Keep it bitter and expose online dating for the ridiculous sham that it is."

"Sure," Gabby mumbled.

"You know, we really should have discussed our main objectives for this trip. I came thinking that through the travails of the hike and our proximity to spiritual beings, I might have a transcendental experience. One through which I might unleash the tether I have to online dating. But apparently Tiffany and Mercy are here for some kind of athletic event in which they out-run and out-last all the competition. As for Sandra— or how is it she pronounces it? Zahndrah?—well, she's just way too old to be with us. And you, little Gabby, do you know why you're here?"

Gabby gulped her drink to avoid answering the question. Hilary didn't seem that interested, anyway. She was already standing up, counting money out of the zipped bag she wore around her waist.

"This high altitude is really getting me down," Hilary said. "I'm going back to the hotel. Coming?"

"I've got a few … things to do. See you back there!"

In truth, Gabriela only had one thing to do. As soon as Hilary was out of sight, she was planning to hightail it back to the Internet café. She really, really needed to check her email. Just before she'd left her condo in L.A. to fly to Peru, a new guy had contacted her. A guy who seemed like a definite possibility, and not a creep at all. And he was interested in her, he said— *only* her.

"On any other morning these old friends would have
sat on the cobblestones of the plaza."

"Hiram Bingham—he wasn't the first outsider
to find Machu Picchu."

CHAPTER THREE

oyam watched the women leave the restaurant, and let out a loud belch. She couldn't digest all the bellyaching she had just overheard. All the sordid details about the women's sexual activities, with the talk about furry penises and crazy men who wear the same filthy shirt for twenty years, and the man who wanted the fox to eat peppers while he pleasured himself with a plastic penis! All these parasitic details churned in Koyam's intestines.

"These women are disgusting," she muttered to Taki. "Maybe they'll infect Rodrigo with their deadly diseases—if he ever shows up. Did you hear the giant woman complain because the man wanted her to have sex with a bear while he watched? They come from a decayed world, no doubt about it. We better keep an eye on our llamas. Who knows what they would do with them!"

Taki had to stifle a laugh, because she didn't want to offend Koyam.

"You heard it all wrong," she said softly, patting her friend's arm. "But you're right—they're all mixed up. They're very confused and sad because they have not found love—for others, for themselves, for Pachamama."

Koyam jiggled her flabby abdomen as though she were trying to shake out the parasitic information she'd just heard.

"You know," she said, her face brightening, "maybe these mixed-up *gringas* meant to talk about our guardian animal spirits, our *ararihua*. The man brought the giant woman a fox skin for her to wear, didn't he? When our ancestors used to have the processions against hail and lightning, they would wear the fox head and skin, and they would yell and strike the fox, blaming him for bringing too much rain."

"Stop, thief!" said Taki, remembering the story. "Wasn't that what they'd shout?"

Koyam nodded. "So when the giant said the man was shouting at her fox skin, he was shouting at her fox of bad luck. I'm sure that's what they meant. They probably saw a drawing of Guamán Poma de Ayala in their books and got all confused seeing all the rain we're having."

Taki shook her head. She didn't think the *gringas* were talking about that, but at least Koyam seemed to be calming down.

"Poor things," said Koyam, burping again. "They have too much time on their hands. By now they should be grand-mothers. Didn't the giant say she was thirty-nine years old?"

"She did. She looks much older than that blond doll, the one who left the café so angry."

"I think someone made her suck on balls," said Koyam. "I wonder what kind of balls they were. Who would be so cruel to such a pretty flower?"

Taki caught Koyam's eye, and they both burst with laughter.

"Balls must mean male eggs," said Taki, nudging her friend. "Well, that's not all that bad—if I recall correctly!"

Koyam elbowed her and pretended to frown, but their laughter grew louder and more raucous, echoing through the half-empty restaurant.

A small, slight foreign woman appeared out of nowhere, suddenly looming over them. Koyam remembered her at once, especially that haughty look on her thin face. She was glaring at Koyam and Taki, her face rigid with contempt.

"*Tu te souviens de moi, n'est-ce pas?*" she demanded. "*Je suis revenue pour te faire souffrir. Tu me comprends?*"

At first Koyam couldn't make out exactly what the French woman was saying, but she'd spent enough time haggling with French tourists to know one thing: the woman was addressing her with the informal *tu* rather than the more respectful *vous*. This was no way to speak to an older woman. Koyam might spend her days sitting on the ground, but she wasn't going to put up with anyone looking down on her, or speaking down to her. Even the uppity-ups of Cusco addressed her formally as *usted* or *mamita*, which were terms of respect and endearment. Sometimes she didn't think that *mamita*—little mother— was respectful enough, but nobody ever spoke to her this contemptuously. The French words were making sense to Koyam now, and she didn't care for them at all. "*You remember me, don't you? I returned to make you suffer.*"

Taki was ignoring the angry French woman, more interested in the twitchy henchman lurking behind her. With his emaciated corpse and nervous movements he would not frighten anyone, but he kept one hand behind his back. This made Taki nervous. What was he clutching in that hidden hand? He looked crazy in his odd costume: balloon-leg white linen pants, a knee-length saffron robe, and a sky-blue Andean poncho.

Koyam spoke to the French woman in Spanish. Rude and informal Spanish, at that.

"Frenchy, we don't have anything to say to you or the skeleton you brought back from hell," she told her. "We were kind to you once, but never again. If you're looking for the beast, go back to hell, because that's where you'll find him. We don't want your kind here. Look, the cops are walking up this way right now. You don't want to be jailed again, do you?"

Frenchy looked confused. She turned to Taki, and started pleading.

"Please, o blessed one, o holy one! Please tell me where I can find Rodrigo! You know he took my money. I must speak with him."

"Your money?" jeered Koyam. "That's all you care about? What about the baby?"

"It was born dead. The authorities cleared me of any wrongdoing. Isn't that right, your holiness?"

Koyam's face boiled with anger. "You mean *she* was born dead, not *it*! She was an innocent baby, you assassin!"

Frenchy ignored her, still gazing at Taki. She didn't look so contemptuous now; just desperate.

"You know that I'm telling the truth," she said to Taki. "Give me your blessing. I beg of you. And tell me where I can find Rodrigo—please!"

When the skeleton man heard the word blessing, *la bendición*—possibly the only word he recognized in Spanish—he reached to Taki with one hand. She signaled for him to lower his head. He bowed low before her, and Taki cupped his brittle skull. She could feel her blessing run through his whole body, not in a vibration, but in a flat line.

"You must accept the fate you've earned," she told him in Quechua, and he said nothing.

Koyam elbowed Taki: they should have nothing to do with this faithless Frenchy. When Koyam whistled for the cops, Frenchy grabbed the skeleton's bony arm.

"*Vite*, swami," she hissed, pulling him away. As his arms flapped in the air, Taki realized why he'd kept one hand behind his back: he was clutching one of her multi-colored shawls. The old thief must have managed to steal it when he and the French woman approached. There was nothing Taki could do now but watch the rainbow shawl flapping its rainforest-butterfly wings as it made its farewell flight.

Frenchy and her scrawny henchman disappeared up the narrow side street. They'd climb the steep slope, Taki suspected, and melt away in the labyrinth of colonial streets, the logic of which defied all tourist maps. Deep in this maze, among the fetid hostels and locked hallucinogenic parlors, this crazy pair could hide for a few days—unless they made trouble. Unless their quest for Rodrigo overcame them like the swelling Urubamba River, and they found themselves drawn into the wilderness, looking for revenge no matter the torrent of consequences.

Koyam didn't like the way Taki was panting after this unpleasant confrontation. Tourists often struggled to adjust to Cusco and its elevation of over 11,000 feet, but Taki was a lifelong inhabitant. Shortness of breath did not bode well.

"Swami must mean 'corpse,' don't you think?" she said, trying to make Taki chuckle.

"No, no," Taki wheezed. "Swami is a term of respect. It refers to a Hindu teacher. Someone who is humble, but a highly enlightened and elevated soul."

"Maybe other swamis are humble, but not that decorated corpse we just saw. These 'enlightened' jokers from abroad with their mishmash costumes are ruining the plaza. Remember the redheaded *gringo* last week? The one wearing a loincloth and clanking his finger cymbals? What nonsense!" Koyam put her arm around her friend. "Calm down, Taki. You let them startle you, that's all. Let me go inside the restaurant and bring you a shot glass of Pisco—no sour. I may have to climb up to the balcony to pay the owner for it with a little tug—but I'll do anything to make you smile!"

Koyam laughed, but Taki still looked fretful.

"Did you feel any benevolent energy pouring out of the corpse?" Koyam asked her. "Hell no! But don't worry, our good old *soroche* will attack him tonight."

Taki and Koyam had seen altitude sickness fell hundreds of cocky visitors to Cusco.

"That bag of bones will never survive a good case of nausea, insomnia, and dizziness," she assured Taki. "I hope his nose bleeds like the Mandor waterfalls after the rains. He'll be sprawled at the airport for the first flight back to Lima."

Taki collapsed like a sack of Huamantanga potatoes.

"Don't wish anyone ill, Koyam," she whispered, clutching at Koyam's hand. "I feel it coming. I don't have the strength to fight it anymore. I can't stop it."

"Sh, sh, sh. If you say it, you'll believe it—or worse, I'll believe it. Shh. The Frenchy's skeleton must have sprinkled some powder on you, like that crazy man in the United States who sent poison powder in the mail. Here, let me dust you off like an old bed. Come on, raise your arms, I'll dust you all over."

Taki didn't move, but Koyam bustled around her, chattering on and trying to lift her old friend's spirits.

"These foreigners are tricky. You invite them to your house and pretty soon *you're* the one sleeping outside. Look at all the restaurants and shops. They are all operated by foreigners! Come on, let's leave the plaza. We've heard enough gossip to last us till summer. Here, let me carry your bundles. I'm younger than you, remember."

"There's nothing to joke about, Koyam. The dusk of our existence has arrived."

"Shh, you're not making any sense." Koyam steered her friend across the cold plaza, struggling to manage both bundles. "You're starting to sound like a foreign swami or swemy, whatever they're called."

"It's all my fault." Taki stopped dead, right in the middle of the plaza. "I should have never testified against Frenchy or whatever her real name is. Do you remember?"

"Assassin, she-devil, vulture."

"No, it's a pretty name, like the name of a flower. She seemed so sweet, remember?"

"I hated her from the minute she approached us in this same spot. Come on, let's move. This spot might be built over some sacred location and we're being cursed. Come on!"

Taki remained immovable. "She spoke to us with such respect the first time. She said she wanted to start a foundation to support the kids high up in the peaks, the ones who can't go to school. She seemed so sincere."

"I know," Koyam said. The wind was growing colder. All the heat seemed to have gone from the day.

"She held my hands and said that she trusted only me, that I was a 'true Inca seer.' *Ooy,* how could I have let my guard down? Why did I let her sweet breath warm my droopy old ears?

Then when she hired Rodrigo to take her on a hike up to the huts where the kids live, a place where no *gringo* ever—"

"Enough!" Koyam shouted. "I'm tired of talking about the beast and about *gringo* tourists and their stupid ways. They all make the same hikes and take the same photos at the same spots. Remember when we saw them at Machu Picchu? All of them standing on the edge of the terraces, holding up their arms in victory, as though they were Hiram Bingham 'discovering' it. What fools—all of them!"

"Hiram Bingham—he wasn't the first outsider to find Machu Picchu," Taki agreed. Still panting, she sat down hard on the ground.

"I want to tell them: people were growing crops in the central plaza of Machu Picchu when Bingham was carried up there on the backs of his porters and said he'd 'discovered' it!" Koyam scoffed. Maybe this would distract Taki, she thought. "How would he have got there if *Don* Arteaga's family hadn't built and rebuilt the bridge?"

"Remember how we used to make the trek up there all by ourselves when we were young?" Taki asked in a soft voice, smiling at the memory.

"We were as fast as pumas!" Koyam said, relieved that Taki was distracted at last. Things were so much simpler then, back when they were young girls running along the mountain paths, dressed in their brothers' pants and ponchos, feeling the crisp air on their chapped cheeks as they climbed the steep summit of Warmiwañuska, the Dead Woman's Pass.

"We ran like the wind," Taki said, her breath catching. "It was in our blood."

"Some of our ancestors were *chasquis*," Koyam reminded her, "the fastest runners and couriers in the empire."

Taki sighed. "But that was centuries ago," she said, frowning. "Now we're tormented by our past actions. Not the deeds of our ancestors, but our own mistakes. We have to make amends."

Koyam dropped to the ground, sitting close to her friend. The distraction hadn't worked. Taki leaned towards her and, eyes wide with worry, started talking in a low murmur.

"After they released Frenchy from jail and she left the country, we were relieved," she said, and Koyam nodded. "Then we heard that Rodrigo took all her money to his island paradise, and we thought we'd never see him again, either. But today, the *gringas* with their broken-heart stories keep mentioning his name over and over; like a demonic clue!"

"It might just be a matter of chance," Koyam tried to tell her, but Taki shook her head.

"Here is Frenchy back again, with the symbol of death in tow. Who is she looking for? Rodrigo. That's not chance. Listen to the mountain spirits—the torrential downpour is upon us. You know we've never had rain this strong. The universe is sending us a terrible message—it is loud and clear, and I must..." Taki couldn't finish. She crumpled onto Koyam's firm plumpness, breathing hard.

Koyam leaned into her friend, holding her tight. She too was exhausted thinking about the infernal gorge today's events had revealed once again. The two women supported one another; stacking each burden so that it wedged perfectly between them, like the Inca stone foundations the tourists so admired. Koyam racked her brain trying to figure out why today had brought the sudden confluence of spoiled *gringas*, psychotic Frenchies, and the beast who was undoubtedly up to more evil. She frowned, trying to recall the details of the sordid and tragic event with Frenchy and the baby. She'd tried so hard to forget. But now Koyam felt she had to get the story straight in her head. It might be the only way she could help avert what Taki saw as an inevitable disaster about to crash down on them.

✳

The afternoon two years ago when Frenchy first approached them, on this very same spot, shimmered in Koyam's memory as glowing in sunlight and flowers, very different from today's shrouding mist and relentless rain. It was August 30th, the feast day of St. Rose of Lima. All the children in town and the faithful churchgoers marched solemnly around the plaza and along the nearby streets. The musicians played beautifully, their hearts full of devotion for their own Peruvian Saint Rose, whose miracles cured the sick. Her statue, surrounded by wreaths of flowers and ornately carved silver candleholders and decorations, was held high by the members of the brotherhoods from surrounding churches. The sound of music and the scent of ancient incense from the priest's swinging censer rose from the plaza, wafting towards the snow-capped Andean peaks. The day's festivities were a sincere veneration of the Catholic saint and the indigenous mountain shrines, and the sun shone down on them all. It was as if Pachamama had silently orchestrated this sublime afternoon.

All eyes on the crowd seemed to be on the procession of St. Rose, but one slender woman turned her back on the statue, seeking out Taki and Koyam. Really, she was seeking out Taki, Koyam remembered, because she walked over and handed Taki a single pink rose. At first Koyam thought she was just a girl because of her slightness of body, but when the woman bent to present the rose, a forced smile on her face, the crow's feet around her eyes announced her age as well past forty years old.

"I bring you this rose, holy one," she said in heavily accented Spanish, "so that you can see that I'm genuinely interested in talking to you."

Taki silently accepted the rose, but Koyam rolled her eyes.

"We are out here all day in the sun, knucklehead," Koyam told the woman, in Quechua. "The rose will wilt in minutes."

The woman ignored Koyam, looking only at Taki.

"I am humbled to be in your presence," she murmured. "My name is Violette, and I had hoped to bring you a bouquet of violets to help you remember my name. I'm sure you, a true Inca seer, must hear thousands of pleas from pilgrims."

Koyam nudged Taki. "Is she a moron or what? Doesn't she know that we use violets as a harsh purgative? All this insincere talk makes me want to vomit. Don't listen to her, Taki."

Violette's eyes flashed with anger, but she kept talking in a cloyingly sweet voice.

"Blessed one," she bleated. "I have been told that only you can help me. While I was very ill back in France, a friend gave me a shawl that you wove and sold to her here on the plaza. She said she told you it was meant for me, and you blessed it for her. It brought me such comfort to be wrapped in the birds and flowers you wove with love. I believe that through the holy power of this mantle, I was healed."

Taki nodded again, though Koyam was sure she couldn't remember the woman who bought the shawl. They sold so many to tourists every week.

"Now I want to help the youngest of the youngest," Violette went on. "I hear that there are children living so high up in a village on the peaks, no roads reach them. These little ones do not go to school. In fact, the government census does not even know how many infants are born up there. Is this right, holy one?"

Taki nodded again.

"I would like to establish a foundation, a source of income, which would pay for the babies to have health screenings, and for the little children to have some sort of early education.

Do you think that you can arrange for me to visit this village? I would love to see the babies—I mean, I would love to help them. I approached the government officials and the NGO's, but they are too bureaucratic—it would probably take years. Can you arrange this visit for me, your faithful follower?"

Koyam could tell that Taki was warming to this woman. After all, people who have recovered from a grave illness want to help others. But when Violette claimed to be a 'faithful follower,' Taki blanched. No one followed her: she simply helped when she could, cupping her knotted hands on the person's head, and speaking the words that came from her heart. Some people said they felt a sunny vibration when receiving a blessing from Taki, but Taki didn't believe them.

"The wishes you express are very generous," Taki told Violette, reaching out to cup the strange woman's head. But Violette brushed Taki's hand away impatiently, and leaned towards her, grasping Taki by the shoulders.

"If you help me with the visit to the children," she whispered, "I will be *extremely* generous with you. Just with you."

Koyam didn't like the way Violette was grabbing Taki. She pushed her away, frowning her disapproval. "Frenchy, you can whisper all you like, but everyone can hear you. There are no secrets in the plaza. Why do you think we sit here? My grandson is an engineer and always says that I know everything that goes in Cusco because I pick the places with the best acoustics and the best view. Now get out of my sight."

Violette edged away, still staring at Taki until the crowd swallowed her up. Koyam and Taki soon forgot about her, because a much more troubling story was sweeping the plaza that day. The dashing Rodrigo Guamán O'Rourke, the forty-year-old Inca trail guide—half-Peruvian, half-American, all trouble—was back in town. His handsome face and dazzling smile had been a female magnet since he was a child—when he could not pass a store or market stall without one of the sales women tousling his hair or pinching his cheeks. These good looks turned smashing and virile as he became a young man with an insatiable sexual appetite—and the finesse to make him a coveted sexual partner. Eventually, as an adult, his enticing appearance of wavy dark hair, deep-set brown eyes, the physical proportions of a Greek god—and his intense charm, made him irresistible to women.

The next morning, the women in every store, hotel, and restaurant in Cusco arrived at work wearing their most provocative clothing. The plaza's cobblestones echoed with the stiletto heels that usually only came out during a fiesta. The old street vendors weren't happy: they knew that Rodrigo fooled around with whoever was available. The sophisticated shop girls were one thing. What worried Koyam and Taki was Rodrigo's penchant for young country girls from the fringe towns around Cusco. These girls believed his sweet nothings and ended up with nothing but a broken heart—or worse. Rumors ran rampant about him fathering children all over the highlands, and there were still worse rumors, rumors of his involvement with infant trafficking. Koyam shuddered. No one wanted to believe a thing so awful, but there were too many rumors for at least some of the stories not to be true.

Before long, they heard that Violette had become Rodrigo's only client. That the more money he demanded, the more she wired to his bank accounts in town and elsewhere. Rodrigo had cheated on the local bank's manager, so she let a few confidential client details float around town. The chatter also confirmed that Violette had been bored stiff with Machu Picchu, one of the Seven Wonders of the World, and that she demanded to be taken to higher and higher peaks—always asking about the babies up in the highlands.

Within weeks the rumors escalated that Rodrigo and Violette were expecting a child and had shacked up in a remote old hacienda. They might have been trying to hide, but it was impossible: Rodrigo's dirty laundry was exposed to all of Cusco. One of his cast aside former girlfriends, who worked at the pharmacy, denied the rumor, insisting that Violette had told her she could never have children because she'd undergone a hysterectomy in France. And anyway, Violette was forty-four years old, the girl said, and far too old to be with child.

In the following April, Taki received an urgent call to rush to a humble hut on a desolate peak. A fourteen-year-old girl had gone into labor and delivered a stillborn infant girl. The elderly grandparents begged Taki to bless the infant and her weakened young mother, which Taki did with all her soul. She attended to the debilitated young mother, swaddled the baby's lifeless body, and sat in mourning for several hours with the frail, grieving grandparents. When the light began to fade, Taki left, promising them that she would return with Koyam and their grandsons who would bring a tiny coffin for the stillborn baby.

But when Taki returned it was too late. Rodrigo had been to the house, and had been allowed to leave with the baby's body. The depressed young mother had admitted to her grandparents that Rodrigo was the baby's father. He had vowed, she said, to make things right by seeing to the baby's proper burial.

The words "proper burial" soon became the most discussed words in Cusco, where claims and allegations flew like a brutal hailstorm. At the inquest, Rodrigo put on the performance of his life. The inquest took its own crooked paths, from bringing up new speculations about Rodrigo's alleged child trafficking, to his shenanigans with young women, to the initial purpose of the inquest: the improper burial of his still-born daughter. Rodrigo stood running his hands through his thick, wavy brown hair, to make sure the female magistrate would notice how gentle and caressing those hands could be.

He had already been cleared of the infant trafficking charges, he reminded the magistrate. He spoke with utmost respect, "Your honor, I beg you to look at any search engine and input: Peruvian infant trafficking—and you will find dozens of names and instances, and not once am I even mentioned or implicated. I do have many children, but I love them and support every single one of them."

He held back his sobs as he described how distraught he had been at seeing his infant daughter dead, carrying her tiny body as he negotiated the many passes, crevices and peaks inaccessible to anyone less experienced and expert. He even cried real tears when he described how he'd laid his daughter to rest at 13,000 feet, past the boggy lake that bordered the vertiginous chasm near Runcu Raccay. He was clearly out of his mind with grief, Rodrigo insisted, but all the same, he was following the ancient traditions when he buried her. He repeated this last sentence in melodic Quechua to remind the inquest's tribunal that although he didn't quite look like them—he was too tall and too fair—he still remained one of them.

But when it was Violette's turn to speak, she claimed that Rodrigo had sacrificed the child to the mountain *huacas*. The magistrate lassoed her in and probed about allegations that Violette forced the young teen to be a surrogate mother, and also insinuated that Violette was part of a baby trafficking ring. Violette screamed at the magistrate that Rodrigo had confided his plan to become the new Tupac Shakur Amaru III, the reincarnation of the two famous rebel Inca leaders. He planned to return to the authentic Inca ways, she said, to ask for forgiveness from nature and to perform human sacrifices in the ceremonial way of the *capacocha*. An infant sacrifice, he'd told her, would bring rain after a drought, and gold would flow from the mines once more.

If Violette was telling the truth, nobody believed her. All through the inquest, she acted like a crazy woman. She screamed out her far-fetched testimony, and growled every time she mentioned Rodrigo's name. She wailed when she insisted that the infant had been buried alive, and that the infant in question was her own daughter with Rodrigo. She changed her story, saying at first that she'd conceived the child while living with Rodrigo in their hacienda, and later that Rodrigo had paid the fourteen-year-old girl to be their surrogate mother. She screeched out accusations that she had transferred all her vast inheritance to Rodrigo's bank account in some Caribbean tax haven.

"That baby came out of my own body!" Violette screamed. "She was French! Get me the ambassador, you primitive savages."

The magistrate reached her verdict and sentenced Violette to jail for lying about the facts and for continued disruption of the inquest, though she only served a few days of jail time. Someone from the French embassy got her out, and escorted her back to France. It was decreed that she would never be permitted to return to Peru.

At the end of the inquest, the gossip dripped, thick as dark oily gunk, at the mention of Tupac Shakur Amaru. The citizens of Cusco were in no hurry to welcome any sort of movement, anti-imperialist or communist, bearing that name. Back in 1572, the first Tupac Shakur, the Royal Serpent, had burned down the Inca's secret city of Vilcabamba rather than let the Spaniards confiscate its treasures. Eventually, a Basque captain and his forty men captured the Royal Serpent, and his head graced the same Plaza de Armas, the very same place where the rumors of Rodrigo's wickedness were now bouncing from arcade to arcade. Two centuries later, the second Tupac Amaru ended up with his noble head also impaled on a pole in the plaza by the Spanish rulers.

Nobody in town wanted to hear talk of any new Tupac Shakur Amaru. Proud citizens of Cusco should talk about its ancient historical and cultural importance, or its university, one of the oldest in the Americas. Violette's crazy testimony horrified the people of Cusco. The tribunal told Rodrigo "unofficially" to leave the city. They couldn't pin any specific charge because other than the deranged French woman's accusations, there was no evidence of his involvement with trafficking in the sale of infants, and during this inquest Taki had vouched that the infant he buried up in the peaks had been still born. Everyone at the plaza agreed with the decision. "Let him go to the U.S.," they said. "He has dual citizenship. We don't want him."

The inquest was so strange and theatrical that now Koyam could only remember it as an hysterical blur. But one thing she recalled precisely was Taki's sworn description of what had taken place in the desolate hut. The infant was stillborn, Taki said, at approximately seven months' gestation. She had massaged the young mother's womb to expel all the afterbirth, and tightly wrapped the girl's breasts so they would not become impacted with milk. Then, Taki said, Rodrigo sat mourning with the family for some time as they sat next to their dead great-grand-daughter. Taki's clear and calm testimony saved Rodrigo from the most severe charges of murder and sacrifice.

After the inquest, Rodrigo left Cusco, and many officials related to the case took long vacations abroad. People chewed on the scraps of this gossip for months, but eventually, all the spicy crumbs were consumed, and the idle talk turned elsewhere.

Now it was a new year, and Rodrigo and Violette were back in Cusco. Koyam scratched her head ferociously as if trying to unearth the one nugget of gold that would illuminate this situation. No one had ever climbed the summits to trace Rodrigo's steps, she thought. Taki had said that she had recurring visions of Rodrigo burying the infant along with many other items. If trackers had followed Rodrigo's trail, they might have discovered the items Taki saw in her vision: a Spondylus shell, known as a "daughter of the sea" and valued by the ancient Incas as an offering for water; and the shawl in which Rodrigo had wrapped the baby—one of Taki's shawls.

Rodrigo had also remembered to leave feathers and bags of coca leaves for the afterlife, Taki said, before he performed a classic *capacocha* sacrifice. "Every detail of the *capacocha* adheres to the rituals," Taki had told Koyam, weeping inconsolably. She knew what she'd seen in the girl's house on the mountain— a stillborn infant. But Taki always trusted her visions more than the evidence of her own eyes. That was why she wept. She experienced inconsistent visions. In some, the infant was lifeless, yet in others—she had been buried alive.

"We better keep an eye on our llamas."

"Way back in 1532, their own Inca king, Atahulapa,
had been garroted byt he Spanish."

CHAPTER FOUR

t dusk the thick Andean fog crept into Cusco's plaza. Its nebulous tentacles reached out to grasp all street corners, alleyways, and arcades. It blurred the massive entry doors of the cathedral and it erased the facial features of its citizens. People passed each other on the street, hunched over, eyes downcast, waiting for the fog to wrap itself around their necks and suffocate them.

Death by strangling was no irrational fear in Cusco. Way back in 1532, their own Inca king, Atahualpa, had been garroted by the Spanish, even though thousands of his warriors were there to protect him; even though he'd filled one room with precious gold and two rooms with silver for the insatiable Spaniards; even though he'd converted to Catholicism. And he wasn't the only one. Modern forensic archaeologists had discovered that the young victims of the sacrificial rite of *capacocha,*

from hundreds of years ago, were strangled. Their long explanations about identifying a fractured hyoid bone—if strangled by hand—or a fragmented thyroid—if strangled by a cord—only increased the communal fear of impending strangulation under the murky cover of fog.

The restaurant proprietor peeked out of the second story balcony, zipping up his pants. He waved unenthusiastically to the *gringa* tourist who had just pleasured him, and watched her wobble away across the Plaza de Armas, still woozy from too many Pisco Sours. Her thick-soled hiking boots splashed rainwater at the two elderly street vendors, but they didn't seem to notice. He squinted down at them, trying to make out what the old women were doing with their hands. Some kind of fist bump, he thought, shaking his head, and watching them march towards the steps of the cathedral.

Koyam held Taki by the elbow, helping her up the steps. "I made that silly fist-to-fist gesture for you—now you have to keep your word. We're going to say our prayers and then we're going to get a good night's sleep, and tomorrow we'll start shadowing the *gringas* to see where they lead us."

Taki said nothing.

"You're not turning into a coward, are you?" Koyam badgered. "You didn't suddenly turn from a puma into a kitten, did you?"

They entered the cathedral through its side door, but Taki did not walk forward toward the main altar. She did not walk in the direction of any of the side altars with their exquisite Spanish Colonial paintings of saints and carvings of angels. She did not kneel, like her fellow street vendors, in front of the sculpture of the dark-skinned Virgin Mary with the kind eyes. Instead, she and Koyam stopped close to the door, dropping their heads in prayer before a large egg-shaped stone set on the ground. Most tourists ignored the two-foot-tall oval stone and walked around it to view the renowned painting of the dusky Jesus. But to Taki and Koyam, and to many others in Cusco, this oval stone represented none other than the Creator.

They glanced around to make certain there were no tourists in sight, reaching into their bundles for the coca bags so they could place a few leaves on the cloth spread in front of the venerable stone.

With each step Taki and Koyam took on their long walk home, their prayers by the Creator were answered, and their resolve turned to stone, as hard as the streets' aged cobblestones. They would do whatever they had to do to stop Rodrigo and Frenchy from causing any havoc. Of this they were certain. All the legal proceedings and deportations and exchanges of money had not kept these two away. Koyam's great-grandchildren might disagree with her, but in her eyes, modern jurisprudence had failed miserably. Now Taki and Koyam would do things the ancient way.

Taki wasn't breathless and fearful anymore: she was ready to confront the oncoming mayhem. The offering she'd left at the cathedral had pleased the Creator and now she was full of conviction. Every drop of blood in her body quivered in anticipation. She knew Rodrigo, and the way he could act with logical, lethal *gringo* stealth to harness the mysteries of the Inca way, causing one huge holy mess. She had to be prepared to react to his dual self, and to deal with two more problems: Violette and her unknown companion.

In this new mood, Taki climbed the hill to her house with legs that felt young again, as lithe as they were in the old days when she and Koyam sprinted through the Sun Gate and down the rocky path to the ruins of Machu Picchu. Despite today's blanket of fog and the incessant downpour, Taki was beginning to see everything with complete clarity. First, she and Koyam had to work out how the whining *gringas* were associated with the demonic trio of Rodrigo, Frenchy, and her skeleton. This time around, the tendrils of fog would not fill their heads and cloud their thinking. This time, Taki and Koyam would remain clearheaded and use the mist and the torrent as weapons.

✳

While Taki and Koyam made their way home, Rodrigo was also padding the streets of Cusco, skulking in the mist and rain. If the rain paused, he ducked into a fog-shrouded doorway, lurking until the downpour began again. Then he stepped into the storm with the agility of an alley cat. The sheets of water obscured him, and anyway, he was dressed like any foreign tourist in dark parka with its hood pulled up, and clunky hiking boots. If anyone inspected the daypack he carried casually over one shoulder, they would find what could pass for eccentric tourist souvenirs: a woven cord, a bronze Inca *tumi* ceremonial knife, and coca leaves, all bundled in a shawl woven with the familiar zigzag pattern.

He approached the guard gate at an exclusive five-star hotel; a former convent built in the 17th century, and slipped the portly guard three one-hundred dollar bills—a huge windfall for a working man. The guard made an about-face, pretending to be checking the opposite door, and Rodrigo walked into the lobby. The two young receptionists greeted him in English, smiling.

"It's raining cats and dogs out there, isn't it?" Rodrigo responded, trying to sound as loud and American as possible. "Phew, I sure could use a hot meal."

The receptionists glanced at each other, unsure about his idiomatic expression and wondering if he was complaining about the mangy street dogs. Rodrigo nodded to them and strode towards the courtyard restaurant. Two years ago, when his face was known to all in Cusco, the baby-faced receptionists had been in high school. He was sure they wouldn't know anything about the case of the stillborn baby, let alone recognize him.

Really, no one would recognize him now. The updated Rodrigo wore his hair in a very short haircut. Gone were the days when he wore an oiled leather hat, or let his thick brown tresses get tousled by the wind, his twinkling brown eyes undressing every woman under forty. He now sported a salt-and-pepper beard and aviator glasses that masked the intensity of his gaze; yet, these two additions could not camouflage his magnetic masculine appeal. Even the young receptionists flirted with him, but his tight-lipped grin ensured that his pearly teeth and flirtatious smile would not give him away. He did not want to look the rakish romantic anymore; unfortunately, his sensual aura could not be restrained.

Tonight, Rodrigo wanted to look like just another *gringo* tourist, albeit a confident one who walked in to the most exclusive hotel in Cusco as if he were entering his usual country club back home in Boston. Before he reached the restaurant, Rodrigo made a sharp right turn and sprinted up the staircase. Any other tourist would have been winded, still adjusting to the altitude here, but Rodrigo was like a duck in water, his breathing calm and steady, completely at ease in the rarefied air of his Andean highlands.

At the terracotta-paved landing, he didn't pause to admire the valuable paintings on the wall. Instead, he slapped himself in the face hard, as a wake-up call and reminder that the bland *gringo* exterior disguised an Inca king on a mission.

For a split second, his sexual urges almost nudged him in the direction of Tiffany's room. Rodrigo had flirted with her on their Skype sessions, and he knew he could easily seduce her. But there was no time for this now. He needed to check in on Sandra, the one who claimed to come from old Yankee money, though her accent and way of speaking were a bit too common to substantiate those claims. Rodrigo was strapped for money, and he had to follow this lead first—weak as it appeared. He tapped softly on her door, but Sandra made him answer numerous questions before she cracked the door open an inch.

"You can't be too sure around heah," she told him in her usual foghorn voice. "Come on in. I'd offer you a scotch, but the minibar prices are wicked high. How about some wahtah?"

Sandra reminded Rodrigo of the cleaning ladies at his summer camp in Cape Cod: heavyset, with bulging varicose veins and a mean attitude. Whenever he was homesick for his mother and the Andean landscape, the grouchy ladies showed no compassion, ordering him to go out with the other boys or they would *whahck him hahd!* He couldn't complain to his Boston relatives. Their only interaction with him was to pay for the month-long camp and his flight from Peru, and then to quickly ship him back to his mother. In the no-nonsense Yankee perspective of his Boston relatives, it was one thing to support the love child of a wayward son, but quite another to have this child— no matter how uniquely handsome—as a constant reminder of their son's carelessness.

Assessing the shrew in front of him, Rodrigo wondered why he'd agreed to let Sandra join this hike, promoted on the Internet as a transformative hike for the high-achieving female alumnae of the Ivy League. Some woman with an anti-online dating blog had posted a link to his old hike-the-Inca-trail website—which included photos of his dazzling, magnetic old self in all sorts of poses—and challenged her readers to take this hike as a group. They could climb to a summit in Machu Picchu, she said, where an effigy of their online dating blunders would be ceremoniously buried by an Inca healer, curing them of this 21st century scourge. Rodrigo understood the irony of her blog, but apparently, no one else did. He was inundated with emails from Ivy League alumnae demanding details of the "online dating effigy hike"—so many that Rodrigo could afford to be very selective. He took his time with the final roster, but now he thought he might have made a grave error with Sandra.

"Are you on crahck, or what?" she screeched at him. "Did you heah what I just said about the train trip? Everyone's saying we are *not* scheduled to go on the fancy Hiram Bingham train to Ollantaytambo. Why not? I paid for a first-class trip and you're going to put me on that fancy train, you heah?!"

"Sandra, the—"

"I told you on the phone, my name is pronounced Zahndrah."

"Sure thing. Sorry. It's a gorgeous name for a gorgeous lady." He leaned against the door frame, wondering if she would invited him in.

"Yeah, yeah, yeah, tell it to the other sad-sacks. You can chahm them, but not me. They have their Hahvad degrees and can't land a man. What a joke! I was married for yeahs, and have a daughter who graduated from Hahvad. Nearly killed me to put her through a fancy school, but she left me anyway. Big deal, right? Am I right?"

Rodrigo flashed her his old flirty smile.

"Yes, beautiful lady," he said. "But now we have much to discuss before our early morning departure. You're going to enjoy all our companions—"

Sandra cleared her congested throat. Rodrigo tried not to wince at her uncouth behavior.

"The only thing I'm going to enjoy is my first-class seat in the Hiram Bingham train, or I ain't going. Period. And if I don't go, I'll take my money back now. All of it. Got that?"

Rodrigo tried to clasp her chapped hands as an affectionate gesture, but Sandra shook him off. His usual charm didn't seem to work with this one at all.

"I did not want to bring up monetary matters," he said in a low voice. "But do you recall what you told me in our emails and phone calls? You said that you would be wiring $25,000 to the foundation that I now have set up in your name. So tomorrow, first thing in the morning, you must go to the bank at the plaza and confirm that your bank has wired the funds. The children are waiting for you with open arms, their kind grandma. I mean," he said, when Sandra scowled, "their loving American *godmother*. I will meet you outside the bank at—"

Sandra spat out phlegm the size and color of a rotting grape. "You fell for that? I was just jerkin' your chain when I made those promises. My daughter told me about this trip— and what the hell, I wanted to join in, but you said that it was only for Ivy League alumnae."

Rodrigo's smile was frozen. "That is correct, Zahndrah, but I included you because you said you have decades worth of Harvard connections—"

"Connections? Ha! The only connection I have is the zillion years I worked in the storage room at the bookstore. I was in my cups every time you called; I wouldda told yah that I was Mr. Hahvad or Mr. Fancypants or whatevah the hell you wanted to heah. Gahd, you're a nincompoop."

Rodrigo's heart was pounding. This was a disaster.

"So you lied about your generosity," he told her, no longer smiling. "You lied about your important contacts. And you still have not paid the balance of this hike. You may do as you wish, but you will not be joining our group."

"Like hell I won't," Sandra said, her expression something between sour and triumphant. "I'll make sure that I get on that fancy train and make them chahge your sorry-ass for my round-trip ticket. Or bettah yet, I'll lock my fat ass in the train's toilet and then they'll have to take me, like it or not. And I'll tag along with *you* and your hot-to-trot women and make you all miserable. I'll turn your fancy trek into a Poison Ivy League hike."

Sandra's cackles turned into a coughing fit, as she gagged on her own phlegm.

"I know how to enjoy my vacations, believe you me, junior," she told Rodrigo. "Get outta heah!"

The door closed in Rodrigo's face, and he stood for a moment, swallowing back his venom. He would strike Sandra later, but right now he couldn't afford such a rash action. He might be caught off-guard by the next woman. If he had misread this weathered harpy so abysmally, and wasn't able to charm her into keeping her word about the $25,000 donation, then Rodrigo really had lost his edge.

Certainly, the last two years had not turned out quite as he planned them. He had mismanaged Violette's inheritance, the money she had gladly turned over to him after he had spent month after dreary month in their love-shack hacienda, his arms wrapped around her meatless body. He had pampered Violette as if she was the one carrying his child, instead of the hick indigenous girl up at the summit, because the more he treated her like a fragile expectant mother, the more Violette loosened her inheritance funds. He told her amazing stories about how they were going to live in various cities in South America. "My precious," he would whisper in her ear as he brought her slices of papaya, "you will live like my queen in Cartagena during the December holidays. Then we will fly down to the island of Florianopolis in Brazil and build castles in the sand. In the fall, we'll drink the best Malbec in Argentina while we tango and make love all night." He would rub her flat tummy with warm oil as if she were carrying the most precious fetus—when, in reality, she no longer had her womb. He would cradle Violette and say, "Our child will speak Spanish, Portuguese, Quechua, French, and English. You just wait and see. I'll invest your funds wisely and we will live a magical life with our baby."

Except he hadn't invested the money wisely. Rodrigo moved Violette's inheritance into this and that financial instrument, until all the funds were in his name only. He had to pay hush money here and there for these transactions to take place, so that they would be kept secret. After Violette was deported back to France, he had to pay a French sleaze ball to keep track of her whereabouts and mental state. He kept a sizeable amount of money liquid, but the young, curvaceous whores and the Caribbean casinos got the best of him. Then, to add insult to injury, the American economy completely tanked and his stocks shriveled to nothing. His investment banking buddies in Boston never returned his calls. The other friends, the seedy ones he hung out with while he was on the lam, pretended they didn't know Rodrigo at all after he could no longer afford to pay for parties on yachts.

Without money and without friends, Rodrigo had to rely on his mother's American relatives. Always kind but poor, they willingly shared their meager meals with him. For the last few months Rodrigo had been living with an old aunt in San Diego, close to the Mexican border. It was there that he came up with the idea of the Inca trail hike for Ivy League women. After the satirical blog linked to his old hiking website, he started reading all the previous blog posts. He ate up the vitriolic comments all these highly educated women made about the heartless men who bamboozled them at online dating sites.

There, on his old aunt's sagging sofa, Rodrigo decided that these foolish women could become his new entourage. He would use his crafty hands to mold their melting broken hearts into something he could use to his advantage. Their excursion along the Inca trail would most certainly be transformative—for him as well as for them. At first Rodrigo couldn't formulate all the specifics of what he hoped to achieve, but the term "pyramid scheme" was broadcasted daily on the TV news, thanks to Bernie Madoff. Rodrigo started to see his own pyramid, one that was about power and money, with himself at the top.

Now Rodrigo lingered on the hotel's second-floor gallery, trying to compose himself. He couldn't let that battle-ax Sandra throw him off his game. He lifted a hardwood bench so one leg of the bench was positioned directly over his left foot, then smashed it down hard. The nagging pain of a mashed toe would be a constant reminder to stay on alert during their hike.

He had to ignore the pain now, and ignore his libido, which was propelling him in the direction of Tiffany's bed. Instead, he was going to knock on the door of each woman according to their rung on his mental pyramid. Sandra he'd already spoken with, and Rodrigo knew now that she was at the bottom of the pyramid, not only because she was old and crass, but because ultimately she had no money or connections.

So his next stop was Mercy. For Mercy, he would have to adopt the persona of a mysterious explorer with a heart of gold. A man she could not take into the law firm's conference room with the partners, but one she could latch onto at a club or an athletic event, a man who would match her own primitive sexual urges. That much he'd discovered from his communications with Mercy; enough to use against her.

Mercy opened the door wearing the hotel's lush bath towel.

"Hmm," she pretended to grumble, the glint in her eye giving her away. "I thought you might show up for a hot appetizer. The others were worried you'd disappeared, but I knew you'd show up here."

Mercy opened the door wide enough to admit Rodrigo into her suite, and he walked straight to the sofa, dropping down into its soft cushions. He patted the spot next to him.

"A hot appetizer might be appropriate for your law firm receptions," he said, "but I don't think you came to this faraway summit to taste the same old flavors, did you? We could sit here and chat, and perhaps you could take copious notes on your legal pad. Or maybe you would like me to quench your thirst?"

Mercy laughed, still gripping her towel.

"Who the hell talks like that anymore? Get real. I get what I want—when I want it."

Rodrigo laughed too, but he pulled Mercy towards him so her hips were close to his face, and murmured to her in delectable Spanish.

She wanted to take charge of the heat of the moment, but it was too late. His calloused hands were rubbing her athletic body, and then, before Mercy knew what was happening, Rodrigo hoisted her onto his shoulders and started satisfying her in ways so raw and lustful that she could only let herself go. Something in his muttered endearments reminded her of her daddy—not in a carnal way, but in the way he always took care of her, his star athlete and brilliant princess. Mercy started to cry uncontrollably. She tried to stop, she wanted to be in command; she tried to grip Rodrigo's head with her muscular legs to dominate him. But he responded by spreading them wider, licking her dripping body. He lapped up her tears and made her scream with ecstasy. For the first time in her life Mercy felt as though she was home, alone with a powerful man, a take-charge man like her dad, and not her usual overgrown boy athletes. For the first time, she thought, she'd found a man who needed her as much as she needed him.

After she drooped, limp and satisfied, in his arms, Rodrigo carried Mercy to her bed and placed her gently on the white cotton cover.

"I'll be back to spend the night with you," he told her, walking into the bathroom to wash his face and hands. "If you'll have me, *amor*. I wish I could take only you on this hike, just to admire your face the second you see Machu Picchu at sunrise. I want to etch your face in my memory for eternity. Would it be terrible of me to cancel the other guests?"

Mercy loved this idea, but even in this blissful post-coital state she couldn't turn off her legal brain. Canceling all the other women might have repercussions for Rodrigo.

"We'll do another hike together in the spring," she promised. "Just you and me."

"Yes, *amor*," Rodrigo called over the splash of running water.

"Once I've arranged the non-profit organization documents for you," Mercy said, wriggling up against the pillows, and reaching for her laptop. Business was taking over her head again. "And I guess I'll have to reduce my caseload. But I can be back here in six weeks."

Rodrigo appeared in the bathroom door, his handsome face beaming and his muscular torso still flush from their love-making. Mercy expected him to join her on the bed, but he put on his shirt and told her he had a few things to take care of. He'd be back later on, he promised.

Hilary was the next name on an energized Rodrigo's pyramid list. Just as he was about to knock on her door, it opened, and Gabby emerged.

"Oh my gosh, you're here!" Gabby squealed. "Hilary and I were so worried about you."

Hilary appeared in the doorway, glancing from her friend to the stranger in the hallway. She couldn't believe it: he *really* was the man of her dreams. She had revealed so many personal dreams to Rodrigo on their emails, and now this Greek god, this Latin Lover, this tall tree-hugger was right in front of her.

"Hil? This is Rodrigo. *The* Rodrigo," gushed Gabby, and Hilary realized she was staring at him with her mouth open. The Rodrigo of the web site pictures was handsome, but not *this* handsome. He looked so suave and dashing and sexy, and his gaze was so intense. Hilary wanted to talk to him—all by herself.

"Okay, Gabby." She gave the other girl a friendly shove into the hallway. "See you in the lobby tomorrow morning, OK? Right, Rod? Can I call you Rod?"

He nodded, looking a little bemused.

"You can call me Pilpintu," she said. "I think that means butterfly in Quechua, and I want to remind myself that I'm on this hike to be transformed; to witness a metamorphosis."

Her freckled chest and neck flushed bright pink with sexual arousal, and Rodrigo struggled to repress a smile. He took a step towards the door, standing as close as he dared to both Gabby and her jittery friend.

"I just really want to be aware of the damage being done to this region's environment—and then help you make others aware," Hilary babbled. "That's what you're all about, isn't it, Rod? The environment? Oh, Gabby—don't let us keep you. I know you want to get back to your book. She's more the literary type, Rod."

"Don't be silly, Hilly!" Gabby clearly had no intention of leaving. With a flick of her glossy dark hair, she turned on her heel and walked straight back into Hilary's room. Rodrigo followed her. "Or what is it we're supposed to call you now? Butterfly? Pilpintu? Do I have the right word, *Rod*?"

Rodrigo couldn't fail to notice the way Gabby smirked when she said his name, or the way her eyes lingered on his crotch. She dropped onto the low sofa and sat staring right at it. Even caged in his tight jeans, his junk had a mind of its own and started to puff up with pride, which made Gabby chuckle.

He couldn't believe that this glamorous and giggly thirty-eight-year-old ingénue was the same woman who wrote the sharp and satirical blog. She wasn't what he was expecting at all.

He must have been staring at her for too long because Hilary grabbed his arm and practically hauled him away.

"Please come sit at the table," she said, turning her back on Gabby. "I was about to order room service. Is there anything you'd like, in particular? I'll just get Gabby some tea. She's always on some diet! She's so short, she has to eat like a bird or else look like a stuffed animal. Right, Gabby?"

Gabby gave a theatrical giggle and stretched on the sofa, like an expensive pedigree cat.

"Oh, Hil," she sighed. "Really, you'd think we were at some speed-dating event, and you're trying to eliminate your competition. Remember, Rod may be cute, but as you said earlier today, you're on this trip to cure yourself from your addictions."

"Well, I …"

"You said you're constantly on the lookout for the perfect Mr. Tree-hugger." Gabby stood up so Rodrigo could get the full effect of her slim figure. "But Rod doesn't look like a tree-hugger to me. Do you think of yourself as simply a tree-hugger, Rod? I think you seem far more nuanced and complex. Not like someone who hangs around online dating services trying to deceive women."

Hilary walked to the door and flung it open, puffing up to her full six-feet-two-inch height to intimidate Gabby. It had worked with Tiffany at the Internet café earlier that day, and she didn't want to be out-played by another woman in her own hotel room.

"Let's talk about this tomorrow," she said. "Good night, Gabby. See you in the morning!"

Rodrigo had seen enough. This little encounter had worked perfectly, as far as he was concerned: both women were desperately vying for his attention. All he had to do was approach each one separately, and then wait for them to eliminate each other.

"We are all tired," he told them. "Good night, ladies. If I think of something I need to tell you, I'll stop by your rooms a little later. Enjoy your dinner."

✳

Thankfully, his throbbing toe kept reminding him of the need to move on. Before Hilary and Gabby could fight over him another second, he was marching down the hallway en route to Tiffany's room. As he approached her door, he did a quick calculation, and realized that Mercy and Hilary would be his best targets for relinquishing their funds to him, but he had to be cautious with both—they were more alert in person than their emails had revealed.

When she opened the door, Tiffany looked pale and distracted, the lower part of her face obscured by an oxygen mask. She didn't look anything like the plastic doll Rodrigo had flirted with on Skype. He couldn't even see the luscious pink lips he had planned on putting to good use during this hike.

"Are you the doctor?" she asked, barely looking up. "This oxygen mask sucks balls. It's not helping at all."

"I'm not the doctor. I'm Rodrigo, remember? How long have you had the oxygen on?"

"How should I effin' know?" Tiffany whined. "The little brown guy told me something about turning or not turning this thingy here."

She pointed to a switch on the tank by her side. Rodrigo could see it wasn't turned on.

"Here," he said, turning the flow of oxygen on, then leading Tiffany back into her room. He pushed what looked like a volcanic eruption of clothes out of the way and settled her on the bed, arranging two pillows behind her head, and one under her knees. Tiffany pulled off the oxygen mask and tossed it aside. Mutely she held up the small piece of candy left by the housekeeper, and Rodrigo unwrapped it for her.

He sat on the edge of the bed, watching Tiffany suck on the candy like a small, greedy child. All these women were more complicated in person than he'd expected. Spending time with them made Rodrigo crave the innocence and simplicity of the teenage girls from the highlands. Their purity of thought and deed made him want to plunge into their sinless bodies, and fuse himself with their righteousness. But the American women on his hike were as trodden as their hiking boots. He would go back to his chaste teens from the highlands as soon as he milked these old cows for their money in exchange for his "rod" and romance and tree-hugging.

"I guess I'm starting to feel better," Tiffany said at last. "FYI, you look older than you did on Skype."

Rodrigo gave a strained smile, and held the mask to Tiffany's mouth.

"I'll come by to check on you later, but if you're not better, you will have to return to Lima."

Tiffany pushed the mask away.

"I know I look like shit right now," she shouted. "But I'm the same hot girl you jerked off to—or have you forgotten?"

"You are very beautiful," Rodrigo said, trying to make his voice as soothing as possible. This one was going to be feisty. "Hot, as you say. Look, I'll fly to Lima in a few days and then we can enjoy each other."

"That's negatory, *amigo*. Don't you know how hard I worked to get here, and how difficult it was to get our little party money? I made *mucho* transactions on my boss's credit cards while he was dicking around with his new mistress. I transferred that $35,000 U.S. frickin' dollar credit, just like you told me. Hopefully my boss won't say shit cuz he knows I'll tell his wifey. But anyways, I'm not leaving till I see Macho Picchu and Ipanema Beach, and dance the effin' tango in Bunos Airs, and get wasted in the Amazon. So get used to being with me, because you and I are going to be attached like effin' Simon-ese twins. Ugh! I think I'm gonna puke."

"The doctor will be here soon," Rodrigo told her. "And I'll be right back."

"Get me one of those little brown girls to rub my feet," Tiffany shouted after his disappearing back. "Then maybe I'll feel better!"

CHAPTER FIVE

he stench of the moldy mattress did not annoy Violette's swami. His olfactory system had shut down some time ago, as had his appetite, and—most assuredly—his sexual drive. His old days as an epicurean, womanizer, and scoundrel were long gone. The rodent droppings sprinkled on the floor and inside the decrepit dresser drawer of his Cusco hotel room bothered him for one reason only: he was afraid that if a rat bit him, Violette might take him to the hospital for a rabies shot. And he never wanted to set foot in another hospital again. Ever.

He was dying. This had been confirmed by all his doctors in France. With each new doctor or hospital he consulted, he lost more and more of his precious time on this earth. The joy he used to feel every time he went for a swim in the sea near his house in Nice disappeared with each ray of Mediterranean sunlight. The salt water and the glistening waves reminded him

of beginnings, and now he wanted to concentrate on endings—
his ending, in particular.

The swami had always been a decisive man who made millions from legitimate and illegitimate businesses, and he knew
how to dispense both rewards and punishment. In the early
stages of cancer, he'd met Violette at a cancer clinic and they
became friends there. They would chitchat about a number of
common topics while they hoped for their quick recoveries.
He would often see her wrapped in a colorful Andean shawl that
seemed to reflect the rainbow's spectrum on her otherwise ashen
skin. As his condition worsened, hers improved. His already pale
skin lost all its color, and his previously corpulent body now
sagged in dehydrated folds. One day, Violette walked past
him and didn't recognize him sitting in a corner waiting for his
treatment. She, on the other hand, exuded vitality, and was
draped in the ever-present Andean shawl. He managed to wave
her over.

"Lend me your magic poncho," he said, only half in jest.
"I need to get better or die."

"Oh, no," she said, pulling the wrap tighter around herself
and perching on the seat next to him. "This is my *lliclla*. That's
what the indigenous weavers call their shawls. It was blessed by
a holy woman weaver in Cusco, way up in the Andes."

"A holy woman?"

"I believe she has the power to heal. She healed my friend
who brought this *lliclla* back and gave it to me. I'd let you
borrow it, but I think I need it right now. I may look healthy, but
I'm suffering a huge financial setback. All this worrying
about becoming destitute is going to bring back my cancer, don't
you think?"

Violette neglected to divulge her additional anxieties—and
her circuitous chronology of events in Peru: her desire to buy an
infant in Peru in 2008, the business with the stillborn baby and

the surrogate mother, her deportation from Peru in 2009, and the revenge against Rodrigo festering deep within her body. She didn't feel like listening to this dying man. She wanted to get to the point right away.

"Money isn't everything, believe me, my *petite*." His voice was weak, and when he tried to sit up straight in his chair, the swami sank back. "I have more that I will ever spend, and I have already been reckless with it. I would give it all up to be healthy for one more year. Believe me, I would try to make a lifetime of amends in twelve months."

Violette snickered. "From what I've read about you, I never figured you were ... religious."

"You shouldn't believe the media. Do I look like such an ogre? Don't you believe that a man, even an evil man, deserves to die in peace?"

He started coughing uncontrollably, and she stood up. "I'll go and call for a priest to come and talk to you."

"Remember what Victor Hugo wrote," he said, clutching his chest. "Faith is a necessity to a man. Woe to him who believes in nothing."

"I didn't realize you were such an intellectual," Violette sighed. "I'll leave you to your lofty and mystical thoughts, my swami. I have other things to worry about now. I have to move out of my flat in a couple of days. Even though I've sold almost everything, I'm still going to be broke in a matter of months. All because I was seduced by the lies of a criminal."

"A criminal? We're not all so bad." He managed a grin. "Look, here's a business proposition for you. Come live with me in my villas, here in Nice and up in St. Paul de Vence, and let me wear your shawl for a few hours every day. I'll either feel better or I'll die. Either way, I'll pay you ten thousand Euros per month, and we'll see what happens."

Violette sat for a moment in silence, her mind whirling. She pictured herself alone with a loathsome old gangster in his cavernous villa—or worse, sharing the hallways with his seedy bodyguards. The thought repulsed her.

"My swami," she said, her tone sarcastic. "Your proposition sounds enticing, but I'm still fatigued from all my treatments. I'll have to pass."

The swami heaved himself up in his chair. "I'll sweeten the pot, then. What if I go with you to Cusco and you locate the weaver? She can bless me right there and then. Hell, I'll even buy all her supply of shawls. If I survive, I'll sell every last shawl to the wealthiest bastards I can find who are on their deathbeds. What a return on investment that would be!"

Violette considered the idea. With the swami's money, she could buy a passport under a new alias; the old crook would certainly have the contacts to make this happen. With a fresh identity she could start a new life and travel freely again. Above all, she could destroy her old enemy. The juices of revenge added a sweet taste to the constant medicinal metallic tang in her mouth.

"But what if you die on me, my swami. Then what do I do?"

"You are a clever *petite*, aren't you? Here, help me up." He reached for her hand, his own bones visible through paper-thin skin, and smiled at her with yellowed teeth. "Let's take care of the business end of this deal right away, shall we? You'll get your money up front, and I'll live long enough to see the holy weaver. I'm a strong-willed man and I'll *will* myself to make it to Cusco. Believe me."

Torrential rain blasted the highlands. Violette huddled with the swami for what felt like hours in their crummy hotel room, waiting for the street urchins to return with any new word on Rodrigo. The swami could afford to pay for any hotel in town, but she would not take any chance that someone might recognize her from her infant trafficking charges back in 2009. She sat fuming on the bed, drumming her feet on the ground and pounding the thin walls of the hotel room.

"That hag of a weaver must know where Rodrigo is hiding," she ranted. "I know that old woman senses these things. She has an innate GPS system." A particularly wild gesture knocked over their only lamp, but Violette decided that the room was more tolerable in semi-darkness. "I spent thousands of Euros keeping track of that louse. I wanted to fly out to the Caribbean to surprise him, but no! By the time I was ready to go there, he was hiding somewhere in California. I'm tired of him always getting away. I want to watch as they torture him slowly, just the way he tortured me."

The swami, only half-listening to her, crowed with delight. "*Oh, la, la. C'est magnifique!* This is marvelous, I must be in heaven."

Wrapped in the *lliclla*, he didn't feel any pain. He didn't know where he was. He forgot who he had once been. He felt immense comfort twirling his bag of bones round and round, wrapped in the rainbow shawl he had stolen from Taki.

"Am I still alive in Cusco?" he asked Violette.

"Yes, my swami. That old witch must have given you one hell of a blessing. Is it true that one feels an immense power surge when she cups your skull and says her magic words?"

"*Oh, la, la—oui.* Yes, indeed. It was like a lightning bolt," he exaggerated. "I didn't really understand her words, but I believe she said I would be cured in a matter of days. Something along those lines. A good crook like me can always read people very well. We have a sixth sense ourselves."

Someone started hammering on the door.

"Hey, *gringos,* we have news for you. Open up," a boy's voice shouted.

Violette reached for the door handle, but the newly energized swami got there first. He held up a hand to stop her, and with his other hand he pulled something from a concealed pocket in his saffron robe; a small, sharp *stiletto* dagger. It had been his constant companion since his teen years in Corsica. He nodded to her to open the door, and two anemic-looking urchins tumbled in. The swami grabbed the first boy and held the *stiletto* to his throat.

"*Arristeti!*" he commanded in raspy Corsican. "Stop!"

Both the urchins held up their filthy hands.

"Shit, lady," the second boy said. "I can't believe you carry your own grim reaper with you. Can we borrow him? He could help us scare some drunk *gringos* into giving us their money!"

Both boys started laughing, and the swami didn't like it at all. They weren't giving him the respect he deserved. So he drew the blade across the neck of the kid in his clutches, exerting just enough pressure to draw blood. The boy cried out in pain and surprise, and the swami felt alive again with the bloodshed of a *vendetta.* There was no better sight than your enemy's blood dripping. That's why he never wiped his blade too thoroughly. He liked to smell the residue of his enemies' blood.

The sight of the blood sent the second urchin into a panic. "We have information for you!" he squeaked, his smile gone. "Some rich *gringas* are going on a hike to Machu Picchu tomorrow. They were at the plaza all day asking for Rodrigo. He's their guide."

The swami released his captive and shoved him away.

"All the *gringas* are staying at El Convento," the other boy continued. "We tried to sneak in, but the guard kicked our asses out."

"Now you know," said the boy with the bleeding neck. "So give us the rest of our money."

Swami couldn't help seeing a bit of his young punk self in these urchins.

"Tell them to come back later tonight," he told Violette. "I want to talk business with them after they get the bleeder patched up."

After she paid the boys, and hustled them out of the room, Violette quickly changed into her foreign-hiker outfit. She needed to check in to the El Convento hotel as soon as possible, so she could follow these *gringas* until they met up with Rodrigo.

Without any light in the room, Violette had to trust the swami's judgment about the way she looked.

"*Petite*, you look better with the dark wig," he told her. "I love women with long dark hair, always have. Why don't you and I just fly over to Rio instead of staying here for your revenge drama? Just give me a few days to get my juices flowing, like the witch said I would, and I'll make you see stars. What do you say?"

"Goodbye and thanks for everything," Violette said, stuffing things into her backpack. "But I have to punish Rodrigo all by myself."

"I swear, hearing your words of vengeance is making me hard. Come on, stay! You won't regret it. Believe me."

Violette slipped out of the room without a backwards glance, but the swami didn't feel dejected or deterred. His mind raced with ideas: how to make more money with the witch; how to stretch his dark criminal hand from France all the way to this mysterious city; how to use the little street urchins to help him; how to satisfy his urges with young brunettes. He had never felt so alive.

✦

Wrapped in the rainbow shawl, the swami rolled back and forth on the squalid floor, over bugs and rodent turds, laughing hysterically. He could see nothing in the darkness but the waves rolling in front of his villa in Nice; he could feel nothing but loud, wet kisses smacked on his face by a young whore, and the Mediterranean breeze brushing his face. The room's black mold and mildew smelled like the freshly cut roses his mother used to arrange in a vase every Sunday lunchtime. Warm blood coursed through his body; and blood never lies.

"I am alive, sons of bitches," he screamed, laughing maniacally. "I am alive!"

The other criminal denizens of the hotel heard the noise he was making; they crept out of their rat holes and walked right into his room. They wanted a piece of whatever was making this fool so happy: women, money, drugs. But what they saw revolted them. A cadaver wrapped in a filthy shawl was curled up on the floor in a fetal position. He had cut open his wrists.

When one man kicked him to see if he was alive, his lips moved. He was trying to say something in a raspy voice.

"Damn you, you lying witch," he hissed, in a Corsican nobody else in the room could understand. What the old crook finally understood was that Taki had double-crossed him. She had put a curse on him—and not the blessing that had him euphoric just minutes ago. The old Mafioso knew he'd been betrayed, and he uttered his last words to Taki and everyone he had ever known, "I'll see you all in hell!"

One of the thugs grabbed the shawl and twisted it around the skeleton's neck, pulling tighter and tighter until the swami stopped breathing. Then they fumbled around for the skeleton's money and passport, and disappeared into the rainy night.

Only one thug stood petrified, his eyes wide with terror. He thought that he might be staring at an ancestral mummy; one of the infamous *mallquis* worshipped by the Incas, which the Spaniards wanted to destroy at all costs. At every festival, from the winter solstice to the summer solstice, the mummified bodies of the Inca ancestors would be carried around in elaborate ceremonial chairs of gold and feathers. These mummies were revered for their wisdom and blessings, and their descendants would rather be killed than divulge the *mallquis'* secret hiding places. Inca rebels on the run from the Spaniards would move the *mallquis* to keep them hidden. Centuries later, the promise of mummies and gold drew foreign explorers like daddy-long-legs Bingham to the heights of Machu Picchu, though Bingham didn't find either. All he could do was identify the trapezoidal wall niches where the mummies once held court. Nonetheless, he spirited away as many artifacts as he could.

Only a select few of each subsequent generation of descendants knew the whereabouts of their ancestor *mallquis*, and they would never disclose this secret. The Spaniards thought they had purged all the mummies from the Inca Empire, but rumors persisted. People still believed that the mummies wielded their power over the living here in modern Cusco.

The last thug left in the swami's hotel room was one of these believers, so the sight of this body on the floor scared him half to death. He couldn't run away like the others: he knew he had to perform some kind of act of respect. What, exactly, he wasn't sure. He'd never gone to school or listened to his biddy great-grandmother when she instructed him in the old ways. His life revolved around thievery, drugs, sex, and rock *en español*, not on putrid ancient beliefs. But he knew he had to do something, or terrible things would happen to him. In desperation, he sprinkled a pinch of cocaine on the skeletal figure, and prayed that the mummy would not seek revenge. He looked around for a bottle of booze, figuring that the *mallqui* would appreciate some *chicha*, but there was no mini bar in the room of this seedy hotel. So the thug could do nothing but nab the only things left to plunder—the bloody stiletto and a blue poncho—and bolt after his accomplices.

The fog and rain obscured their trail, so they appeared to emerge in the plaza like wraiths formed by mist. It was as if the far-reaching tendrils of fog were rewarding the thugs for garroting yet another victim, reminding everyone that the *huacas*, the sacred spirits of the peaks, were disappointed with the mess their descendants continued to make of their ancient empire. Emboldened by their escape with so much booty, the gang decided to start drinking—and raising hell in town.

But the fearful one in their group didn't feel like celebrating. He'd recognized Taki's handiwork on the woven shawl covering the body on the floor. He didn't dare tell his confederates about Taki's powers, but he knew that her rainbow shawls conveyed truths about the wearer. The color white symbolized time. The skeleton had rolled around in ecstasy until he was so smeared with feces and squashed bugs it was impossible to see the white panels of the shawl anymore. Taki had designed the shawl so that *if* the white panels were kept white, then the wearer lived a long clean life. But the old crook was as dirty on the inside as the outside. He had cut a child eager for a few coins in exchange for gossip, he had plans to organize an international infant trafficking ring, and he thought nothing of double-crossing anyone who got in his way. That was why Taki knew that he had to accept his destiny, and that he had to die a death commensurate with his stained life.

People thought that Taki only gave blessings, but in the anguished mask of death on the skeleton's face, this thug had seen the markings of an ancient curse: you must accept the fate you've earned.

"He thought he might be staring at an ancestral mummy."

CHAPTER SIX

Constant rain filled the otherwise charming Spanish courtyard of the El Convento hotel with a lake of stagnating water. It stopped the guests from taking the usual photographs of the lush courtyard garden, so picturesque with its umbrella trees and bright flowers. The dormant waters kept guests well away, as though its murky gloom might be contagious. The more adventurous ones peered into the water and saw no reflection of their own worried faces; this made them worry even more.

In this mysterious city, where every aspect of nature seems to contain an ancient symbol of life and death, no one dared ask any questions about the atrocious weather conditions—and what they foretold. The guests at El Convento tried to repress their sinking feelings, but vague, anxious questions kept on swirling around in their heads. Eventually they'd start whispering to one another.

"Do you think we could change to a less challenging hike?" asked one elderly gentleman, gripping his walking stick with white knuckles.

"How foolish of us to think we could hike these unforgiving peaks during the rainy season," murmured his wife. "Surely there must be regulations ensuring the expertise of the tour operators—don't you think?"

Outside the thick walls of the former convent, distant thunder crashed and the slate clouds overhead threatened to descend. The hotel's attempt to distract their guests from the horrendous weather with a weaving demonstration was a disaster. Every time the lightning flashed, the two young weavers stopped and made the sign of the cross, their young faces terrified. Both girls were still teenagers, and they had never experienced these tempestuous conditions.

The atrocious weather should have deterred the Ivy League hikers. But the women who gathered inside the restaurant just off the flooded courtyard chattered affably as if they were certain that their Rodrigo—the real-life man of their dreams, and not some online dating jerk—was going to transform their lives on this hike, whatever the weather.

Tiffany, not Hilary-Pilpintu-the butterfly, stood out like a flighty moth. She wore a hot pink velour jogging outfit and hopped from one breakfast buffet item to the next, commenting on each item.

"Euww! Gro-oss, I don't even want to ask what this is. I'm only eating bananas and the trail mix I brought from Newps. This stuff is fattening and euww! We don't even feed our dogs this mystery meat!"

The other women ignored her, flashing each other false smiles that hid a multitude of new secrets and dreams. Not a single one mentioned having seen Rodrigo the prior night.

Sandra, the last one to arrive to breakfast, marched in shouting. "What a nightmahre this is turning out to be!" She dragged a chair back from the table they were sharing and hurled her denim patchwork purse onto the floor; it hit Gabby's leg. "That piece of work Rodrigo bettah show up this morning. And what's this crahp about leaving our suitcases in the storage room of the hotel while we're hiking? The little bellboy told me I could only take a backpack on the train? I thought we had porters to carry our crahp? If we leave our cases here those brown Stackjacks will steal everything."

Hilary put her fork down with exaggerated care. "Zahndrah, please refrain from using derogatory terms about anyone, especially the locals."

Sandra stomped towards the buffet table, ignoring Hilary's comment.

"Who cares what she says?" Tiffany slid her plate, piled high with sliced banana carefully picked from the fruit basket, onto the table. "I don't even understand what she's saying half the time."

Sandra, plate already in hand, turned around to face the group.

"A Stackjack is a short, stocky man with a short haircut, and as for brown…well, just look around." She pointed to the dining staff and snickered, then grabbed three rolls. "I didn't have no suppaahh last night. At least this food looks good. It's included in the room chahge, am I right?"

She didn't wait for an answer from the other women, not that any of them were planning on replying. They didn't want anyone to know such a boorish person was part of their group, so they sat eating in silence, gazing down at their plates.

Gabby threw Hilary a challenging look, and Hillary gazed straight back. They were pros at hiding any perceived advantage—or disadvantage. They had perfected these competitive talents at their respective Ivy League colleges, and at their intense and demanding jobs. Both knew that they hadn't climbed to the top of the socio-economic ladder by revealing their cards too early in the game.

Gabby broke first.

"So, Hill," she asked, with exaggerated politeness, "how was the rest of your evening? Did you play solitaire or Sudoku?"

"Um ... ah," said Hilary, taking too long to answer, "I ... I had a pretty mellow evening, I guess. How about you?"

"Memorable, definitely memorable. I feel totally invigorated this morning. But you look kind of tired. Would you care for some more of this coca tea—you know, to perk you up?"

"No, thanks. I'm not tired at all. I'm totally acclimated to the altitude now." Hilary sounded defensive. "I was bewildered for a second there. You caught me off guard. But I'm alert now—ready for anything that comes my way."

"That's good." Gabby gave her most innocent smile. "We need you at the top of your game. I was starting to get worried about you. Mercy was saying that she vaguely remembers you back at Harvard, and that you were pretty introverted then. You weren't really part of any group."

Mercy kept eating. She wasn't joining in this weird, tense conversation. At least it meant that Hilary and Gabby weren't asking her any awkward questions. Hilary raised her powerful arms, as if stretching.

"You could say I was a late bloomer, I suppose. But I've always been physically fit and mentally alert." Hilary punched the air to illustrate her point. Tiffany, her mouth full of banana, looked unimpressed. "And thankfully, I've never had any self-esteem problems or eating disorders. Nothing personal, of course. I'm glad to see that you've overcome your ... issues. You're a good weight for a woman who's ... short."

Gabby's smile showed an excess of teeth. She looked like an animal about to attack.

"Oh, did you get that from my blog? I think I posted an *ironic* eating disorder entry a couple years ago." Gabby lifted a piece of bread, but changed her mind and set the roll down. She couldn't let Hilary get away with this. "You know, I have to keep the blog entertaining for all my readers. It's really starting to pay off. I'm monetizing it in some innovative and profitable ways."

"What does 'monetizing' mean?" Tiffany asked. "Is it a good thing?"

"Really good," Gabby said "Just like my size and shape. They say that good things come in small packages, and I think most men agree. They seem to prefer petite women. Right, Tiff?"

Tiffany glugged from her bottle of water. This conversation was boring, and she had other things to think about. Why hadn't Rodrigo returned to her hotel room last night to check on her one more time? All the guys in Newps were just the same. They used her and then dumped her. She was going to have to try harder to entice Rodrigo with her hot body, or she would find some other dude to party with all over South America.

There had to be other guys around somewhere. Her girlfriends back home had told her that lots of old rich guys like to hike in faraway places, and Tiffany thought Cusco counted as pretty far. Although she'd slept for most of the flight here, she thought Peru must be "like as far away as Costa Rica." She'd had an awesome time in Costa Rica last fall with that old dude. If Rod ignored her one more time, she'd bail on him and latch on to some random rich guy. Unfortunately, random rich guys were not ever as hot as Rodrigo. Some of them had wrinkles where their abs used to be.

"Gross, but whatever," she said aloud, and banged the bottle onto the table.

Sandra, back with a piled-high plate, misunderstood.

"You can say that again, sistah," she said. "I mean, what is so fancy about this whole damn mess, you tell me? Like you said, it's gross." Sandra speared a sausage and then gestured at Gabby and Hilary with her fork. "We got Mutt and Jeff ovah heah sparring with them fancy words. Then we have the legal eagle who only talks when people pay her by the hour. She's probably bringing her laptop on the hike!"

"I don't think there's WiFi up there," Tiffany pointed out. Mercy didn't even look up.

"You know," Sandra continued, dropping her fork so she could pick up a sticky pastry, "I'll take a Nor'easter any day over this weathah. Am I right? And by the way, I told Rodrigo that I *am* going on the fancy Bingham train, come hell or high watah. Damn skippy. You're not riding on the ratty train, are you, Pinkie?"

Tiffany grimaced. "Duh-uh! Do I look like I belong with goats or chickens or whatever they carry on their trains? We're going first class on the Big One, absolutely!"

Hilary had heard enough from these two bozos. "Listen up," she barked. "We all paid the same amount of money for an all-expenses-paid, customized, small group hike on the Inca trail. We all agreed to follow the guidelines of this trip. Therefore, we will *all* go on the same—"

"What?" Sandra managed to say, despite a mouthful of food. "Are you the leadah or what? Shut the f-up or get ready for a C-Town Beatdown!"

Gabby and Mercy couldn't help grinning: the thought of broken-down Sandra pouncing on Hilary's ripped body was comical.

"There will be no 'beatdowns' on this hike," Mercy said, trying not to laugh. "I haven't heard that expression in years."

"Why would you have evah heard it?" Sandra challenged Mercy. "You was all cozy in college, in the People's Republic of Cambridge. You never left the Square, did ya? What would you know about beatdowns?"

Mercy took a deep breath. "We are all going to be challenged enough by the hike," she said in an even voice. "So let's get a good start, okay? Let me refresh your memory. We had to be in shape for this—"

"Are you saying we're not fit?" Tiffany interrupted. " Cuz them's fightin' words Right, Sandra?"

"I can take care of myself, Pinkie Pipsqueak," said Sandra. "I'm going on this hike, you just watch me."

"What ev-er, but don't ask me to help you," sniffed Tiffany. "You're just *way* too old and too fat to be a part of this group. There, I said it. Deal with it."

"First things first," said Hilary in her bossiest voice. "Let's clear the air once and for all. Tiffany and Zahndrah, which colleges did you attend, exactly, and how did you receive the Ivy League alumnae invitation?"

"What damn difference does it make at this point?" Gabby asked. After last night's encounter and today's verbal joust, she now considered Hilary her primary adversary.

"Here's the difference. If Tiffany and Zahndrah lied about their Ivy League affiliation, there may be other pertinent information we don't know. Obviously, at least one of them is not in any shape for this hike—frankly, there's no way that she can make it up Dead Woman's Pass."

Tiffany was up off her chair now and hopping like a boxer before a match.

"You don't intimidate me one bit, bitch," she told Hilary. "So what if I'm not Ivy League. I went to OCC, and the only reason I didn't get a degree was cuz I had to work three jobs, okay?"

Tiffany's eyes were tearing up: she was feeling sorry for herself, getting picked on by these snobs. There was only one thing to do, and that was attack. "By the way," she said, sniffing loudly, "Rodrigo stopped by to see *me* and check on *me* last night. He sat there and massaged my feet until I felt better."

This information didn't have quite the desired effect. Tiffany had expected Hilary to look annoyed, and Gabby to start pouting, but everyone just sat there smirking, as though they each knew something she didn't.

"I feel *so* awesome now," Tiffany went on. "My trip is all paid for, and Rodrigo is super-psyched that I'm coming. Believe me, he wants me on this hike—he needs me by his side."

"Whatevah," groaned Sandra, who seemed more interested in wiping sticky residue off her face than hearing about Tiff and Rodrigo.

"Like I told you yesterday," Tiffany said. "You'll all be lean-ing on a rock crying with pain while I steam past you. I'll get to Macho Picchu before all of you effin' snobs."

"You know Tiffany," said Gabby, spotting the opportunity to eliminate a very beautiful competitor for Rod's attention. "If you're worried that our group will slow you down, you may want to hire your own hiking guide. I'd be willing to refund you the full amount—immediately. I can give you a check right now. How does that sound?"

"That's a generous offer, Gabby," said Mercy. She didn't want to believe Tiffany's story about Rodrigo. Why would he go back to see Tiffany just before he returned to Mercy's room to make love to her all night? Tiffany was obviously a liar. "I'd be willing to chip in ... in cash, so Tiffany can make her solo arrangements."

Tiffany flipped her middle finger at the women. "Chip this!" she said, and stalked out of the dining room.

Sandra picked her way through one final pastry and said nothing during the money talk, although she had plenty of choice words she wanted to get off her chest. She'd like to know how Gabby could get her hands on so much money, and why she was willing to blow it all on getting rid of Tiffany. Sandra figured that Gabby had gone to college on a full scholarship, like all the brown kids who lied on their admissions applications, and now she most likely had a fancy-schmancy, high-paying job, while Sandra had killed herself working long hours to supplement her daughter's tuition remission.

If Gabby was so loaded, there must be some way Sandra could get in on the action. How could she get this pretty brown girl to pay the balance Sandra owed Rodrigo? As Sandra licked her sticky fingers, she resolved to make this little grease ball, with her precious shiny black hair and sparkling dark eyes, pay. This, Sandra thought with a smile, could turn out to be a free vacation of a lifetime. A vacation where she could harangue Rodrigo and the women all day and night. They wouldn't be able to escape her tongue-lashings, the way her daughter and ex-husband finally did. This made Sandra so happy she decided to help herself to a third serving of the breakfast buffet.

Violette sat at a table at the far end of El Convento's restaurant, studying the clusters of tourists. Every ten minutes or so she strolled to the buffet tables, pretending to select another item, so she could eavesdrop on various conversations. She thought she had pinpointed the group of women the street urchins had mentioned, but before long a group of men joined them. Married couples were no use to her. Rodrigo's prey—and therefore hers as well—was an all-women group.

That left one all-female group in the restaurant. They were loud and boisterous, Violette thought, so that meant they were probably American. One, in a terrible hot-pink outfit, kept bouncing up and down like a child. Three of the women looked like the kind of wealthy foreign hikers who stay for a few days in Cusco using the opportunity to wear expensive parkas and matching accessories, but the other two women—one quite haggard, and the bouncy blond prostitute—didn't seem to fit with the rest of the group.

Violette checked her watch: the vans would soon be picking up the hikers to take them to the Poroy train station and the start of their hikes. She edged closer to the loud group of American women, and heard the woman in pink mention Rodrigo's name. Violette's skin prickled. This was indeed the group she was looking for.

Violette detested Americans: they were raucous, crass, and arrogant. And she particularly hated the sound and slangy words of American English, though she had learned it for her job in Nice. After the woman in pink gestured obscenely at the other women and stomped out of the restaurant, Violette followed her.

"Hello," she called after her. "I love your pink clothes. Where did you buy them?"

Tiffany smiled. "Thanks! I got them in Fashion Island. That's in Newport Beach. Where are you from?"

"Ah, I am from Paris. Yes, Paris. Have you been there?" Violette tried to smile in the American way, with a wide-open mouth, not in the usual reserved, tight-lipped French way that Americans seemed to find off-putting.

Tiffany beamed at her, relieved to find someone friendly in this dismal city.

"Oh, yeah," she told Violette. "I was there last summer with my boyfriend. We had an awesome time shopping and eating, and well, you know." Tiffany winked at Violette and lowered her voice. "And screwin' like French bunnies, if you know what I mean."

Violette tried to keep smiling, though everything about this blond woman was distasteful.

"What is your boyfriend's name?" she asked. "Did I hear you say he was named Rodrigo?"

"Oh no!" Tiffany looked stumped. "Um, I forget the guy's name from Paris. It was so last-year, you know? Rodrigo is … well, he's someone else. And he's not my boyfriend—yet. But I'll have him wrapped around my little finger in a day or so."

Tiffany giggled, and Violette wanted to slap her. She hated all these American idioms. She didn't have time to figure out what the little finger and the wrapping meant. The bell captain was announcing the van for the first group of American hikers, the ones with the men in tow. The group in question was bustling about in the lobby, looking flustered and apprehensive. The men were carrying backpacks out, while the women pointed out their suitcases to the polite bell captain, badgering him about how securely their precious belongings would be while they were away on the hike.

"So tell me," Violette said quickly, "are you meeting this Rodrigo right now? Is he here?"

Tiffany shot the French woman a suspicious look. Why was this stranger champing at the bit about Rodrigo? She had enough competition with the other snobs, and she wasn't going to add a snooty French woman to the lineup.

"I gotta pee, sorry," she said, and darted off in the direction of the restroom, leaving Violette standing alone in the lobby.

Violette didn't dare ask the hotel staff any questions; she couldn't risk someone recognizing her from the hideous dead baby incident. Besides, what would she ask? "Where can I find Rodrigo?" No, it was too risky. If she accomplished what she had planned as a punishment for Rodrigo, Violette didn't want anyone to be able to identify her later on.

So there was nothing else to do now but lurk between the lobby restroom and the dining room, and wait for the woman in pink to return. She seemed to be taking a long time. Violette felt nerves twist her stomach, and the suffocating dark wig made her scalp hot and itchy. It wasn't possible to hear the Americans in the restaurant now, not with heavy rain pelting on the roof, and thunder rumbling.

Before the pink girl emerged, the haggard older woman came waddling out of the dining room. Violette tried another one of her American smiles.

"Hi!" she said. "I think they called your van. They are ready to take you to the train station."

"Sorry, I can't understand a word you're saying," Sandra said, frowning. "You have a terrible accent. Whe-ah you from?"

Violette tried to speak more slowly and clearly. "Sorry! I am from France. I think that your van is here to pick you up to go to the Poroy station."

"You don't say—"

"Yes, I do say the truth!" Violette said. "Your van is here."

Sandra nodded. "Gotcha. I'll get the rest of my group. Are you going on the fancy train, the Hiram Bingham, or the regular one?"

"The same train as you," Violette said, her heart racing. "May I ride with you? My van is late."

"Sure, but you'll have to pay your share. That's ... er, fifty dollars US. You can just give it to me. I'm the unofficial leadah of the group."

"I can give you fifty Euros," Violette offered. "That is worth more than fifty American dollars."

She held out a bill and Sandra yanked it from her hand.

"Just remembah this," said Sandra. "I'm doing *you* the favor and not the other way around. Now tell that Stackjack van drivah not to leave without us."

Violette sat in the front seat, barely turning around when the other women piled into the van. She introduced herself as Camille, though none of them seemed very interested. She'd chosen the name on the spot, sure that these imbecile Americans would miss the literary allusion. The fictional Camille, in *Don Quixote*, was seduced and betrayed by Lothario, a legendary scoundrel, just like Rodrigo.

Nobody said much during the twenty-minute ride to the Poroy train station. They would have had to shout, anyway, over the sound of heavy rain, the hiss of the wet roads, and the squeak of the windshield wipers. At the station, Violette trailed behind them, keeping an eye out for Rodrigo. But the sinewy indigenous man waiting for them was a stranger, with a voice so soft they all had to stand in a tight circle, leaning in to hear what he was saying.

"I am Choque," he told them. "You please to wait over there."

He pointed to a man kneeling on the ground and arranging leaves on a small white cloth. "You to wait for bless," Choque continued, "then you to go on train."

He tried to step back, but both Hilary and Sandra blocked his way.

"Hold on theah, Chuck," Sandra boomed in her usual foghorn. "That's your name, am I right? Which way's the Bingham train? It's supposed to be blue and that train over theah ain't it, my man."

Choque looked confused. "You to wait for bless," he said again, "then you to go...on train."

"Where's Rodrigo?" asked Hilary and Gabby in unison.

"Rodrigo, he wait for you at camp." Choque squirmed out of the circle of howling hyenas and disappeared into the sea of wet tourists, vendors, porters, tour operators, and a gang of puny street urchins darting among the crowd.

The urchins were frantically looking for a skinny French tourist with short hair. There were too many cops around, which meant it was too hard to hop illegally onto either the Expedition or the Bingham trains. They had to find her somewhere in this crowd of doughy *gringos* milling around the platform, here for the 7:45 a.m. departure. The boys still felt the sting of the humiliating cut to their comrade, and the sharper sting of returning to the hotel late at night only to find a dead body, and no money. The tiniest of the urchins remembered that the nasty man had called the French woman Violette, so he started shouting it through the station with the same shrill voice he used to sell gum in the plaza.

It was hard to be heard over the racket of the farewell band, which had just struck up a jovial tune, and the Andean dancers entertaining the crowds. But Violette, rigid with nervous tension, heard him. She ducked down and leaned into Sandra for protection.

"Well," said Gabby, "we might as well go and get a blessing. They're not allowing anyone to board the train just yet. Who knows? Maybe the shaman's blessing will help turn all this around."

"The only one turned around is you," Hilary hissed. "The *despacho* is not a blessing, but rather an offering, and there are more than three hundred types of *despachos*. From the way the *misayoq* is starting to arrange the coca leaves, sugar, and rocks counter-clockwise, I believe this is an offering for protection. Do you see how he is only using his left hand?"

The shaman was concentrating on arranging the symbols for preventing floods and for physical survival. He fanned the incense and focused on showing reverence to the mountain spirits, then asked those spirits to help the travelers align their hearts, minds, and bodies with all beings in the universe. Everyone stood at a respectful distance, except Tiffany. She squatted next to the shaman and put her arm around him.

"Say tequila, or whatever you drink here," she said, holding her cell phone aloft and clicking several times. For one shot she stuck out her tongue and gave the horn-hand sign, like an aging rock star. "Dude, you're lucky to be in a photo with me."

Hilary grabbed Tiffany by the arm like a rag doll and hauled her away.

"Don't you have any respect or decency?" she demanded.

Tiffany glanced around at the other women. They all looked disgusted with her, but she couldn't back down. She took out her phone again, and clicked a group shot.

"I need a photo of y'all," she said. "You gotta be the winners of the most boring people contest."

Then she turned her back on them, and pretended she was texting. On Tiffany's list of diversionary tactics to be employed in awkward and embarrassing moments, this pretend-to-text ploy was her all-time favorite, just ahead of the drop-my-handbag trick where she could very effectively show her booty.

When no one seemed to be glaring at her anymore, Tiffany wandered off, strutting around the platform and smiling at the older men, until their wives noticed and pulled them away. Whatever! Tiffany couldn't find one available guy in this entire train station, and that wasn't good. She always liked to have a backup plan. Now she would be forced to rely solely on

Rodrigo for her South American party with the funds she took from her stupid boss. The trouble was, all those snobs in her group seemed to have the hots for Rodrigo as well.

Hilary had tried to apologize to the shaman, but when she stood too close he fanned the incense furiously toward her face. She understood his message: step back. He'd lost his concentration. The foreign women were gnawing at him like hungry foxes, and he couldn't believe that the band playing at the station included a trumpet player. This sound frightened him. Didn't the musicians remember that in one of their old Inca myths, Cusco was once besieged by a month-long torrential storm? The giant, who represented the swollen waters, was asked by King Pachacuti not to play the trumpet, for if he continued to play, a deluge would surely follow.

The oblivious trumpeter at the train station blew with all his might, and the shaman lost his own internal balance. Without thinking, he added white cotton to the offering. Hilary couldn't help correcting him.

"Sorry to bother you, but doesn't white cotton symbolize rain?" She wiggled her fingers in a semblance of raindrops, to the amusement of the small crowd observing the *despacho*. "We don't need any more rain. Can you please add some llama fat so we get some sunshine? Does anyone know how to say 'sun' in Quechua?"

The shaman added more and more *huayruru* seeds to ward off the alarming negative energy. His left hand, which shook with fear, placed miniature tin llamas and condor feathers in the *despacho*; anything to balance the offering. He sensed the intent of the women around him as cloudy and cruel; each one of them was off-balance in some way. Their heavy black energy frightened him; their darkness overwhelmed the white of the cloth spread on the ground, its whiteness representing the clarity of the universe. In their faces and tightly wound bodies he saw slimy envy, the wrath of a viper, the gluttony of a tapir, greed, loneliness, and a throbbing pink opening that spoke of a volcano of lust. These visions formed tangled lianas in his mind and he couldn't maneuver through the vines threatening to dig their roots through his skull. His head bowed, he implored the mountains, whose glaciers provide water, to do anything necessary to bring balance and reverence back to these women's lives.

Violette couldn't pay much attention since her scalp was itching uncontrollably. When she thought no one was looking, she inserted a pencil behind her ear and lifted the side of the dark wig while she scratched. One of the urchins noticed. There was something about this woman's pinched face that seemed familiar. He told the smallest boy in his gang to accost her.

"Call her Violette and ask her for money," he whispered. "And try to pull her hair."

The urchin bumped up against her and tried to do as he was told, but he was too small to reach her wig.

Violette flinched when the boy started jumping up at her like an over-eager dog.

"Please help me with this pesky child!" she asked Sandra. "You are a strong American woman!"

"Sure," Sandra said, and shoved the tiny tough guy across the platform. "Don't come back, you little greasah!"

This scene confirmed to everyone at the train station that this group of hikers was abominable and should be avoided at all costs. Everyone turned their backs on the group and walked away. Even the shaman wrapped his *despacho* in a colorful shawl and unceremoniously ran off. Normally, he would have shaken the colorful shawl bundle and added a blessing for each passenger. Not today. Today he fled the foreign women lugging doom.

The train personnel were allowing people to board, but Violette had not bought her ticket yet since Sandra kept insisting that they were going on the Hiram Bingham train, which had a later departure. But the other women were boarding *this* train, and Violette didn't want to be left alone. Across the platform she thought she saw the gang of urchins, and she was afraid that they would somehow get in the way of her plans to punish Rodrigo. Violette couldn't allow this to happen. She was on Rodrigo's trail, so close that she could almost smell him, and she couldn't lose that scent.

Sandra stood on the platform, shouting up to the women already in the train.

"Suit yourselves, you sad sacks, but I'm going on the fancy train. I won't be too fahr behind. I'll catch up with you, don't you worry."

Hilary, Gabby, and Mercy let out a collective sigh of relief. They even traded jubilant fist pumps.

"We'll arrive two hours before her," Hilary told the others. "Thank goodness! Sandra will be nothing but trouble on this trip. Do you want to agree now whether we should wait or *not* wait for Sandra, or do we need Tiffany's vote? Where is she, by the way? The train's about to leave."

Violette knew where Tiffany was. She'd spotted her boarding a different coach of the early train. Given the choice of following Tiffany or following Sandra, Violette decided to stick with Tiffany, however poor her company. The blond bimbo would act as her sparkly Rodrigo bait.

Tiffany was looking for a seat far from the other women, to work on her back-up plan. As soon as she saw a trio of men traveling without women, she followed them along the aisle, bouncing into the empty seat in their group of four, and launching into some shameless flirtation. Violette waited to board the train with a conductor, so she could buy a ticket directly from him. She was hoping that many tourists had cancelled because of the dismal weather, but she made certain of obtaining her ticket by slipping him a twenty-Euro tip for his trouble.

Before she looked for a seat, Violette peered out the window at the half-deserted platform. The urchins stood in a gaggle, pointing at her.

"We're following you, *gringa!*" screamed the little one. "You can't escape us!"

All the other passengers roared at the outrageous mini-gangster's braggadocio, but not Violette. She knew from personal experience that even the most weak and insignificant persons could find the strength to climb mountains and cross raging rivers, if they were driven by desperation and revenge.

CHAPTER SEVEN

rue to her threats, when Sandra boarded the Bingham train she headed straight to the bathroom. She locked the door, wedging her backpack against it, and stood listening to the courteous staff seating the other guests. She smiled smugly when she heard a conductor tell a man to go ahead and change seats if he wished.

"We have had many cancellations," the conductor said, "but we will still have a wonderful trip. Do not worry about the rain."

"Fine, we'll change seats," said a male American voice, and Sandra raised her fist in triumph. "But first we need a drink. Where's the bar?"

After the train pulled out of the station, Sandra grabbed her backpack, swung open the door, and pushed her way toward the bar car. When the conductor approached as if to ask her for her ticket, she went on the offensive.

"You theah," she said in a loud voice. "Someone is sitting in my seat, so I'm going to sit at the bah. Don't bother me again, got it?"

The conductor cleared his throat.

"Yes, madam. May I please see your ticket?"

"Don't 'madam' me! What's wrong with you? I just told you that some moron is sitting in my seat. I want a refund immediately and bring it to me back at the bah, you got it?"

The conductor studied the cantankerous worn-down foreigner, and decided that it would be much easier to leave her alone; she would drink herself into a stupor, and his three hours would pass uneventfully. He'd seen too many argumentative *gringas* on this train, and they made his working days long and miserable.

"Please enjoy the train," he told her, smiling broadly. "They are playing beautiful music back at the bar."

"Sounds like cats meowing to me. Don't bothah me again." Sandra pushed her bulky body and overstuffed backpack past the conductor, hurrying towards the safety of the bar.

By the time the Bingham train made its series of switchbacks leaving Cusco, Sandra had finished her third whiskey. She gazed out the window at a landscape blanketed by dense fog and drenching rain.

"What a nightmah, am I right?" she called out to the sprinkling of tourists in the bar. No one answered her. Sandra staggered from her bar stool to a corner table at the front of the car, where she could collapse spread-eagled, kick her backpack out of the way, and doze off. When she began snoring thunderously, the musicians moved to the back of the car and played as loudly as possible to drown out her obnoxious presence.

✳

Meanwhile, her fellow hikers in the earlier backpacker train had already descended to the lower-altitude Sacred Valley. They passed the inundated agricultural terraces of Jaquijahuana, but due to the torrential weather they missed the colorful villages of the Andes. Hilary, the group's self-appointed tour guide, pointed out the terraces and towns obscured by the fog and rain.

"It's a shame we couldn't see the town of Zurite," she told them. "That's where the Inca king, Atahualpa, was born. Back then it was known as Tumibamba. Did I tell you how the Spaniards imprisoned him until his subjects could fill three rooms full of—"

"Believe or not, I did study that factoid at little old Brown," Gabby snapped.

Hilary ignored her. She turned to Mercy, who was busy on her laptop.

"Prepare yourself, Mercy," she said. "The train is entering a deep gorge carved by the Pomatales River. Soon we'll see the Urubamba River—did you hear me, Mercy?"

"Yup," said Mercy, clearly distracted. "Thanks for the travelogue, but I'm working on a memo. Would you please find Tiffany? I suggest we four vote now on whether to wait for Sandra or just get started on the hike. And maybe we should offer Tiffany the refund one more time."

It was evident that the women were only interested in the end game: to have Rodrigo at their side. They had learned through years of chasing the brass ring of American success, which their Ivy League education had also affirmed, that they were women who could defer satisfaction. But this trip was the end of the line for them, though they would never admit such a maudlin sentiment. They had wasted fifteen post-college years by being off track with unworthy men, and now they were on the Inca trail hike to find their one and only soul mate.

Hilary did not like to take orders, especially not from Mercy, the golden athletic girl who everyone had always loved or admired, but she was eager to get rid of the toxic Sandra.

"Good idea," she said, her tone sarcastic. "I'll go fetch her, boss."

It didn't take Hilary long to find Tiffany: the bimbo had her legs propped up on the knees of an obviously gay man in the opposite seat. An oblivious Tiffany had pulled down the oversize zipper of her hot pink sweatshirt to reveal over-tanned cleavage.

"Sorry to bother you," Hilary said, nudging Tiffany's bony shoulder, "but we need your vote on the Sandra situation."

Tiffany glared up at Hilary, then heaved a melodramatic sigh.

"Fine, I'll come along." She winked at the handsome men. "But don't let anyone take my seat, you gorgeous hunks!"

"I didn't realize you were into gay men," Hilary muttered as Tiffany stood up.

"What?" said Tiffany, swiveling to look at her seat mates. They were laughing, mimicking her mannerisms. Tiffany looked furious. "Okay, so you fooled me three times, shame on me! But don't fool me again. Because that would be shame on ... shame on you."

Hilary almost felt sorry for Tiffany. She was so oblivious, completely unaware of things. Hilary decided that she wouldn't say anything about this to Mercy and Gabby. Perhaps if she tried a more compassionate approach, Tiffany would decide to take the offer of the refund, and hire a different trail guide for her solo hike.

"They got me good, I admit it," said Tiffany, as they staggered along the aisle. "My gaydar isn't as good as yours. I guess you knew right away they were gay cuz you're a tranny, right?"

Hilary couldn't believe she'd been feeling sorry for this girl. She shoved Tiffany against the train's windows.

"You are the most insensitive, uneducated, and crass person I have ever met," she hissed. "You *cannot* talk about people the way you do—not about their skin color, not about their gender, not about their weight—nothing. From this moment on, do not make one more comment or observation about anyone. Just hike with your mouth shut or let us pay you to find your own way. Your behavior is reprehensible!"

Tiffany ducked under Hilary's extended arms.

"My gaydar is working just fine now," she shouted, followed by beeping sounds like a sonar submarine or radar. "And you should be proud to be a tranny!"

While the rest of the passengers peered out the windows at the snow-capped Verónica peak, the Ivy League hikers ignored the view. A malaise had muddied their minds and hearts, and each one was preoccupied with understanding their respective growing uneasiness.

✳

Mercy wished she'd allowed Rodrigo to turn the hike into a romantic trek for two, as he had suggested. She yearned to hear his seductive words, and to feel his firm touch. Mercy snapped her laptop shut; she was through playing games with jocks. She resolved to take a chance and reveal her broken heart to Rodrigo, a man her father would have admired as a fellow macho; a dying breed, as her dad used to say.

Hillary still felt the sting from Tiffany's comments. She had always resented her strapping six-feet-two-inch body: it had won her lots of praise as an athlete, but it had also alienated most guys. Inside she felt delicate and soft, but everyone expected her to be the opposite. In Rodrigo she saw a mature man from a spiritual culture, a man who could appreciate her unique feminine soul trapped in this huge masculine frame. Hilary pictured herself running a consulting firm from Cusco and leading hikes along the Andes with Rodrigo. All she needed to do was present herself as more alluring and compliant, so she wouldn't intimidate Rodrigo with her height and powerful personality. She would try to channel the softer Hilary from her college days, and show Rodrigo that inside this Amazonian exterior fluttered a delicate butterfly.

A morose Tiffany sat with her eyes closed. Though she wasn't as hyperactive as usual, her thoughts darted restlessly. One second she felt like accepting the refund from the snobs, and the next she wanted to shut them up by racing to the top of Machu Picchu, leaving them all in the dust. But now, with all the rain and mud, she was afraid to fall. The one idea that kept flashing back in her head was how she was going to party all over South America with Rodrigo. She wished she had paid more attention to all the charges she made on her boss's credit cards, and to all the frequent flyer miles she had redeemed. Tiffany had followed Rodrigo's instructions, and before she knew it, she had e-tickets to all the cities they were going to visit, and the hotels and the boat cruise down the Amazon prepaid. She had even managed to get credit to buy her backpack and hiking gear. Luckily, the memories of ripping-off her boss made her feel buoyant and desirable again, so uplifted that she decided to make a move for Rodrigo the minute they arrived to camp.

It was Gabby's cheerful voice that got everyone's attention. "Okay everyone," she said, "in a few minutes we'll be getting off the train. We all recognize that we've had kind of a bumpy start, but I propose that we take a couple of votes and then proceed with our hiking trip with total commitment and enthusiasm. What do you say?"

Mercy agreed. "Sure, let's just put the first item on the table. Without disparaging Sandra, please."

She flashed Tiffany a significant look.

"I don't even know what 'disparaging' means," Tiffany retorted, "so I'm not saying anything about that old hag."

Hilary opened her mouth to speak, but Mercy got there first.

"Is it fair to summarize," she said, "that since Sandra opted to take a different train than the one agreed upon, and that since said train will arrive three hours after the approved train   this train, then she has violated her travel agreement?"

"I agree," said Gabby. "Let's put it to a vote, and let's honor the final decision. Call for the vote, Mercy!"

"Those in favor of proceeding on the hike without Sandra, raise your hands."

All four hands shot up instantly.

"Let the record show," Gabby concluded, "that all four other hike participants agreed to proceed without Sandra. Furthermore, let the rec—"

"That's all we've agreed to, Gabby," interrupted Mercy. "Ultimately, our tour leader could choose to wait for her. So we'll proceed to the camp and meet up with Rodrigo."

At the mention of Rodrigo, Hilary pulled her shirt collar up like a turtleneck. She didn't want the sizzling flush of sexual desire on her chest to reveal itself to the others, her tough competitors.

"What's the second vote?" asked Tiffany. "You said two votes, and that's plural. More than one, duh-uh?"

Gabby looked at Hilary and Mercy, but they pretended to not understand the question.

"The second vote is as follows," Gabby told her. "Raise your hand if you agree to immediately refund Tiffany the full amount she paid for the hike. This way, she can—"

"Kick your ass with my stompin' boots!" Tiffany said. "Yeah, I'll vote for that. Don't even think about it. I'm on this hike—no ifs ands or buts. Frickin' snobs!"

The other women thought it best not to push the issue any further and create even more of a scene.

*

Meanwhile, the well-heeled travelers on the Bingham train paced back and forth from the elegant dining car to the bar car. They had lost all interest in the music, the traditional drinks, or the alpaca steak. They were worried about the rising waters from the raging Urubamaba River, the banks of which paralleled the train tracks. Its waters now threatened to rise to the tracks.

The cluster of tourists lounging in the dining car ignored the announcement that they were now passing Corihuaynachina, more commonly known as Kilometer 88, or the trailhead of the Inca Trail. They laughed nervously when they heard that the normally visible section of the now abandoned highway, once used by muleteers between Cusco and the Amazon rubber plantations, was underwater. Every announcement from that point on elicited jeers or sighs. The bar car emptied because of the drunk, argumentative miscreant who kept insisting that someone had stolen her passport and her wallet. Once she fell back asleep, the conductor tied her backpack to the pedestal of her table, in plain view of the other travelers.

Despite the gloom of imposing granite mountains and two dark tunnels, the travelers cheered when the announcer welcomed them to Kilometer 110 and the town of Aguas Calientes. From this station they would travel on a brief, harrowing bus ride up to the citadel of Machu Picchu, and to the aptly named Cielo Lodge, a seventh heaven hotel for the fortunate few.

The hapless and drunk Sandra managed to stagger off the train, foaming at the mouth both at the conductor and another employee escorting her onto the platform.

"You are a crazy old lady," the conductor told her, no longer charming or polite. "Leave now or we will take you to the police station. You just took a free ride on an expensive train. Get lost!"

They abandoned Sandra among the wet crowds who ignored her rants. Without a clue about where to go or who to call, she was distracted by a pizza sign. Groggy with drink, she decided to step inside and order some take-out. The helpful young man behind the counter told her to check at the hotel across the street.

"Is it the fancy hotel?" she asked him. "I ain't staying at no dump, you get me?"

At the old and rundown hotel, she insisted that they give her the best room with the best view.

"Madam," the receptionist told her, "our best room is the honeymoon suite on the second floor. It has a large balcony overlooking the Vilcanota River. But perhaps someone of your years should take a room on the ground floor near the reception. This way I can help you with anything you need, yes?"

"Hell, no! Gimme the best room and take my backpack upstairs, while I carry my pizza…and bring me a six pack of beeah…and call Rodrigo to come and get me, damn Stackjacks."

Late in the afternoon of January 29, 2010, hell and high water did come to the Inca Trail. The railroad tracks, the only way in and out of Machu Picchu Pueblo, were damaged by the swelling waters. When the mudslides swamped villages, roads, and agricultural fields, cutting off all communications with Cusco, people panicked. Sandra, miserable in her honeymoon suite, marched downstairs to admonish the hotel manager.

"There's no watah in my suite!" she yelled. "Fix it right away."

The manager had already charged her card for the full three-day stay, and she had signed the charge. He'd dealt with *gringas* before and he knew that it was better to lie to them than to confront them.

"Yes, of course, Madam," he said. "My son is at the hardware store this very minute buying the, uh, the pipes. He will come up to fix your room in a few minutes. Yes."

"Not good enough. I'm gonna buy some bottles of watah and some whiskey across the street, and when I return that faucet bettah be working. But why is everyone out in the street running in circles? You people scamper like rats."

"We are not rats," said the manager, affronted. "We are worried because there is a major flood and we have no way out of here."

"Well, did you find Rodrigo for me?" Sandra demanded. "Is he coming down or up or wherever I am in relation to where he and the others are?"

"Madam, if your friends arrived to Kilometer 88 early this morning, they are already on their hike. God bless them on this muddy and slippery trail. We have no way to contact anyone. Madam, please stay calm until they rescue us."

"What do you mean *rescue* us?" Sandra screeched. "Where's Rodrigo? I need my refund!"

"Do whatever you want," the manager said, turning his back on her, and he walked into the back office and slammed the door.

Sandra strolled out to the street with the confidence of someone who expects civil servants to arrive with sirens blaring and fix the problem. Any problem. But the only sound she heard was a boy's braying voice.

"Hey, old *gringa!* I told you I was going to come after you."

Sandra searched the crowd for policemen, but there were none in sight. She ran into the pizza joint, but the waiter shooed her out.

"Where's the skinny *gringa* who owes us money?" the urchin hollered.

Sandra grabbed the waiter's arm and insisted, "You gottah help me, heah!"

"Sorry," he told her. "I must go home and get my children. You go back to hotel."

Sandra pointed to the boy who'd shouted at her. He and his urchin friends were waiting for her outside the pizza joint.

"Are you on crahck? Those thugs will kill me."

The waiter yelled at the street urchins and they walked away. When he tried to shake Sandra's hand, she rejected it.

"Good luck," he told her. "Go back to the hotel, quickly."

He cursed the urchins once more, and Sandra hustled back across the street. In the hotel she panted and huffed up the steep, rickety stairs to the honeymoon suite. The hotel seemed deserted. Although she yelled for the manager, "Help me, heah! I'm being followed by some little greasahs!"—no one answered her pleas.

In a panic, Sandra unlocked the door but dropped the room keys on the floor; she could hear hoofbeats and the braying of beasts hunting her down. She pushed the flimsy door open and practically fell into her room. There was no point in locking the door or even screaming any more. All she wanted was to reach her backpack and take out her hidden U.S. dollars, the same dollars she'd accused the train conductor of stealing. She would throw them to the beasts, and that would appease them.

But the urchins chasing her up the stairs couldn't be pacified quite so easily. Their animalistic ire demanded blood. Their entire sordid short lives had taught them to inflict pain on others in equal measure to the pain they had felt all their miserable lives. They didn't have shelter, they didn't eat regularly, and everyone pelted them with rocks and vile words. Now it was payback time. Instinctively, they made a line of attack, pushing Sandra towards the balcony. She kept throwing wadded dollar bills at them, and the smallest of the urchins gathered them up, but each handful of dollars just made the boys bray louder and louder.

Sandra retreated to the balcony and peered down to the swollen river, grasping the overstuffed backpack as a shield. In one instant Mother Nature decided her fate. The entire balcony collapsed into the raging foul-mouthed waters of the river.

CHAPTER EIGHT

hoque and his team, three porters and one cook, stood in a cluster away from the other hiking guides. They were waiting for their five *gringa* hikers to arrive from the train stop at Kilometer 88, and they wanted to stay clear of the insults hurled their way from the other porters. Since his teen years Choque had grown accustomed to snide remarks and taunts. Each low blow had toughened him up, and helped make him the foremost porter and guide in the region. He had complete trust in his team of porters, whatever others might think of their debilitating physical flaws. He understood their drive and determination—and their allegiance to Rodrigo. When Choque had been down and out, it was Rodrigo who pumped him up and promised him something Choque didn't dare to dream of as a possibility, something that gave him a ray of hope, and because of these promises Choque remained loyal to Rodrigo.

Each group of porters knew their place on the hierarchy of tour operators and they clustered only with porters of equal prestige. Choque and his team waited on the outskirts. They were approached by two doddering elderly men, who looked fragile and almost effeminate. Choque felt sorry for these old men. He assumed they were there to sign up as porters or cooks, but this didn't make any sense: they were too old, too flabby, and no one had ever seen them work as porters before. Choque didn't want them to be ridiculed by the hotshot porters with the elite tour operators. He certainly didn't want anyone to think that these unmanly men were his relatives, because then they would really amp up their contempt for him. And then Choque would have to sneak up on those hotshot porters while they slept in their sturdy tents, and cut them down. Cut them good and deep.

Choque saluted the old men.

"What brings you out on such an awful day, uncles?" he called to them. "We don't need any help."

The skinniest old man pulled his woolen *chullo* hat so that the long ear flaps and forehead section almost covered his entire wrinkled face.

"Nephew, you're a good man to ask about our welfare," the old man said. "We are looking for Rodrigo, that is all. We are old acquaintances, and we heard that he might be back leading hikes. What have you heard?"

"We haven't heard anything, have we?" Choque turned to look at his motley crew of misshaped porters.

The hunchback porter-cook shook his head no, shuffling closer to the old men.

"I think I've seen you two at the Plaza de Armas," he said to the plumper old man. "You're always hanging around the women street vendors. You've never worked up on the trail, have you?"

"Nah, that wasn't us at the plaza," the old man said too quickly. "We work on the very private hikes for the super-rich. We know trails that you runts could never climb. Go ahead, and ask me any question about any of the secret trails!"

The mention of runts outraged the three dwarf porters.

"Watch your filthy mouth, you *pongo-camayoqs*," one of them hissed, "or we'll cut out whatever measly eggs you have left."

All three dwarfs roared like howler monkeys, and one grabbed his genitals. "At least we still have both our huge eggs—and our rod!" he said.

Before anyone could say another word, Choque gave his three porters a few swift kicks. "Enough of your cruel antics," he spat. "You are men, like me. Our bodies or our body parts do not define us. We are men, damn it, and we are the top-notch porters of *Don* Rodrigo Guamán O'Rourke..."

He immediately regretted mentioning his boss's name, though he was so proud to work for Rodrigo. When the porters mentioned the word "rod," it reminded Choque of the first time he and Rodrigo met. Rodrigo had shaken his hand and looked him in the eye.

"Choque," he said, in a matter of fact way, "your name means golden rod. You were destined to use that rod for pleasure, but evildoers took that possibility from you."

Choque had cried like a girl, but Rodrigo had no patience for such self-pity.

"From now on you will behave as a complete man," Rodrigo told him. "A full man. I promise you that I will pay for your surgery and that you will be whole again." His day in the sun was in the horizon.

The slight old man approached Choque cautiously.

"It is all right, little nephew," he whispered. "I understand your anger and your pain. It is all right."

Choque tried to shove him away, but the old man had already placed his firm hands gently on Choque's skull.

"You did not deserve the cruelty done to your body. Pachamama will reward you if you behave honorably from this moment forward."

Choque pushed both old men away from him, and the frailer old man tumbled to the ground.

"Let's get the equipment ready to go—our *gringa* hikers are arriving!" he shouted to his crew. Then Choque turned to face the old men. "If I ever find out that you two limpy-dicks are asking about my Inca, I'll cut you down."

He stomped on the hand that had blessed him, and the old man writhed in agony. One of the dwarfs ran forward, hitting at the old men with nettle branches. But the plump old man, still on his feet, yanked the nettle branch away and hit the dwarf square on the face. The dwarf ran back to his posse, howling in pain.

Koyam lifted Taki from the ground and wiped the mud as best she could from Taki's poncho.

"¡*Ooyooyooy*, we are deep in mud now. Now we do look like our poor brothers." She was trying to make Taki smile at their comic appearance, but Taki still looked preoccupied. "Maybe we should forget this outrageous plan and go home and weave some bright yellow coca bags. We need sunshine in our old age."

Taki rubbed her hand. "You know that is not our destiny. We have to set things straight. Rodrigo is back and now we know who his porters are. We have to stay on their tracks and determine his sinister plans—and then put a stop to them."

The two women made their way to a large boulder with a granite overhang. Once their bundles were hidden in the nearby shrubs, they could settle down to observe Choque and his men from a distance.

"I thought that there weren't any *pongo-camayoqs* left in Cusco?" Koyam whispered. "Why would we need any now since the *acllahuasis* were destroyed hundreds of years ago? Who needs eunuchs to guard the Brides of the Sun, when they no longer exist?"

"That's precisely my point," Taki said, nodding. "Our people are all mixed up about the Inca ways, the corrupt present days—and no one cares about the future."

"You're right." Koyam batted at an invisible fly. "My great-grandchildren think their technological gizmos are the answers to everything. But why would anyone castrate Choque?"

"In the ancient days, eunuchs were needed to guard the young virgins. They were the intermediaries between the Brides of the Sun and the Inca, and they lived long, long lives, like eunuchs often do. They were trusted guards. But there is no need for them now."

"But why would Choque work for Rodrigo? And why would his team of porters be such a mangy group bound to attract attention wherever they go?"

"Perhaps it is a warning. Perhaps they are meant to instill fear." Taki wanted to change the conversation. She was afraid to speak about what she suspected were Rodrigo's motives. "Did the nettles sting?"

"Nah, they were wet. But did you see my lightning-speed reflexes? I impressed myself. I hope I didn't blind the litle hothead."

"You know," Taki explained, "in the olden days, in *Camay*, what is now our month of January, the boys were elevated to adult status. In those days, the dwarfs whipped the boys with nettles to affirm their adulthood…or so I think. *Ooy*, I'm getting all mixed up myself."

Koyam pulled out her flask, the one a slaphappy tourist had given her, and took a swig of moonshine. She was concerned about Rodrigo's symbolic warnings. She didn't dare ask Taki the extent of the dangers they were facing.

"Take a little swig," she told Taki. "It won't do any harm."

But Taki shook her head. Koyam put a bit of moonshine spit on her palm and rubbed Taki's swollen hand.

Choque counted the hikers approaching him and his porters, waiting until they all stood in front of him, looking wet and unfriendly.

"Are we still to wait for one more hiker?" he asked them. "I think she is the older lady, no?"

The women looked at each other and for a moment no one said a word. Finally, Hilary spoke up.

"The fifth hiker was Sandra," she told Choque, "but she decided to take the later Hiram Bingham train."

Rodrigo had warned Choque about Sandra's erratic behavior, and he had promised that he would eliminate her from the hike. His boss always accomplished what he set out to do.

"Did she decide to go straight to Machu Picchu?" Choque asked. The women shrugged.

"Well, she really wanted to ride that train," said Gabby. "Are you saying that she may have stayed on the train all the way to Machu Picchu?"

Now the group was all smiles.

"The witch is gone for good!" cheered Tiffany. "Yahoo!"

Choque was alarmed. "She is a witch?"

Tiffany slapped him in the chest. "Of course not. There's no such thing as witches. But she was one crazy bitch, for sure. Hey, can we get going on the hike? Rodrigo is waiting for me."

Choque's almond eyes squinted. This pretty little blonde was in for a big surprise. She didn't realize she was a small insect in his boss's vast and complex web of plans.

"Should we to wait for Missus Sandra?" he asked them.

Gabby glanced at the other three. "In view of the fact that she is more than likely in Machu Picchu by now, I think we all agree to go ahead without her on the hike. That is—if you're sure she's safe in Machu Picchu Pueblo?"

How can anyone know for certain, Choque thought, but he wasn't about to say this to the *gringas*.

"The pueblo is called Aguas Calientes," he told them, "and it is safe. I'm sure that Missus Sandra is very, ah, how to say, very strong."

"Enough talking about Sandra," Tiffany complained, making a face. "Let's get this show on the road. Where are our porters?"

Choque pointed to the misshapen men.

"You're kidding, right?" Tiffany said. "This must be one of Rodrigo's little jokes." Tiffany looked at the other women. "Rodrigo likes to play all sorts of games and pranks on Skype with me. Not only is he *huge*, and hot, but he has a sick sense of humor."

Hilary was ready to pounce on Tiffany if she made any rude comments about the small porters, though secretly she was worried about their ability to carry all these heavy backpacks.

"Well, I don't mind carrying my own pack," she said. "How about you, Mercy?"

All Mercy could think of were the possible legal ramifications. She had to remind herself that they were not legally responsible for any details of this botched Peruvian trip.

"Sure, I'll carry my own backpack," she said, then turned to interrogate Choque. "How soon will we join Rodrigo? Is there any way to contact Sandra and let her know that we won't be meeting up with her at all?" Mercy thought they should at least feign concern.

Choque replied in so soft a voice that none of them could understand his answer.

"What?" Tiffany hollered. "Did you say that we may not meet up with Rodrigo tonight at camp? Why the hell not?"

"He is very important man," Choque said with pride, puffing out his chest. "He has too many responsibilities. He will meet us soon."

Choque tended to mirror his boss's self-importance and pretension. Rodrigo had taught him that a real man never listened to women: they used women, because women were dispensable. Choque admired his boss, his Inca, for having young women like plentiful chinchillas all over the peaks and valleys. His powerful seed had produced dozens of children. Rodrigo had told him that on this hike he was escorting lonely foreign women so desperate that they begged for men on their computers. So far, everything his Inca had promised him had come true.

"He is important like Inca of long ago," Choque continued. It felt so good to puff oneself up like a virile rooster, to stalk like a puma. "We listen and we wait. He have too many wom—"

"He has too many *whats*?" screamed Tiffany, throwing her pack to the ground as though she was ready for a fight.

Koyam skulked as close as she dared to Choque and the hikers. Then she hurried back to Taki.

"Let's pick up our bundles, the hike is beginning," she muttered. "Did you hear the pretty flower scream?"

"What was she shouting about?"

"She won the lottery." Koyam giggled.

Taki elbowed her. "Stop being such a joker. This is the most serious hike of our lives. We are in danger, sweet sister. We are in dire danger."

Koyam swallowed hard with fear, but she was determined not to show it.

"You've been trying to scare me with your predictions since I found out you had a third teat, a witch's teat." She grinned at Taki. "So far in our seventy years you've only been correct about nine out of ten times. That proves you're no witch. Come on, pick up your bundle. We have to shadow them."

Gabby sat down next to her pack and tried to start up her laptop.

"Just give me a few minutes to write down some ideas for my next blog," she said, frowning at the screen. "My words sting the most when I'm feeling frustrated and disappointed—as we all are, I'm sure."

Hilary and Tiffany rolled their eyes to the sky.

"I agree with Tiffany," Hilary said. "Let's get the show on the road."

Mercy was pulling all sorts of items from her backpack, scattering them across the damp ground. "Did anyone notice where I put my laptop?" she asked. "Surely I put it back in my backpack, didn't I?"

"Oopsies! I guess your Harvard brain wasn't working, was it?" Tiffany giggled and broke into a mock-cheerleading routine. "Let's go, Ivy Leaguers, let's go!" She kept chanting and clapping, jumping around in the mud. Without Rodrigo around, Tiffany had to get her kicks one way or another, and right now there was nothing she enjoyed more than getting under the skin of these snobs.

Hilary helped Mercy reorganize her backpack, but they couldn't find the laptop.

"I'm so sorry, Mercy. I guess you left it in the train." Hilary leaned closer to Mercy and lowered her voice. "That darn gnat Tiffany should go on her own. Want me to suggest it?"

Mercy wanted to say yes, but she didn't want to get in the middle of yet another fight—not to mention a potential legal morass with a ding-a-ling like Tiffany.

"I think Tiffany will burn out in a few hours," she whispered to Hilary. "I hope so, anyway."

"Oh, no, this is too much!" Gabby cried out. "Now my battery is dead!"

All three women checked their cell phones. No one could get a signal.

"Do you think that we'll get cell reception at camp?" Hilary asked Choque.

Choque could hear Rodrigo's advice: "Tell them very little, but keep them mildly happy. Lie, always lie to *gringas*."

Choque smiled. "Oh, yes, we usually to receive cell in camp."

"Let's get a move on, people." Tiffany, showing no sign of burning out, clapped her hands. "That includes the teensy guys, too."

Hilary slapped her on the shoulder. "Watch your mouth," she snapped.

An annoyed Tiffany pushed her back, and Hilary almost tumbled into the mud. The porters stood around ridiculing the women's behavior. Choque had warned them about these crazy *gringas*.

Tiffany wasn't finished, and she certainly didn't care if these mini-men were laughing.

"I once decked a bouncer bigger than you," she told Hilary, her face red with anger. "It was at the Ocean Blue Club. Gawd, I would love to be there right now, sitting at the bar drinking a giant Lemon Drop Martini, and not here with Chuck and his three *dwarfs*."

Hilary hastily apologized to the men, in case they had understood Tiffany's remarks. The men ignored her, busy picking up all the gear without any apparent effort. Hilary knelt down next to them, though even kneeling she still seemed to tower over them.

"Please call me, Pilpintu, butterfly," she told them, smiling. "The Incas respected men of short stature like you, right?" When no one answered, she kept talking. "I took this course about the Spanish chroniclers, and Bernabé Cobo wrote that the penitents would go wash in the river accompanied by a short person who was deformed. I mean who had a ... anyway, that person would whip the penitents with nettles. You have an amazing history. What other important roles did little people play in society?"

The men ignored her, but Tiffany had an answer. "To carry our frickin' crap," she told Hilary. "Now shut the f-up and move. Rodrigo is waiting for me, and I don't want to disappoint him."

Choque suppressed a smile, and pointed to the path they'd be following; a path that shrouded unimaginable pitfalls for trusting hikers. He knew Rodrigo better than any of these silly *gringas* ever would, and Rodrigo had no intention of being disappointed ever again.

"The spirits of the dead he'd been forced
to rob were punishing him."

CHAPTER NINE

 t the Kilometer 88 train stop, Violette waited for the American hikers— all as mad as March hares, in her opinion—to descend from the train. She fell in with a group of tortoise-pace hikers, the prudent ones who questioned the wisdom of continuing this journey in such brutal weather. They were Swiss, and responded with an aloof politeness to Violette's inquiries about joining their group. This suited her perfectly, because it meant they wouldn't start asking her awkward questions. The indifferent guard at the warden's hut barely glanced at their passports and their group pass, waving the hikers through.

Violette made sure she walked at the tail end of the Swiss group, and slowly distanced herself as they approached their smiling guides, who greeted them with warm hand towels and even warmer coca tea. She slumped her shoulders, pulled up her neck gator, and yanked down the hood of her parka, surveying which guides looked available—and bribable. She anticipated that their response would be: "Sorry, we can't help you. You should have paid for your reservation for the hike before reaching Kilometer 88." But Violette could also count on the enticement of the five hundred Euros she would offer—*after* the guide agreed to her requirements. Her short apprenticeship under her slimy swami had taught her the power of greasing the palms—or even drawing blood—in order to accomplish her goals.

Before approaching her targeted guide, Violette bid a flamboyant adieu to the Swiss hikers to demonstrate to the soon-to-be-hired guide that she was not totally alone. She had met some of the better-known guides standing around here a year ago, when Rodrigo had bamboozled her with circuitous hikes that always ended up in or near Machu Picchu, never in the faraway peaks that nurtured a tiny baby, any baby, her baby—the child she so craved to hold as her own. Just thinking about this now, reliving the miserable memories of the baby and Rodrigo made the hollow space where her uterus once resided cramp with phantom pain. Violette thought of her swami's Corsican proverb: *Ciò chi un tomba ingrassa.* He was right: what hadn't killed her had made her stronger.

She advanced towards a middle-aged, roughhewn man she had not met before, and found it easy to persuade him—too easy, she thought, for such a rainy day. He yanked the bundle of Euros she proffered and immodestly stuffed it into his underpants. Although repulsed by the guide's response, Violette could almost hear her swami say: "If you want the pigeon to carry your message, remember to wet its beak." Her pigeon was now ready to do her bidding.

The guide rounded up his scraggy porters. Their defeated faces revealed that their hands would never grasp any of the

Euros; instead they would peck at a few crumbs thrown their way. These men would never grace the online photo galleries of the first-class trekking outfitters' websites. They were the exploited porters, the ones whose backs had endured all the burdens of the first-world travelers, like the porters who now trudged silently behind Choque's crew and his fast-paced American hikers.

Violette gave a series of convoluted directions to the guide, and tried to explain. "The reason I want to follow the group of women—"

"No need, no explanation," the guide responded. He adjusted the wad of Euros in his crotch, and picked up his pace.

The guide did not question why she didn't want to stick close to her Swiss friends. He suspected she had a specific reason to be following Choque's gelding scent, although it was a stench he found abhorrent, and which confirmed all the despicable rumors about Choque, Rodrigo, and the rest of their plagued porters. When he had heard that Choque had been castrated nine years ago, when he was a fledgling thirteen-year-old, in retaliation for the debauchery his father committed against women in the highlands, he had no pity for Choque. In fact, he admired the unknown "surgeon" attackers. In the scant few months since Choque had first been engorged with semen as a young adolescent, he had spread it around forcibly, just like his father.

The curse put on Choque's testicles was not a novelty to the guides who were experts in the legends, facts, and sacrileges of the Inca Trail. A related curse had been inflicted on one of the men in Hiram Bingham's exploration party of 1912. After being forced to excavate the graves of his ancestors in Machu Picchu, a local man named Alvarez developed incapacitating problems with his testes. He cried out in agony so his American oppressors would hear and understand that the spirits of the dead he'd been forced to rob were punishing him. But Bingham's osteologist, Dr. George Eaton, only concerned himself with ancient indigenous bones, not the soft testicular tissue of a living being. Eaton may have thought that he was involved in an unholy and profitable quest, but he continued to stuff chests with skulls and tibias and miniscule metacarpal bones, the tiny hands of child mummies, and other treasures from Machu Picchu, and shipped them back to the U.S. Spindly-legs Bingham, the Ivy League promoter who lived off the wealth of his wife's family, brazenly hyped Machu Picchu by writing: "It is unknown and will make a fine story." What he didn't realize or didn't care about was that in his greed for notoriety and priceless artifacts he forced his local grave robbers to violate a taboo so thunderous that even Illapa, the god who controlled weather, could not restore the balance of the Andean universe with the crack of his lightning.

Choque, on the other hand, was now a twenty-two-year-old eunuch who brooded and cracked heads whenever possible. He had always been pugnacious, but lately his aggression had been directed towards his own men. His lack of testosterone did not diminish his male rage at all. While he waited for Rodrigo to get enough money to make him a whole man again, he practiced his manly aggression on his porters. He punched and kicked them, and they, in turn, took it out on anyone else. His little men waited until the other hiking groups were asleep, then they pounced on the most exhausted of the porters and inflicted surface cuts and welts. Most of the victims retaliated in kind, and unbeknownst to the foreign hikers, these violent attacks occurred regularly on the Inca trail. The leaders of the elite hiking groups laid down the law by distancing themselves from

Choque's group, not because of fear of the impotent henchman, but because they feared his omnipotent leader, the reputed demigod Rodrigo.

None of the guides openly refuted the growing rumors of Rodrigo's celestial powers. They allowed the outrageous gossip to float up into mountains where the Andean elements would determine their validity. Little by little, the guides learned to be guarded with anything related to Rodrigo. The crimes attributed to him, particularly the infant trafficking charges, were always shot full of holes and eventually blown sky-high, and he was exonerated—yet again. His unearthly presence continued to be felt on the Inca trail, each time with more fear, respect, and—for people like Choque—with reverence.

When the scandal over the missing infants implicated Rodrigo since he was the reputed father of said children, he was able to prove, once again, that he had been in the United States during the time in question. When an eighteen-year-old girl's belly was sliced open in 2006 and her baby forcibly removed by a baby-peddling ring, the rumor-mongers tried to link Rodrigo to the evil deed, but again he had an alibi: he had been away from Peru for months. Nonetheless, people feared a repeat of the case charging a German man and his Peruvian wife with selling a baby for $16,870 to a German woman a few months earlier. The guides could not erase from their minds these ghoulish deeds and their possible connection to Rodrigo, so they stayed far away from him and his confederates.

In time the accusations and sagas of Rodrigo's escapades became legend. An old guide would tell another: "I saw Rodrigo up in Huayna Picchu, reigning over all of Machu Picchu, like an Inca of yore, and yet my brother swears he was drinking *chicha* with him in Aguas Calientes—at the same time."

After the last inquest, when Rodrigo appeared to have left Peru for good, one or two guides babbled that they had spotted him in Lima and Cartagena, surrounded by a dozen gorgeous women at a beach club or on board a yacht. No one really believed them: in this day and age, when everyone owned a camera phone, they couldn't produce a single photo to substantiate their claims, so they soon became the laughing stock of the Inca trail guides. But lately, with the arrival of the worst storm in decades, the gossip that a Rodrigo-like phantom had been sighted in the Plaza de Armas in Cusco, or near the highest spot of Dead Woman's Pass, sent chills up the strong backs of the trail guides. These phantasmagorical coincidences proved that anything was possible in the Andes, anything.

The livelihood of the guides depended on Machu Picchu and its rewards of unparalleled natural splendor and generous foreign tourists. The guides also regarded the flip side of Machu Picchu—its malevolent acts of nature and the vengeance of man—with a similar awe. Those were the precepts of their Andean cosmology. They revered paired opposing forces, the principles of duality that governed their days versus nights, wet versus dry, cold versus hot, male versus female. Thus, Choque upset their worldview since he did not have an opposing force, and he could not be balanced. Life demanded equilibrium, but Choque's presence threatened that. The other guides didn't like it. They demanded balance on their hikes. In the old days, they tolerated Rodrigo because he kept to himself; he was just a big-mouth cad leading hikes along the off-beaten paths that were too risky and rigorous for most foreign trekkers. In due time, they learned to fear Rodrigo, but Choque was way off-kilter and they weren't afraid of him at all. They simply wanted him to disappear.

Violette kept her eyes on the American hikers, only half-listening to the monotonous spiel of her trail guide.

"Soon you will see the old Inca ruins of Patallacta," he told her. "They were first uncovered by Hiram Bingham in 1915 and further excavated in the 1970s by the Cusichaca Trust."

When she didn't seem interested enough, the guide began reciting facts and figures to impress her.

"Hiram Bingham's men collected 200 skulls and 6 mummies wrapped in cloth from this site. There are 116 buildings and five baths, and a canal feeds the baths...." He paused for her reaction, but Violette was adding up figures of her own: one, two, three, four women, plus Choque, plus four of his men. She had to remain focused on this entourage of nine—and nothing else—until they met up with Rodrigo. Although Violette's revenge plan only included Rodrigo, she would mow down any of this group of nine misfits if they got in her way. She had paced her revenge slowly and methodically—like the tortoise in the fable—and she would demolish Rodrigo at the end of their race. Today, for the first time, Violette could see the finish line. Her swami had taught her all about the satisfaction of a vendetta.

Violette and her guide climbed a steep path. Her damp wig weighed down her head, intensifying her headache.

"Please notice to the many bromeliads on the cliff wall." The guide pointed to the slippery ground cover. She wished he would stop droning on. The porters all looked bored to tears at having to listen endlessly to the same facts. "There are more than 2,000 types of orchids.... The chinchilla is a rodent and is the smaller cousin of the viscacha.... In five kilometers we will be in Wayllabama village, but we will not camp there. We will camp near the American hikers. Is this correct, yes Miss?"

He raised and lowered his eyebrows several times, as if his hairy brows were sending her secret signals, and Violette glared at him. She didn't care for his attempts to fraternize with her. He had no idea what she wanted, or how medieval a punishment she had in store for Rodrigo. It had been a long day, and Violette wanted to throw away the wet, itchy wig. But her mind was still alert, and she was focused on her plan of action. To her relief, the Swiss hikers stopped for the night in Wayllabama, but the Americans forged ahead, like the arrogant hare of the fable, marching at a breakneck pace towards an undisclosed location. Luckily, they didn't notice that Violette was hot on their heels.

DECEPTIONS

CHAPTER TEN

hile the American hikers waited for their porters to set camp, Taki and Koyam sat safely hidden, nuzzled within a deeply concave boulder. Had this been a true cave, neither woman would have entered for fear of disturbing the beings that dwell in such places. Koyam pulled out a large space-age blanket from her bundle.

"My engineer grandson gave me this," she said. "I think he said the astronauts took one similar to it to the moon. Here, let me wrap it around both of us."

Taki felt its stiff waterproof side. "I hope it doesn't keep us too warm. We must stay alert. I have a feeling that Rodrigo will sneak into the camp like a mountain tapir in heat." They both chuckled. The size of a tapir's testes and sex drive were notorious. "Rodrigo thinks he can burrow past our keen eyes and noses. We'll catch him when he goes in to sting the *gringas*. All that beast ever wants to do is pierce women."

"*Ooy*, Taki," Koyam teased. "You picked this spot so you could watch all his nasty shenanigans with the *gringas*. Shame on you at your old age!"

"Why do you insist on acting the clown on this serious mission? This could be a life-or-death situation. Don't you believe me?"

"Of course I do!" Koyam protested. "You've got the all-knowing third titty, haven't you? It's just that if I'm going to die soon, I'd rather die laughing."

"Ah," Taki sighed. "Who knows how this is journey is going to turn out? Unfortunately, we have to wait for Rodrigo to make a move since he's the center of the spider web, and—"

Koyam slapped her soggy leg. "Aha! That's how you divine what's going to happen in the future. You use the hairy spiders, don't you? You keep them in a clay jar, like they did in the ancient days. If you pull one big one out and you see all eight legs extended, it's something good. But you must have seen the spider's legs withdrawn, so now you know it's all going to be bad. It's all an uphill battle from now on, isn't it?"

"You've known me my whole life. When have you ever seen me play with spiders?" Taki kept her eyes on the *gringas*, clambering into their wet tents.

Koyam counted the fingers on her left hand one by one. "So you don't use spiders, you don't use pebbles, you don't chew coca leaves and spit the juice on your palm—so how do you know what's going to happen? Come on, you can tell me. I've never asked you before because I figured I was always safe next to you." Koyam started to choke up. "But n-n-now you tell me this journey could be my last one, and well, I'm not ready to d-die."

Taki elbowed Koyam. "Don't get all teary-eyed now. You're tough as a long-nosed armadillo. Who knows how I know some things? I just do. Let me tell you once and for all—I am not a sorceress or a witch, despite what you say about my extra teensy teat. All I know is that throughout my entire life, I've only tried to help people with whatever gifts I have."

All the *gringas* had all but disappeared, sealed up and dry in their tents, but Taki could see a shadowy figure moving around their small encampment.

"Whoa, whoa, whoa!" Taki nudged Koyam again. "Who's that fifth woman monkeying around the *gringas'* tents? Do you see her, the one with the black hair? Why is she spying on them?"

"She would make a terrible spy—look at her, practically leaning into each tent! I think she's a thief. A skinny thief at that." Koyam yawned and flexed her arms; they were strong from the years of hauling heavy bundles up and down the steep terrain of the highlands. "You know how it is. Wherever there are *gringos*, the pickpockets are not far behind. Although that skinny one looks like a *gringa* thief, doesn't she? Look how fair her skin is."

"Hmm, I don't like the looks of this. She's not a thief, I tell you. She's eavesdropping. Were there five *gringas* on the train?"

"Who knows? I just counted four women, the same four that we saw in the Internet café. I'll let your magic third titty figure it all out for us." Koyam yawned again. "I'm going to sleep for a couple of hours. I'll take the second shift."

She leaned into Taki in their usual two sacks of potatoes fashion. Throughout their decades spent together out in the marketplace or as street vendors, they had learned how to take a warm snooze leaning against each other, however cold and wet the weather.

Taki remained alert and on edge throughout the night. She didn't want to struggle to explain her visions, her entire heightened sensory awareness, to Koyam or anyone else. She refused the labels others gave her: clairvoyant, seer, healer, shaman, priestess. Taki didn't care about praise or insincere pleading from disingenuous self-interested fools. Eventually, people, *her* people, asked for her blessings. Over the years Taki had learned to transmit her understanding and love with words of truth that made people walk away with a deep sense of solace palpitating through their bodies. All she was trying to do was to keep one person at a time in balance with the universe.

As youngsters, Koyam learned to wait whenever Taki froze into a trance while trying to make sense of the perplexing visions or sounds or feelings she was experiencing—and Koyam never asked Taki to explain herself. Instead, she punched and scratched those who ridiculed Taki's slobbering spaciness, and then used her own shawl to wipe Taki's drool or the tears her friend shed, terrified of her own bewildering gifts. Later, as young teens, when they were in the Cusco plaza, Taki would mention her visions. Sometimes she'd ask Koyam: "Did you see those beautiful girls who just walked by? They're on their way to the Sun Temple in the Machu Picchu citadel."

Koyam would say she'd had her eyes closed, or that she hadn't noticed. Their other friends would have said: "Are you insane? We're in the middle of Cusco, not in Machu Picchu." Eventually, Taki learned not to blurt out her visions, like hairy tarantula spiders used for divination, she kept them covered in the clay pot of her mind. But Koyam never told her she was crazy. When Taki mentioned the girls walking to the Sun Temple, Koyam asked her what they were doing.

"I think they were singing together and one was lighting a torch. Are you sure you didn't see them?"

Koyam, always practical, would poke fun at Taki. "I'll take your word for it," she would say. "Just don't try to sing along with them, because you have a terrible voice."

This was Koyam's constant taunt. "I still don't understand how they could have named you 'song' when you can't sing. Taki, Taki, song, song!" She would always sing the last four words.

In time, after both women had married and had children, a small group of elders came to visit Taki. They took her away on a strenuous and secretive five-day journey into Machu Picchu. This retreat took place in the days when very few tourists dared to make the trek to the citadel. Taki returned to her home as if nothing had happened, but little things she said to Koyam dropped clues that some important transformation had taken place.

One day, not long after her expedition with the elders, Taki took Koyam aside. "Now I know why they named me song," she whispered.

Koyam knew better than to act too interested. She preferred to give Taki plenty of time to let the cat out of the bag. A few minutes passed before she pressed her friend to continue.

"Does it mean 'silent song' because I can't hear the rest of your story?"

Taki hesitated for a moment. "It means a trill, a vibration," she confided, then paused again. "Apparently I not only feel, you know—uh, special things, but I also give out certain vibrations. What do you think?"

Koyam gave Taki a hard slap on the back. "Why do you think I sit so close to you?" She giggled. "It's like getting a massage—all day long."

Decades later, when the hordes climbed breathlessly to Machu Picchu to experience the renowned vibrations emanating from its granite foundation, hoping the quartz within it would cure their ailments, Koyam reminded Taki of this conversation.

"Come on, Taki," she said, "let's go sit by the Sun Gate. As soon as the tourists arrive, I'll charge them to grab your hands to reenergize their bodies. Now *that* will make them quiver with elation!"

Taki rolled her eyes in disgust at Koyam's money-making scheme, but Koyam persisted. "We'll be rich in no time," she told Taki. "We'll have enough money to go to Miami Beach and wear thong bikinis so our butts can shiver. Come on, Taki, show them what a mystical throb feels like!"

Those had been the golden days of Taki's gift. One day she evoked a wondrous image of Andean condors with their ten-foot wingspan gliding in and resting on the edge of Huayna Picchu peak, affirming their role as king of the birds. Another day she saw the condor flying through the sky with a fox on his back, soaring higher and higher through the clouds. Hours later that same well-fed fox descended from the clouds alone, without the condor's assistance. The fox splattered all over the terraces of Machu Picchu and left the seeds of the banquet he had feasted on in the sky, and soon the fertile soil sprouted grains.

"Aha," Taki said, smiling. "So it is true that the mischievous fox did help to spread seeds of quinoa and corn for us to eat!"

In the late afternoons of the best epoch of her life, Taki would see rosy sunsets diffused in the glowing light of the sun god, Inti, which reminded her to sacrifice a guinea pig the next day. Sometimes Taki yearned for those days when the melancholic sounds of a *zampoña* flute made her smile at the child at her breast, and predicted healthy crops and peaceful dawns. Back then, these vivid images had augured magical beginnings.

Now, at the dusk of her life, a somber drum thumped a hollow beat, as if it were Taki's last distress signal. Taki wanted to close her eyes and rest her head on Koyam's shoulder, but the terrible visions—of peaks drenched in blood, and bone shards poking violently from funerary caves, and an angelic child marching to her death—thwarted any hope of sleep. Every time Taki dozed off, she woke up in a panic over the cherubic child with the gold filigree hair and twinkly emerald eyes forging ahead to the jagged peak.

She shivered violently and cried out, waking up Koyam.

"What's the matter, Taki?" Koyam asked, still half asleep.

"I'm all right. Go back to your dreams." Taki didn't want to alarm her friend, or to reveal how murky and treacherous her visions had become. She opened her mouth in a mute sob at the apparition of cascades of water and mud overflowing bridges, roads, and railroad tracks. She broke out in a cold sweat at the sight of a balcony of a contemporary building in Aguas Calientes falling into the Vilcanota River, its churning waters swallowing a big woman in its hungry crests.

Then the suffocating vision of the present-day perils of the raging river flowed in reverse like a slow-motion movie rolling backwards and backwards to the past. This time, Taki saw another child, an indigenous boy, carrying heavy scientific instruments on his tiny back, while being urged by two *gringos* to cross the rising Urubamba River. The boy, like any young child, was shaking with fear at crossing the river ahead of the men. He was a native of the land and he knew that this was not the proper place to cross this river, but he heard the *gringos* yelling at him to cross, to be the guinea pig, the sacrificial lamb, in order to determine the depth of the waters.

Taki heard the long-ago boy say: "It is too deep, *Señor* Hendrikson. I am afraid, Engineer Tucker." But the men persisted, and the river smacked its gluttonous lips in anticipation. On the child's first misstep, the swift currents collared him—for eternity. Taki covered her eyes; it pained her to watch the boy from decades ago drown. His poncho floated on the water until it came to rest on the rocks downriver next to the long metal tube that the *gringos* ran to rescue while letting the boy drown. Tears rolled down Taki's cheeks: she couldn't believe the men chased after the hard metal object instead of trying to save a flesh-and-bones child.

Years later, spindly-legs Bingham would write about his escapades in Machu Picchu, and about the repairs Hendrikson made to his wet alidade, but he never opened his mouth or inked his pen—in sympathy, in agony, in humanity—for the loss of the tiny child his own men sent to do a man's dangerous job.

That last tragic vision exhausted Taki and she fell asleep next to Koyam. Although they still felt as spry and strong as forty-year-old women, their older bodies obviously needed the rest. In their deep sleep they were oblivious to the silent activity taking place in the camp. Their keen eyes and ears missed the arrival of Rodrigo, slithering like a serpent into one tent and then another to play with the *gringas'* minds and their bodies.

For his first port of call, Rodrigo selected Hilary's tent: she was the woman who craved the most attention, and he would need to depend on her physical size and strength later on this journey. He snuck into her tent and put his index finger to his lips.

"The boy was shaking with fear at crossing the river
ahead of the men."

"Shh," he whispered, smiling at her. "I only have a few minutes to spend with you. I must return to town, because the rain flooded the condor rehabilitation facility and I must help rescue them."

Hilary sat up from her oversize sleeping bag.

"I'll go with you," she volunteered. "I'd love to help."

Rodrigo lay down next to Hilary and pretended to moan with back pain.

"It's been backbreaking work," he told her, "but I knew you would understand. You have a heart of gold, my gentle butterfly."

Hilary melted at these soft-hearted words. She was so pleased that Rodrigo saw her as delicate and kind and loving. She started to rub his back, listening intently to his moans of gratitude. She let her hands slide lower and lower, but just when she reached down to pleasure him, he turned and kissed her passionately.

"I would do anything to stay here with you, just you," he murmured. "But I must do what is right. You do understand, don't you?"

Hilary nodded like a high-school girl, though she was bitterly disappointed that Rodrigo was going to leave after just one kiss.

"I admire what you're doing," she told him. "Will we see you in the morning?"

But Rodrigo slipped away with an enigmatic smile, and no promises. Hilary lay back in her chilly sleeping bag, her heart fluttering like her butterfly namesake.

Rodrigo waited a few minutes before ducking into Gabby's tent, where he did a repeat performance. She was a bit too talkative, so he had to kiss her for a longer period of time.

"Without letting the others know that I was here," he asked her, "because I was desperate to see you and only you for just a few moments tonight, can you please convince them to keep going on the hike until I meet up with you all later tomorrow night?"

"Sure, of course," Gabby agreed, but then she started plying him with annoying questions. "Why can't you stay with us tonight? Why don't you send Choque to help at the condor rescue center? We really need you. After all, you're the guide we hired. You wouldn't want us to demand a refund, would you?"

Rodrigo didn't like the tone of this last question. Gabby wasn't entirely under his spell yet: her tone was that of a demanding American consumer, one who saw him as a hired hand and a Latin lover, not the god-like presence he'd like to be. She might be one who could make trouble for him, even before he drove these women like cattle to his specially selected Inca trail. He didn't need this pushy little character to make trouble; he needed her to be the one who herded the women farther and farther into the trail he'd chosen.

"All your questions are very perceptive," Rodrigo told Gabby. "They show how bright and caring you are. In fact," he added, kissing the palms of her hands, "you have all the qualities that I have always dreamed of in a soul mate."

Gabby loved what she was hearing, but she was very wary about trusting any man with such quicksilver emotions. This, at least, she'd learned from all her online dating disasters.

"Hmmm," she said. "You present a bit of conundrum, don't you? I like what you say, but paradoxically I'm both attracted to and suspicious of your words."

Rodrigo looked downcast.

"I was a fool for revealing my heart to you," he murmured, and retreated out of her tent.

"Rodrigo—wait!" Gabby cried, but he didn't come back. The only result was alerting all the other women. When Gabby wriggled out of her tent, hoping to find Rodrigo standing there, she discovered Tiff, Hilary and Mercy, all roused from their slumbers. The women had slipped on their heavy parkas over their thermal underwear. While they stood shivering they craned their necks trying to spot Rodrigo in the darkness of the camp. Tiffany had managed to slip her bare and tanned legs into her moist hiking shoes, but she weathered the bitter cold in order to clear things up.

"OK—so which one of you just said 'Rodrigo, wait'?" Tiffany demanded, as her legs shook in the chill of the night. No one said a word. "Because let me tell you all one thing for sure: if Rodrigo had been in camp, he wouldda been in my tent."

Tiffany marched from tent to tent pointing her powerful flashlight inside each one in turn. She'd bought all sorts of camping gizmos on her boss's credit card, and at last one of these gizmos was giving her power over the geniuses. After her tent-search turned up nothing, she beamed light into each woman's eyes, the way the cops always scrutinized her at the Pacific Coast Highway sobriety checkpoints back in Newps. She fixed the light longest on a surly-looking Hilary.

"Rodrigo is not inside *anyone's* tent," Tiffany declared, "but whoever is dreaming about him and shouting out his name better forget about it. He's with me."

The other three women looked forlorn and disgusted. They were cold and damp, standing shivering outside their tents in this camp in the middle of nowhere, staring at this determined and bumptious airhead from Newps. However smart and successful they might be, they had all fallen for Rodrigo's Inca trail website and its promises of transformation and adventure lacking in their professional lives. Now the reality of their situation was beginning to sink in. They were way out of their depth here in this craggy, forsaken land.

Hiram Bingham, the women's fellow Ivy Leaguer, had compensated for his lack of academic success by promoting himself as the discoverer of Machu Picchu, the supposed lost city of the Incas. One hundred years later, these three women of varying physical size tried to project an image of Amazonian vigor in order to camouflage their broken hearts. But in this, their final quixotic quest to find true love in a faraway land, they neglected to do basic sophomore research on Rodrigo. And this academic error was already coming back to haunt them.

They'd all assumed that someone else had vetted Rodrigo's outlandish claims, because otherwise his website would *not* have been linked to an Ivy League-quality site. Lured by his syrupy chocolate eyes gazing out from his home page, the women had logged on to their laptops and asked their virtual oracle: "Will I find lasting love on this expensive and rigorous hike on the Inca trail?" The wording of each query differed a little, but the cyber oracle could identify past patterns and project desires: its state-of-the-art predictive analytics examined the frequency of their visits to online dating sites, and was able to forecast the women's behavior. So this cyber oracle, like all oracles, uttered obscure and ambiguous advice. "Your heart aches for an elevated love that exists at the top world," it said, and recommended various websites. Their eager and educated fingers clicked from one website to the next trying to make sense of the advice they'd been given. When the cyber oracle offered up Rodrigo's Inca Trail website, with its magical photos of the elevated city of Machu Picchu, the words "elevated" and "top of the world" seemed like a mystical message. All the women were smitten with the idea that their soul mate waited for them in the land of the Incas.

Tiffany's experience as a cheater and scam artist didn't persuade her to analyze her past decisions; she only listened to the rage within. She paced the campsite, beaming her flashlight into every bush and along every pathway. Finally, something in the mud grabbed her attention.

"What the hell! Whose frickin' size-12 footprints are these? They're certainly not Chuck's or one of his mini-men." She swiveled around, pointing the light at each of the three women. "I'm no Ivy League genius, but I'd say Rodrigo *was* here and he *did* go in to see one of you bitches. So fess up now, OK?"

The other three stood frowning at her. None of them were admitting anything. Tiffany's rage swelled.

"Chuck!" she hollered. "Get your ass out here! You have some explaining to do. We want to talk to Rodrigo right now!"

She marched over to where the porters were sleeping, beaming her flashlight at their heads and kicking them awake. They were all a pile of arms and legs covered by their ponchos and a cheap plastic tarp, which they had set up under the foliage of a large Queñua tree. As a native Californian she knew some Spanish—mainly from watching TV commercials—so she barked her commands in Spanish, just like the Chihuahua who wanted a taco.

"*Yo quiero el radio,*" she told them, raising her voice even more when they pretended not to understand. "*Yo quiero el teléfono.* Give me the phone, you little twerps!"

Choque sat up, shielding his eyes from the bright beam.

"You'd better bring out the solar power radio," Tiffany ordered, "and the two-way radio with the five-mile radius, and the smart phone app with the uploaded topograph-whatever maps that beam our location to your headquarters. Bring out all the bullshit you advertised on the website *now!*"

Choque and the porters refused to move, but Tiffany had the eyes—and mind—of a shoplifter. She spotted Choque glancing at his backpack, dumped a few feet away. When he sprang up to reach it, Tiffany's six a.m. Newps boot-camp workouts paid off. She got to the bag first, grabbed it, and ran back towards the other women.

Choque and his men were all standing up now and looked enraged, but Tiffany held him at bay with the flashlight.

"Don't come near us, Chuck," she warned. "We're going to call Rodrigo."

She threw the backpack towards Hilary, Mercy and Gabby.

"That's how you deal with these little a-holes," she told them. "Now one of you frickin' geniuses figure out how to use the communication equipment."

But when Hilary started emptying the bag onto the damp ground, all they could find were pornographic magazines and a lonely chipped transistor radio. Tiffany, her face white with shock, flew into a rage.

"Chuck, you lying son of a bitch! I'm going to kick your ass." She stood glaring at him, but Choque seemed more amused than afraid. The porters snickered, and walked away beyond the range of her flashlight into the blackness of the night.

Hilary turned the radio on and moved the old fashioned dials. None of the women owned a transistor radio, which they regarded as a relic, a piece of archaeological potsherd that Bingham would have surreptitiously packed inside his chests to send back to New Haven before the Peruvian government put a stop to his pillaging. They were dismayed at being reduced to listening to news on a radio. They'd prepared and researched for this trip, but tonight neither their laptops nor cell phones could connect them with the world outside this soggy mountain top.

Tiffany yanked the radio from Hilary. "Are you a moron or what? I can't believe you're trying to find something in English." Tiffany deftly found a news station in Spanish. "Shhh, pay attention."

Mercy and Gabby seemed to awaken from their catatonic state, and translated for the other two.

"The roads are closed," Mercy told them, "and the river has destroyed the train tracks."

She didn't want to mention Sandra, who had insisted on going on the later train, but they all realized the implications. Hilary couldn't contain her tears. "Do they say if the trains arrived to Aguas Calientes safely?" she whimpered. "Poor silly Sandra—I mean Zahndrah."

Gabby shook her head. "Well, they're saying that around 2,000 people are in the town of Aguas Calientes," she said, straining to listen to the news announcer. "And the Peruvian government has plans to helicopter them out of the area...as soon as the rain subsides."

Gabby paused, not wanting to upset Hilary further. She was surprised at her own empathy. Until a few moments ago, Hilary had been her rival for Rodrigo's attention.

Mercy picked up where Gabby left off. "They don't have an exact count on the hikers currently trekking on the Inca Trail, but they say that the ancient Inca paths have been around for hundreds of years and have excellent drainage."

The women looked at the muddy ground and worried about the rest of the terrain. They turned off the radio to save the battery, and to avoid any more bad news. They had nowhere else to go but forward on this ill-fated hike.

✹

Tiffany's angry shouts had woken up Taki and Koyam.

"¡Ooyooyooy, that little doll is definitely related to howler monkeys," Koyam said. "What has been happening? What did I miss?"

Taki, who'd been fast asleep, sat rubbing her eyes.

"I can see that you're no night watchman," said Koyam. "I knew you'd fall asleep."

"I did, but let me stretch out." Taki struggled to her feet and walked to the far side of the boulder to relieve herself. As her eyes adjusted to the darkest part of the trail they'd taken, she saw Choque and the porters busily pushing rocks and tree branches around, covering up the path. Taki narrowed her eyes. She knew what they were up to. They were attempting to create a small mudslide that would prohibit anyone else from passing.

The genius of the Inca paths was their extensive reach and solid stone construction: the network connected all four corners of their empire, their Tawantinsuyo, from Quito to Argentina. Its shortcoming, from a modern perspective, was that in many sections the roads were alarmingly narrow and steep. Choque and his men had selected one of these narrow sections to create an impasse.

Taki tiptoed back to Koyam, signaling to get up and to keep quiet. The two women shouldered their bundles and walked higher up the path to a point where they were safe from Choque and his malevolent road crew, but they could still see the *gringas*.

Taki stated the obvious. "The women seem upset. Just look at the bouncy doll! Choque must be thinking that the women will try to return the same way they came and head back towards the warden's station. That's why he's blocking the narrow road."

"Do you think that Rodrigo was at the camp and then disappeared, the way he always does?" Koyam asked.

Taki could predict where this question was going. "Yes, I'm sure he was at the camp visiting one of the—"

"Visiting? Did you say *visiting*? Rodrigo doesn't visit. He comes in like a fox and takes any chicken he wants. That's what he did with my great-granddaughter, or have you forgotten? He used her anytime he wanted until he got bored. My poor little girl went to Miami looking for him and we've never heard from her since."

Taki reached out to hold Koyam's hand. There was nothing to say to provide comfort. The pains of the past and fear of the impending doom kept them wide awake as they watched the *gringas* retreat to their respective tents, and as they saw Choque and his men return to their roost, to keep vigil on these four women their boss needed in order to accomplish his great feat.

CHAPTER ELEVEN

odrigo addressed the porters from the relative comfort of his tree platform. "Did I not tell you that these American women attack without provocation?" he hissed. "Even the prettiest among them turned out to be a blackback coral snake, didn't she?"

"Yes, *Don* Rodrigo," the five men replied.

"I've told you how to properly address me, haven't I?" Rodrigo asked with theatrical patience, shaking the distant branches of his tree platform to remind them that he perched above them like a god in the sky. He employed this method of camouflage during his nocturnal hikes. He either climbed to his strategically constructed platforms or stayed at an elevated covered spot to watch the action of his tour groups from a distance. Rodrigo grew bored easily playing the dashing adventurer, brimming with historical and anthropological facts during the day, by night recounting eerie campfire stories to entertain his tour groups. He loathed hearing the foreigners' trite observations about the Incas, the topography, and the current state of affairs in the world. Their arrogant first-world view irritated him, and he fantasized pushing them off various precipices throughout the perilous hike. Rodrigo's only consolation from *gringo* overload was that the tree platform was also an effective love shack where he could bring his sex partners when he had more than one woman to satisfy on a trek.

The foreign women he bedded up here, on the platform's sisal mat, relished the painful rug burns on their knees as they pleasured Rodrigo, their special cloud-forest lover. They performed sex acts with him they would never dare to do back home, not that they could ensnare such an accomplished and handsome lover elsewhere. They tolerated the pain knowing that soon they could show their scabby knees to their girlfriends back at the office, standing around the water cooler and describing, in lurid detail, what Rodrigo had done to them—and vice versa. The women would be able to recount how they howled with the monkeys and other cloud-forest animals as the eyes of a curious viscacha studied their lovemaking in the tree. What the women could not recount was their carnal abandon, which they treasured like a love song, and which drove Choque and the other porters insane with unsatisfied lust.

Rodrigo wasn't finished interrogating the porters. "I've told you how to properly address me, haven't I?" he asked them again.

The men looked at each other and then gazed up at Rodrigo's platform, hoping to read some directional sign in his eyes, but the opaque night muddied everything. Confusion and exhaustion fogged their brain, and they couldn't recall which one of his titles Rodrigo preferred nowadays.

Since they had first met him, he had slowly transformed from a lascivious thirty-three-year-old man known simply as

Rodrigo to a proper Spanish gentleman, *Don* Rodrigo. Then their boss decided to claim his Inca heritage, demanding to be called Rodrigo Guamán Poma de O'Rourke. One of the porters ridiculed the appropriation of the famous name—Guamán Poma de Ayala—by calling him "Mr. Falcon Lion." This was a feeble pun: Guamán meant falcon, and Poma meant mountain lion. When Rodrigo heard this nickname, he struck the porter with such force that he perforated the unfortunate man's eardrum. This handicap meant the porter could barely keep his balance for the duration of the hike.

"Next time you lose your balance," Rodrigo had threatened him, "I'm going to push you all the way down the cliff."

Finally, one of the porters flashed onto Rodrigo's latest name preference.

"Yes, my Inca, you told us that the *gringas* would bite and not let go, just like a coral snake." He raised his voice, in case Rodrigo had missed the honorific title. "My Inca!"

"Precisely, my man!" Rodrigo continued his lecture as if he were a professor in a lecture hall. "The American female never ceases to amaze with her erratic behavior. Don't you all agree?"

"Yes, our Inca," they answered, but Rodrigo was not satisfied.

"I am your Inca, that is true, but am I not more than that? Have I not proven to you that my powers exceed those of a mortal?" The men, who had never gone to school and had worked as beasts of burden all their lives, didn't know what to say. All they knew was to answer yes to all Rodrigo's questions, or face the consequences of a beating. All they wanted was for him to go to sleep for a couple of hours so that they could do the same.

Rodrigo assumed that his men only lived to please him, giving him their admiration and loyalty because of his obvious superiority. He knew his looks and muscular body were the envy of the trail guides, and his knowledge of the Inca trail flora and fauna was unrivaled, which was why his porters and clients showered him with praise. Rodrigo didn't realize that when his rivals patted him on the back and said, "What a macho! They don't make strapping Incas like you anymore!" they were actually mocking him. After every false compliment, Rodrigo would swat his porters and demand, "Did you hear that? Didn't I tell you that even the premier guides see me as their superior?"

Up in the tree platform, Rodrigo aimed his sling directly at Choque and hit him with a small jagged rock. His mother's people had given him his symbolic sling or *huaracas* when he was a young teen. At that time Rodrigo had been told to sling a rock at the beginning of the rainy season, but he liked the pain and blood the sling extracted from his human targets better. When his latest shot stung Choque, his right-hand man had said nothing, ignoring the hot blood dripping from the fresh wound on his shoulder.

"Answer me," Rodrigo demanded again. "Am I more than mere mortal?"

"Your accomplishments and talents exceed those of any man," Choque said, because his men still seemed dumbstruck. "That is to say, they exceed those of any mortal. You are our Inca, but you are also the god of lightning—our Illapa."

"What am I capable of doing?" Rodrigo asked. The porters could hear him selecting another rock; they did not want to bleed like Choque.

"You are a warrior in the sky," called the cook-porter. "Your sling stone is the lightning bolt that broke your sister's ceramic water jug and brought us rain from the skies. That's who you are, *Don* Guamán Poma."

This was the wrong title. The sling hurled its second blood-thirsty rock, and the cook grabbed his leg in pain.

"You are unique and perfect, thunder god Illapa," he croaked, so confused that he couldn't recall any details about Illapa's silver cloak of lightning.

"Whatever happened to the name Pachacuti II?" one of the slower porters asked. "I thought you were going to name yourself the second cataclysm. Since you are making the world anew, I think that would be a good name."

Rodrigo seemed pleased with that suggestion. There was no movement on his platform, though the men below him still cowered in fear and subservience. All but the cook felt themselves hopelessly inferior to Rodrigo. The cook had enough self-esteem left to feel confident of his one skill: a talent for creating savory dishes out in the wilderness of the trail. He was particularly proud that his food had never given any tourist the runs for more than one day.

For a few minutes, while the rain stopped and the howling winds subsided, the porters relaxed enough to doze off, assuming that Rodrigo had done the same. But this peace didn't last long.

Sharp pebbles zinged from Rodrigo's sling, a demand for them all to pay attention. "Am I on top or at the bottom of the pyramid?" he wanted to know.

Choque, who was tired and still smarting from the first sling attack, let his quick temper get the best of him. "Neither," he snapped. "We're freezing here below your warm tree platform. What pyramid are you referring to...Illapa?"

Normally Rodrigo would have clambered down to beat the insubordinate Choque to a pulp, but right now he needed to articulate his pyramid scheme. It had lost its primary benefactor in the missing-in-action Sandra, and Choque was the only one of his minions who could begin to understand the subtleties of Rodrigo's supreme plan. This plan would install Rodrigo in the pantheon of the Inca gods for this new millennium. He'd told that scrawny French woman, Violette, who had latched on to him like a pernicious parasite two years ago, that he planned to make his earth-shaking entrance as Tupac Amaru III, but now Rodrigo had higher aspirations. That was one reason he wanted to constantly remind others that he dwelled high above them. Tonight it was an ordinary tree platform, but in two days' time it would be the zenith of the highest peak, as the new Inca god.

"Where did I leave off?" Rodrigo asked.

The exhausted porters snored their responses. Only Choque was still wide awake.

"You said that you had aimed too low," he told Rodrigo, "by wanting to lead as Tupac Amaru III. You said that the first Tupac Amaru had escaped the Spanish in 1572, deserting his citadel in Vilcabamba, but that he had been captured because of his lack of conviction. Instead of forging ahead of the pursuing Spaniards, he waited by the Urubamba River for his pregnant wife to be moved gently."

"You have a great memory, Choque." Rodrigo was pleased. "Once we get your reconstructive surgery completed in Brazil, you will impress all the women. Young beautiful women, not these used-up *gringas*. Go ahead—tell me more about the worthless Tupac Amaru I and II."

"You said that because of Tupac Amaru's weak decision to wait for a woman, the Spanish captured him and gave him a bogus trial. He was beheaded… a fitting end for a weakling, in your estimation, my Inca god." Choque struggled to suppress a giant yawn. "You also consider Tupac Amaru II a usurper. The only worthwhile thing he did was to kill 575 Spaniards in 1780, for which he was also quartered and beheaded…your highness, Illapa."

Rodrigo was not about to let the tired Choque fall asleep: Rodrigo himself was wide awake and wired on cocaine, and whenever he was in this state, his minions were expected to stay awake with him. He woke the porters with well-placed sling bullets. "Stay awake, you simpletons! You, cook, tell me which one of the *gringas* should I go after first? Which one has the most money?"

The cook shrugged. "I'd have to say it is the giant. She seems very kind and well-mannered, and I think her family must have spent a fortune to feed her. She looks as docile as a lamb, but although she is all muscle, that rump of hers is prime beef...and she also owns an expensive camera."

Rodrigo was disgusted with the simpleton cook's rudimentary evaluation, and felt it was his duty to chastise him. "Cook, you'd better stick to food preparation and that is all. In fact, this is your last trek with us—you're just plain stupid. A stolen camera will only bring a few hundred *soles*. What I'm talking about is $50,000. Do you understand what that amount of money can buy me?"

The cook finally looked alarmed. He feared losing his job, meager as it was; he had children to support. He looked at Choque as an ally, but Choque was ignoring his pleading, watery eyes. Choque enjoyed watching the cook and the porters get a beating from Rodrigo, because it meant the heat was on someone else.

The cook wasn't giving up. "The fifty thousand U.S. dollars would be enough money to fund the new Virgins of the Sun temple you will establish. It would let you house lots of beautiful young girls to satisfy the rich male tourists." The crew of porters had been hearing this story from Rodrigo for years.

Rodrigo zinged a rock at his head. The cook saw stars, but he also remembered how people said that Rodrigo financed his lengthy vacations to the Caribbean.

"I suppose," he continued, "that you, as the new Inca god, will be selling babies again, like you used to. Am I right?"

Fortunately for the cook, Rodrigo had run out of rocks and jagged pebbles.

"Don't think you're getting away with something, cook," he snarled. "Your last comment will not go unpunished. You will feel the pain—you can count on that!"

The other porters admired the cook's daring. Rodrigo was a known cad, a Don Juan of immense proportions, but he was also notorious for the clandestine selling of babies to foreigners. He had his own children all over the highlands, uniquely adorable infants and toddlers whose features combined the best of Rodrigo's Irish and Peruvian ancestry with the grace and golden skin tone of their young indigenous mothers. Rodrigo took great pride in fathering lots of children. To each young girl he impregnated he would say, "You will go down in the history books. Did you know that two of our greatest men in Inca history are the Inca Garcilaso de la Vega and Guamán Poma de Ayala?"

But this meant nothing to the pregnant girls. "I can't read and I don't know anything about these men," they would say. "Why are they famous?"

"Both men were half Inca and half white," Rodrigo would tell them, flashing his brilliant smile. "Just like me."

The gossip in the highlands was that Rodrigo would visit the hamlets where he had fathered children, give the baby's family money, and take his newest child away with him. He'd promise to take care of the child, but no one really knew what he would do. Most of the infants' mothers had already fled Peru to work as maids in Spain, leaving their children in the care of overburdened grandparents. The rumor was that these women had been tricked into thinking that they would be taking care of elderly Spaniards, and able to send a lot of money back home. The reality was that once they arrived in Spain their passports would be snatched by their smugglers, who then forced the girls into a life of prostitution.

Rodrigo's porters had been envious of the children who were taken abroad by eager parents who could not have any babies of their own. When the porters had been youngsters, no one had volunteered to rescue them from their miserable lives; not one soul had ever wanted to adopt a tiny dwarf baby. But the porters kept their rancorous thoughts buried inside their hardened hearts and never revealed Rodrigo's baby trafficking to anyone.

Instead of continuing his Socratic-Method inquiry, Rodrigo told his flunkies his truths.

"The *gringas* we have in camp tonight are the brightest of the brightest from America, can you believe it?" He frowned, more annoyed with himself than with his sleepy and thick-headed men. "Don't answer that question. Believe it or not, you fools are *not* at the bottom of my pyramid. That base level is made up of all the people who will follow our lead as the neo-Incas, the empire that will cover the four corners again. Our Tawantinsuyo will be ruled by me and for our benefit. What do you think of that?"

The men looked at each other in panic, unsure if they were supposed to answer or not. Choque cleared his throat, and prepared to say something, but once again Rodrigo barked at them to shut up. So the men fell asleep—all except Choque. If Choque had known how to write, he would have been taking notes from Rodrigo's maniacal rant.

"In the Illapa pyramid scheme," Rodrigo roared, "the *gringas* are the ones who will bring me the money. That is the only thing these people are consumed with anyway. Even that pretty little brunette, Gabriela, who I intend to ravish tomorrow night, told me in her endless emails that her blog was in the process of being monetized. Monetize, finance, credit swaps, capitalize, IPO. The jargon of money-hungry, greedy bastards is getting more and more interesting, don't you think?"

Choque cleared his throat, just in case, but Rodrigo clearly didn't expect him to reply.

"Sandra fooled me once," Rodrigo continued, "but I tricked Violette more than once. It is amazing how easy it was to spend thousands and thousands of Euros, but I sure enjoyed myself. I guess the universe is even-steven now, wouldn't you agree?"

"Yes, Illapa," Choque whispered.

Rodrigo laughed. "That's why you're my almost main man, Choque. In a few months, once you return from your surgery, you will be my complete main man. We are going to plunge our golden rods deep and hard, long and cruel into every crevice we want. What do you say?"

Choque's moan of primeval desire rang into the night and Rodrigo joined him in a lewd duet—briefly. Rodrigo wanted to finish outlining his pyramid scheme, mainly for his own benefit since he needed to fine-tune it before he proceeded the next day. These *gringas* and their strong-willed ways had mystified him more than he expected. The giant, Hilary, turned out to be a softy when he had counted on her to be his brutal enforcer. The face and body of Tiffany did not arouse him the way he had anticipated. Touching her plastic breasts and kissing her plumped-up lips was like making love to a store mannequin. He had obviously melted a glacier of desire in Mercy, and this was gratifying, but her ability to turn into a business lawyer seconds after he had satiated her meant Mercy was too unpredictable. And the chipper brunette, Gabby, whose vivacious brown eyes scrutinized him too closely, was still an enigma.

"Where was I in my pyramid plan, Choque?" he asked.

"You were telling me how you are going to get the money for my operation…I mean, for the pyramid plan to work, Illapa."

"Stop thinking about yourself, Choque! Don't piss me off, or I'll cut off your rod, too. Here's what I was saying: These *gringas* are graduates from the Ivy League, the smartest of the smartest, and do you know what they do after they use their big brains to make lots of money? You don't know, do you? Well, I'll tell you. They go on their computers and they beg for men. Can you believe it?"

"Hmm," was all Choque dared to utter.

"That is exactly what they do. They go online and they beg for men to meet them and to screw them. These women have everything the rest of the world wants. They are attractive, they are educated, they are well-fed, they can buy whatever they like, but they cannot find a man. Why do you suppose that is?"

"Illapa, Inca god, should I answer or not?"

"Go ahead, idiot!"

"Their men are like me, they are not potent. Are their rods limp?"

"A stupid answer, Choque. No, their men are potent and even those who aren't take pills that make them rock hard—"

"Then why have you not bought me these pills, Rodrigo?" Choque shouted.

Rodrigo jumped down from the platform and pummeled Choque with the cook's pan.

"Don't ever question my decisions again or I will kill you," he spat. "I am the god of lightning."

Rodrigo turned to the sleeping porters, kicking them awake with punches and kicks. They scrambled to their feet, cowering with fear. Rodrigo commanded them to help him back up to his perch, where he resumed his lecture, as if nothing had happened.

"As I was saying, these *gringas* are hypocrites. They have all the best qualities but they lie about themselves to the men on the computer. They send photos that show them at their best when they were much younger. Even beautiful women like Mercy or Gabriela fabricate their pasts. Did you know that Mercy is really a Latina?"

The porters all shook their heads.

"You should have guessed this truth. Doesn't she speak to you in Spanish all the time?"

The porters nodded again.

"You little donkeys really depress me." Rodrigo gave a melodramatic sigh. "I was counting on you to find out which one among the *gringas* was the richest, and all you can tell me is that the giant owns an expensive camera. Now I have to charm them one by one to find out which one has a trust fund or blue-chip stock that they can sell immediately to help me start the Illapa Foundation. I'm going to try the scheme that worked with Violette, although I'll have to tweak the plan. Listen to this carefully, because I will ask you to repeat it to me."

Choque and the porters gazed up at Rodrigo, straining to see him in the inky night, and fighting exhaustion. It was too late for a test.

"Violette wanted a baby of her own so badly she would do anything to have one. Mind you, she had thrown away her own fetuses while they were still in her womb. She thought she could have a baby when she was good and ready, but it doesn't work that way, does it?"

The confused porters shrugged their shoulders.

"You'll never guess what she proposed we do," Rodrigo continued. "She wanted to buy three babies, one to keep as her own and two to sell back in Europe. I went along with her plan because it required that she transfer her money to me, first for her own baby, and then for the rest. But we double-crossed her, didn't we? By the way, has anyone else smelled that perfume she used to spray to cover up the stench of her putrid body? I've been it smelling all night."

Violette, he knew, preferred her namesake in her perfume. One porter had smelled the strong scent of violets, which was unusual since they were not in bloom in January, but he didn't dare tell Rodrigo. He didn't want Rodrigo to break his nose as well as perforate his eardrum.

"Do you have any questions before I proceed to tell you the rest of the pyramid plan?" Rodrigo asked, his voice low with cunning.

The porters were petrified: anything could happen now. Rodrigo had always been boastful and demanding. He'd always treated them as his possessions, expecting them to forsake everything for him. They had listened to his fantasies about how he was going to lead as the new Inca, and gone along with his stories of unlimited success with women. Sometimes the best porter would get a prize: Rodrigo would let him take his cell phone behind a shrub and look at videos of his naked foreign women so that the little man could pleasure himself. For so long the porters had thought of Rodrigo as an entitled man who paid them a pittance, but who at least paid them something. But tonight's grandiose and erratic behavior made them fear for their lives.

Rodrigo pointed to the deformed back of the cook.

"Cook, why don't you let your hunchback do the thinking? Ask me a question *now!*"

"Why don't you promise the *gringas* that they could become your *mamaconas* at the temple of the Virgins of the Sun you're going to start?"

"Proceed," said Rodrigo. "Give me more details, lumpy."

"If the *gringas* are as smart as you say, then they would appreciate knowing that in the old days, when we were a great empire, the *mamaconas* were in charge of the *acllahuasi*. They trained the young virgins, and they managed the gold and textiles and all the wonderful things that Inca emperor gave them. If you ask them to bring you their money, I think they know how to transfer money from bank to bank. And the lady at the bank in the Plaza de Armas in Cusco, the one who used to scream with frenzy when you…? She could give you the money."

"In some ways, you're more simple-minded than I thought. Do you think that just because I satisfy these women with my long tongue and my longer golden rod that they are just going to wire their money to me?"

"It is possible." The cook sounded sulky. "You are the Inca god, not me."

"Yes, you are powerful and a great talker," chimed in the porter with impaired hearing. "Why not make the *gringas* feel guilty? They are almost forty years old and they have no children and no husbands. Tell them that they must give you the money to help the children. And when you invite the old rich men to lie down with the young prostitutes in the house of the Virgins of the Sun, maybe they might also like to go to bed with the old *gringas*. The *gringas* won't have to lie to the computer anymore. I think. Perhaps."

He cowered behind the cook's hump in case Rodrigo tried to attack him again. But when nothing happened, another porter dared to speak.

"Why don't you impregnate all four *gringas*?" he asked. "They will stay here with their children and bring all their money. You could even threaten to sell their children and they will bring you more money to prevent you from doing it. Women are simple-minded like that."

Rodrigo remained silent. This silence worried the porters and they nudged the one porter who hadn't spoken. He looked down at the ground and refused to speak until Rodrigo's voice came booming from above.

"Tell me your idea or I'll pick you up and throw you off a cliff."

The tiny porter cleared his throat. "We have been talking about the male organ all night long," he said. "Is that why you picked the word *pyramid*? Is the top section of the pyramid you and your hard golden rod, Illapa? Is that how you are going to conquer?"

His brain befuddled, Rodrigo tried to make sense of the puzzle pieces offered up by his peanut-brained porters. Aspects of each suggestion made some sense, and each idea could possibly be monetized, as the *gringas* liked to say. But on the whole, his pyramid scheme needed the foundation of money to turn his dream into reality.

The roar of a distant puma sent shivers up his spine. His ancestor had just spoken to him as clear as day in the middle of the night, and Rodrigo understood that in order to become a god he had to perform a god-like act. This had to be an act of immense sacrifice that would please all the mountain spirits, one that would make his people realize they must return to the ancient ways.

"The sacrifice must be immense," he said aloud. "And it must honor the ancient rites."

CHAPTER TWELVE

Neither Taki nor Koyam would admit to one another that the leaden and sleepless night had weighed them down completely. They felt the aches and pains of their seventy years, and their earlier conviction that they could defeat Rodrigo was beginning to wane. They weren't even sure if they could stay awake until the battle lines were drawn.

From their perch just off the trail, they could see below to the camp, but no one could see them. They knew every vantage point and hideout from their decades of making pilgrimages along the off-beaten track of this and other secret paths. These were not the paths the tourists would ever discover since they led to nowhere their clouded foreign eyes wanted to see. Narrow and vertiginous, the paths would paralyze anyone not brought up to tread cautiously along these spiritual arteries. Even among most of the indigenous people of the region, these paths were unknown.

Every hundred years or so, one of these Inca trails presented itself to the world. In 1997, after forest fires, such a trail was "discovered" on the back of Huayna Picchu, but this was as rare an occurrence as Halley's Comet, the comet that the Incas claim foreshadowed the destructive force of Pizarro. The paths revealed themselves only to a few; those initiated to the mysteries of the trails and committed to secrecy. These were the roads that Taki followed.

To the novice eye, the path along which Choque had led the women was not immediately evident from the Inca Trail: they'd had to sidestep around a giant boulder that hid it from the main trail. Stout shrubs and trees further obscured its enigmatic beginning. These paths were the genius of the Inca engineers, who not only constructed the main Inca trails with granite steps, studding them with well-spaced inns or *tambos,* but also designed the secondary and tertiary passages that later enabled Inca rebels to elude the evil yoke of servitude of the Spaniards.

These were the backdoor paths that had helped Manco Inca escape from the Spanish conquistadors in 1535. Pizarro and his men had stormed into Cusco and pretended to respect Manco as the Sapa Inca, but he knew that he was under the control of Pizarro and his guns. Manco escaped with his troops along these hush-hush trails that led to his secret town of Vitcos. Once established in his new capital, Manco led a major revolt throughout the highlands, but the Spaniards pursued him through the known and unknown Inca trails, destroying the strategic bridges along the way. Manco had tenacity and a sense of purpose, because he was fighting for his people and their way of life, but in time, the Spanish chased him out of Vitcos too. Manco took to the road again, going from one secret route to a clouded path, and settled his rebel capital in Vilcabamba, far from the gunfire of the Spanish. The vines and lianas of the cloud forest took over the road leading to Vilcabamba, where Manco ruled his people and ignored the Spanish in Cusco.

But the Spanish would not rest until they captured Manco. First, they captured, raped, and then lanced his sister-wife, Cura Ocllo. Her cold body was put on a balsa raft and sent floating down the Urubamba River until she reached Vilcabamba and the arms of a heartbroken Manco. Eventually, it was Manco's overconfident and kind heart that did him in. In 1544, he welcomed some Spanish renegades into Vilcabamba, saying that he knew what it felt to be hunted down by the rapacious Spaniards. But they turned out to be cut from the same Spanish cloth. They returned Manco's favor by spearing his son and stabbing Manco. He lived long enough to make his last words of advice to his people ring true to the present day.

"Never forget our ceremonies," he told them, "and hide the rest of our icons and our precious ancestors, for they alone will speak the truth to us."

Throughout the years, Taki and Koyam would tell each other these legendary tales of escape, pursuit, and treachery; above all, they recalled the acts of infidelity. Koyam's sense of devotion to Taki and her mysterious ways always made her renounce the double-dealing Spaniards in the legends of Manco Inca and Tupac Amaru I and II. Each time Taki told their stories, Koyam shouted, "¡*Ooyooyooy,* how I wish I could have been there to fight those double-crossing Spaniards!"

Taki would take Koyam on hikes into the cryptic caves and crags surrounding the clearings. Koyam would accompany her to certain spots, but then Taki would ask her to wait, sometimes from dark till dawn, until she returned. Their bonds of friendship, which were as intertwined as the lianas to the granite boulders, meant Koyam would never ask Taki to explain her absences. Besides, Koyam enjoyed the distraction from her days at the plaza. She listened to the birds, mimicking their sounds while she studied their vibrant colors. These colors she would include in her textile designs once they returned to Cusco.

From their observation point, Taki and Koyam could observe Choque's obvious anger with his porters. The small men perplexed Taki. She couldn't decide if they were harbingers of demonic afflictions, as some claimed, or if they were spiritual beings, like the soldier-angels of the Spanish artistic tradition. In the brief time with the porters, when she had met them at the Kilometer 88 porter stand, she had not absorbed their essence.

"I should have tried to bless the little men," she told Koyam, scratching her head. "Their emptiness haunts me."

"You blessed Choque. What did you feel?"

"An immense animosity. He's a puma trapped in a miniscule cage." Taki wheezed out a long sigh. "I should have spent more time with him, too."

Koyam opened her sleepy eyes. "Now is not the time for regrets, Taki. I'm no sage, but those tiny demons have attached their talons to Choque, and he's a parasite who feeds off Rodrigo. Isn't it enough to know that together they are all up to no good?"

"I've never rushed to judgment on a potentially disastrous encounter as I am doing with Choque and his men. I'm not getting any visions as to what to do. I'm truly scar—"

Koyam put her rough hand over Taki's mouth. "Enough with the doubts. We made a decision to stop Rodrigo, and now we must remain vigilant. Come on, let's stand up. We're getting moldy, like potatoes left out in the rain."

Koyam started to do her mountain calisthenics, lifting her right leg and then her left. With every lift, the legs reached higher and higher, just as they used to do before they ran in the mountains in their youth.

"Look at me," she said. "I should have been a ballerina."

Taki smiled at Koyam's *jetés*. "Just don't go falling off the cliff. I'm not carrying you to safety."

"What safety? I'm with you, aren't I? That's all the safety I need. Come on, Taki, you have to move. You're going to sprout mushrooms if you stay on the moist ground."

Koyam began sparring with an immobile Taki. Every three or four punches, Taki would block Koyam's jab, just as she used to do in her younger days when she practiced boxing with her grandson. In the rustle of the leaves, she heard his high-pitched, preadolescent laughter again. He'd tell her she had quick reactions for a tiny granny, and she would wrestle him to the floor, giggling like a young girl.

"That's what I like to hear," said Koyam, "you laughing again! Only don't laugh so loud or we'll draw the attention of Choque and his men."

"Watching your silliness reminds me of my little alpaca, Khipu. Don't you wish we had our animals to keep us warm tonight?"

"Just the ones with two arms...like the old days!"

"Those days are gone," Taki sighed.

"Just one more night with a warm-blooded, two-armed animal would be fun, don't you think?"

Taki ignored this question, and began practicing her own calisthenics. They had learned to do this athletic routine each day at dawn, before they walked down to the plaza to sit for most of the day. Taki stretched her legs, wishing she hadn't brought Koyam along on this dangerous journey. As she watched her lifelong friend do her jumping jacks under a starless sky, Taki resigned herself to the darkest days of their lives. For the first time in her life, on a night when all her senses were on heightened alert, Taki felt nothing in her heart and saw nothing in her mind and soul. This void filled her with a bottomless grief.

Koyam interrupted Taki's reverie. "Do you see what those crazy porters are doing?" she whispered, pointing, and Taki peered down to the camp. The men were jumping up at attention as if Rodrigo were commanding them telepathically to rise and line up. Then Choque seemed to be wrestling and punching one or two of them for no apparent reason.

"Perhaps all their bizarre up-and-down behavior keeps them alert at night," Koyam suggested.

"Those are men who have been dealt bad luck in appearance and in genital mutilation," Taki said. "This undoubtedly makes them intractable warriors full of hatred at the world for their misfortunes."

"Yes, I suppose they have a right to be angry at the world. They must have it even worse than the ordinary porters for the other tour groups. Do you know that at the weigh stations they routinely let the porters pass with packs that weigh over 40 kilos?"

"That's unbelievable." Taki shook her head. "I thought the labor law and the porter's union had a limit of 25 kilos? Are you sure you have it right?"

"Yes, my great-grandson told me. There was a funeral for one of the young porters whose lungs gave out because of the weight of all the items the tourists demand on the hike. He also said that even the elite tour operators try to get away with paying the men 90 *soles* a day instead of the minimum 150 *soles*. No wonder the little men look so angry! What do you think they are going to do with the *gringas* on this hike?"

Taki didn't answer. Koyam wondered if Taki had gone into a trance that would illuminate their next step, but her friend was simply exhausted.

Koyam did not mention to Taki that if Choque and his men were to be their adversaries, she felt powerless to defend herself against them. She knew that Taki considered her as a type of bodyguard, but this was a role she could no longer play. Koyam knew that the fear she instilled in men, women, and children around the Plaza de Armas was well-founded. In her youth, she had no qualms in cracking a head or two, but here on the Inca trail she had always been a different person. For Koyam, the Inca trail hikes had been an escape from her daily routine, and the burden of her ever-expanding family and their demands and entanglements. Koyam and Taki's days of running at full speed along the Inca trail had passed them by eons ago.

Koyam elbowed her friend. "Do you remember how we would play *chasquis* on the trail?"

Taki nodded.

"You were the lead *chasqui* because you were a faster runner and could get to the half way station first. Then I would run and announce the message from the emperor, remember?"

Taki finally snapped out of her funk. "How can I forget your hilarious messages?"

"Which ones do you recall? I could use a happy memory—tell me!"

Normally Taki would have recalled one of Koyam's funny lines, but this time she just frowned. "This is no time for laughter. The sun will soon be rising and we have not thanked the mountain *apu* for keeping us safe."

Taki pulled a few coca leaves from her textile bag, and blew on them gently, reciting her words of gratitude to the mountain spirits. She held the pale green leaves upright between her fingers and pointed to each direction of the mountain peaks, blowing air on the coca leaves towards each peak. She asked the *apus* to bless Choque and his porters so that they would return safely to their homes with calmer hearts. She pleaded with the spirits to repel Rodrigo and send his evil ways plummeting to the bottom of the Urubamba River. Above all, she asked the spirits to keep vigil over the bitter *gringas,* whose problems Taki did not comprehend, but whose destiny had brought them under the sinister influence of Rodrigo. Their plight worried her the most, so she sent them blessings of harmony and peace. They were strangers to the Andes, and had no idea of the infernal danger that awaited them.

Taki touched Koyam's skull. "I'll be back in two hours," she said. "Whistle loudly like the Andean Cock-of-the-Rock if the hikers start to move out of camp. I won't be far."

Before Koyam could reply, she walked off, following the trail in the direction of one of her secret nooks.

Koyam stood for a while and practiced whistling various bird sounds. She could hear Taki in the distance repeating the sounds, and this made Koyam feel a little safer. But she was still on edge. The women in the camp below were all in their tents, but the porters had started to prepare for their departure. All her life Koyam had been vigilant about anyone who might harm Taki because of her gifts; this was her role in balancing the universe, and her protective instinct helped her to feel at peace. But as she watched Taki climbing the narrow path with the gait and appearance of a man, Koyam realized that Taki was just an ordinary person—an elder with a gift, but an old woman nonetheless. They were both ancient like the granite boulder on which she was leaning, and it dawned on Koyam that if she were to die today, then this would be the perfect cemetery. She would become part of the soil and granite of her ancestral land. Her soul would rise with the melodic sounds of the birds and reach the peaks; perhaps her laughter would please the *huacas* and she would rest eternally with a view of Machu Picchu.

Koyam whistled in the dulcet and showy style of a Russet-crowned Warbler, and then she answered that call with the two-syllable tweet of the Golden-crowned Warbler, knowing that Taki would be smiling at this song of nature, and the way Koyam could mimic it.

From a distance, Taki heard Koyam's zany bird songs, and was grateful for her friend's eternal optimism and joy. Although she trusted Koyam with her own life, Taki could never reveal the secret that had brought her to this godforsaken cave all these years. Initially she had lied to Koyam about the destination.

"You and I must contribute to the *apachita,* the pile of stones at the hidden pass," she'd told her. "But you must not tell anyone about the fork in the Inca Trail that brings us to this place. Can I trust you?"

"With your life. But don't think that I don't know there's more to your distant hikes than paying your respects to the *huacas* at the pass. I'll get it out of you one day." Koyam never tried to uncover the secret because she respected Taki, and knew her place in the universe.

Every time Taki disappeared into the mountain, she would return to Cusco and the problem or situation that had been troubling her would resolve itself one way or another. Koyam assumed that on this hike the answer to the poisonous Rodrigo problem would require an equally venomous solution. Koyam waited and whistled—and expected the worst.

Taki got down on her knees and crept through the narrow opening of the cave. She paused for a moment, waiting for her eyes to adjust. Ages ago wise elders had moved stones to enclose most of the cave opening, protecting it from human intruders. The many bats that made this place their home were busy elsewhere with their nocturnal wanderings. Bats did not frighten Taki, because she understood that these creatures represented both life and death, both fecundity and destruction. Their dual image fluttered in her mind and she began to understand the significance to her current dilemma. She had a vision of Rodrigo hanging upside down in the cave, his large wings undulating every couple of seconds. Then the face of the golden cherubic girl appeared in Taki's vision, smiling up at the Rodrigo vampire bat. He smiled back with his pearly white fangs.

Taki rubbed her eyes and stood up, and wiped the bat guano off her pants. She moved carefully through the sticky and malodorous cave towards a barrel shape wrapped, with great care, in wool and cord. When she found the corded barrel, no larger than a cask of wine, Taki knelt in the dung and lowered her head until it almost touched the ground, her nose inhaling the feces and urine of thousands of bats.

"I come to pay my respects, beloved ancestor. We are facing a great danger, and I beg your wise counsel," Taki struck her own skull to eliminate the vision of the Rodrigo vampire bat, now winking at her as he languorously masturbated. She felt her breathing constrict, and her voice sounded shrill. "A demon is among us, just like in the days of yore. His past actions are as reprehensible as those of the criminals who destroyed the empire you ruled."

She waited for the ancestor mummy, the *mallqui*, to grieve for his beloved people before she went on.

"Your presence among us guides us to this day. Your descendants showed kindness to the Spanish and they stabbed you." Taki slapped her forehead trying to banish the vision now playing in her mind—a horrific scene of the sadistic copulations of Rodrigo, Choque, and the *gringas*.

Taki was panting with fear and panic, thinking of her impending combat with Rodrigo and his minions.

"Your highness," she implored the mummy. "Please give me a sign as to what I should do. I have watched over you in this sacred grave for fifty years, but it is probable that I will die today."

Saying these words was a relief, like the lifting of the heavy rock of burden.

"Granted," she continued, "I did not take you out and march you in front of the people or dress you in sumptuous textiles, feathers, and gold. But I kept you warm with the tunics we wove for you, in the imperial designs you deserve. Koyam found a picture of the tunic you might have worn. That tunic is now in a museum in Chicago.... I am sorry."

Taki's eyes adjusted to the darkness, and a single ray of dawn light illuminated the mummy bundle. She smiled at the ancestor, hoping that the state of the woven tunic wouldn't be held against her. It had been a bold regal red when she'd brought it to the cave. Now it was rotting, oozing with bat dung.

"Koyam and I ground up hundreds of dried up cochineal insects to make the red dye for the alpaca yarns of the background, and she wove the white birds and the gold Inti pattern, with all her love. Look how lovely it still is!"

This was a lie. The once imposing Inca was now reduced to a humdrum, run-of-the-mill, bag of bones. In his golden age, as a recently desiccated mummy, the ancestor had dazzled his subjects with his gold and jewels. His descendants cried and mourned for him during his wake, and during the days of his *piccha*, the five-day floating spirit, when his soul roamed among the living. He had been accompanied in the subsequent annual ceremonies of *puruc raya* by all his mummified wives and attendants. As he was carried in a royal litter, his orange feathered headband reminded all that their ruler still lived among them. This was the sovereign mummy daddy-long-legs Bingham was desperate to find, so he could shove it into a ship's chest on its expedited way out of Peru. But Taki's ancestors, those with the all-knowing gift, had hidden him in this secluded cave.

"I did not take you out and march you in front of the people or
dress you in sumptuous textiles, feathers, and gold."

"I come today to ask for your forgiveness," Taki said, trying to steady her breathing, "for I have not selected another to follow in my steps."

Tears rolled down her wrinkled face like the muddy tributaries of the great Amazon River. "Not a single one of my descendants could begin to understand the significance of keeping you among us," she whispered. "They would conspire to send you off to some foreign museum or science laboratory."

Taki would never allow him to become some Third World skeleton in the closet of yet another North American institution. She would not give up the reins that would turn her ancestor *mallqui* into a relic brought out to pick the pockets of donors during a museum fundraiser or capital campaign. The Waspy huckster Bingham would have said, "Mummies sell, so bring them out to raise the funds for the good of the institution, by golly! Yes, siree."

Taki would rather see her *mallqui* entombed forever in his native grotto, with its god-awful smelling bats than reside in the hygienic laboratory of a soulless institution abroad. She had lived long enough to remember that the treasures of Machu Picchu and the Andes had been pilfered or destroyed by foreign conquerors. First the Spanish arrived and burned all the *mallquis* they could find in the realm, knowing full well that for the Incas there was no greater death than to be burned, even if one was already a mummified corpse. Then Bingham arrived in 1911 with visions of his own type of conquest. When he saw the great carved niches within a wall in Machu Picchu, he knew that the important mummies had been installed there to rest. He forced men to dig up their own ancestors in search of the perfect Inca emperor mummy to take back to New York, but all he found were the remains of numerous female mummies. The imperial ancestors had been carried away by the faithful, never to be found. Always the great promoter, spindly-legs Bingham had decided that the skeletal remains of the women must have been those of the Brides of the Sun. The imagined sexual hijinks of one Inca king and hundreds of young virgins would sell lots of newspapers back in United States.

Twenty years ago, Taki remembered, research into the skeletal remains revealed there had been as many men as women in Machu Picchu, and that the bones and spinal columns pirated by Bingham suggested that the women had worked slavishly, carrying heavy weights. In other words, these could not have been the skeletal remains of the privileged Brides of the Sun. The truth didn't affect Bingham's career or reputation. After his Machu Picchu exploits, Bingham went on to become a governor, a senator, and an even wealthier man, all on the worn-out backs of the Incas he pillaged.

In the dark cave, Taki's visions had become as clear as the quartz crystals abundant in Machu Picchu, and this clarity made her hyper-alert to everything around her. The ancient oracle within the *mallqui* whispered a harsh truth that punctured her ear like a glinting sliver of mirror. She not only saw the reflection of her own visions in this mirror: she witnessed the horrific act Rodrigo was about to commit. The shard vibrated in her brain, and Taki realized that she and Koyam were no match for the demonic Rodrigo.

Taki's vision subsided at the sound of flapping velvety wings. The vampire bats were returning to the home they shared with the Sapa Inca. They would be his only fitting companions now as Taki would need to carry out the other delicate *mallqui*, the benign female one who had guided her with an open heart. The arrogant Inca *mallqui* had never mentioned his eternal companion sitting at his feet in the cave; the loyal and benevolent *mallqui* that had been his constant mate throughout the centuries. The first bats barged in unabashedly and banished Taki from their home. Life and death, fecundity and destruction, past and present: they all thrived in the balanced universe of the secret cave.

She could also hear a more obnoxious sound, the Andean Cock-of-the-Rock warning her to get back to their vantage point above the campground. Taki blew her nose on her poncho and inhaled the fresh dew on the branches outside the cave. And she caught a nearby whiff of a violet fragrance, a scent that could not exist in nature this time of year. The smell shocked Taki back into the here and now. Taki placed coca leaves, enough for eternity, in front of the macho *mallqui,* and crept out of the cave carrying the tenderhearted ancestor—who purred encouraging words in her ears. Taki's entire body shivered with energy and lethargy, courage and fear, conviction and uncertainty. Here on the brink of death, she had never felt so alive.

CHAPTER THIRTEEN

s the light of dawn illuminated the campground, the acrimonious atmosphere of the hikers transformed into a congenial sunrise of friends eager to continue their trek. The rain and fog were gone, and so were the snide comments and bad feelings of the day before. The arc of a faint rainbow appeared above the campground, its distinct bands of color a reflection of the patterns woven into Taki's shawls.

The women, busy repacking their gear, were all eager to share their intensely vibrant dreams of the previous night. Tiffany started recounting her dream as though it had been a ray of sunshine beaming just for her.

"I'm telling you dudes, that little humpback chef put some wacky weeds in our food. And I didn't eat anything but the bananas. I mean, I was flying over these mountains like a condor. Now I know exactly how to get over the next pass."

She pointed up the steep Dead Woman's Pass. "And up to Macho Picchu! This is what we have to do —"

Mercy held up her hand, trying to stop the flow of words from Tiffany's mouth.

"Why don't we let Choque take us on the Inca Trail?" she asked. "Rodrigo has entrusted us to him for a reason, don't you think?"

"As a matter of fact, good old Choque has taken us *off* the main Inca Trail," retorted Tiffany. "We shoulda stayed with the Swiss hikers back in Wayllabamba. I don't know why he dragged us this way, but if you follow me I'll bring us back to the Inca Trail so we can catch up with the Swiss guys. They were kinda cute, don't you think?"

"I didn't notice," said Mercy while she zipped up her parka and cleaned her sunglasses.

"I'm telling you," Tiffany insisted, "Choque is going to take us on his own hike to nowhere, probably cuz he's lazy and hates my guts, by now. Let's just leave him behind and take the stubby porters along. I'm a super-good hiker and I swear I know how to get to the pass. I saw the whole thing when I was flying in my dream. It felt great to be a condor."

Tiffany ran in between the tents, flapping her arms and leaping up and gliding down. The other three women couldn't help laughing along with her.

"I know what you mean about the clarity of last night's dreams," Hilary said. "In my dream, I was flying with hundreds of species of butterflies. You wouldn't believe the vibrant blue in the Blue Perisama butterfly! I even remembered that there are over 278 species at the six elevation levels from 1,500 meters to 4,000 meters—"

"You actually dream statistics like those?" asked Gabby in disbelief.

Hilary laughed at her own hyperbole. "No, of course not. I was interjecting some facts I recalled about the butterflies native to Machu Picchu, that's all. I read up on so many interesting facts about Machu Picchu before coming here … you wouldn't believe how much I've been looking forward to this hike."

Mercy didn't feel like listening to the facts that she was certain Hilary was ready to spout like last night's rain. "Tell us about your dream, Hilary," she said quickly.

"Oh, yeah, sure. In this dream, the profusion of butterfly colors and sizes overwhelmed me. They almost frightened me until I saw them fly together up into this clear sky, where they formed the word HILARY. My name was floating in the sky in every color imaginable. They must have been welcoming me, don't you think?"

Mercy smiled at Hilary. "Undoubtedly, they were acknowledging you as a fellow butterfly. Or as someone who cares for the welfare of the environment. That's a formidable dream, Hilary. I'm happy for you."

Tiffany wanted to hear more dreams from the other women the way she always wanted more and more martinis back in Newps. She wanted everything in excess, and she wanted everything instantly—and she never wanted to pay for it. And why should she? She was hot and some guy would always pick up the tab. Duh! On this day, she was tempted by the description of the dreams, her own and the others', and she was determined to have her temptations satisfied on the spot. She prodded Mercy.

"You're not telling us your dream cuz it was horny, wasn't it?"

Mercy almost declined to incriminate herself, but this morning was so happy and harmonious, she knew she had to relax and share. "You're a mind reader, Tiffany. I had the most incredible sexual dream of my life, but unlike you two I wasn't anywhere near the sky—or even in the atmosphere, for that matter."

"What? You're not going to give us details?" Tiffany demanded. "No way! Out with the trashy dream, girlfriend. Wet dream,
wet dream, we wanna hear the wet dream!"

"It was wet all right," whispered Mercy, trying to ignore
Tiffany's manic dance: the thirty-something blond girl was hopping from foot to foot. "I was underwater and I was a manatee
mating with a shark. Impossible, I know, but I wasn't frightened
of the shark…whatsoever."

Gabby couldn't tie her hiking boots, she was laughing so
much.

"Why weren't you afraid of the shark?" she asked Mercy.
"Was he eating you?"

This bawdy comment made the other women holler like
jocks.

"Well, was he? Is that why you weren't scared?" Gabby
persisted.

Mercy paused—a long, reflective, legal pause—before she
answered. "No, I wasn't scared because between…well, between
the oral sex, he sang to me in Spanish!"

The women were beyond hysterics at the image of
a Spanish-singing, cunnilingus-performing shark. Hilary, who as
a lanky, lonely child had learned to look for connections in
dreams, to find symbolism in names, and to reflect on the
serendipity of life, had an inkling that the lyrics of the Spanish
song must hold some significant meaning for Mercy. If she could
get Mercy talking about that meaning, then perhaps they could
all talk about other issues: serious issues such as their online
dating dependency and their lack of a love life. They had all
postponed so much until some indefinite date, until after their
Ivy League years and graduate school and successful careers.
But now they found themselves alone and damn near forty—
and wanting something very different. These were the topics
Hilary had hoped to discuss with like-minded women over their

trek on the Inca Trail, rather than trade backbiting insults. Maybe things were about to change.

"What song was he singing?" she asked.

"An old mariachi song my dad used to sing," Mercy answered.

"Fascinating," mumbled Gabby as she finished stuffing her items in her backpack and Hilary fussed with her camera lens. "But your dream has elements of the Electra complex, don't you think, Mercy?"

Tiffany answered for Mercy. "Don't start with anything electrical—"

"This had nothing to do with electricity," Gabby corrected.

"Who cares? I'm still pissed about last night. These ass clowns don't have any of the advanced electrical equipment we were supposed to have on the hike. Their Inca Trail website is ghetto."

Gabby stifled the urge to reprimand Tiffany for being foolish and rude.

"Let's just keep the jokes rolling," she said, "and we won't even feel the burn of trekking up to Dead Woman's Pass. Shall we tell Choque to get started on the hike?"

"I'm telling you, Choque took us on the wrong path." Tiffany was pouting. "I saw the whole thing when I was a condor flying in the mountains last night. Honest!"

Gabby wished she'd jotted down all these gems of idiocy flowing from her fellow trekkers' mouths. How did she end up with a condor-flying dingbat, a giant who thought she was a butterfly, and a nymphomaniac whose daddy must have messed her up emotionally? And that wasn't including the awful Sandra, who seemed to have disappeared. All Gabby had done on her blog was to suggest that a group of women hikers destroy the effigy of the typical online dating male pariah, and then linked her blog to Rodrigo's Inca Trail website. In a matter of days her suggestion had gone viral. When she was inundated with requests, Gabby had restricted the hiker list to Ivy League alumnae, and this was the strange group with which she'd ended up.

As the others finished their packing, Gabby scribbled down ideas for her blog. She would love to skewer every single one of the observations made by her fellow hikers. When she got home, Gabby vowed to herself, she'd transform her blog into an extraordinary, multi-faceted opinion site that others would clamor to visit. It would be a site reflecting her Renaissance talents and interests. Her satirical bite would make people call her a twenty-first century Jane Austen, parodying the plight of women in her time.

There was no time like the present. Gabby needed to get started today in the old-fashioned way, with pen and paper, until her laptop was operational. She tucked her notebook into her jacket pocket and started thinking that her satire could extend way beyond the online dating phenomenon. If she could turn her talents to lambasting other contemporary issues, she'd be able to monetize her site in no time.

Choque appeared, unsmiling.

"We go now," he said gruffly. "We walk. Come."

Tiffany refused to move.

"Choque, I know for a fact that you are not taking us on the Inca Trail." She pointed in the opposite direction. "We were tired and wet last night, but I know that you went past Wayllabamba and to the left. So now we have to backtrack, got it?"

"No go back. We go forward." Choque pointed towards Dead Woman's Pass. "Come."

"Choque, what time will we arrive at Dead Woman's Pass?" Mercy asked. "Is that where we'll meet up with Rodrigo?"

Choque's eyes darted from left to right and back again. He heard Rodrigo's voice tell him to lie.

"We go this way," he mumbled, "and we meet Rodrigo early. Very early."

Even Tiffany seemed placated by this. The women all fell in line and walked at a good clip behind Choque. The porters, bringing up the rear, snickered at the colliding energy waves caused by these women. These men had spent their entire lives in this energy-bound corner of the world, and they could easily detect the women's jittery excitement at just the mention of Rodrigo's name. Their boss was a king or even a god as he claimed last night—a god who would be frolicking with all the women, in any way he wanted. The porters picked up their own pace, excited by the thought of what their boss would be doing with these beautiful *gringas* in just a few hours.

The women heard the rushing sound of a river.

"Is that the Llulluchapampa River we hear?" Hilary called to Choque. "Will we be crossing a traditional rope suspension bridge?"

"Yes," Choque said. "And—no."

Hilary had read a huge amount about the upcoming steep hairpin bend, and she was looking forward to taking photos at the bridge before entering the unusual cloud forest. The Inca engineers had mastered the construction of different types of bridges, but the one that Hilary was hoping to cross was the famed suspension bridge made of *ichu* grass. In the days of their empire, the Incas replaced these rope bridges annually. Hilary decided to share her knowledge of the indigenous flora and fauna with the other trekkers.

"We are so fortunate to see this many orchids," she enthused. "Do you see that bright pink one with a white center? That's an *epidendrum secundum*. Priests named it the crucifix orchid, but the locals call it Wiñay Wayna—right, Choque?"

"Yes."

"Gosh, can you tell us more about the plant life we're seeing?" Hilary asked.

"No."

"I guess you're tired," she said, smiling. "This must be a very challenging job. Do you belong to the porter's union?"

All the porters, Choque included, smirked at this question, but they didn't answer Hilary. She tried not to feel rejected—again—but their curtness deflated her enthusiasm to learn about other cultures. On her various online dating profiles, Hilary had listed this personal trait as one of her best attributes. She'd also posted a head shot of herself holding bird-watching binoculars. Although she'd received some interested emails, the men always asked for a full body photo as well. Hilary had researched the statistics for this cyberspace-dating behavior and found out that 97% of male participants demanded to see a photo. She also found out that 82% of women posted a touched-up photo or glamour photo, and that many women posted photos that were ten years old.

Hilary had expected sincerity and kindness in the online dating game, but some of the men had told her that she was just "too needy," when she saw herself as genuine. Her research also revealed that when she would hit forty, in just a year's time, statistically the only men who would date her would be over fifty-five. Now, thinking again about all these statistics, Hilary felt so distracted and depressed that she lost her footing on a slippery hand-hewn step. Tiffany was right there in a split second, holding Hilary's arm until she regained her balance.

"Little David just lifted the giant!" Tiffany screeched. "What's his name, you know— like Jack and the Beanstalk."

"Thanks, Tiffany." Hilary took a chance at being sincere. "Obviously, I wasn't concentrating on where I was stepping. I was thinking about the purpose of this hike—you know, our online dating obsession. It just dawned on me that the only men who may possibly want to date me are going to be closer to my dad's age. How depressing is that?"

"Sucks balls, for sure," said Tiffany. "But why do you tell them your real age? Just say you're thirty-two. I always say thirty and, you know, that was seven years ago. Men don't care—they just want to see if they're gonna bone you or not. So post a younger photo of yourself. It works, trust me."

"Don't you think that the whole virtual medium is based on words, and charm, and seduction?" Gabby asked. "It's not all physical attraction."

"For men, and quite honestly for me, it's all about the physical chemistry," said Mercy. "That's why a photo is the first screening process."

"On my blog," Gabby said, "I get all sorts of comments from women who say that after they meet someone face-to-face, they're often turned off by the guy's idiosyncrasies, like facial tics or weird voices or even ugly hands. I think that as we get older, if we're still single, not by choice, we turn bitter and take it out on the poor guy who's just met us. You know, it's a defense mechanism. We pick them apart just as they're picking us apart. We're the problem."

"We're just discerning, that's all," Mercy said. "We've been chasing the elusive brass ring all our lives. That's why we went to Ivy League colleges and then on to the best graduate schools and then on to successful careers. So why should we settle for some guy we don't want?"

"Duh! For his money!" Tiffany giggled.

Hilary looked down at the river and spotted the most vibrant birds. She stopped to catch her breath, admiring the emerald-green feathers of a Booted Racket-Tail hummingbird, and decided that this sighting was a blessing. Not everyone was privileged enough to see this bird's long, long tail feathers in this mystical cloud forest. Perhaps she would also beat the odds among these beautiful women, and be the one Rodrigo selected as his mate.

"It's not always about the money, Tiffany," said Mercy, frowning. "We all have well-paying careers."

"Maybe *you* all do," Tiffany said, "but I don't, and I can tell you that it's always about the money. The richer the man, the younger the woman at his side. The more beautiful the woman, the richer the man. You don't need a graduate degree to get the basic laws of nature."

"You make a valid, yet cynical point, Tiffs," Gabby told her. "I love it. May I quote you on my blog?"

"Sure, girlfriend. I'll even let you upload a super-hot photo of yours truly from about eight years ago." Tiffany howled as she gave all the women high fives and knuckle pumps.

"Tiffany, you are an incorrigible flirt, you know that?" Gabby said.

"Well, if I knew what 'incorrigible' meant, I would know whether to say thanks or not."

"You're hilarious," Gabby said, laughing. "Hey, why don't you co-write some of my blog posts? We could get people interested in your fresh and zany perspective. What do you say?"

"I don't like to write, but you can put me on YouTube if you want. You really think I'm funny?"

"Refreshing and hilarious," said Gabby, and all the women cheered for Tiffany.

"Okay, thanks you guys! But I always thought that I didn't lasso a rich guy cuz I wasn't super-smart and classy. But you guys are, so where did we go wrong?"

Hilary silently thanked all the spirits and the mountain *apus* and Pachamama. This was the moment she had been waiting for: a group epiphany on the perils of online dating. She wanted this cathartic moment to last, so she jumped into the conversation with her confession.

"I, for one, can get a bit clingy with the men that show an interest in me," she admitted. "I send them lots of emails, and maybe I use too many emoticons. It freaks guys out."

Mercy didn't want this hike to turn into a bitch session or a pathetic woe-is-me club. "We all made mistakes with our online dating experiences," she said briskly. "We have to move forward, and there's no sense in rehashing our past mistakes."

Gabby didn't appreciate anyone telling her what to do, so she decided to follow Hilary's lead and volunteer her mistakes. "Well, I have to check my emails all day long to see if Mr. X or Mr. Y wants to meet me in person. Then I make all sorts of graphs of the available guys to determine which one best intersects with my qualities, according to my guidelines."

"Are you saying you rank the guys?" Tiffany asked.

"Yes, but I do it in a very complicated way."

"So how do you decide on the winner?"

"No one wins. By the time I've compared and analyzed, the guys have moved on."

"Okay, that's just plain freaky." Tiffany screwed up her face. "I mean, if you got good results then I'd get the point of your rankings, but all you do is wait too long. It's all about timing."

"Genius observation," Gabby said. "Looks like we've all missed our moment to select from a field of men. We wasted those days in graduate school or in our careers when we called the shots with men. Now the ball is in their court."

Gabby's realization made her pick up the pace, and the others followed suit. Soon they were all panting, climbing higher and higher up the trail.

"We're no better off than women two hundred years ago," she continued. "Now we're destined to be the wallflowers, the spinsters, the old maids, waiting by our computers hoping that some guy selects us. And as we get older, fewer and fewer men want to date us…except eighty-year-old seniors. That's incredibly depressing."

"Don't get too theatrical, Gabby," Mercy said. "We're still in control in many ways—"

"Such as?" asked Gabby.

"It's going to sound crude, but we control who we have sex with. We can choose to have a non-consequential hookup, a late-night booty call, a friend with benefits, a—"

"But don't you all think that if one is looking for cyberspace romance, and not just hooking up for sex, then deception is unavoidable?" Hilary asked. "Deception by others *and* self-deception. As you say, Gabby, when you were in the driver's seat, you drove with abandon. You picked who you wanted to be with, but now the tables have turned on us and what do we do?"

"We go on multiple online dating sites," Tiffany suggested, "and lie, lie, lie."

Mercy shook her head in disbelief. "Seriously, now! What we have to do is realize that we've all passed up opportunities for love, for real romantic relationships. We set our standards too high, and we became hypercritical of any prospective love interests. But I think now that we recognize the error of our ways, we have to go forward with conviction of what we want."

"The keyword in your comment is 'real,'" Hilary agreed. "There's nothing real about a cyberspace romance simply because that's where disembodied communication takes place. What we're yearning for is a flesh-and-bones real man."

"You mean a hottie like Rodrigo?" Tiffany asked way too eagerly. She'd given herself away, and now the other women knew with certainty that she was going after Rodrigo, just like she'd said she would.

They stopped, glancing at one another. Tiffany had struck a raw nerve—again. When they heard Rodrigo's name mentioned, Choque and the porters stopped too. Up until that point, they had ceased trying to follow what the women where whining about.

They were close to what the women assumed was Dead Woman's Pass, so they all stood pretending to admire the breathtaking views. The cliff was a riot of color, covered with dozens of varieties of orchids, but no one, not even Hilary, commented on their beauty. Birds circled overhead, each one squawking or singing its exclusive tune, but not one of the hikers bothered to look up to the sky. The faint rainbow that had radiated harmony and understanding had dissolved, and the women were oblivious to their surroundings. Once again, they were concentrating on how to best attract Rodrigo.

The women were not unlike the carnivorous Heliamphora plants of South America, primed to attract insects with their visual and chemical signals, trapping their prey in their waxy scales. Each one of the women exuded undetectable but undeniable pheromones, charging the air with desire and lust.

The porters detected this chemical whiff and grew agitated. They thought they smelled violets in the air and that enraged them: that scent reminded them of the French woman who had caused such a ruckus for Rodrigo and consequently for the men who had been unemployed for months until Rodrigo returned. The aroma in the air made them insane with longing and they cursed their physical defects and each other, but the women didn't even notice the little men arguing. They were too consumed with their own competitive strategies.

Mercy's legal mind reasoned how to eliminate her competitors and present her case with flair to Rodrigo. She would seduce him in Spanish and satisfy him as he had satisfied her. She would not hold back in any way. By the end of her closing statement, Rodrigo would realize that she was his perfect mate.

Gabby dismissed Mercy and Hilary as competitors. They were both too set in their ways. One was excessively logical and the other was too ambivalent. Only Tiffany, with her keen, unorthodox insights, had impressed her. She would have to keep her eye on Tiffany, and to point out her flaws to Rodrigo, if necessary.

Hilary would have been the only one to notice that they had not hiked in the direction of the famous pass. They had definitely hiked for three hours, but their obsession with their own heart's desire made them overlook the fact that Choque and his porters had led them onto an extremely narrow path; a path that none had seen in the maps they studied before the hike.

It was evident that the women were only interested in the end game: the top of the mountain and, above all, the open arms of Rodrigo. After years of chasing after the brass ring of academics and professional employment, they had learned to defer satisfaction in order to achieve a goal. The uphill battle required hardened Spartans, not jelly-bellied whiners. Here, on the narrowest section of the path, they each stood deep in their own thoughts: they all knew in their guts that this hike represented the end of the dating line—at least the era of dating in which they called the shots. They would never admit such a maudlin sentiment to anyone, but privately they all acknowledged that they had wasted the fifteen years of post-college graduation on a series of inappropriate men. They had gone through too many men, and all their graphs and pie charts and animated bar charts indicated that their days of being the ones who selected men were over.

In their aggressive charge to the top rung of their careers, the women had ignored their yearning hearts. They acted as brazenly as their male counterparts, and thought they could find the perfect match when they were good and ready. They'd bought into the potential of cyber dating because it was a numbers game, a target-rich audience, and they reasoned that if enough candidates saw their photos and descriptions, and vice versa, then they could select an ideal mate from interested candidates. What they did not consider were the myriad problems of online dating: people didn't fall in love with categories; people deceived others with their old photographs and with false descriptions; and everyone dragged along their dysfunctions and unrealistic expectations as a silent third party. It was a fatally flawed, *ménage à trois*.

As the orange-feathered Cock-of-the-Rock cried its cacophonous song, the women realized that they were irreparably burnt out with online dating. That, in fact, unlike the Inca rope suspension bridges that were renewed every year, the women's Internet connection to disappointment was permanently severed. Their only reality was this dead-on moment of clarity near the 13,700-foot pass in the Andes Mountains. They were here on this spot trying to find love. This was their last shot, and none of the women was prepared to lie down in defeat like the famed woman of the Dead Woman's Pass. Each was struck as if by a lightning bolt, and understood that if there were such a thing as a soul mate, he had to be here on this Inca Trail—or no such thing existed at all.

CHAPTER FOURTEEN

Flashes of insight abound in the intense atmosphere of the Andes Mountains. The women hikers were not the first to experience a real eye-opener about their lives. Visitors often found themselves making pronouncements shallow and deep, generous and miserly, deadpan and frivolous—all in accordance with the time-tested duality reigning among these high peaks. Certain epiphanies might appear as a mere physiological reaction to the altitude: as the body receives less and less oxygen, blood flow to the brain is increased, causing not only headaches but sparks of short-lived wisdom.

This new clarity about finding their soul mate on this specific hike did not shock the women. Had they been back home in their polished and perfect modern environment, they would have ridiculed their own sentiments, their own leaps in logic. But high up on this trail, the women inhaled their profound awareness that their soul mate waited for them around the bend.

✳

Other proclamations of insight at this high altitude reveal the speaker's inflated ego. Such was the case of that Ivy League adventurer, Hiram Bingham. With big dreams of making his mark and his own money—instead of leeching from his wealthy wife's trust—Bingham set off to Peru determined to discover Inca ruins. Only a huge find would satisfy this tall man's needs. In anticipation of the skepticism he might encounter when he would later claim that he "discovered Machu Picchu on July 24, 1911," Bingham brought along a camera to record his discovery. Bingham later wrote that when he first laid eyes on the deserted site, he was glad that he had a good camera and that the sun was shining. Never mind that on that day the sky was actually overcast and drizzly; never mind that he overlooked the fact that people were living at the site and growing crops when he startled them with his camera (a stalk of corn is visible on the edge of his pictures); never mind that a Peruvian graffiti artist had carved his Basque name, Lizarraga, and the date, 1902, on this ancient site. Bingham's tenacity and skewed perspective on his self-importance motivated him to promote himself as the discoverer of Machu Picchu.

Thankfully, the hand-hewn stones of the citadel were impossibly heavy, otherwise Bingham might have reconstructed Machu Picchu on the icy streets of New Haven. After all, one can visit the ancient city of Pergamum in the heart of Berlin and not on the shores of the Aegean Sea, or view the magnificent manuscript of the 17th century Peruvian chronicler Felipe Guamán Poma de Ayala—in Denmark. Something is definitely rotten, not only in Denmark but in the international peregrination of ancient treasures. The motto "to the victor go the spoils" might have been Bingham's silent desire, but since there was no war—just greed—he simply took what he wanted.

"They probably saw a drawing of Guamán Poma de Ayala in their books and got all confused."

Bingham was not the only foreigner who coveted a personal transformation courtesy of his voyage to Peru. The Spaniards before him had climbed peaks and crossed passes in search of an El Dorado that would convert them from simple soldiers to wealthy noblemen back in Spain. Many present-day tourists to Machu Picchu also seek a mystical experience to help them make sense of their soulless lives back home. When their desiccated emotional auras collide with the antediluvian energy emanating from Machu Picchu's granite heart, perplexing and macabre incidents occur: a nondescript Ivy Leaguer loots a country's treasure; a king is garroted despite filling rooms full of gold and silver as ransom; children are sacrificed in times of great upheaval—and intelligent women jockey for position in the race for a scoundrel's heart.

The women hikers stood on the narrow path, their sweaty backs resting against the cool rock face of the cliff. They caught their breath and allowed the revelation of their ultimate purpose to sink in: they were on nothing less than a quest for their very future; they were on a sacred pilgrimage for love. In front of them a steep precipice served as the stage for birds of rainbow colors and floating vines dripping with purple orchids. It almost beckoned the women to step off the ledge and commit their mortal bodies to the boundless treasures of the Inca Trail.

In a normal situation, the women would have behaved much more cautiously when confronted with such a cliff. Instead they remained inches away from the unprotected edge of the cliff, transfixed by their own paradoxical awareness. They resolved to abandon their addiction to online dating, yet they still embraced the hunt for their soul mate. In defiance of all logic, each woman envisioned herself as Rodrigo's soul mate, the woman who would bewitch him for eternity. A surge of endorphins flooded each woman's brain and heart, and each woman totally forgot all the heartache she had already endured as a result of her impetuous love pursuits. Whether online or face-to-face, all their most recent love affairs had been short-lived, painful fiascos that left them scarred.

Even though each woman could recite the signs of true love, such as commitment and trust, compassion and nurturing, open communication and similar belief systems, they were all as clueless as Tiffany in their deluded reactions to Rodrigo. Instead of analyzing the way their own behavior had contributed to their past romantic failures, the women brainwashed themselves with a surge of saccharine visions that turned their minds to mush. Even Gabby, who had skewered this exact type of behavior on her blog, now looked as moonstruck as a teen.

Each woman took out her camera to photograph the rushing river, the vampire orchids, and their own wide-eyed expressions of lust and longed-for love. As they adjusted their lenses for a wide-angle shot of the panoramic cloud forest, their pupils enlarged with sexual desire for Rodrigo. They reviewed their digital images and discovered that instead of a full shot of the lupines and snapdragons, each one had managed to also include an unflattering shot of one of the other women. Just as the photo of corn stalks invalidated Bingham's claim that Machu Picchu was deserted, the women's photos of their rivals broadcast their real focus: the upcoming competition for Rodrigo's attention.

This was a photographic Freudian slip, an unconscious and unfavorable depiction of their newly identified enemies. In some shots slender Tiffany looked bloated; in others, the light on Mercy's alabaster skin revealed brown blotches. Even petite Gabby looked troll-like in some of the photos. The women leaned back on the rock face and inhaled the malignant pleasure of seeing their enemies at their worst. Instead of deleting the bad shots, they deftly clicked the crop icon, so their competition appeared in their atrocious pose, on the full screen—and they saved the cropped image.

Tiffany had stolen an expensive camera from her boss, but she'd forgotten to charge the battery and the camera was dead.

Instead of admitting her mistake, Tiffany pretended to take better photos with the long zoom lens. She'd had enough of feeling inferior to these snobs and it was time to bitch-slap them.

"Enough with the photos, bitches!" She elbowed Hilary's thigh. "Let's get moving."

Hilary's gigantic feet extended past the edge of the cliff, and she wouldn't budge when Tiffany jostled her. She was preoccupied with the overwhelming abundance of nature in front of her. She had always known that she belonged in this sweeping panorama, picturing herself as a steward of its creatures and plants. She would use her training and professional experience to assure the preservation of this ecosystem, and she would be accompanied on this journey by Rodrigo. This was the out of focus bird's-eye view ever-present in Hilary's mind, and now, feeling safe in her protective environment, she prayed to the river *huacas*. All she wanted was a sign from her deities that would confirm that she would soon realize her dream.

Hilary snapped pictures with delirious speed as if that would help expedite a mystical sign. And it seemed to work. A large iridescent feather glided past Hilary's knees, brushing her kneecaps like the delicate filament of a spider's web, and Hilary attempted to kneel down and reach for it. Her inner butterfly was certain that this maneuver by a giant woman standing on a narrow, steep path would be possible, but, alas, she had underestimated her girth. The other women saw the potential catastrophe, but none reached out to block the fall. None dared risk her life when she was so close to finding her singular soul mate; none would admit that one fewer competitor was to her benefit. To the victor go the spoils!

Only the hunchback cook, standing further downhill, said something.

"*Pilpintu, Pilpintu*, butterfly—look at me!" he shouted. Hilary glanced at him, and at the last minute her large-framed body tumbled towards his voice and not towards the abyss.

No one rushed to help Hilary, not even the helpful cook. It wasn't cruelty that made them ignore her bleeding face and scraped elbows and knees. She was now a log blocking the path. She couldn't get up and no one could help her.

Choque spoke quietly to the porters. "We should have used her body to block the path last night," he said, and they all laughed boisterously.

Tiffany could kick ass with the best of them; she'd learned how to defend herself in all the foster homes and at juvenile hall. Right now she wanted to beat the little men to a pulp for cruelly laughing at Hilary, and for doing nothing to help her.

"Come and help, you little shits!" she screamed, but the porters didn't move. "Whatever! Hilary, don't move until I tell you, okay?"

Hilary's mouth was bleeding profusely, so all she could do was nod. Tiffany tossed aside her day pack and clambered over Hilary's pack and her twisted legs, grabbing hold of small rock outcroppings to keep her balance. It took her a few minutes to position herself, and to help Hilary untangle her long limbs.

Tiffany told Hilary to sit up and to tilt her head backwards, and poured water over Hilary's face to determine the extent of her cuts.

"Dude, you look like shit," she said with brutal bedside manner. "But you won't need any stitches. I know all about stitches since I had my eyes done last year. You're gonna bruise…a lot, I'm not gonna lie. And your teeth, dude, they're gone. They're swimming with the fishes…if you know what I mean."

Hilary started to cry, and Tiffany crouched next to her. She'd pulled off her T-shirt and pressed it against Hilary's forehead. Years ago Tiffany had taken a class in first aid, and although she hadn't really paid attention, she vaguely recalled something about applying pressure to stem bleeding.

"Sorry about your teeth, but you can get awesome implants. While you're at it, you can get some fillers here and here." Tiffany pointed to the marionette lines around Hilary's mouth. "Here, bite down on my gross t-shirt to stop the bleeding."

After Hilary had composed herself, Tiffany talked her through standing up.

"Okay, girlfriend, it's all about your core and you've got abs of steel. Do you do Pilates? Never mind, don't talk. So we're going to concentrate on the abs to do all the work of standing up. Your legs are bruised, but so what? When you get back home you'll go to a tanning salon and they'll spray you with a golden tan, like mine." Tiffany shook her left leg over the edge of the cliff to show Hilary it was safe to stand up.

But Hilary didn't get up. She was considering a more permanent solution to her problems.

Hilary, who had a prodigious memory, was thinking of the story of the priestess Sarpay who decided to jump to her death into the Apurimac River from a cliff not far from this very precipice. When she'd first read the story, Hilary could not understand why anyone would fling herself off a cliff. But now, sitting here slumped and humiliated, she had new respect for Sarpay.

Sarpay was the priestess in charge of the famous Inca shrine to the river goddess Apurima and, by affiliation, to Mamacocha, the goddess of the ocean. The Andean peoples revered rivers, streams, and mountain springs, so their shrine on the banks of the Apurimac River was laden with solid gold idols in the shape of breasts, and was given sacrificial blood in order to keep the waters flowing throughout their kingdom. When the Spaniards set out to destroy all pagan idols, they targeted the golden breasts attached to the sacrificial pole inside the shrine—not so much for religious reasons, but out of sheer greed for gold. They did not care that without the blood-engorged breasts the oracle would no longer speak to the people, and their pleas for water for their crops would not be heard. The people would not be able to implore: O Mamacocha! Give me water without ever stopping!

Hilary whispered the same prayer now, and was overheard —and misunderstood—by Tiffany.

"OK, Hilary," she said, gently raising the canteen of water to Hilary's swollen lips. "I'll give you water, but not too much, cuz then you gotta pee. And there's no frickin' toilet, like there's no frickin' GPS, and it looks like no Rodrigo."

She glared in the direction of Choque and the porters, and slipped the canteen back into her pocket.

"Come on, up," Tiffany told Hilary, taking her wounded Goliath's arm, and managed to help her to her feet.

With Hillary walking again, the hike continued slowly up the perilous path. The birds that had previously welcomed the women with chipper songs flew away from the forlorn party's jittery vibrations. Wind buffeted their bags and dangling cameras, and each woman stepped with exaggerated care, shaken by what had happened to Hilary. One by one they silently followed each other's clodhopper stomps, raising a dust cloud of confusion and sadness—a misery so visible that it revealed their whereabouts to a fuming-mad French woman picking her way up the trail in their wake.

Violette took long and confident strides on the hazardous path. She didn't bother to stop and take in the awe-inspiring views. She only stopped to spit out chest phlegm, a side effect of the chill she'd suffered after too many hours in a wet wig—a wig she disposed of moments ago over this very cliff. The unprotected edge of the cliff did not frighten her whatsoever, and she tested her resolve by leaning her tense, bony body over the verge like some one-woman game of Russian roulette. "Go ahead and pull the trigger," she dared the Inca Trail's perilous paths. With every bullet she dodged, she mimicked her swami—"I'm alive, sons of bitches, I'm alive!"—and picked up her pace, ignoring the birds who serenaded her lonely journey.

She was following the tracks of Rodrigo's whores, the American women he had obviously entangled in his erotic fantasies. As she climbed she rehashed all the incidents of their relationship, the way he dominated and then discarded her. Soon she was almost marching, like a soldier heading into battle; she would topple this dictator, no matter the odds.

But Violette knew, deep down, that she had not been enough for Rodrigo, even after she gave up her baby daughter—granted, an infant born from another's womb, but her daughter nonetheless. Rodrigo had presented the gestating infant as a virtual baby he had conceived with Violette, and had convinced her, a shrewd French woman, that the infant was, in reality, hers. Did she not feel her infant fluttering in her womb? Did she not see that her golden and wavy hair matched her own? Rodrigo asked her questions like these over and over, until she believed he was speaking the truth. In their desolate hacienda he had massaged warm oil on her cold, barren body, and shown her an image of her beautiful golden-haired baby on his computer screen. She had slept clutching a printout of her infant's avatar, one that would soon transmute from a cyberspace infant into her own pudgy and cuddly baby.

This euphoria only lasted as long as money flowed from her accounts into Rodrigo's hands. After the baby was stillborn, and Rodrigo had depleted all her funds, Violette snapped. At the Cusco inquest she attempted to present her own spin on the infant's death, and to tell the world that Rodrigo was involved in the trafficking of beautiful Peruvian babies, the very same children he had fathered with countless young girls in the highlands. But her hysterical and outlandish accusations only resulted in her immediate deportation from Peru.

Her swami, the Corsican crook, was the one who hatched the Byzantine revenge plot against Rodrigo—with a large profit margin for himself, of course. While they waited for their cancer treatments at the clinic in Nice, he said, "*Petite*, there are many ways to inflict pain with my stiletto, but let's be creative, shall we?"

"I could kill Rodrigo with my bare hands, if only I could enter Peru on a different passport," Violette told him.

"*Oui*, I can see that," said the swami, gripping the edge of Taki's shawl draped around Violette's frail torso, his sick mind busy concocting a plan. "Why don't we channel your rage, use Rodrigo for a while, recoup your lost money, and *then* you can have the satisfaction of stabbing him...multiple times?"

"What an incredible plot!" Violette scoffed. "Why didn't I think of it? I'll just fly to Cusco with a morbidly ill crook and intimidate Rodrigo into giving me the money. Easy! By the way, I'm sure the money is all gone."

The swami coughed at his pain and laughed at her anger. "What if said crook cleared up all your passport problems? Would you take him first to get the blessing of the healer or witch, or whatever she is? Then said crook would arrange for—"

Violette jerked the shawl away from his ghoulish hands. "Get to the point or I'll do it myself."

The swami yanked the shawl away from Violette and wrapped it tightly around her neck.

"Listen up, *petite*, or die," he hissed. "This is how it's going to go down. Got it?"

Violette nodded yes, but calmly unwrapped the tight shawl from her neck and folded it, setting it down out of the swami's reach. He laughed, as though he had just watched a mouse take a bite from a cat. He leaned close to her ear.

"It's a simple plan," he whispered, his breath foul. "You introduce me to the witch, I get her blessing, we give it a little time to work its magic, and abracadabra! I'll soon feel like my old stud self. Meanwhile, you meet with Rodrigo, and get your fill of his *saucisson*."

Violette climbed the last stone stairs leading to the summit, and grimaced at the memory of the swami grabbing his decrepit genitals and making crude thrusting motions. His behavior, much like the grand plan he concocted, was so idiotic. She paused for a moment to catch her breath, looking down at the series of acute switchbacks awaiting her descent, and laughing at her own foolishness. Why had she allowed the crazed swami to convince her that they could entice Rodrigo into organizing an international infant trafficking ring—by selling his own children?

On the flight over from Nice to Lima, the greedy old crook had scrawled a plan on the drink napkin. On the next flight, from Lima to Cusco, he showed Violette the potential profit margin, all the zeros preceded by the number three.

"What if Rodrigo refuses?" she asked him. "What if he's not in Cusco?"

This enraged the swami so much that he tried to choke her with his bare hands, but he was too weak to do any damage. He slumped back in his seat, muttering some Corsican saying that she didn't understand. Since he was picking up the tab, Violette had to go along with his madness, but secretly she had an alternate plan for Rodrigo, one only she could execute.

The party of nine hikers kicked up so much dirt and shook so much vegetation that Violette would have been blind not to notice. She took off downhill with renewed energy, reminding herself that the American hikers were her map to Rodrigo. Violette's swami had taught her to aim high, to extract everything out of life, and to act fearlessly, just as he had done when he snatched Taki's shawl in the plaza from Taki herself. When the hiking guide Violette hired refused to climb this dangerous trail, she dismissed him, determined to track Rodrigo on her own. Soon she would fulfill her goal when Rodrigo's head was impaled, just like the two previous Tupac Amarus, and displayed at the top of Huayna Picchu, a peak so often photographed that it had become the iconic image of Machu Picchu.

Taki and Koyam were ahead of the women hikers by two switchbacks on the path. If necessary, they could have stuck more closely to the group of nine hikers, but they had anticipated where Choque would set up camp for that night, and they wanted to get a good spot nearby, so they could see and hear what went on. The path they were on was the most dangerous and therefore the least traveled by the locals, and it was never traversed by foreigners. At certain points they could see the hikers in the distance and count the number of people in the party. When Koyam spotted a lone figure three switchbacks behind the American group, she knew something was wrong.

"*Chuta!* Damn it!" she exclaimed. "There's a skinny white person following the *gringas.*"

"It's the French woman," Taki said without any hesitation.

"Finally, the third titty predicts something useful. What does that Frenchy want?"

"I'm not sure—"

"Let me talk to the tiny titty," said Koyam. "You obviously are not paying attention in your old age. You used to be able to predict so much more in our youth. Remember how you told me not to marry Cuntur?"

"Of course, poor boy!"

"Yes, yes, yes, he died young. Boo! Hoo! We cried about it. But what does Frenchy want now? And how come she doesn't look like herself?"

"Don't tell me you can see her features from here." Taki peered down the trail. "I can't even see if it's a man or a woman."

"Hmm, I can see that you're avoiding my question. What does Frenchy want with the *gringas*? How did she find this secret path? Is she a … well, you know, a little like you?"

"No, she does not have my gifts. She is a woman full of hate for Rodrigo, and through that hatred she found this path. She's been following the *gringas* for a couple of days." Taki rubbed her forehead as if cleaning the windshield. "I see her at the train station in Cusco and on the train with the other women. I … I don't like the rest of what I see. Please don't ask me anymore about what I see…it's awful."

Taki was practically whimpering, stumbling along the path.

"Take it easy," said Koyam. She reached for Taki's hand. "Let's walk a little slower. Don't get so agitated. But you really should tell me what we are up against. Don't you think I should know?"

Taki gripped her friend's hand. "My visions are not like a movie. They don't have a big Hollywood beginning, followed by a chase scene, and then the hero wins. They're more like watching a little bit of one horror movie, then a scene of a love story, followed by … by a nightmare, and then back to the beginning."

"Start with the love story, then."

"I keep getting flashes of the most beautiful little girl you can imagine. She has wavy golden hair down to her shoulders and she has glowing bronze skin, like ours...when we were young, that is."

Koyam wanted to get past the pretty little girl, the golden *wawa,* and get to the dangerous part, to the vision of where and when she would have to fight someone or something, because that was what Koyam did to defend Taki or any of the weaker street vendors, for that matter. She had always been the enforcer and she had the scars to prove it.

In their youth, when the street punks thought they could jump them from behind as they walked home with their bundles full of unsold souvenirs, Koyam would wait until the men got so close that she could smell their alcohol *chicha* breath. The punks thought they could just tumble her and Taki to the ground, lift their full black skirts without a fight and rape them. But Koyam clutched jagged fist-size rocks in her hands, her very own protective *huacas* that she had chiseled into a mace-like weapon, and she knew how to use them—until she heard the bones of their attackers crack.

Taki continued describing the golden child with the twinkling emerald eyes with hints of gold.

"What is the golden *wawa* doing?" Koyam asked.

"A very tall person is carrying her in a litter, a miniature copy of the one that carried our ancient king Atahualpa, before the Spaniards attacked him, before they garroted him, even though he put up the ransom of gold and silver." To Koyam's surprise, Taki started giggling like a child. "The golden *wawa* is laughing so hard that she is throwing her head back and you can see all her dazzling white teeth. Her hearty laughter makes the veins on her delicate neck pop out and...no, oh no, no!"

Taki dropped to the ground and started crying, covering her eyes and nose.

"I can't stand the stench of violets," she whispered, and bent over to vomit by the side of the road.

Koyam sat down next to Taki, but kept her eyes focused on the nine hikers and the lone French woman. They were getting closer, too close, she decided. She grabbed Taki by the arms and forced her to stand and walk.

"Let's just walk and head for where they should all make camp," she said. "No more talk about any visions, all right?"

Unfortunately, the visions were uncontrollable and Taki had to spew them out in disjointed spurts. Koyam didn't dare stop to ask for Taki to make sense; she just picked up the pace so they could reach camp quickly, letting Taki talk all the poisonous visions out of her system. For a moment, at least, Taki was smiling again.

"Oh, look, the golden *wawa* is playing with the nice lady who almost bought your friendship bracelets by the Internet café at the plaza. Now the golden *wawa* is in the arms of the other lady, one of the pretty blond ones." Taki hesitated, and Koyam had to grab her arm again, to drag her along the trail. Taki resisted, protesting. "Wait a minute! I count nine people hiking the trail, but in my dreams the pretty flower, the one that is a cousin of the howler monkeys—she's not in the group. I can barely see her profile in the darkness."

Koyam didn't care if any of the *gringas* disappeared from Taki's dream or from the face of the earth. Along with their sordid sexual fetishes that they couldn't stop talking about at the café, they brought with them a deluge of frightening visions for Taki, visions that had obviously put her in danger. She was coughing and wheezing as she walked, her shoulders slumped and right foot dragging. When she started to speak again, Koyam silenced her.

"Let's just get to the rest stop and wait there," Koyam told her. But Taki had to get something ominous and heavy off her chest. She tried to moisten her dehydrated lips with her dried tongue, reaching for Koyam's face with clammy hands: Taki had to reassure herself that she was still alive, and Koyam was still alive, despite her dreadful vision.

"There are bodies falling off the cliffs," she cried. "I can't tell who they are...but I can't see the golden *wawa*. What have they done to the golden *wawa*?"

CHAPTER FIFTEEN

odrigo's ebullience was evident from the campsite to the trail. In his luscious voice, a tenor ambrosial and melodic, he sang a song of everlasting love. Mercy was the first to hear the word *corazón*—sweetheart—and she stopped dead in her tracks. The troubadour could only be Rodrigo, singing the exact words he'd moaned as he made love to her at the El Convento Hotel, the same words the shark had sung underwater in her dream. The lyrics were Cupid's arrows to her heart. *Espérame en el cielo corazón*, Rodrigo sang. Wait for me in heaven, my sweetheart, if you should go before me. He was singing with the intense emotion of someone struck by Cupid's legendary gold and lead-tipped arrows of true love and erotic love. The way he sang these words pierced Mercy's soul with uncontrollable desire, for she was convinced that he aimed his arrows exclusively at her. At the hotel, Rodrigo had said so much more, both raunchy and tender, but it was the lyrics of this old song that really moved her. It was one of her father's favorites, a song she'd known for years. Somehow Rodrigo had telepathically realized its importance to her.

Mercy's analytical and well-grounded mind surrendered to her visceral yearning to run into Rodrigo's arms. Instead of feeling fatigued by the hike or shaken by Hilary's near-death stumble, Mercy felt buoyant and optimistic. Why couldn't she take time off from the vicious billing cycle of her law firm? Why not allow herself a well-deserved mid-life crisis? Why not roll the dice? Other male partners had been forgiven similar missteps.

As she picked up her pace, Mercy decided to submit to Rodrigo's passion and respond in kind. Let the chips fall where they may; she'd have her last go at true love. Over the years she'd demonstrated to the other partners her legal talents and her judicious nature. On her time off, she'd sown her wild oats for far more years than any of her colleagues, male or female, though thankfully she'd never caught any STDs to attest to her promiscuity. She'd even ceased feeling avenged every time she dumped each WASP jock, yet another scapegoat for her father's financial failures.

In the thin-aired atmosphere of this mountainous region, Mercy felt ashamed of the harsh treatment she'd doled out to countless pleasant men who'd shown a real interest in or affection for her. She'd dismissed them after a month or two, when she was satiated. Mercy had no intention of making the same mistake with Rodrigo. She would approach him with an open heart and allow their obvious chemistry to evolve into something genuine and lasting. For once she'd give her legal mind a rest and allow a softer side to emerge.

The fact that Tiffany claimed dibs on Rodrigo did not worry Mercy. That was just a reflection of Tiffany's immature desires, not a sign that Rodrigo had misled Mercy. After all, he'd spent the night at the El Convento Hotel with her, not with Tiffany. How she wished she could access her emails this very second so she could review her correspondence with Rodrigo. Prior to this hike he'd shared meaningful and intimate observations in his emails to her, enough to let her know that he yearned for a lasting relationship. Mercy would have to be patient with Tiffany's infantile outbursts, to demonstrate to Rodrigo her own maturity and understanding of their significant connection. Mercy was certain of that bond. The overpowering chemistry that she and Rodrigo shared was as real as the snowcapped peaks chilling the air.

The hikers didn't care that Choque's trail did not stop by the Runcu Raccay Inca ruins.

"Pumasillo Peak is 19,915 feet high." Choque pointed up, looking more bored than the women. He flicked his index finger at the marshy tarns that dotted the landscape, stifling a yawn. "Look, many Andean gulls."

When he asked Hilary if she wanted to see more ruins, Tiffany answered instead.

"Shut up, Chuck," she snapped. "You're an idiot for bringing us on this dangerous path. Can't you see that her face is ruined?"

At the beginning of the hike, Hilary had expressed interest in stopping at the ruins of Sayac Marca, but after her accident, she didn't want to go anywhere near the sheer cliffs that framed the three sides of the ruins. Instead of looking at the scenery, all she could see were her own swollen lips, pursed with distaste at her own foolishness. Her inflamed lips, missing teeth, and scratched forehead only served to reinforce the realization that she had been a grotesque figure for many years, even back at college.

At the consulting firm, Hilary's talents as a quantitative genius and an effective communicator had propelled her to management level in record time, and this had built her self-confidence. However, her larger-than-life frame and demure nature made others think of her as an asexual gentle giant, a panda of a woman who did not need any physical or romantic love. When the last online dating guy tried to engage her in the furry-costume sexual debacle, she understood that she was indeed a grotesque figure.

That was why the notion of destroying an effigy of the online dating jerks during this hiking trip had appealed to her. Hilary wanted to annihilate the effigy of the monsters who trawled online dating sites, picking up women desperate for true love. She had been one of those love-hungry freaks on an impossible quest, and men had exploited her vulnerability, and sledge-hammered her soul. Hilary had been looking for a sign of one thing or another on this trip—and throughout her life, for that matter. As it turned out, she had been her own symbol all along: a symbol of the outcast. She was the frightful Gorgon with serpents for hair, and tusks, and scaly skin; the very sight of her turned people to stone. She bit down on the cushy inside of her cheek and drew blood, a taste she would learn to like from this point forward. From now on Hilary would become the Gorgon, the lioness, the fearless puma of the Andes, and she would protect other innocent fools, easy marks like the sucker she had been.

At the sound of Rodrigo's distant song, Hilary wished that she'd brought earplugs. She didn't want to hear one more mellifluous sound from him or the birds, and certainly not from Tiffany, who kept on asking too many questions.

"I hope you're feeling better than you look," Tiffany said. When Hilary ignored her, she tried to get Hilary to laugh. "Let me hear you say, 'I thought I saw a pussycat,' please."

Hilary ignored this as well, so Tiffany repeated it, this time with a lisp to mimic how Hilary would sound until she got her teeth fixed.

"Okay, I was just kidding," she said at last, when she couldn't raise a smile from Hilary. "But you really should look on the bright side. Now you can take a good look at yourself and decide what other touch-ups you should have done. I did that after my last breakup, and see my new girls!" Tiffany pointed to her breasts that bulged like coconuts from her athletic bra. "You're really cute, but you need an extreme make-over...I'm just saying."

Gabby maintained her usual skepticism about Rodrigo's sappy song and his subsequent playing of the evocative Andean zampoña pan flute. She didn't buy his welcoming musical interlude or his unilateral selection of a different trail and frightening overnight campgrounds, forced on them by his proxy, Choque. The pit in her stomach told her Rodrigo was staging this evening, or perhaps the entire hike, with some ulterior motive in mind.

But what bothered her the most was that the same pit in her stomach fluttered with excitement about seeing Rodrigo again. Gabby wanted to erase his words from her mind, but she kept hearing the words he said to her last night in her tent: "You have all the qualities that I have always dreamed of in a soul mate."

Gabby wanted more time to plan her next encounter with Rodrigo. She didn't want to be the first to arrive to camp, so she allowed Mercy and Tiffany to trip over themselves to get there first. She hung back, behind Hilary and Choque and a couple of the porters.

Gabby hadn't grown into a skeptical person because of some intellectual sense of doubt. Rather, she'd learned this attitude the hard way. Certain benchmark events in her life had shaped her into a skeptic, and then into a cynic, and eventually into a multi-layered skeptic-cynic-satirist. At college Gabby had still been an idealist who believed everyone was her friend, but after her roommate and her then-boyfriend stabbed her in the back, she saw everyone as an enemy until they proved otherwise. Even as late as her first professional job with a multinational luxury goods corporation, Gabby believed that most people acted for the good of the company or for the good of the group. When she realized that this wasn't the case, and that human conduct was motivated by self-interest, the cynical Gabby was born. Now, listening to Rodrigo setting the stage with a little too much premeditation, all she could think was: "What's the catch?"

"Welcome, my beautiful ladies!" Rodrigo greeted each woman with a European kiss on each cheek. He whispered a special brief message to each one, but did not give them a chance to respond. Instead he glided over to the next woman, and handed her a moist towel to wipe away the grit from the trip.

"Please sit down and relax," he said, pointing to the stone benches covered in woven textiles and positioned around a campfire. Tiffany started to say something, but changed her mind, nodding to Rodrigo as if answering some silent question. While the women settled themselves on the stone benches, Rodrigo ordered Choque to serve them drinks, which were already poured into wooden cups. He instructed the porters to set up the tents, and they scurried around the campground, erecting each tent a good distance from the next, and far away from the comfort station and outdoor shower.

With gentlemanly care, he escorted Hilary to a bench he had positioned behind the weathered remains of an Inca wall that hid her from public view.

"Shh," he murmured. "You do not have to say anything, my butterfly."

With remarkable tenderness, Rodrigo wiped the dried blood from Hilary's face and hair. He applied a butterfly bandage to close the small gaping wound on her forehead.

"See, a tiny butterfly bandage for my delicate butterfly." He didn't ask what had happened, and Hilary refused to utter one single word. She wanted to figure out Rodrigo, to determine what made him tick, to analyze his actions—and to challenge herself to remain as silent as a Trappist monk. After her near-death experience on the cliff side, Hilary understood the significance of losing her front teeth. The mountain *apu* had shown her harshly that she must keep her mouth shut: she was a know-it-all who blurted facts like an encyclopedia, a windbag who bored others to pieces. Now she was in pieces, and she wanted to make amends. There on the cliff side, while everyone had expected her to do cartwheels down to the abyss, the luminescent feather brushing her knee had murmured to her: *silencio*.

That was the mountain *apu's* message: silence or you will die. Be silent and learn from us. Through her silence, she could truly listen to the Andean deities, begin to know herself, and learn how to live in harmony with the awe-inspiring Andes.

Rodrigo knelt down to clean the dust and pulverized gravel flecking the wounds on her knees, dabbing her cuts with disinfectant and applying Band-Aids.

"Oh, I missed a section here," he said, and he licked the inner part of her knee. Without thinking, Hilary jerked her leg away, and Rodrigo stood up, moving behind her. He massaged her shoulders and talked about the damage the torrential storm had caused. From this vantage point, he could observe the other women on their stone benches. Gabby was writing on her notepad, and Mercy and Tiffany were speaking in low voices.

"You would think that we Andeans would be better prepared for the storms that wreak havoc every few years in the highlands, wouldn't you? But such is our trust in our Earth Mother, our Pachamama. Some years she gives us too much rain and some years our crops dry to dust." Rodrigo grasped Hilary's shoulders. "You understand about the duality of life—the frailty of life—don't you, my butterfly?"

Hilary wanted to say so much about the conundrum she was experiencing that very minute: how, on the one hand, she couldn't trust what Rodrigo was saying to her, but how, on the other, it felt good that he had shown immediate interest in her. She wanted to ask him why he hadn't instructed Choque to take them on the wider and less hazardous path. But she didn't ask him anything. She just let Rodrigo continue massaging her, and talking about Andean beliefs. These were traditions and facts with which she was familiar from all the books she'd read, but Rodrigo was explaining them in the most captivating way.

"You are the only one who can appreciate the significance of all the rain we've had. Everyone else has forgotten the demands of our gods, that they give and they take away. Don't you think?" Rodrigo massaged her neck and cranial bones with dexterity. He splayed his fingers and rubbed Hilary's head from her widow's peak down her hairline and behind her ears. With his strong thumbs, he applied pressure at the base of the skull, with all the confidence of someone used to manipulating heads, like a massage therapist or a backwoods butcher.

"That is why our monthly festivals and our sacrifices were so vital in maintaining a balance in the empire," Rodrigo continued. "Now look at us! There is no reverence for traditions; there is no fear of our taboos. We lack the will to make heart-wrenching sacrifices. Although I believe that you are capable of making great sacrifices to save our earth, our Pachamama, wouldn't you?"

He froze his hands on Hilary's skull, his fingers locating all the pressure points on her temples. Hilary said nothing.

"You've already left your blood on the rocky soil of the ledge," Rodrigo murmured, "as a fitting tribute to the mountain *apus*. There is no greater gift for the gods than sacrifice. To sacrifice is to make sacred, wouldn't you agree?"

Still Hilary said nothing, so Rodrigo told her about the ancient festival of Camay that took place during the second month, now known as January.

"The Inca would come out on the square, surrounded by the *huacas,* especially the *huaca* of the Sun. We would bring one hundred alpacas, especially those with a white head and brown body, and we would sacrifice them in front of the *huaca* of the sun. But in years of great drought or of floods, like the one you just witnessed, we would sacrifice a small and perfect child."

He felt Hilary's neck and shoulders contract with fright, so he changed the subject deftly—and swiftly—to the fruit fights the warriors used to have during Camay. While he talked on and on, Rodrigo continued massaging her shoulders. The porters and Choque were running interference every time one of the women stood up to see what Rodrigo and Hilary were doing.

Although Hilary was half-listening to Rodrigo, her mind kept flashing back to her brush with death on the trail. She realized that she was experiencing typical post-traumatic stress symptoms. Immediately after the fall, she had been in shock, and perhaps she still was. That was why she'd had an out-of-body experience when Tiffany explained how to get up slowly and safely: she'd seen herself from an aerial perspective, rising up like a Gorgon of mythical proportions, and she had cringed. Hilary had trouble believing what had really happened to her on the trail. She'd looked down into the chasm and seen butterflies fluttering. She hadn't felt the pain of falling, or of having her teeth reduced to jagged stumps.

"I promised you that I would show you peaks and views that only a select few ever see, didn't I?" Rodrigo waited for an answer. Hilary felt anger rising at him, at her fall, and at her now horrendous mouth, and she shrugged rather than reply. Rodrigo stopped massaging her back. "Would you like Choque to take you back to the warden's gate by Kilometer 88? If that's what you'd like, I'll arrange it. But I would love for you to stay on the hike until the end. You don't have to say a word—I can feel what you want. Didn't we agree in our emails that you and I have a special connection with the environment, with these ancient mountains, and…with each other?"

Hilary's reaction to Rodrigo's comments confused her immensely. She didn't want to believe another word from him, yet she wanted him to continue telling her about the dual beliefs in the Andean world.

"Do you want to know why *you* understand the profound meaning of sacrifice? Let me tell you." Rodrigo slid his hands from her shoulders and down to her pectoral muscles, where he began gently massaging her breasts. "You and your Ivy League friends relied on technology as the answer to your emotional needs, and where did that get you? Nowhere—because today's world has forgotten what is sacred: love is sacred …and to revere sacredness requires sacrifice."

Hilary's mind ricocheted with paradoxical ideas, a confusion that she thought might be a result of her accident, but when Rodrigo continued to rub her shoulders, she relaxed and he sensed it immediately. He leaned into her back and she felt his erection push against her as he licked the back of her neck. Hilary didn't want her body to react excitedly, but it did and she buckled. He swayed his body left and right, back and forth, rubbing against her and letting out a low moan.

"This is how we will dance—just the two of us," he murmured, wrapping his arms around her waist. "Stay here until you feel like joining the others. I will never let you out of my sight, ever again, I promise. We will be as intertwined as the vines over there."

He pointed to the dense vegetation of lianas wrapped like boas around a large boulder. The rock was crowned with sensual blood-red orchids opening up their hinged petals and sticky packets of pollen to entice hungry bees. In the texts she'd read on the Early Greeks, orchids were powerful aphrodisiacs and predictors of fertility. Hilary wondered if the people of the highlands also associated the orchid with virility and fertility. She wanted to ask Rodrigo that question, but decided to maintain her vow of silence.

Hilary tried to disregard the symbols flashing in her mind about her current predicament. The more she tried to ignore them the more the symbols shouted out their meaning: her teeth were ruined as were the ruins of the wall that shielded her from the prying eyes of the other women; her emotional state was tied in knots just as the lianas choked the rocks, and her female organs were orchids dripping with desire for Rodrigo's virility. Hilary ran her tongue along the rough edge of her teeth hoping to discover the fangs of the protective puma she wanted to be, the fangs of a lioness ready to pounce on predators trawling dating sites. She tapped her teeth stumps, hoping to feel an electric shock of pain that would impel her to leave this perplexing Andean trek, but although her teeth were badly broken, the nerve endings were not exposed.

Hilary nodded acceptance of her fate. The *despacho* by the shaman at the train station had worked its magic. Her Andean protective deities had not allowed her to plunge off the cliff, and they had not seen fit to turn her into a guardian puma either. Rather, they were insisting that she stay and submit to the cosmic duet she was obviously, unquestionably predestined to dance with Rodrigo.

CHAPTER SIXTEEN

he cook had prepared an Andean stew of delicious potatoes and quinoa. After serving Rodrigo's portion, he sprinkled powder on the remaining stew—a powder Rodrigo had supplied to "relax" the *gringas*, he said, while he entertained them by the campfire.

Before dinner was served, Rodrigo picked up his pan flute again, but before he could play Tiffany interrupted him.

"Cut the crap, Rod," she screeched. "You have lots of explaining to do. Why didn't you lead the hike like you promised? And why aren't we on the real Inca Trail? Hilary almost took a flying leap to hell up on the ridge. And did you ever find out what happened to Sandra? Explain. Now!"

"Hmm, you do ask many interesting questions." Rodrigo pretended to look pensive and concerned. "The most important thing is that you are all here safe and warm and dry, as is Sandra.

She made it on the expensive Bingham train to Aguas Calientes and is nestled in the honeymoon suite with a lovely view of the river—"

"So, you spoke with her?" Tiffany frowned. "Let me use your phone so I can call her."

"The hotel manager got the message to the warden's kiosk and they let me know. Surely you realize that the torrential storm and mudslides have killed all communication from this location?"

"Whatever! Just explain yourself."

Rodrigo felt he did not owe anyone an explanation, now or ever. Does a god talk to a gnat?

"On to your next question—and this is a very crucial point," he said, making sure he sounded commanding. "You all signed up for a unique opportunity to hike the off-beaten paths of the Inca trails in order to destroy the effigy of the evil suitors who have tormented you. Believe me, you would not be able to accomplish this goal from the crowded Inca Trail. You saw all the porters and the other hiking groups that follow one another like dumb sheep, didn't you? Wouldn't you all feel rather silly, pathetic even, destroying the effigy of those who've spurned you?"

Mercy and Gabby absorbed his callous words, but did not answer Rodrigo. He smiled and spoke softly, allowing his chocolate brown eyes to tear up.

"You are all too special to be treated with disdain," he told them.

Tiffany wasn't convinced. "What's so special about—"

"Dinner is served nice and hot," interrupted Choque, and he and the cook handed a two-handled soup bowl to each woman.

The hearty stew satisfied most of the women, who were ravenous, even Hilary, whose portion had been mashed. Tiffany turned up her nose at it, choosing instead to munch on the trail mix she'd brought from Newps.

While they ate, Rodrigo sang and two of the porters played the pan flutes. Choque walked behind each woman, carrying alpaca blankets.

"I wrap nice and tight to keep you warm—just pull out arms and hands," he said. Each woman allowed him to wrap and tie the soft and warm blankets around them until they were swaddled like infants, calm and toasty around the campfire. Choque had to raise his voice to be heard above the loud singing.

"Our leader is good singer, but he is better storyteller. Would ladies want to hear happy story or scary story?"

"Shut up, Chuck," Tiffany said. "We're not in kindergarten, you moron. We want Rodrigo to explain his actions."

Mercy yawned. "How about a brief scary story? I'm almost ready to go to sleep in my tent."

She thought she was being sly, but her seductive voice got everyone's attention. All the other women noticed the longing look directed at Rodrigo.

Gabby felt obliged to cock-block Mercy's transparent plans. It was always this way: Mercy locked eyes with whomever she desired, and then she left Gabby behind at a party in L.A. or at a ski resort in Deer Valley while she cavorted with new sex partners. They both attracted attention wherever they went, but Mercy's sexual charisma seemed to overwhelm men. Tonight Gabby refused to play second fiddle.

"Naw, make it a long and interesting story, Rod," she said. "Don't leave any details out."

Gabby was sure that the whole campfire scenario, and the soon-to-be executed effigy, were good material for some tantalizing blog entries. If she uploaded a video of the whole event, she could further her marketing opportunities. It might even go viral, and soon her brand would attract the funding she deserved. Gabby pulled out her camera to video Rodrigo's story-telling, but her fingers felt very thick and clumsy and she soon gave up on the idea.

Hilary shrugged, indifferent to the whole event. She had already experienced Rodrigo's undivided attention and was satisfied with the decisions the Andean deities were making for her. She formulated the rules of her self-inflicted vows of silence and decided that she would allow herself to display only a few easily understood hand and head gestures to communicate with her fellow hikers. She figured that by concentrating on remaining silent, she would allow her other senses to sharpen and to teach her insights about her character and her life. Plus, she didn't want to open her mouth and display her jack-o'-lantern teeth. She gave everyone around the campfire an enigmatic Mona Lisa smile, but rested her eyes for too long, too lovingly, on Rodrigo. Gabby took envious note of the private time Hilary had already spent with Rodrigo.

"Okay, start the damn scary story," Tiffany commanded. "But it better be super scary so we can get pumped up about destroying the whatever-you-call-it that represents all the a-holes we've met. What's it called again, Gabby?

"An effigy. It's a rough figure that represents the hated person or group."

"So where's the frickin' effigy?" demanded Tiffany.

"Do not worry about minor details, Tiffany," Rodrigo said. "We will get to the destruction of the effigy. First, let me tell you about life and death in the Andes."

Unlike the other women whose eyes were half-closed after eating the sedative-laced stew, Tiffany was as jumpy and boisterous as usual.

"Just hurry up and scare us, or we're going to bed. You hear me, Rodrigo? We, as in you and me, are going to bed, like you promised."

Choque and the porters snickered at Tiffany's desperate sexual need for their virile boss, their Inca god awaiting his coronation. After the imminent bloodletting they too would be potent; they too would get a taste of power. The Incas of yore always rewarded those men who sacrificed their most valuable possessions—from their llamas to their wives to their flawless children—for the good of their Inca. Rodrigo had even told his men that at the ruins of Pachacamac they found the bodies of hundreds of young women, still dressed in the finest alpaca weavings, their delicate necks strangled with the cords they'd woven themselves. The porters imagined hundreds of graceful women weavers who gladly died for the greatness of their Inca, and their male eggs swelled with desire, proud that they were near a future great Inca who would pass on rejected women to them. Underneath their thick ponchos, they rubbed their penises in anticipation of the writhing and supple female rewards they would soon ravage.

The porters reasoned that this was the way it had always been. The remains of countless women were entombed all over these mountains, some with gold and silver llama amulets to accompany them into the afterlife, others with the finest alpaca blankets and feathers still hugging their once-noble bodies. All had one thing in common: while alive they had been the most beautiful women in the realm. The Inca only selected the most perfect young maidens to sacrifice to the gods, either as young girls or as young women. Those who lived long enough to marry noblemen would be buried alive along with their deceased spouse. Such were the polarities of the Inca world: one's beauty would bring about an ugly death, but also eternal bliss.

The Spanish tried to put a stop to such practices, but soon decided that it might be to their advantage to marry such noble Inca women. The women's cleanliness and grace appealed to the sensual desires of the Spanish men, but they also regarded liaisons with Inca women as a way to increase their own wealth and status. Women in the Andean world, either low or high status, served the desires of the Inca and of his male subjects. Rodrigo had told his men that he aimed to bring back this dictum: the women in his realm were to please their men. Among his first projects was converting the ruins of Machu Picchu back to a compound for the Virgins of the Sun. Rodrigo had asked his men: "Can you imagine the millions of men and the billions of dollars that would come to our condor's nest of a village in order to deflower young and beautiful girls?"

The porters did not want to guess a dollar amount; they just wanted to be a part of this great plan. Rodrigo told them that they would be following Inca tradition since that had been the main purpose of Machu Picchu way back when. Rodrigo twisted the writings of Hiram Bingham, who had advanced the idea that the citadel had been an *acllahuasi,* a convent for the Brides of the Sun. Bingham wrote that in the Andes the people wanted to please the sun god above all else, which was why they constructed numerous *acllahuasis* the length of the thousands of miles of their empire.

"I am not an egomaniac like Bingham," Rodrigo had told his men. "I just want to enjoy one kingdom with one fully stocked *acllahuasi,* right here in Machu Picchu. I would share the women with our paying guests. Don't you think my goals are noble?"

His men had nodded in agreement. When Rodrigo wanted to keep Choque, the only full-sized man in his troupe, happy, he told him: "Choque, you will be in charge of all the guards in our palace. Do you know that Bingham quoted from the sixteenth-century chronicles of Pedro de Cieza de León, and wrote that the guards at the *acllahuasis* were men of your kind? Only eunuchs, that is to say noble *pongo-camayoqs*, were trusted with guarding the women."

Choque looked as if he wanted to stab Rodrigo for humiliating him in front of the smirking porters.

"Don't act so offended," Rodrigo had told him. "*Pongo-camayoq* simply means a door man or guard. Some have twisted its meaning, but once you are fully restored, you can prove them wrong, and do as you wish with the women. You're my trusted general."

For the porters, Rodrigo's schemes were the vehicle for all their disjointed and depraved dreams. Everything he told them eventually came true. After the heavy rains of many years ago, archaeologists had discovered dozens and dozens of female skeletons, women who had been sacrificed by strangulation at a site in Túcume. The porters weren't surprised since Rodrigo told them that this is the way it should be: women, beautiful women, were sacrificed to bring about the wishes of the Inca and to appease the gods. Illapa, the thunder and lightning god, either ordained an excess of rain or a dearth of rain. It was up to the Inca to command the human sacrifices to satisfy Illapa and the other gods. But the ruling Inca always rewarded those who gave up the most.

The porters craved such a reward and were prepared to submit to the sacrifice demanded. They were accustomed to the ritual bloodletting fights Rodrigo imposed on them. Either he forced them to fight one another until they drew blood or he would pounce on them until he saw their vital fluid hit the soil. Once their blood spilled on the Inca trail, Rodrigo could hike with confidence, knowing that the rest of the journey would be uneventful since the blood of his men had nourished the earth. Rodrigo always acted like a ruler, and soon he would rule more than this band of weak little men.

"In the States," Rodrigo was telling the women around the campfire, "you do not live with death like we do in the Andes. Death is always among us as a constant lively companion. This doesn't make any sense to you, does it?"

Rodrigo didn't care about the women's opinion: he simply wanted to see which ones were still fully alert, to work out how much longer he would have to wait until the calming effects of the stew took hold.

Tiffany was the only one who answered. "So far you suck at storytelling, Rod. Let's just call it a night and go to bed. We can get up early and arrive in Macho Picchu at sunrise. I've had enough of this awful hike. I'd rather see the rest of South America with you. Wouldn't you rather do the tango with me in Bonos Airs?"

She winked at him conspiratorially.

"Later, but for now," Rodrigo replied, playing for time. "For now, what if you were to find out that the dead speak to us high in the Andes, as clearly as you are hearing my voice? Would you like to meet such a talking dead person?"

"Gawd, Rod," Tiffany sighed. "You're not going to describe a damn zombie movie you saw in a stinky movie theatre in Lima, are you? Cuz we're all from California and we know all about movies: zombie movies, vampire movies, slasher movies. Nothing scares us anymore, does it, Gabby?

"It would take a lot to scare us, that's for sure," said Gabby, only half-awake.

Rodrigo's jaw tightened in anger and he signaled to his men to play an eerie tune on their pan flutes. "Okay, I see you ladies are a tough group to entertain, but I am no court jester. The story I am telling is a truth more real than any movie can ever depict. Are you not all alone, without any communication to the outside world? Do any of you really know your exact location? And could any of you fight off evil bigger than a vicious jaguar roaming these mountains?"

Mercy was groggy, but she did not like the sound of Rod's veiled threats.

"Rodrigo," she said, her voice slurry with sleepiness, "it's one thing to try to scare us with your hijinks on this hike. It's quite another to insinuate that we're lost in the wild and that we're in some kind of danger. That is a threat, and I'll have you know that my international law firm knows *exactly* where I am at all times."

Rodrigo flashed them his dazzling pearly smile. "Ladies, we have much to accomplish tonight, what with the destruction of the effigy and other matters. Let's not waste our time with arguments or talking about threats. However, I do like to be accurate and precise, and in fact there is no one on the outside who knows where we are…unless you have a GPS beacon embedded in your body, Mercy, and I know you do not."

"What exactly are you saying?" Mercy tried to sit up and look authoritative, but she felt very groggy.

"And we have some serious hiking to do tomorrow," Rodrigo continued as though she hadn't spoken. "Do you or do you not want to hear a scary campfire story? Isn't that what you all do at summer camp? Come on, let's learn about the frightening facts of life in the highlands. Information you would never ever discover on the traditional Inca Trail. You are privileged to be in the hands of Illapa."

"Who the hell is Illapa?" demanded Tiffany as she adjusted herself on the stone bench. Gabby scribbled ideas on her notepad, while Mercy lounged on her bench waiting to hear the rest of Rod's story.

"It is my nickname. It means god of thunder and lightning, and—"

"And just tell the story because so far you're slow and nothing whatsoever like lightning." Tiffany giggled, pleased with herself. Hilary's eyes were closed and Gabby's eyelids were half-shut. Mercy rubbed her eyes with fatigue, but Tiffany's eyes sparkled with excitement about teasing Rodrigo.

"I take it that your silence means that you do wish to learn more about our mysterious corner of the world," Rodrigo said. "You North Americans! You assume that everything will go as planned. We Andeans, on the other hand, believe that fate will preempt all the best plans in the world. For example, you presumed that the online dating sites would net one perfect match for you, didn't you?"

Gabby and Mercy shrugged, and Hilary gave him the thumbs-up.

"But instead, technology matched you up with liars who believed your very own lies or exaggerations, and soon this accumulation of lies created a false cyberspace image of all the participants in the game of dating deception. We Andeans look at the clouds and know that rain is coming, our crops should grow. But we don't assume they will yield record crops. The results are not under our control, the gods decide. It's terribly fatalistic and archaic, isn't it?"

Hilary gave Rodrigo two thumbs up but Gabby and Mercy seemed to have dozed off. Rodrigo was undeterred. "I know you don't want to admit this, but you began to believe in your new and improved online dating avatar, didn't you? And you liked the avatar's enhancements and its camouflage of your greatest faults, didn't you?"

Rodrigo didn't want the women to fall asleep yet, so he motioned to one of the porters to run behind each one and bang his drum. Once the women were alert, Rodrigo could continue.

"You all thought that once you met your ideal mate—your soul mate—he would find the *real* you through the thick-skinned avatar you created, but guess what? Technology fooled you over and over and over again. The cyberspace lies of these men matched your own set of lies. The jumble of electronic untruths and false profiles and photoshopped pictures and unscrupulous websites spawned an online dating monstrosity. Two liars do not create one soul mate, do they? Am I right? Come on, admit it. I'm very astute, aren't I?"

His porters quickly answered, "Yes! Our Inca."

"I'm talking to the ladies, idiots. What do you say, ladies? Am I right?"

"I say your storytelling is getting worse, Rod. Plus look around. We're all half asleep." Tiffany yawned to make her point.

"I'm trying to take the high road here," he said, sounding wounded. "I'm trying to illustrate to all of you how you arrived at this specific crossroads in your lives. How you survived a precipitous route to get here and how you will comprehend that you must make profound sacrifices to achieve greatness."

Hilary recalled all the types of fallacies in argumentation, the Latin classifications floating in her mind like loose stones from the Coliseum. Was Rodrigo's conclusion a fallacy of *ignoratio elenchi* or of *tu quoque* or of *consensus gentium*? She couldn't decide, and even if she could, how could she use hand gestures to communicate disagreement? Hilary gave Rodrigo another thumbs-up, partly out of pity for his leap in logic, but mostly because she knew that her Andean deities were looking out for her well-being. What could she possibly have to fear?

The veins on Rodrigo's neck bulged. He was angry with these women who had not paid attention to his wisdom or appreciated his analysis of their poor choices. He decided to lure them to his prepared scenario with a bloody tale.

"In the old days, during our month of Camay, which is your January," he told them, "we would make a feast and dance for days. Not for happiness, mind you, but to repent our sins. Men and women would all hold on to a long rope that looked like a snake made of four colors: red, black, white, and brown, with the head made from a ball of red wool. The women would wear a special white feather from the *tocto* bird on their heads. And what do you suppose we did after the long rope snake dance?"

"Nobody cares, Rod," said Tiffany. "If you had a real snake, that might be a shocker, but dude, you're boring us."

Rodrigo signaled to the cook, who carried over a gunnysack and placed it on a flat stone surface in front of Rodrigo. Something inside the gunnysack squirmed and squealed. Rodrigo hacked at the coarse bag with a butcher knife, and the high-pitched squealing echoed through the mountains. The women were all awake now, their eyes wide with fright.

"Now do I have your attention?" Rodrigo demanded. He signaled to the cook again, this time to put an end to the squealing with one final stab.

"What the hell is the matter with you, Rod?" Tiffany panted. "What did you just kill?"

"An effigy of something I hate, of something I must destroy, of something whose nourishing blood the earth needs."

Gabby pulled nervously on her hair. "Honestly, Rodrigo, that was disgusting. When we said we wanted to burn an effigy of the lying guys we've met online, we were talking about an effigy made of straw. Didn't the Incas used to burn those straw effigies? No, no—I remember now! The Incas used straw effigies and then threw arrows at them, right?"

"Ah, so you wanted to get rid of the men who broke your hearts and soiled your bodies with their infected sperm by simply burning straw. Why come to the Andes to do that? Why not do it in Los Angeles or Boston or any town U.S.A?"

"Because we are civilized, that's why!" shouted Mercy.

Rodrigo laughed. "Do you really believe that your society is advanced socially, culturally, and *morally*? That is the definition of civilized, isn't it?"

"We certainly don't just butcher whatever animal you just slaughtered." Gabby shuddered.

"I hope that you are being facetious, my little Gabby. Do not embarrass yourself and your great Ivy League university by uttering such inane and uninformed comments. Our ancient rituals of sacrifice have great meaning. We know that as humans we are nothing, and we pay our respects to our gods by our rituals of sacrifice. In your society people kill each other by the thousands for trite reasons, or for no reason at all. Isn't Los Angeles the capital of the drive-by shooting? Your people kill innocents overseas, and they use advanced weapons as though they were playground toys. But let's narrow our conversation to the effigy you asked me to prepare for you, shall we? You asked me to conduct an Andean ritual that would transform your lives, did you not?"

"I was being ironic, as in saying something in the opposite way that is expected." Gabby glared at him. "Obviously I did not mean that we should kill some innocent animal."

"Are you sure you saw correctly? I do not see any dead animals here. Where is the blood?" Rodrigo pointed to the soil around the stone slab.

"We all witnessed your violence," Mercy told him.

"Violence? Violence? It is not violence. It is a sacrifice." Rodrigo nodded to the cook who lifted a heavier gunnysack, one the size of a small tire.

Hilary's voice was stuck in her stomach, and she could not make herself scream. She shook her head violently and shut her eyes when Rodrigo stabbed and stabbed the helpless animal inside the sack. Its deep bellows resounded inside the women's heads and paralyzed them with fear.

"You asked me to create for you a life-altering trek on the Inca trail, my own Inca trail," Rodrigo told them. "You asked me to design an effigy that you could all destroy. You demanded that

I make this experience one that would convert your dependency on technology into an awareness of the fragility of your very soul. You expected me to pour my manhood into each and every one of your many orifices, and I have and will continue to comply, but first you must keep your end of the bargain."

Mercy tried to stand up: she wanted to run from this lunatic, this megalomaniac in their midst, but she was unable to do so. While the women had been horrified by Rodrigo's violent attack of the animals in the gunnysacks, they had not noticed that the porters had not only removed the empty stew bowls; the team of men had grabbed the long ties hanging from the women's blankets and attached them to a heavy log on the ground.

Rodrigo stood up and walked over to Mercy. "You pride yourself in being logical and strong…and you are. But you also use and throw away men like banana peels. Your character is off-balance and it teeter-totters from depraved to kind—and back. You are also a very passionate lover, and therefore I will allow you to be the first to begin her transformation from a promiscuous slut into a caring *mamacona*."

Rodrigo held up the bloody knife, and Mercy shook her head in horror. "You cannot coerce me into doing anything cruel or crazy, Rodrigo," she said. "I refuse to do as you wish. I don't even know what a *mamacona* is." Mercy squirmed, trying to free herself from the swaddled blanket Choque had tied like a straightjacket. Her hands were free, so she managed to grab one of the tiny porters, pulling him in front of her to use as a shield against Rodrigo.

Rodrigo yanked the porter away from Mercy and kicked him to his corner.

"A *mamacona* was an honored matron in charge of the convent of the Brides of the Sun. Soon we will have *mamaconas* in these very mountain citadels."

Gabby came to Mercy's defense. "Let's all calm down, please. Rodrigo, we understand that you interpreted our request for the destruction of an effigy too literally. We're sorry for the misunderstanding, but we would like to forget about the effigy altogether. I think I speak for all of us when I say that this hike has been too arduous for us, physically and emotionally, and we would like to return to Cusco at sunrise. Can you do that, please?"

"Very nicely worded, Gabby. But in one word: no."

"Why the hell not, Rod?" Tiffany looked annoyed. "Gabby, Mercy, and Hilary want to leave, so let them. They're tough bitches and they can make it out of here on their own, believe me."

"Precisely for that reason, Tiffany. They would be leaving as they came, as self-absorbed, thoughtless women with delusional disorders. The three of them suffer from a predominant erotomanic-type delusional theme   "

"Just let them go!" screamed Tiffany.

Rodrigo marched up to her and slapped her across her face.

"Next time, I'll draw blood to make you pay, Tiffany," he said, pleased that he'd finally managed to shut her up. "Now, let me finish my psychological analyses of these whores. They crave an idealized romantic love, but they lie to any prospective mate. They crave a spiritual union but they engage in the most depraved of sex acts. Hilary, you wanted to mate with an animal, a wimp of a man dressed as a bear, didn't you?"

He loomed over Hilary, who did not want to get slapped: her face was already in so much pain. She nodded yes, but Rodrigo slapped her anyway.

"Tonight you will mate with a real beast," he said. "A roaring, clawing, skin-puncturing, and venomous beast."

Hilary, bent double, saw three drops of blood hit the ground. She looked up at Rodrigo, and gave him two thumbs up.

He rewarded her sacrifice with a painful French kiss that drew more blood from her wounded mouth.

"You sluts broke my train of thought," he said. He walked over to Mercy and stood staring at her. "You, you are a piece a work. A highly trained attorney who still experiences persecutory delusions on behalf of her father. Give me a break! You only mate with white men because you hate your own race, but you can't admit it. Yet you are an amazing lover; I'll give you credit for that. You're on my top one-hundred list, isn't she, boys?"

"Yes, Illapa our god!" the porters shouted, and Mercy's face burned red with shame.

Rodrigo walked from one woman to the next, kissing them passionately. "I'm sorry I lost my temper. Please accept my deepest apologies. You paid for a transformative trek and you will have a transformative trek. If we allow you to leave, then we have all failed in our promise, and we keep our word in the highlands. In order to arrive here in the manner that you did, I had to make sacrifices to the *huacas* so you would be protected. What do you think that the *huacas* demand as proof of one's sincerity?"

No one answered Rodrigo. He said, "Let me show you one proof!"

He pulled up his shirt and lifted a Spondylus shell pendant from his chest. Hilary remembered that this type of shell was revered because it came from the ocean, from Mamacocha, and therefore the source of water. Under the shell, Rodrigo's self-inflicted wound dribbled blood. The women flinched.

"You asked me for a long and detailed scary story, didn't you? Well, here it is. We Andeans believe in bloodletting. Please notice that I am using the present tense of the word 'believe' since it will be significant to you shortly. You can visit our museums and study our ceramics and our textiles and you will see depictions of men carrying their own dripping head in one hand and a *tumi* knife in the other. You will see streamers coming out from all bodily orifices that continue to ooze blood. You will see flayed skin allowed to weep blood directly into the soil of our Earth Mother. She gave us life and we must reciprocate."

During Rodrigo's lecture, both Gabby and Mercy were trying to free themselves of the tight blankets. It was impossible to read what Hilary was thinking: she sat immobile, a wistful smile on her face. Tiffany's body twitched wildly with nervous energy. She did not appear to be tied as firmly as the other women, yet she didn't seem to be attempting to free herself. She had learned from the various juvenile detention centers that sometimes it was better to appear entrapped so people would leave you alone while you planned your next move.

Rodrigo had no intention of letting the women just walk off. They had to keep their end of the agreement, and one way or another they would make a sacrifice tonight. He was intent on forcing the women to perform this one sacrificial act before he enlisted them in the more solemn acts of his kingdom. He needed to illustrate to them the rigorous steps required to fully transform one's life.

He'd undergone a hard-earned transformation himself, and it had been painful every step of the way. As a youngster, when he shared his fantasies of power and success with his camp counselor in New England one too many times, the counselor referred him to a psychologist. It was decided that his Narcissistic Personality Disorder did not include self-destructiveness or characteristics of impulsivity or aggression, so they allowed him to return the next year. Rodrigo hated the camp, and took it upon himself to display the same offensive characteristics that the psychologist described. He learned to cut himself, but the camp director did not send him home. Finally, when he attacked a weaker boy and drew blood with a spiny shell, he arrived back in Cusco a month early. Upon witnessing the awful cuts on his body, the wounds she was certain other boys must have inflicted, his mother refused to ever send him back to the States, and his father's Boston relatives never contradicted her. Rodrigo's transformation had taken him years, but in time he'd found others who believed in his brilliance and talents, in his godly attributes. Soon his transformation would be complete, and he would become their god.

Rodrigo stood laughing at the four cowering women who thought they could dictate a revelation, who thought personal transformation could be ordered online and paid for like an overnight delivery.

"One step at a time, that is how you will be transformed," he lectured them. "Just as you arrived at this point by taking one painful step along the precarious path, by hiking on *my Inca Illapa Trail*, that is how you will untether yourself from all your online addictions and your psychotic disorders."

Rodrigo gazed out at the black night, unsure of what he was going to say or do next. The one thing he did know was that he had not broken the women down sufficiently to command them to do his bidding—in particular, the very critical next step—so he backed off. He had until dawn to brainwash these Ivy League women, so he decided to punish and reward them, to pit them one against the other, to make love to them and to beat them down in order to make them draw blood. Then and only then would they be ready to commence the sacred procession to the peak.

"His porters quickly answered, 'Yes! Our Inca.'"

"Can't you just picture her marching up to the
peaks in the *capacocha* procession?"

CHAPTER SEVENTEEN

¡*Alalau!*" Taki exclaimed. "These poor women don't know the evil they're dealing with. We have to move in closer to them, even if the little men catch a whiff of us."

The old women were crouching on a ledge near the campground. The blackness of the night blanketed all the surrounding paths, jagged boulders, and roaming beasts sharpening their claws while they hunted for their next meal. The only glow came from the campfire that illuminated the ruins of the stone wall, which in turn created a false sense of security and of a cozy familial hearth. The porters played their pan flutes and Rodrigo's words lulled the women to sleep. Except Rodrigo was punctuating his monologue with a bloody weapon, a dagger with which he stabbed the air in exclamation marks composed of a vertical gray blade and its descending drops of thick red blood. This strange nocturnal scene, featuring anxious hikers and malicious porters, painted an authentic Andean tableau of harmony and discord.

"Move, Koyam," Taki insisted. "We must get close to the women and try to save them."

"That's exactly what I've been telling you since last night, but now that Rodrigo is yards away from us, I'm truly afraid, ¡Alalau!" Koyam rolled her eyes. "What did the mallquis tell you we should do? Surely our wise ancestors gave you good advice?"

"¡Ooyooyooy! How did you know about the hidden mallquis? It's a secret I've kept to myself all these years."

"I've shadowed you for the last seventy years. Of course I know that you were selected as the steward of the mallquis. They are the oracles that answer the questions posed by those gifted ones, such as yourself. I've always tagged along with you when you hiked into the caves that only you know about. I figured that if I accompanied you long enough maybe in time the mallquis would speak to me, but either they've clammed up or I haven't heard what they whispered. Hell, I don't even know where you've kept them hidden all these decades! By now I know who I am, and I am not the seer, I am the doer."

Koyam waited for Taki to give her instructions, but Taki said nothing.

"If you don't tell me what to do right now," Koyam told her, "I am going to start throwing the little men off the cliff one by one. That is the only plan I can come up with."

"It's all so convoluted in my head, Koyam. The mallquis don't tell me blow-by-blow what I should do. They speak to me in riddles and visions and scents and sounds. It is up to my heart and my mind to somehow piece it all together. It's as if my mind is composed of pieces of my great-grandson's puzzles. Lately, I've been thinking that the mallquis are here just to help us concentrate on our problems and our own solutions, because they never have interfered with my actions."

"¡*Chuta!* Damn it, Taki! No more riddles, no more doubts, it's time for action, not secrets. We all know that many of our ancestors are still among us in mummified form, but if they won't interfere, if all they do is talk in riddles or give vague clues, what good are they then? I say we should do it my way."

"The *mallquis* are with us, as always, but we should not question their judgment or reveal their whereabouts to others — ever. Do you want to know why they have never spoken to you? You and your big mouth are worse than the foreign scientists who find one of our *mallquis* up in the peaks or inside the caves and they broadcast it to the world. Next thing you know, our ancestors are sent off to Washington D.C., displayed like freaks in their fancy museums, making millions of dollars for them. It turns my stomach the way they treated the poor frozen maiden from Ampato. Remember—back in 1996? The fools even named her Juanita." Taki shook her head with disgust.

"That wasn't the worst of it," Koyam said. "Their president said that Juanita was so good-looking, if she were alive and he were single, he might ask her for a date! It's revolting how they treated her." Koyam spat out the sour taste in her mouth.

"Poor frozen maiden," Taki said. "Can't you just picture her marching up to the peaks in the *capacocha* procession, the solemn sacrifice that was her destiny? They say the sacrificial maidens had a large entourage of priests and priestesses that accompanied them until the moment of their death. Sometimes they offered them *chicha* so they would be numbed and less frightened. The victims each wore a beautiful tunic tied with a *chumpi* belt around the waist, and they wore a shawl, a *lliclla,* around their shoulders held in place by silver *tupu* pins. Finally, they wrapped the maidens in very tight mantles while musicians played…"

Taki cocked her head, listening intently to the music drifting up from the campsite. "¡*Alalau!* ¡*Alalau!*" she exclaimed. "I think that Rodrigo is planning a *capacocha* right now!"

Koyam left their perch to creep closer to the campsite, fearing that Taki's message from her oracle had revealed the most horrific news. A *capacocha* of ancient times followed certain ceremonial steps dictated by the Inca and the gods. The one thing mandated in a *capacocha* ceremony, without any exception, was a human offering to the sun or one of the other gods, such as Illapa, the god of thunder.

Koyam looked from the women to Rodrigo, who appeared to be lecturing them instead of singing. None of the *gringas* looked as though they were in the midst of any ceremony, and they certainly didn't look like victims. Perhaps Taki's interpretation of the mummified oracle's advice was all jumbled up in her old brain.

The women, Koyam observed, were sitting around the campfire wrapped in warm blankets. Three of them seemed to have dozed off, but the pretty flower with a monkey's voice and hyper personality was as jittery as ever. She seemed to be interrupting Rodrigo's speech, and one of the porters slapped her across the face with the nettle branch. Koyam gasped at this cruelty, but she wasn't about to rush down there to protect a loudmouth *gringa*. She did have her mace handy, in case she had to take down Choque or Rodrigo. The little men didn't worry her too much: she could lift them and throw them over the cliff without any hesitation.

Taki gathered her heavy bundle and followed Koyam's lead, edging closer to the campsite. She set her bundle down as though it were a valuable and fragile package, then wedged it for safekeeping between two boulders. Koyam was even closer now, squatting by the ruined wall where Hilary had sat earlier while Rodrigo massaged her neck and filled her head with promises he had no intention of keeping. Taki crept up alongside her.

"Did Rodrigo strike the giant woman?" she whispered. "She has cuts on her face."

"I didn't see him hit her, but she looks like she could strike him right back, so don't worry about her. But that scruffy little porter slapped the pretty flower with the nettle branch."

"Throw him off the cliff first when the time comes!" Taki recommended.

"With pleasure. Can I first swing him round and round?"

"Can't you ever be serious?" Taki elbowed Koyam, then paused to study the scene. "Everything we are looking at here does not add up to a *capacocha* ceremony, does it? I must be getting senile. What was I thinking? There is no young and perfect child here ready to be sacrificed, and these women are far from perfect—and anyway, they're too old to be offered to the gods. Should we leave?"

"Naw, let's stay and punish Rodrigo if he tries anything. I've wanted to break his arms ever since my great-granddaughter fell under his spell and went to Miami looking for him. Who knows what's happened to my child in that foreign land?"

Taki did not have the heart to tell Koyam the truth about her great-granddaughter's fate. Taki had a frequent vision of the young woman alone in a small room, man after man arriving to feast on her nectar, her eyes as glassy and opaque as the cheap quartz sold in the Plaza de Armas. Taki rubbed her eyes furiously to wipe away this ominous revelation, but another totally nonsensical vision took its place.

"My days as a seer are coming to end," she muttered to Koyam. "You won't believe what just popped into my mind."

"I have no idea, but I hope it's a detailed action plan that shows us winning this fight. In case you haven't noticed, we are just two old ladies preparing to fight six men. It's a death wish."

"¡*Ooyooyooy*, all I see is death. Bodies flying in the air and into the abyss. Blood splattering on the ground. A woman crying in pain—"

"Does that woman crying in pain look like me, by any chance?" Koyam nudged Taki.

Taki, staring into space, did not laugh at her friend's gallows humor. "I see hundreds of black llamas slaughtered—"

"Tell me something I don't know. One hundred black llamas have always been sacrificed to stop the rain. Someone faithful to the old ways must have slaughtered their black llamas today since the rain has stopped. What else do you see? Which one of the little porters do I have to fight first? Give me a heads-up, will you?"

"Can I tell you all the nonsensical bits and pieces I see?"

"Sure, but if you see me jump in to crack Rodrigo's bones or throw little men off the cliff, get out of the way and go hide in the *mallquis'* cave."

Taki leaned into Koyam. "I see feathers of all colors, and young beautiful girls laughing as older women wrap their heads with feathers. I see their families smiling and dressing them in tunics of the most remarkable woven patterns." Taki grabbed Koyam's red poncho and inspected its pattern. "The shawls are made-up of the sacred diamond-shape lake pattern. You know how we revere the glacier-fed lakes."

"Yes, the shawl and the lake patterns sound beautiful, but how am I going to win this fight? Which one of the *gringas* do I save first? Can you please fast-forward the movie in your mind because Rodrigo is starting to move around. Look! I think he's asking each one of the women something unpleasant."

"But if I try to watch Rodrigo and simultaneously try to read my mind, I won't be able to do it."

"I understand. I'll keep my eye on Rodrigo's movements," Koyam suggested, "and you tell me all that you see or smell or whatever else happens to you when you go into your trances."

Taki paused for a moment, and then started speaking again very softly. "Someone is putting coca leaves in the little girl's mouth, and he is also storing her nail clippings and strands of her hair in a bag made from the testicles of a llama. Now he's setting the bag next to the little girl. Isn't that unusual?"

"Not as unusual as us getting thrown off the cliff because we didn't make the first strike against Rodrigo. Maybe you should forget this slow-motion vision and skip to one that shows me and you cracking bones, instead of some little girl from way back when getting dressed in pretty clothing."

"¡Alalau! They're making her sit down with her knees drawn up to her chest. A man is going behind her tiny neck with a thick cord...I can't bear it, I can't bear it, he's strangling the little girl." Taki rested her head on Koyam's shoulder and began to sob.

"Shh, shh, the porters might hear you. The little girl's sacrifice was eons ago, remember? This does not happen anymore. We'll cry over a Pisco Sour at the Plaza de Armas tomorrow. Shh, Taki, please be quiet."

Taki choked back her sobs, determined to finish describing her trance. "They're wrapping the lifeless little girl entirely with a colorful mantle, then with another mantle of complex geometric patterns, so that she resembles a bundle, and no longer the happy child."

Koyam said nothing, but she knew that her friend's visions were no help to her whatsoever with the situation at hand. Rodrigo's actions had turned from bizarre to abusive—now he was slapping each of the women. Koyam gently pushed Taki away so her head was resting against the wall that their ancestors had carved and painstakingly installed one stone at a time, not knowing that their descendants would use it as a protective shield against an evil force like Rodrigo.

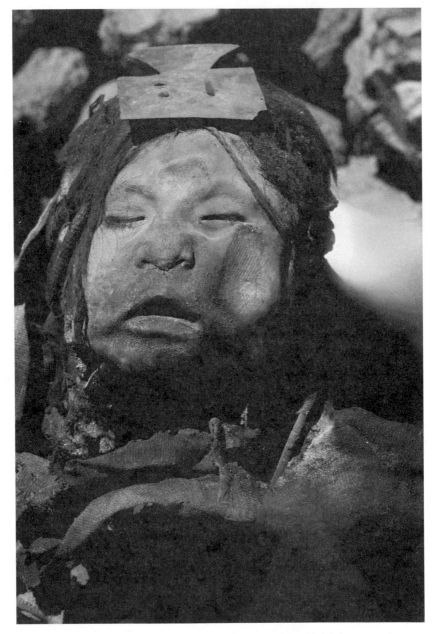

"Someone is putting coca leaves in the little girl's mouth."

Koyam clambered to her feet and swung her mace a few times to remind herself that this brawl with Rodrigo and his minions might be her crowning fight, her last hurrah, her final performance as the protectoress of Taki, the only remaining guardian of the secret *mallquis* of the Inca empire.

In the past, Koyam had never dared to regard herself in such high esteem. She'd given all her loyalty and friendship to Taki, whose benevolence was widely known, but tonight Koyam would prove to the mountain gods, to the holy *huacas*, and to her ancestors, that the mighty body she had been given by them would be used to extinguish the malevolent beings present at this campsite—whatever the cost.

Rodrigo walked back and forth among the women, who seemed confused by his maniacal questioning. He paused in front of Mercy, leaning over her until their noses almost touched.

"Are you ready to destroy your effigy now?" he demanded. "Have I proven to you that sacrifice is sacred?"

When Mercy didn't answer, Rodrigo strolled over to Gabby and stroked her pretty hair as if she were a kitten.

"Little Gabby, what will it be? Pick one of the gunny sacks." He marched to Choque's side and grabbed one squirming gunnysack. "What do you suppose is in the sack? Take a satirical stab in the dark—or should I say take a wild ironic guess at it? In other words, figure out the opposite of what you think. From the size of the bag it could be a piglet or a human infant—which is it?"

Gabby cringed, and this seemed to both delight and inflame Rodrigo.

"Gaaabbyy, you're not guessing! Do I have to remind you how many men ridiculed *your* intellect, and your morality—

and who knows what they did to your tight little opening. Shall I take a teensy look?" Rodrigo laughed, reaching down to remove Gabby's panties, but Choque had fastened the blankets too tightly and Rodrigo couldn't do it with only one hand free. His men laughed along with him. "You told me you'd like to jab the online dating men in the back. Well, here's your chance. Go ahead and cleave your very personal effigy!"

Rodrigo swung the gunnysack, containing some sort of squirming, grunting beast, in front of Gabby's appalled face. Hilary tried to catch her eye: she gave Gabby a two thumbs-up sign, and then stuck out her thumb as if she were hitchhiking. She couldn't believe that Gabby didn't understand her clear message: there was obviously no child in the bag, so make a run for it and I will cover you. But Gabby just slapped at Rodrigo and at the sack in a hysterical, childlike way, while all the men laughed and slapped at each other in sarcastic imitation.

Hilary's silence and her immobile pose set her apart from the other women, who were trying to squirm their way out of their blanket-cum-straightjackets. So while Choque kept his eye on them, he no longer bothered with surveillance of Hilary. She sat listening to her Andean deities whisper in her ear from miles away at Huayna Picchu peak.

"Butterfly," they whispered, "break the glass from the binoculars in your vest pocket, and cut the back restraints from your blanket. We will watch over you and throw sand in the eyes of anyone who comes near you."

Hilary had never believed in anything as much as she believed in a nonexistent voice that the pre-dawn Andean morning blew her way. She would do exactly as the deities said.

Meanwhile Rodrigo had skipped over to Mercy, handed her the dagger and started coaxing her into stabbing the gunnysack. Mercy's eyes blurred red with anger. She thought of her father's strong hands and how they would have choked Rodrigo and killed whatever was in the sack before either beast harmed his princess. She had always made him proud, and at this moment in her life, she knew that he would want her to go to the limit, no matter what. Surviving this ordeal would make her dad proud.

Mercy reached for the gunnysack with the dagger and pierced it deeply. Rodrigo jumped up and down in demented joy as blood poured from the sack.

"High five, Mercy," he shouted, but as she reached to high-five Rodrigo, she swung the dagger at him as well, aiming for his other arm. Rodrigo swung the sack at Mercy and knocked the dagger onto the ground. One of the porters scurried over to pick it up.

"Did I tell you to pick it up? Does a god need help from a tick? Well, does he?

"No, our Inca Illapa," answered the porter.

Rodrigo handed the gunnysack to Choque and wiped his bloody hands on his pants.

"Okey, dokey," he said, as though they were playing a happy game. "Let the ladies rest and relax before we enjoy their bodies. We can entertain them some more. It's time for a fight in the octagon, my loyal subjects."

He pointed to two porters, who moved slowly to the center of the campsite. Despite the reluctance on their weathered faces, soon they were punching and kicking each other with a vengeance, imitating the moves of professional fighters they had seen on satellite television, until they drew blood. They knew that this was the moment that pleased Rodrigo the most, and the sooner it happened, the sooner he would lose interest in their fight and let them go back to their corners.

"Olé!" Rodrigo shouted as though this were the bullfights, when he saw blood splatter onto the dirt.

One of the exhausted porters saw his one opportunity to live free of Rodrigo's cruelty. He opened his heart to the *huacas* and felt the morning dew drizzle on his face. "This is your last chance at being human again," it told him, "but you must escape now."

The porter took one last punch to the face, and while Rodrigo howled his approval, leaping up and down like a mad man, the porter took off. He ran as fast as he could away from the camp. Choque realized what he was doing and started chasing him, but he was encumbered by the gunnysack he was holding, and tripped on a stone slab. The large viscacha writhing inside the gunnysack managed to escape, racing away as confused and frenzied as the fugitive porter.

"Let the weak link break away," Rodrigo shouted. "We're better off without him. He'll never make it past the cliffs, or the pumas that will smell his blood or his own stupidity. He never said a word, nor did he entertain us, did he? At dawn we'll find pieces of him."

The fragrance of violets permeated the air, and Taki and Koyam sniffed, nodding to each other.

"It is Frenchy's scent, of that I am certain," said Koyam. "But it must be some piece of her clothing that Rodrigo is carrying with him, don't you think?"

"I smell Frenchy's body and not just her clothing," muttered Taki. "Rodrigo must have brought her to this very spot and taunted her just as he is taunting the *gringas*. It must be Violette's trapped anger and fear that the boulders and soil are finally releasing. At least that is how I am seeing her in my vision. I see her behind a boulder, but she looks very haggard, as if she is going to die."

"Well, I hope she is dead already, and then soon we won't have to smell her at all."

"Your heart is full of hate," said Taki, "even at a time when our very existence hangs by a thread, you should—"

"*Ooyooyooy*, Rod just lifted the little flower right out of her blanket!" Koyam said. "He has no shame. He is fondling her right in front of his men. She looks as terrible as the giant. Her face must have swelled up with the stinging nettles the porter used to strike her."

Rodrigo was gripping Tiffany's hair with one hand; with the other hand he roughed up her breasts. "Your breasts are wonderful, but your face has welts all over. Lucky for you, I don't care what your face looks like as long as your lips do their professional best. Are you ready to show the ladies how you earned your keep?"

"Shut up, Rod!" screamed Tiffany, wincing with pain. "I'll do whatever you want, but let's do it inside the tent."

"Ladies, today you will see how your Inca god is capable of transforming an exhibitionist hooker into a submissive little hiker," bragged Rodrigo. "Indeed, you will be astonished by how quickly I can convert Tiffany from a devil to an angel. Our hiking companion Tiffany has never told you how she managed to join this illustrious Ivy League group, has she?"

Tiffany attempted to break free from Rodrigo, but when she could not elude his grip, she let her body go limp. This forced Rodrigo to let her fall to the ground, like a heavy blanket falling from a bed. He stood menacingly over her.

"Here's the blunt truth about Tiffany," he told the others. "She is a slick liar and a wily thief. While she provided sexual—oh, excuse me, I meant to say 'escort services'—to very wealthy old men back in California, she also managed to steal many valuables. She eventually became quite the blackmailer, threatening to divulge her client's nasty little habits to their wives. Isn't that so, slut?"

"Go to hell, Rod," Tiffany spat.

"You have to hand it to Tiffany—she's full of spunk, isn't she? Could it be because she's learned to do whatever it takes to make ends meet? She's a real renaissance woman, you know. She can perform any kind of sexual trick!"

"They don't care about that, idiot. Let them go and I'll do whatever you want," screamed Tiffany, still flat on her back on the ground.

Tiffany had known all sorts of sadists in her life, but never one as crazed as Rodrigo. Her mind was whirring. She knew that she would somehow land on her two feet, because she had the suppleness of a cat with nine lives, but Tiffany wasn't so sure about the other women, the snobs she'd grown to like. These women, sitting trapped and helpless in their seats around the fire, had been the students at the Ivy League colleges of her dreams. But despite their intellectual arrogance, they didn't have the fortitude of a foster kid who had learned to tune out everything horrible happening to her body while she dreamed of being a smart student at one of those exclusive ivy-covered colleges she'd seen in a magazine at a doctor's office. On this hike Tiffany had been pretending to be one of those students on a college trip abroad, because she'd never had the chance to do anything like that when she was a teenager.

She had first learned about the Inca Trail hike while she waited for one of her johns to finish using the bathroom. She'd poked through the items on his hotel desk, and then scrolled through his emails. One of them read: "Hey buddy, want to slay lots of smart and desperate women? My alumni newsletter sent this Inca Trail website. Let's do it for the hell of it!"

Her john returned, demanding her services, and Tiffany complied expertly. But her mind was full of Andean vistas of icy peaks and llamas cavorting among the smiling women hikers she had seen pictured on the Inca Trail website. Tiffany felt she deserved a shot at making at least one of her lifelong dreams come true: she would pretend to be a college grad from one of the Ivy League schools, and she would make new friends.

Of course, it was turning out to be a short-lived fantasy with a tragic ending, no different than all the experiences in her life.

It was time to make her final move, to take care of number one, and the first step was luring Rodrigo down on the ground with her. Tiffany reached out her arms to him, licking her lips and wriggling out of her jeans and panties. Rodrigo obliged, shouting at the porters to watch and learn. She straddled him and kissed him passionately, writhing on top of him to put on a convincing show. All the other women shut their eyes, but Choque and his men howled and hooted and applauded their Inca's latest conquest, and the next step on his pyramid plan.

But before Tiffany could do more than thrust and groan, a blurry figure emerged out of the darkness. A reed-thin woman swinging a dainty stiletto knife—a memento given to her by her Corsican swami—ran towards Rodrigo, yelling in Spanish and French.

"*Salaud!*" she screamed, exploding with rage. "Rotten bastard! Filthy womanizer! You thought you could get rid of me so easily? You thought you could replace me with these mangy whores?"

Before Violette could reach Rodrigo and Tiffany as they coupled shamelessly, Choque and one of the porters tackled her to the ground. A stunned Rodrigo lay underneath Tiffany, flinching at the sound of Violette's high-pitched yelps, not to mention the startled screams from the other women, and the manic confusion of the porters, all of whom were trying to restrain the furious Violette.

"I am the god Illapa," he cried, glaring at Violette. "Do you realize the thunderous punishment that awaits you?"

Rodrigo would never admit this to anyone, not even himself, but his obsessive belief that he was an anointed new Inca and Illapa was starting to waver. Only a true *capacocha* sacrifice, he decided, would prove to everyone that Rodrigo Guamán

O'Rourke had majestically transformed from a talented man into the god of thunder. Still squashed beneath a half-naked Tiffany, he raised his right arm and cried out, as though he were commanding the thunder and lightning to strike down the hysterical women around him.

Gabby and Mercy took advantage of the melee to try to yank free of their restraints. Mercy managed to pull one leg out, but her other leg was firmly wrapped and tied to the log. Gabby's futile efforts to free herself left her limp and slouched. With her small frame, she looked like a child sent to sit in the corner. Only Tiffany had the animal-survival instincts to flee. Like a feral cat, she jumped off of Rodrigo, gathered her panties and jeans, and ran past Gabby and Mercy.

"Help me, please!" Mercy called to her, but there wasn't a second to lose.

"Sucks to be you!" Tiffany hissed, avoiding Hilary's outstretched hand. Hilary was actually trying to hand her a glass fragment from her broken binoculars, but Tiffany was preoccupied with grabbing her own day pack.

"Use your frickin' giant size to defend yourself," she said, flipping Hilary off. "Dumb bitch!"

Tiffany was in full survival-and-attack mode now, the state of being she'd been forced to adopt for most of her life. After the beatings, the sexual abuse, and the endless foster homes, the soft, sensitive little girl had metamorphosed into the seductive vamp Tiffany, and the woman who never allowed herself to feel anything. Every time she allowed herself to care for someone, to let a weakness show or to reveal doubt, someone else had taken advantage of that frailty. Tiffany had learned that in her flashy new-money "fake it till you make it" crowd in Newps, to be a beautiful but vacuous blonde was an asset, her shallowness as desirable as her new silicone enlargements.

Tiffany took one last look at the fragile, brainy snobs with their paws still stuck in Rodrigo's traps, and bolted down the path. She promised herself that if she saw the missing porter on the way down, she'd kick his ass off the cliff without any hesitation. She would never show any vulnerability or kindness ever again.

As she jogged down the trail, a sliver of sunrise illuminated the horizon. Tiffany smiled to herself, picking up her pace with the agility and self-confidence of an endangered Andean mountain cat just released from captivity.

CHAPTER EIGHTEEN

"**Y**ou insane son of a *pute*," screamed Violette, struggling to elude Choque's steely grip. "You thought I would disappear after you abandoned me and took my money? You imbecile!"

"I am the god Illapa," Rodrigo shouted at her again in his most menacing manner, trying to drum the information into her crazy head. "Don't you realize the thunderous punishment that awaits you?"

Rodrigo scrambled to his feet, adjusting his clothing after his interrupted encounter with Tiffany, and raised his arm again. This time a porter read his mind and handed him his bullwhip. Rodrigo strode around his mountain stage as if he trained circus animals, but he didn't immediately crack his whip or shout any further commands. He was stupefied by Violette's sudden appearance here in the mountains. He had not given her a thought since the day she was deported, but now she was back, screaming at him, and he couldn't predict what she wanted. No matter, he was the one in charge, and he would decide what to do next. He strolled around the restrained women, staring at Violette and Choque.

He cracked the whip once for dramatic effect. "Violette, I didn't recognize you," he said, his voice thick with contempt. "You're as scrawny as a resurrected corpse. Tell us why you've come back from the dead. Have you returned to steal another baby?"

Violette stared wild-eyed at the three remaining women.

"Do you know that he has fathered dozens of children from poor young girls?" she asked them in heavily accented English. "Or that he sells his own children to the highest bidder from your country?"

The captives didn't quite understand what Violette was saying. They were bewildered and exhausted after all the tribulations of the last two days. Rodrigo cracked his whip again.

"They don't care about any babies, do you, ladies? Gabby's had a couple of abortions, if I recall an old blog of yours correctly. Or was that another satirical entry?"

Gabby didn't answer Rodrigo because she had stopped understanding specific words. All she could hear was her own blood coursing through her veins and lulling her into a daydream-like state. Between the carnage with the poor animals in the gunnysacks and the vicious fight between the porters, Gabby had been forced to consider, and to appreciate, her own lifeblood. She wrapped her arms around her torso, trying to protect the heart pumping blood through her slight, trembling form. She blocked out all the other sounds around her, relieved that she no longer had to listen to all the earlier accusations: everyone seemed to blame her for promoting this nightmare Inca Trail hike on her website. Gabby had felt overwhelmed with guilt; she'd felt dirty and tainted by Rodrigo's pawing at her panties, and dirty and tainted because of her excitement at his touch. Now the palpable evil around the blazing campfire frightened her, and made her blood run cold.

Rodrigo strolled up to Mercy, as arrogant as ever.

"Introduce yourself to Violette," he commanded. "You two have much in common. You're both man-eating swine, did you know that? Don't bother to answer—you're both liars, too. Show us what a good lawyer you are. Defend yourself, Mercy."

There were many avenues of persuasion Mercy could employ right now, hoping to defuse the increasingly terrifying scenario. But Rodrigo was way beyond megalomania, her earlier diagnosis. He clearly displayed all the contradictory traits of a menacing psychopath. Reason or logic would not work with him, and neither would compassion or total submission to his will. So Mercy decided to take a chance with a soft-toned, measured line of questioning.

"Rodrigo," she said, trying to keep her voice steady. "Would you please tell us what you hope to achieve by restraining us here?"

Rodrigo cracked his whip. "Are you saying I don't know what I'm doing here?" he shouted.

"On the contrary, it's obvious that your men follow all your directions obediently because you're a strong leader." She looked him straight in the eye. "It's just that we three don't know why we're restrained. If you would explain it to us, we would have a better understanding and not react fearfully, as we have thus far."

"Do not let him sweet talk you, like I did," Violette screamed, thrashing around in Choque's grasp. "He made me believe that I would soon have my own baby. This is what he does! He will love you and compliment you intensely, and then he will abuse you. Do not let him talk you into doing anything for him. You cannot imagine how depraved—!"

Choque applied additional pressure on Violette's neck until she stopped talking. Rodrigo picked up where Violette left off.

"So far you are not a very effective attorney, are you, Mercy?" he sneered.

"Are you asking me to speak for or represent Violette? If that's the case, can you please allow her to answer my questions as well?"

Rodrigo bent over laughing. "You *gringas* are hilarious, especially when you don't even try to be humorous. Is that irony, Gabby? Is it? Let me ask the jury." He pointed to the porters and Choque. "What say you, my loyal subjects? Shall we let Violette speak?"

"Whatever you say, our Inca Illapa, sir," replied the porters.

"Proceed, counselor." Rodrigo waved at Choque to loosen his hold on a purple-faced Violette.

Mercy waited a few seconds to come up with a line of questioning that would amuse Rodrigo, something that would entice him until the intensity of the present moment diffused. Clearly Rodrigo's erratic behavior had worsened since the escape of Tiffany and the porter. Rodrigo was incapable of thinking rationally: that was obvious. His hair-trigger reactions thus far had been violent. For all they knew, he could be on the verge of murder.

Mercy felt ashamed and mortified that she'd let a maniac dehumanize her. She was powerless in the face of the trauma he was inflicting on all of them. Gabby sat with her arms wrapped around her chest, her eyes shut, as though she was in a semi-catatonic state. Hilary, on the other hand, maintained a beatific smile directed at Choque and the porters, but Mercy observed her hands moving ever so slightly behind her back.

Only Mercy seemed to be entirely present in this catastrophic moment, and she feared for her life, for all their lives. The sensation of powerlessness washed through her again, and she realized that it had been quite some time since she was the brilliant golden girl outwitting other attorneys, always coming out on top. She had never stopped to assess her own decline, because she'd been blinded by her past glory. In letting her guard down on this hike, Mercy realized that she had allowed an animal to dominate her and humiliate her.

An impatient Rodrigo cracked the whip, and Mercy asked her first question.

"Violette, please respond to my questions in a calm voice so everyone can understand your perspective. Would you please tell us why you ran into our camp and attempted to stab our hike leader, Rodrigo?"

Mercy saw that Rodrigo smiled at the mention of "our camp" and "our hike leader."

"I have thought of nothing else but revenge for the perpetrator who killed my baby," spat Violette.

"You are as barren as the Nazca Desert, Violette," sneered Rodrigo. "You were never pregnant. I simply wanted to make you happy, so I lied to you about trying to adopt a child. That is all, and this line of questioning is boring me to tears. Make it quick, Mercy."

"Violette, if Rodrigo decides to show mercy on you, although you clearly wanted to harm him, will you depart calmly if accompanied by Hilary, Gabby and me?"

Rodrigo guffawed. "You are ridiculously funny, Mercy. Let me see where you are going with your questions. Get to the point."

Violette's morbid hatred for Rodrigo was obscuring her judgment: she didn't realize that Mercy was trying to tell her to be docile, and to apologize to Rodrigo. Mercy glanced to one side, noticing that Hilary appeared to have released herself from her bindings, although she still remained seated. Mercy knew she needed to ask Violette something that might engage Rodrigo's attention instead of his ire.

"Violette, are there any words of clarification or *apology* you would like to extend to Rodrigo?"

At last Violette seemed to catch on. Going against her Gallic pride, she decided to play along.

"Yes," she sniffed. "I would like to let Rodrigo know that I came to Cusco accompanied by my sponsor, an extremely wealthy man who wishes to become a partner with Rodrigo. He believes that there is a huge market for the sale of healthy babies who are partially white, like Rodrigo's many, many children. My business partner believes this new venture would be immensely profitable. He says that only a select few have historically benefitted from Peru's precious assets, and that since Rodrigo is an expert in the Inca Trail, he would understand this reference."

Violette's swami had spoken bluntly, but truthfully, since he understood the magnetic attraction and incentive of a favorable profit margin, particularly one gained illegally. Centuries ago, the myth of El Dorado lured the Spanish to the mountain peaks of the Andes, and they indeed took all the riches of the Inca Empire and destroyed the advanced culture they found here in the highlands. Then, centuries later, through sleight of hand , another opportunist was able to produce documents purportedly allowing him to export archaeological treasures out of Peru. But those antiquities were not enough, so the spindly-legged adventurer paid a shady Cusco antiquarian a hefty sum to purchase over 350 smuggled Inca artifacts. One bad deed led to another, which in turn led to a mountain of bad deeds and a tangled paper trail that would take one hundred years to unravel until most of the artifacts were returned to their homeland.

The mention of a business proposition intrigued Rodrigo. After he completed his *capacocha* procession and sacrifice at sunrise, he would be the undisputed Inca and thunder god, Illapa, but where would his financing come from? His pyramid scheme required funds. He knew that Violette's were all used up, and the *gringas* were most uncooperative, not at all like the submissive, love-hungry, sex-deprived saps he was expecting. These whores were not easy prey as he'd hoped, and he suspected they would never turn over their money to him—with the exception of the battered Hilary. But it would not be the huge amount he needed. He turned to Mercy.

"Ask your client how soon I can meet her partner. Can he walk up here? I don't want to go back to Cusco for quite a while."

Violette loosened herself from Choque, but was careful not to lunge towards Rodrigo—yet. "He is a very savvy business-man," she replied, "but he is a bit sickly. He would like to seal his business deal with you over a ceremony that money cannot buy. They say that a *capacocha* ritual can be performed to heal the sick—an eye-for-an-eye type of ceremony, where Rodrigo would offer up one of his many children in return for the good health of my business partner."

Rodrigo cracked his whip furiously. "A *capacocha* ceremony is reserved for an Inca or for a god, not for a sick and depraved foreigner," he roared. He took a step towards Violette to slap her soundly for her impudence, but she lunged at him and bit him on his hand. Choque and one of the porters grabbed her by her arms and legs.

"Where's my baby?" she shrieked. "Did you bury her alive?"

Violette's piercing screams stunned Gabby back to reality. Hilary, sitting nearby, saw Gabby rouse herself and, in a moment of sisterly compassion, threw the glass from the binoculars to her.

Violette's body rattled like a bag of bones as Choque and the porter lugged her squirming body towards the edge of the cliff. A second porter ran alongside, ready to strike her on the head with a rock.

"Make sure that she is dead," Rodrigo shouted. "I never want to see her again."

When the cook heard Rodrigo's command, he was enraged: was there no end to this boss's cruelty? Violence was not in the cook's blood, and he could not decide if he was capable of attacking Rodrigo and putting a stop to the madness of this terrible hike. He glanced at his cooking equipment, considering which one would inflict quick and terminal injury: a butcher knife or his heavy skillet. He had already packed all his utensils in readiness for their departure at sunrise for the procession. A *mock capacocha*—that was how Rodrigo had described it on the first night of the hike, and not this debauchery.

"These stupid *gringas* are going to believe that it is a real human sacrifice," Rodrigo had told the porters. "We'll take them up near the closed path by the ruins of Phuyu Pata Marca. The old route is overgrown and has vertiginous views of the Urubamba valley, which should make them jittery. But don't you worry—it will all be a pretend sacrifice. We're just going to scare those *gringas* into giving us their money in exchange for allowing them to live. You all trust me unquestionably, don't you?"

The cook had nodded along with the rest, but he'd suspected that Rodrigo spoke with a forked tongue, and that he was planning something truly heinous and reprehensible, quite probably a real *capacocha*.

That night, the cook had dared to ask a question. "Illapa, the *gringas* are the smartest women from the best universities. You yourself have told us that. How will they ever be fooled into giving us their money?"

Rodrigo had lifted the lid of the frying pan and struck the cook on his delicate humpback.

"You are not allowed to utter one more word on this hike," he shouted. "In fact, on the last night I'm going to cut you to pieces and feed you to the pumas that bear my former name: Guamán *Poma* de O'Rourke!"

"We will do as you command, our Inca," responded the porters, just in case Rodrigo needed help punishing the cook; none of them relished being food for the hungry pumas.

Now, as Violette shrieked obscenities, the cook stood immobile. He didn't know what he could do to stop the insanity uncoiling its tight anaconda body through this forsaken campsite. As a simple cook, he had confidence with a butcher knife, but he wasn't sure he could turn a utensil that chopped tasty turnips, yucca, and potatoes into a weapon of death.

By the time the cook settled on how he would attack Rodrigo, the second porter was raising his slight yet strong arm, preparing to strike Violette with the jagged rock. The porter aimed for Violette's head but at that precise moment Choque swung her too violently over the cliff's edge, and she and the rock wielding porter nosedived together, screaming, into a chasm of fire and brimstone.

CHAPTER NINETEEN

oyam lunged forward, her instincts telling her to try to rescue the despicable Violette, but Taki's tight grip held her back.

"Do not meddle in the decisions of the *apus*," Taki scolded her. "It is a fitting end. Violette's stinking soul rotted everything and everyone around her when she was alive. Let her decaying body fertilize the vines that will creep back up the side of the cliff looking for the energy of the sun."

"*¡Chuta!* Damn it, Taki. If we're not here to rescue the *gringas* and we're not here to punish Rodrigo, what is the purpose of risking our necks?" Koyam demanded. "If Rodrigo finds us, he will punish us the same way he got rid of Frenchy, that's for certain."

"The purpose I see will give meaning to our lives."

"Enough, Taki. Say exactly what you mean—now."

"I keep seeing something so reprehensible that I cannot believe it could take place."

Koyam was exhausted, at the end of her rope with Taki. "Tell me what it is and we'll decide what we can do about it. Just remember that Rodrigo, Choque, one porter, and the cook are still alive and angry. So we either make a move to release the women, and face Rodrigo's wrath, or we scatter down the path and let them all meet their destiny. Which is it?"

Taki remained silent and tiptoed over to her bundle cradled by the two boulders. At a distance she heard Rodrigo's long-winded rant about the power of Illapa; she listened to him crack his whip repeatedly near the terrorized women. Taki felt obliged to follow the time-tested steps since in doing so she would make sure that she pleased the *huacas* and her ancestors, and in return they would intervene in the calamity. She caressed the child-size bundle within the larger bundle and she rearranged its rainbow-colored mantle. She whispered incantations and delicately dusted off some fallen twigs and leaves the wind had kicked up as it whirled around the stone ruins and cliffs, howling its cries of dire warning.

Taki returned to Koyam, who was warming up her aged body by swinging her stone mace, Koyam's unique version of calisthenics.

"It's now or never," she told Taki. "What is holding you back? If you see me dead in your dream, so be it."

Taki's body shook. "¡*Achachay*! It is so cold. I cannot believe my icy vision, but it must be true as it has been repeating itself in my mind. It is not about fear for you or me, although I do not see what is going to happen to us. It's what I see happening to the child, the little golden girl, whose charming lilt brings a smile to everyone's face."

Koyam looked from behind the ruins and saw Rodrigo passionately kiss Gabby, who made no effort to push him away.

"Who knows what depraved games these people play?" Koyam said. "The little dark-haired woman is wrapping her arms around Rodrigo's neck as if nothing occurred a couple of minutes ago, as if witnessing two people fly over the edge of a cliff is an ordinary event."

"Perhaps she is trying to distract Rodrigo," Taki murmured. "In my dream, I see all three women marching up the hill taking turns carrying the golden child who is chattering and playing with the feathers in her hair. We must not intervene with Rodrigo's group until we see him leading the group to the top of the pass. Once we hear Choque whistle to the ancestors, then we move in quickly to rescue the child and the women. You will not act before it's time, right?"

"Easy-breezy," Koyam answered.

Rodrigo's screams startled everyone. He pushed away from Gabby's embrace, writhing and grabbing at his upper back. Choque ran to his boss and saw the blood running down between Rodrigo's shoulder blades.

"Do not move, Illapa," he said. "You have a piece of glass stuck in your back."

Without waiting for Choque to pull the shard from his back, Rodrigo spun around and whipped Gabby mercilessly. As the women cried out for Rodrigo to stop, and Choque cheered his boss on, urging him to strike her harder, no one noticed that a little girl with wavy golden hair had wandered out of one of the tents and stood crying in the middle of the camp.

She was no taller than thirty inches and her whimpering lips formed only one word, over and over.

"*Taita, taita,*" she sobbed politely. She rubbed her sleepy eyes with tiny bronze hands. Her angelic voice was almost inaudible, and since no one responded to her words, she began to cry louder. Only the cook had the wherewithal to approach the tiny child. He knelt down next to the little girl and spoke to her in Quechua.

"*Wawa*, child, please stop crying. Your *taita* is busy right now. Well, he is, uh—do not worry."

The cook picked her up and walked away from Rodrigo's frenzied whiplashing. The golden child rested her sticky, wet hands on the hump of his upper back. He had not felt any gentle hands on his deformity since his own sweet children had touched it as toddlers. With every year that he worked harder and harder—in small restaurants where he could hide in the back kitchens—to provide a living for his growing family, his own children became more and more ashamed of his increasing hump. Eventually, no one ever touched him with kindness, and as his hump grew, no one would hire him in the city anymore; the only job he could get was as a cook for a madman hiking guide.

Her ethereal face buried in the cook's neck, the golden child continued crying softly. Her tears dripped from her cheeks onto the rough, dry-skinned chest of the sentimental cook. He tried bouncing her and singing a soft lullaby his own children loved, but she continued to cry.

"¡*Taita, taita, achachay!*" She was a child of the highlands, accustomed to harsh weather, but all the screaming and whiplashing had woken her up, and she cried out that she was cold and wanted her father. "¡*Taita, taita, achachay!*"

She reached out for Rodrigo, and this gesture—her very presence—seemed as natural as the iridescent feather that had brushed Hilary's knee on the precipice, yet the golden child's shivering cries sent an unsettling wave of vibrations through the air. The wind accelerated its corkscrew direction, and Hilary mouthed a silent word of desperation: "Help!" This was always the case in the Andean highlands: a miniscule and innocent action could cause an avalanche of lasting and painful reactions.

One day in July 1911 a long-legged adventurer was crawling on all fours across a rickety Inca suspension bridge, just six inches at a time. He was petrified, but followed the lead of a small boy—a youngster who had cared for him, showed him how to climb the dense vegetation of the terrace walls of Machu Picchu, dodged the lance-headed vipers, and proudly revealed the royal mausoleum of his Inca ancestors hidden within a semicircular stone structure. This minute act of kindness by a child was returned a hundredfold with acts of greed and deception. Hiram Bingham emptied out every skeletal remain, potsherd, and artifact from Machu Picchu. He was so blinded by avarice and his need to make his mark among his fellow Yankee adventurers that he totally forgot the helpful hand of the little boy. Some say this little boy was the same child who tearfully carried the Yankee adventurers' equipment across the river rapids and into the mouth of the mighty Urubamba River — never to be seen again.

"I'm going to clobber Rodrigo right now," declared Koyam. "I have to take advantage of the fact that he is wounded and Choque is distracted, busy attending to the boss. Let me go squash two monsters now!"

"Not yet, Koyam!" Taki said. "You will not defeat three angry men. Would you ever step into a pit with raging mad pumas?"

Koyam looked at the positions of the three men in the camp and realized that she could not surprise-attack them, her usual tactic of revenge against evildoers. Not only would they tear her apart with their fangs and claws, but Taki might be compelled to try to defend her, and all would be lost. The surface wound that Gabby had inflicted did not warrant the beating she got at the hands of Rodrigo.

Choque had moved in closer to Rodrigo, trying to calm him down, and to remove the shard of glass from Rodrigo's back. He unrolled a bandage and attempted to wrap it around the wound.

Taki rubbed her eyes and focused on the cook who was rocking back and forth. "Koyam, my eyes are failing me. Why is the cooking swaying? Why isn't he trying to help Rodrigo?"

"¡*Ooyooyooy!*" Koyam exclaimed. "Your vision reflected the truth. He is holding a child with long golden hair! Where did she come from? Why haven't we seen her on the hike earlier on?"

"Because Rodrigo must have gone to pick her up from her mother when we passed the village of Wayllabamba. That must have been why I was so fearful on the first night of the hike." Taki grabbed Koyam's hands. "I finally understand my vision. Now will you follow all my instructions? This is our last and final chance to end Rodrigo's exploitation of these poor and lovesick country girls and forcefully spilling his seed all over the highlands. It is our last opportunity to prevent his madness towards the *gringas*."

✻

"Come my precious flower, my little K'antu," Rodrigo spoke with a perfect calmness after his raging storm against Gabby. He approached the golden child, who was still clinging to the cook. Rodrigo smiled from ear to ear.

"*Taita* was just kidding around with the nice lady," he said, handing the whip to his only remaining porter. Rodrigo bent down to whisper in the porter's ear. "Let's get started, up to the platform. You and Choque tie Mercy and Gabby together so they don't try to run away down the path. Don't worry about the giant. She will follow all my commands. She knows who her god is!"

"Yes, Illapa."

Choque was standing guard over the women who sat slumped and dejected on their stone benches. The porter shuffled up to Choque to give him Rodrigo's instructions. He mimicked Rodrigo's gestures, and repeated his final command: "Go tie the two women together, you dumb ass."

Choque did not find any humor in the tone of the command, or in the porter playing the big part of his boss. He grabbed the small man and dragged him near the wall ruins where Taki and Koyam were hiding. The women saw them coming and drew back even further, making sure they were out of sight. Choque threw the porter against the wall and stomped on his genitals.

"Don't you dare scream or I will end you," he threatened. "I've had to listen to your loud mouth ridiculing my manhood for too long. You are the last porter alive and I will make your life miserable until Rodrigo gets my member fixed. Then I am leaving this wretched place forever."

Choque walked away and left the porter writhing in silent pain. The little man bit his own hand to muffle the painful cries. Taki had already witnessed this scenario in her dream. She reached into the bundle that she had safely ensconced between the boulders, and took out the wrapped funerary bundle.

"Do you now hear the commands from our *mallqui*, our revered ancestor?" she said, peering into Koyam's eyes. "I have broken a solemn vow to never remove the *mallquis* from their hiding places in the *machayes*, the cave tombs, but this is the only way to combat Rodrigo. Come, let's go quickly!"

Taki held the mummified ancestor out and walked up to the porter still struggling to stand after his beating from Choque. She grasped the cord which was wrapped around the alpaca mantle of the mummy, and held it in front of her head and torso. The mantle and her own poncho blended into one long cloak, making it look as though the mummy were talking to the porter.

"Little brother," Taki whispered, her own face obscured by the desiccated face and skull of the *mallqui*. "You must do the right thing. You must not sacrifice the golden child or harm the foreigners."

To emphasize her command, she shook the *mallqui* like an Andean windstorm swaying a mossy tree and then backed away, leaving the porter dumbfounded.

Koyam followed Taki up the path as fast as a scurrying *viscacha*, all the while genuflecting to the *mallqui* out of equal parts fear and respect. When they reached a distant-enough ledge where they could still make out the details of activity at the camp, Koyam got up the nerve to speak.

"Can I look at our revered *mallqui* or will I go blind?" she asked Taki.

"I did not bring out the fiercest of the *mallquis*," Taki reassured her. "He inhabits the darkest of caves surrounded by bats that protect him, the bats that have frightened away all the intruders through the centuries. Who knows what he might have done to all of us if I had brought him along? But this gentle *mallqui* must have been a patient little girl. She will guide us with love and compassion. Come take a look at her."

Koyam did not dare raise her eyes to look at the *mallqui* until Taki lifted her chin.

"Dearest ancestor," Taki said, "please allow my loving sister who has protected me for seventy years to look at you and thank you for the guidance you have given us throughout our lives."

A gust of air revolved around them like a whirlwind, and in its motion Koyam's cloud of fear lifted. She felt like her old brazen and outspoken self—her young audacious self, someone she hadn't seen in decades.

"Hey there, grandma. Why didn't you protect me when my husband knocked my tooth out? Why didn't you prevent my great-granddaughter from rolling in bed with Rodrigo? Where is she now?" Koyam was nose-to-nose-cavity with the mummy and she punctuated her questions by knocking her forehead against the *mallqui's* skull. "I'm seventy years old and you expect me to beat the shit out of three men and protect three stupid *gringas*? You'd better tell Taki the whole truth about what I have to do right now—because I can't hear a damn word you're saying. ¡Chuta!"

Koyam stared down the mummy with impunity, daring her to strike her dead or dumb, but other than the gust of air that lifted her heavy poncho, her brother's old poncho, nothing else happened. The more Koyam stared at the mummy, the less she was afraid. She was looking at a *mallqui* with a bit of tight dried skin around its skull, a simple cadaver with a good set of chompers, and dark, hollow eye sockets. The rainbow pattern and colors of the *mallqui's* mantle were the design of one of Taki's famous *llicllas*, and the mummy's hair was plaited with a long alpaca cord, in the same fashion of the black alpaca thread woven into the now-famous ice-maiden mummy's pigtail. These were all interesting details, but they didn't provide a single survival clue to Koyam.

Koyam walked away, concentrating on the action taking place at the camp. She had always focused on the here and now, doing her best with the matters at hand, and through her example her descendants had progressed intellectually to the point that their logic led them to disregard their old-fashioned matriarch and her ancient beliefs.

"So be it," Koyam said, swiveling to point accusingly at the *mallqui*. "You didn't utter one word to me like I was always told you would do, and—"

"You have to listen with a pure heart," Taki told her. "Then and only then will our ancestors speak to us and give us good advice."

"I'll do what I have to do. So be it!"

Taki wrapped the *mallqui* back into her bundle and bent over to whisper to her.

"Yes, I heard all the words you blew in the wind circling Koyam. Yes, you are very clever to get her upset and angry. You brought her warrior blood to the surface. She will be able to fight the evil and spill its blood into the thirsty soil of our mountain range." Taki made kissing sounds in the air, the same way her ancestors had always done when they communicated with their *mallquis*.

Even after the Spanish thought they had burned or dismembered all the *mallquis* from the Inca Empire, grave diggers in every century thereafter found more and more funerary bundles in caves and the sides of cliffs. Whenever Taki heard about this sacrilege during her morning gossip session with the other street vendors at the Plaza de Armas, she rushed up to her hidden caves to check on her charges. No looting hands had ever touched her *mallquis* and on each occasion Taki filled the dank cave with loud air kisses of gratitude.

As recently as the 1990s, looters found mummies of the Chachapoya cloud people in the dry, cave-like niches around the Lake of the Condors in northern Peru. As looters are prone to do, they destroyed the cloth wrappings of the mummies in their lust for jewelry and valuables. Rumor had it that a few of the cloud-people mummies made a run for the border and managed to immigrate to the private collection of an American connoisseur who built them an ostentatious, climate-controlled mausoleum on his property, hoping to decorate it further with Inca antiquities that magically appeared on the art market with freshly printed "old" provenance records.

A few years later, in 2000 or 2001, more Inca mummies appeared on the scene. These *mallquis* were found 82 feet below the ground, this time in the upper walls of a limestone cave, their bodies wrapped tightly for eternity in a flexed sitting position. They were removed by the authorities for further study of their health, diet, medical practices, ancient diseases, and religious practices. But still looters and their foreign financiers keep skulking around the cloud forest in an endless search for mummies to line their pockets by fueling the ongoing fascination with mummies, and selling them on the black market for a hefty profit. Mummies satisfy a need to connect to the mysteries of our ancient ancestors. In their open screams and long-nailed claws, we witness their terror at death, and yet we believe that their preserved bodies still host the soul that can communicate blessings or curses to us, their still breathing descendants. In our proximity to their corpses, we feel a malicious satisfaction, as we squeeze our still plump and pulsating bodies.

Taki and Koyam always shooed away ingratiating looters and their foreign-money men anytime they saw them around town asking the whereabouts of past *mallqui* legends. The looters heard that Taki was able to communicate with the oracles of her ancestors and that was why her blessings contained truth and power. They directly approached Taki and offered her obscene amounts of money for her stories. Koyam would ask Taki: "Let me tell them a story from hell and take their money. I'm good at storytelling. I'll send them hiking on a maze of paths that will end with their plunge into the sides of the cliffs." Taki would not allow it, so Koyam would chase them out of the plaza by throwing well-aimed rocks at their legs.

But what modern-day descendants of the mighty Incas have forgotten about their mummified ancestors is that whether the skeletal remains were burned or dismembered by the Spaniards or destroyed by looters, their organic composition, their very essence, eventually fused and morphed into the nearest landmark of nature—a tree, a boulder, a mountain peak. And in their decomposition, the *mallquis* became the *huacas* their descendants venerate to the present day up in the Andes Mountains. The *mallquis* and the *huacas* are present to prevent the sinister appearance of someone who does not fear their taboos; someone whose abhorrent actions break every prohibition; someone who does not stand in awe of godly punishment. Even if that someone claims to be Illapa, the god of thunder.

CHAPTER TWENTY

hen Rodrigo saw the rays of sunshine reflect off his daughter's golden waves, he realized that he had to rush the procession.

"Dress K'antu, now," he instructed the cook. "We must begin the procession by sunrise."

"My Inca, I do not know about dressing little girls. Please do not make me do this," the cook begged Rodrigo. "Please allow me to ask the giant to help me."

"Fine, but get K'antu dressed in her full regalia and force her to drink a few sips of *chicha*."

"*Chicha*? Please don't ask me to give *chicha* to a child."

Rodrigo wanted to whip the cook, but his daughter had latched on to the hump on the cook's back and would not let go.

"Dress her or get yourself ready for a long jagged jump." Rodrigo smiled benignly at his daughter, and she mirrored the same dazzling smile. K'antu had her mother's glowing bronze skin, but her sparkling green eyes were a genetic throwback to an ancestor from the Emerald Isle.

The cook was mesmerized by the pure innocence of her eyes, the only respite from his otherwise bottomless despair at having aligned his pathetic life to that of a psychopath. The verdant sparkle of K'antu's eyes reminded the cook of the legendary ostrich-egg-sized emerald that the Incas hid from the rapacious Spaniards. They coveted the giant emerald egg and demanded that the conquered people bring them all their emeralds, their daughter emeralds, as a gift to the mother emerald, not realizing that the people revered the egg-shape as a symbol of the creator. Instead of thinking about the loftier significance of the egg emerald, the cook recalled the emerald's association with love and its protection of love. He was a simple man who had been beaten down because of his physical condition and bad luck, but cuddling the green-eyed golden girl, he remembered what pure love felt like, and was overwhelmed with the urge to protect the girl from the dangerous rages of her father.

The cook approached the giant. "Pilpintu, please help me dress the child. She will be joining our hike this morning."

K'antu looked up at Hilary and opened up her arms to be carried by her. When Hilary lifted her high, K'antu giggled and fluttered her hands. "Pilpintu, *Sumaj k'achitu!*" she said. "How beautiful!"

"Hilary, please release us!" Gabby and Mercy shouted, but Choque tightened the rope that connected to the nooses on each of their necks.

K'antu, seeing the women attached by a rope around their necks, looked startled. The cook instantly sensed her fear.

"Don't worry K'antu," he told her. "We don't want the nice ladies to fall down during our walk. We will keep them safe when we hold them by the rope."

K'antu giggled at Hilary, who in turn smiled back, revealing her broken teeth. Others may have gaped in disgust, but K'antu's delight in everything around her seemed contagious. She touched Hilary's cheek with her chubby hands. "*Sumaj k'achitu!*" she said again. "How beautiful!"

Gabby gingerly touched the welts on her cheek and wished the golden child would touch her, healing Gabby with her innocence before Rodrigo hurt her again or before Choque sadistically threw her off the cliff as he had done with Violette and the porter. Aside from the physical pain from Rodrigo's beating, Gabby felt a crushing sense of defeat because of the way she'd lived her adult life, because of the accumulation of misdeeds that had brought her to this moment of epiphany. When she stared at the distant sunrise, her squinty vision saw the round eye of *The Seven Deadly Sins and the Four Last Things*, a painting by Hieronymus Bosch that she so admired back in college. In the handheld mirror of her memory, Gabby witnessed all her acts of lust and pride. She saw the fetuses she'd aborted without remorse, and she saw a man about to kill a woman as a result of wrath. In the painting's pot of gold she saw her own body boiling while she held on tightly to her laptop in a last-ditch effort to monetize her blog. Gabby saw all her impetuous decisions, her entitled behavior, her disregard for the men she'd led astray with lies, things she had said and done simply because she was an Ivy League grad. Finally, she looked up at the clouds above the high Andes Mountains, and saw in them the Latin inscription in the Bosch painting: *Cave Cave Deus Videt*. "Beware, Beware, God Sees."

Mercy had not lost all hope: her mind was busy conjuring up many possible scenarios as to what would happen next in Rodrigo's insane plot. But any attempt to loosen the rope was met with a lashing of a nettle branch on her bare arms. She called out to Hilary, who was heading towards the child's tent as if everything were as normal as the sunrise rising along these mountain peaks.

"Please, Hilary, we have to save ourselves," Mercy cried, but Hilary strolled away, apparently oblivious. "Hilary, we have to save the little girl! He will harm her!"

Hilary stopped midstride, gazed back at Mercy with a totally blank look, and ducked into the tent.

The extent of Rodrigo's insanity soon became apparent to all but Choque and the golden child. Rodrigo emerged from the tent wearing a poncho woven with cheap silver metallic fibers, with none of the organic tones, or the art and subtlety, of a genuine Andean poncho. On his head he wore a silver diadem with an orange pompom in the center, his crude attempt to reproduce the royal *mascaipacha* crown of the Inca. His narcissism showed no limits as he pranced in front of his physical and emotional captives, demanding exaggerated praise and striking the porter on the head.

"Your awe of me is obvious, but don't just stand there, boy," he demanded. "Recite a poem about the power of my reign."

"I never went to school, Illapa. How would I know about poetry and such things?"

Rodrigo kicked the porter. "Don't be such a small-minded fool! For once think like a full-size man, and praise your god."

All the porter could see and hear was the talking skull of the *mallqui* that had appeared in front of him after Choque's beating. It had said to him: "You must do the right thing. You must not sacrifice the golden child or harm the foreigners." But the weak and defeated porter could not begin to think how to protect the child and the foreigners. The last of his strength had been used up beating the other porter, the one who had enough sense left in his broken spirit to escape down the treacherous path. The porter thought he would try the same tactic, though that would not help rescue the child or the *gringas*, but he couldn't come up with anything else. He had always been a sheep and never a puma; his destiny had been to follow and do as he was told.

Rodrigo swaggered in front of Gabby and Mercy.

"I know I have stunned you with my godly presence," he said, with a theatrical wink, "but you can thank me later when we reach our special sacrificial stone."

The chiseled facial features that had so captivated the women when they first saw Rodrigo, now seemed singularly distorted and repulsive.

"Don't even think about harming us any more than you already have," Mercy hissed, brandishing her dead cell phone. "My law partners just texted me and they know our exact location and are sending the rangers or *federales* or whatever they are called here."

"My whip, Choque!" Rodrigo demanded. "I have to break a stubborn filly."

Choque jogged over to the cook's supplies, where the porter had dropped the whip. In that instant, the porter saw a window of opportunity to behave heroically, to do the right thing, just as the *mallqui* had instructed him. He jerked free the women's leash that was attached to a boulder, and Mercy and Gabby were free. Mercy grabbed Gabby's hand and dragged the other woman up the path.

"Hilary run away!" Mercy shouted. "We've escaped!"

A stunned Rodrigo turned to run after the women, but the porter flung himself towards Rodrigo's feet and grabbed his right leg. Rodrigo dragged the porter for a few feet, trying to shake him off the way he'd shake off a small, annoying dog. When the little porter wouldn't release his grip, Rodrigo bent down, picked him up, and unceremoniously threw him off the cliff.

"Choque, I have gotten rid of the last vermin among us," he shouted. He dusted off his poncho and cracked his whip.

"Let's move on, we have an empire to create. We must follow our original plan."

"But Illapa, the two rich *gringas* have run up the path. I can't see them on the path anymore; they are fast runners—"

"Keep talking like a spineless wimp, and I'll never have your member fixed. The reason you don't see them is because they either fell down—in which case, good riddance—or they got tangled up and are stuck in the brush. Either way we don't need them, other than for your eventual enjoyment."

"What about the money they were going to give you—the money for your pyramid plan, the money for my rock-hard penis?" shouted Choque, outraged.

Rodrigo cracked the whip so that the tip almost touched Choque's arm. "You are bordering on insubordination, which will be punishable by death in my new empire. Tell you what, Choque, you get a head start and stop the *gringas* from escaping. I'll be the rear guard and proceed with the *capacocha* ceremony assisted by cook and the giant—and, of course, the tiny guest of honor." Rodrigo laughed thunderously at his own wicked plan.

Inside the tent, Hilary and the cook dressed K'antu with great care. They copied the image from a torn magazine page that Rodrigo had placed next to her clothing. The picture showed computer-generated images of what the young female victims of the ancient *capacocha* ritual wore the day they were sacrificed. Hilary had never dressed a wriggly child and she didn't bother reading the English captions; she was going with the flow and letting her deities decide her next step. The cook didn't know how to read, so together they peered at the images and, with meticulous care, layered hand-woven textiles on the happy girl. Both were totally oblivious to the fact that they were following a ritual: dressing a perfect child for her sacrifice.

First, they slipped on a pale yellow *acsu*, a dress patterned with plum and red. The skin on K'antu's body and face was flawless; not a freckle or minute birthmark marked her. Time seemed to stand still for the cook and Hilary: they could both see and feel, in their hearts, that they were in the presence of human perfection. In ancient days parents of such flawless children often offered their child as a sacrificial victim. This was a great honor for the parents and the child's community.

"Bring K'antu out now. We have to start our procession," Rodrigo shouted, and then started playing his pan flute.

Hilary wasn't quite sure how to wrap the *acsu* and fasten it with a belt, but the cook figured it out. Next they covered K'antu's shoulders with a *lliclla* of rainbow colors, like the ones that Taki wove. This *lliclla* was fastened with a silver *tupu* pin to which they attached tiny bells. Finally, they tried to attach a white feather headdress, but spunky K'antu took the headdress in her hands.

"Pilpintu, *Sumaj k'achitu!* How beautiful!" she giggled, and these words warmed the hearts of the cook and Hilary. Rodrigo stuck his head into the tent.

"Cook, let's get a move on. The giant will carry K'antu, and you lumber after them. I'll be right behind in case she decides to disobey my orders, like her other friends." Rodrigo glanced at the bruised giant holding K'antu and she gave him the thumbs up.

"You're a loyal subject, Pilpintu!" Rodrigo complimented her, but he did not notice her grimace at this insult.

✷

Tangled in the dense underbrush of vines and bamboo obscuring the untouched path, Gabby and Mercy edged along the side of a cliff, clinging on for their lives. Mercy, the former star athlete, figured out the steps she needed to take to extricate herself, but Gabby's rope had to be cut off, and they had no way to do that. They both had their feet on the path, and this meant they were stable, but they needed a third person to cut the rope ensnared in the haywire underbrush. Both women panted, heaving with exhaustion after sprinting up the mountain path, and from their futile efforts to loosen the rope.

Taki and Koyam had earlier scrambled from their perch near the sacrificial stone landing kept secret for centuries. Now Taki approached the women from farther up the path. She didn't want to scare them, so she tried speaking in her best street vendor English.

"No problem," she said. "I make you good price."

Mercy and Gabby remained motionless.

"If he comes any closer," Mercy whispered to Gabby, "lean into the side of the cliff and I'll try to kick him like in my old soccer days. Trust me, my dad taught me to kick like a man."

Koyam, standing just inches behind Taki, understood the word soccer.

"Goooaaalll!" she cried.

"Are you kidding me?" Mercy muttered. "These two old fools must be insane. Let me offer them my useless cell phone."

She tried to hand over her dead cell phone as a bribe, but both Koyam and Taki shook their heads. When Koyam handed Taki a knife, both Mercy and Gabby screamed.

"Please, old men, don't hurt us," Mercy begged in hesitant Spanish. "We are not your enemies. Please."

Taki put down the knife and showed Gabby the friendship bracelet around her wrist.

"I friend, yes? You buy at plaza," she said, trying to remind Gabby of their interaction in Cusco.

Koyam wasn't so patient. She removed her brother's old poncho and lifted his dirty shirt to show the women her sagging breasts.

"We women not men," she told them. "We hate Rodrigo. We kill him now. You come."

Gabby began crying uncontrollably. Here atop the peak of a godforsaken land, an ancient old woman, dressed as a filthy old man, had just flashed her decrepit breasts, and was now dangling off the cliff-edge hacking at the snaked rope trapping Gabby. The old woman was holding on with one hand to the bulging back bundle hanging from the other old woman's back. This was a moment of heroic and remarkable significance, Gabby knew, one which her old professors would have called the actions of a Greek hero: a true hero who, despite an Achilles' heel, will face peril and forge ahead with determination, ready to sacrifice herself for the common good. Gabby was overcome with admiration for the old woman's heroic efforts, and for the first time in many long hours felt the will to live surge through her body. In this moment of life or death, Gabby chose to live and to lead a heroic life. She cheered the old woman with the only word that made sense at that moment.

"Goooaaalll!" she blurted out, swallowing back her sobs.

Koyam burst out laughing at the *gringa's* gallows humor. "¡*Chuta!* Damn this rope and damn my arthritic hands, but if I die now, at least I'll go down laughing."

Once the tangled rope was cut, Taki and Koyam helped the younger women crawl up the path to the landing of the sacrificial stone. From this point they could see the zigzag path to another pass.

"Sun gate to Machu Picchu," said Koyam, pointing. "You go now."

Gabby was still shaking after her ordeal and could not stand up. Taki understood her predicament and put her hands on her head and blessed her.

"You change life," she told Gabby. "You do good now."

"Yes, yes, I will do good." Gabby smiled at Taki through her tears. "All I've thought about is the fact that we were all missing in Machu Picchu and no one would find us. But what we've been *missing* is the purpose of our lives. Don't you agree, Mercy?"

"We've all been self-absorbed for too long," Mercy said, her heart pounding with the exhilaration of being free. "When we undertook this trip, this quest, we did it with insincere goals, and thus far we've failed all our challenges. Now we have to rise to the final test and rescue Hilary."

The old Mercy would have stomped off without a backwards glance, but the Mercy who'd survived this ordeal knew she should ask the old women for their advice.

"We want to help our friend, Hilary," she said slowly, raising her arm to remind them that Hilary was the tall woman. "How can we free her from Rodrigo?"

"We ask ancestor," Taki said, and pulled the *mallqui* out of her bundle. Gabby screamed.

"I think they are insane," she told Mercy. "We've been rescued by lunatics—nice women, but they must be crazy. Who hikes with a skeleton?"

Taki kissed the air and gestured for Mercy to do the same.

"Is this hell or what?" Mercy frowned. "Does she want me to kiss the skeleton?"

"She said it was her ancestor," Gabby said. "So OK—I'll do it."

She kissed the top of the mummy's skull, and Koyam roared with laughter at her audacity.

"This little *gringa* has guts," Koyam told Taki. "Nobody would ever dare to kiss a *mallqui*—and live to talk about it."

She gave Gabby a fist pump, but there was no time for celebration—Rodrigo's tenor voice announced his imminent arrival. Taki hid the *mallqui,* while Koyam gestured at Gabby and Mercy to crouch behind some high outcroppings and surrounding shrubs.

"You stay," she hissed, and went to meet her enemy. *Mallqui* or no *mallqui,* she would rely on her own time-tested surprise attack.

Koyam had had enough with Taki's hesitations and excuses. One had to cut off the head of the snake, so in time the body would stop moving. She watched the procession approaching the sacrificial ledge, and determined that she had to wait until the giant holding the golden child arrived at the wide landing. This meant that Choque would also be standing next to them, since he was the leader. Once they were safely on the landing, she would take down Rodrigo and bounce straight back to destroy Choque. The cook and his humpback would probably hightail down the path; if not, Koyam would deal with him after decapitating the snake. Once Koyam had visualized her battle, she remained on guard like a puma prepared to pounce.

Taki crouched downhill from Koyam and she had the *mallqui* out of its bundle right next to her, just as it had instructed her. Choque passed her, marching up the hill and making a left turn towards the wide landing. The giant and the golden child also walked by, taking slow and careful steps. Behind them ambled the exhausted cook, and several yards farther behind strolled Rodrigo in his silver regalia, cracking his whip over the precipitous edge of the cliff. When Rodrigo's song reached its ear-splitting crescendo, he gazed up at the heavens for dramatic effect, indulging his megalomaniacal delusions. That was all the time Taki needed to make her kissing sounds at the cook, who glanced to his left and saw a *mallqui* staring down at him. The *mallqui* did not say anything other than generate a gravel-filled gust of air, but this was enough to terrify the poor hunchback.

"Move your hump, or I'll sacrifice you instead," Rodrigo threatened. But instead of moving forward, the cook made kissing noises back at the no longer visible *mallqui*. His final act, he decided, would be a brave one that would make his ancestors proud.

"Butterfly," shouted the cook. "Don't let go of K'antu. Rodrigo wants to sacrifice her!"

The cook turned around on the narrow path and charged for Rodrigo's legs. At the same time, with all her might, Koyam aimed her mace for Rodrigo's temple. Choque, hearing the ruckus, tried to knock Hilary down to the ground before rushing to Rodrigo's aid. But Hilary's trunk rooted itself in the soil of the sacrificial arena, and Choque's forceful punch did nothing more than make her sway. She never loosened her grip on K'antu.

Rodrigo's outsized ego could never have anticipated that a short, hunchbacked cook would be able to tackle such powerful legs, drawing on nothing but a residue of pride and love for a child. Rodrigo could never have dreamt that the ancient great-grandmother of an inconsequential girl he ravished years ago could harbor such a strong desire for revenge that she would willingly lie down on the edge of a mountain top and reach out to strike him with a lightning bolt to his temple.

This was the precise blow that Rodrigo had been planning to use on K'antu as it had been the most common way to extinguish the thousands of flawless children the Incas sacrificed to their gods. He had toyed around with the idea of strangulation, but even in his madness, he knew he did not have the courage to accomplish this. But a blow to the head from Illapa, the god of thunder and lightning, seemed ideally appropriate.

Choque arrived too late to save his beast-of-prey boss. He saw a flash of silver tumble and crash off the cliff, and in Rodrigo's demise he also saw all hope of ever regaining his manhood. For a few suspended seconds he thought he saw Illapa rise as a god and gain flight, but it was only Rodrigo's light-weight silver poncho lifting with a gust of air.

Soon after, Choque stood above the collapsed body of the cook, resting his foot on the cook's hump, reveling in the power of knowing he could dominate another being. This is what he had allowed Rodrigo to do to him: to lie to him, to step on his back, to crush his lusty dreams, and to take them to his grave.

From her ledge above, Koyam could see Choque standing on the path but she could not readily reach him to give him his final blow. She lay down and tried to strike him, but missed. Choque's years of fighting and drawing blood from his opponents had sharpened his bellicose skills. He tried to grab Koyam's arms and yank her free of the ledge, so he could hurl her over the side of the cliff.

On his first try, she struck his hand with her mace, but he recovered quickly and grabbed her forearm and began tugging her towards the abyss.

Taki pulled Koyam's legs back towards the landing, but real-ized that Choque's strength would win out. So she raised up her venerable *mallqui*, an ancestor she had promised to protect and maintain for future generations so that they might benefit from her wisdom. Her gentle *mallqui* had shown her what she must do, yet until this very moment Taki had been unable to do as the *mallqui* instructed.

Just as Choque pulled Koyam close the edge, Taki called out his name and made kissing sounds.

"Choque, you did not deserve the cruelty done to your body—"

"Shut your mouth, you old witch!" shouted Choque. "I'll tear you apart next."

Taki swung the funerary bundle of her *mallqui* by its strong cord and hit Choque squarely on the head. He tried to block the *mallqui* and regain his footing, but a well-placed kick from Mercy, the Ivy League-champion soccer player, sent him over the edge. As Choque fell backwards, he saw the mummy-bundle languidly gliding above him making kissing sounds of love and forgiveness for a man who had been violated as a child, and now deserved a painless death.

CHAPTER TWENTY-ONE

"K'antu, *wawa*, child," murmured the fallen cook. He turned his head slightly away from the roughness of the path, swallowing gravel and blood from the mortal stomp Rodrigo had administered.

Koyam, still full of rage, ran down the path and punched him with her powerful hands, but she wasn't able to roll him off the cliff. Taki begged her to stop.

"Koyam, control your rampage. It is over!"

"Please, uncle, I am dying," murmured the cook. "I must see that the golden child is alive. Please show her to me...."

"*Sunsu,* idiot, I'm a woman, and the child is fine. So die, or I'll finish you off!"

Taki hurried down the path to pull Koyam off the decimated cook's back.

"The child, I must see the child…"

Koyam tied the cook's calloused feet together, an unnecessary act as his breathing was painful and shallow, but she was exhausted and knew she could no longer face an adversary of any size. She listened to the cook's raspy pant, and walked away, resisting any compassion; she was a warrior, not a seer like Taki. She would let Taki take over and decide the cook's fate.

Taki crouched next to the tied feet of the cook. He lay head-down on the downhill slope of the Inca trail, and when Taki tried to look at his face, it was blocked from view by the hump of his back.

"The mountain *apus* know that you've endured much pain in your life," she said, taking a handful of coca leaves from her pouch and setting them on the back of his legs. "Your disease reduced your lung capacity, yet in your diligence you carried food and supplies up these peaks, even though that stole your breath one trek at a time."

Taki smoothed out the coca leaves and added her textile friendship bracelet to the makeshift *despacho*, the offering, she was conducting. Up on the ledge, Gabby and Mercy looked down, holding each other tightly in admiration of the kindness Taki showed the cook. Taki scrounged through the gravel path until she found a stone, a triangular brown stone resembling their almighty mountain peaks, and added it to the *despacho*.

"You've made many mistakes in your life," she continued, "but you've also walked in disabling back pain—and our mountain spirits felt your agony."

Taki blew gently onto the coca leaves and motioned at Koyam, standing further up the path. Koyam rifled through her bundle and brought additional offerings for Taki to use.

"The *wawa*, please…" muttered the cook.

"Your eyes are facing our mountain peaks and you will not be able to turn your head to see her...but she is safe." Taki patted his paralyzed hand.

Koyam handed her a hotel-size mini bottle of whiskey that she must have gotten from a tourist. Taki opened the bottle and sprinkled the whiskey on the *despacho*, and then Koyam took her mini bottle back.

"*Wawa*...."

"Let me have the giant bring her closer so you can hear her voice," Taki agreed. "Koyam, please have the giant and K'antu come closer."

Koyam did not want to leave the cook as she suspected that he might be feigning his demise, but she knew she had to obey Taki. The giant, however, refused to budge, even when Koyam shoved her. Her stabilizing roots grew deeper and deeper into the granite mountain. She was holding K'antu, letting her unpluck the white feather headband she was supposed to wear at her sacrifice—the sacred ritual her insane father had orchestrated with an unsuspecting entourage of brilliant but dysfunctional women, and with the coerced reinforcement of broken men.

As Illapa, Rodrigo had planned on releasing a bolt of lightning against K'antu's unconscious head. He had selected the perfect inaccessible cave where he would leave K'antu in her regal funerary bundle. The precious objects he would bury beside her and the elegant woven mantle in which he would wrap her were all stored in his backpack, now lying on the ground near the cook's head.

All Rodrigo's demented plans had drained from his head when he fell—and landed on a jagged rock in the most impassible bend of an overgrown corner of the cloud forest. This sepulcher was a death-trap of a place where no one would ever find his broken skeletal remains. All the crazed ideas that had cluttered his cranium for years spilled onto the stone and the soil, and provided the lifeblood demanded by the mountain *apu*. His native soil would absorb his twisted soul and appropriately channel its remaining energy into the lianas whose nature was equally twisted, but whose strength provides the vertical support to teeter-tottering trees. In life Rodrigo had used debilitated men with impunity, but as part of the cloud forest lianas, his remains would spend an eternity supporting the wobbly and the weak.

K'antu giggled as the breeze wafted feather after feather above Mercy and Gabby's heads and down the path, past the dying cook's prone form.

"I hear the *wawa's* giggles!" the cook cried with joy.

"I am making this offering on your behalf so that you are well received for doing the right thing," Taki said. "You sacrificed yourself so K'antu could live." Taki added strands of her hair to the coca leaves and blew again. She needed more items for her offering and gestured for Mercy and Gabby to give her strands of their hair to add to the *despacho*.

K'antu's laughter filled the air.

"*¡Sumaj k'achitu! Sumaj k'achitu!*" she cried out. "How beautiful!"

The white feathers that K'antu released floated away like a hollow hail storm, and landed softly, one by one, on the craggy mountain peak rising from the cook's back. Engulfed by the glacier of feathers, soothed by the musical trill of K'antu's voice, the cook closed his eyes and saw his own children surrounding him, blowing kisses. He wanted to tell them he loved them, but all he could manage was a rapid succession of short, sharp, hard sounds from deep in his throat. Taki blew once again on the coca leaves and left the cook cradled by the downy softness of the feathers, and of the soil of his ancestors as he rattled his last breaths.

✳

For the remainder of the hike the women followed Taki's silent lead and concentrated on nothing else other than the simple experience of alternating steps—right and left, right and left—as they rejoiced in feeling the pressure of their heels and toes against the ground. Periodically, Taki would take in deep, loud breaths, and each woman down the line would also inhale deeply, all the way back to Koyam on the tail end, who belched strong whiskey. During this meditative walk, their focus was on the many sensations jogging their memory, awakening them to the fact that they were alive, and that they had survived the chaotic madness of Rodrigo.

Hilary's zombie-like steps gradually elongated as she imitated the athletic smoothness of Mercy's gait. Bearing the weight of the sleeping golden child tired Hilary, and when Gabby offered to take over, Hilary silently agreed. An hour later Mercy took hold of K'antu and carried her lovingly. Throughout the hike, the three continued taking turns carrying the golden child, just as the *mallqui* said they would.

Taki's zigzagging path eventually intersected with the official Inca Trail. The junction was not far from the Inca terraces and stone ruins at Wiñay Wayna, a location named after the forever-young orchid always in bloom. At many times of the year this location would have been crowded with tourists, but today Taki and Koyam were able to lead the women to a desolate, enclosed stone storage area. Here they camped overnight, sharing blankets and bites of food that Choque had horded in his pack.

At sunrise Taki and Koyam rounded up the *gringas* and K'antu, and they headed for Intipunku, the famous Sun Gate entrance to Machu Picchu. Koyam and Taki were wearing their rainbow-colored shawls instead of their brothers' old ponchos.

They wanted to look their best in honor of their survival against the evil spirits inside Rodrigo.

Together they climbed fourteen steep steps past the old watchtower, and then stood in awe of the majesty and incomparable vastness of Machu Picchu, allowing the view to take their breath away.

Hilary moaned and cleared her throat as if she had been holding back a flashflood of words until the moment she could make a significant pronouncement. But she stalled, standing with her mouth wide open. Before leaving California to fly to Peru, she had memorized stanza after stanza of Pablo Neruda's poem about Machu Picchu. She had read Jules Verne's *La Jangada* and Conan Doyle's *The Lost World,* and had planned on acting on Sir Arthur's famous quote: "The more you knew about South America the more you would understand that anything was possible—anything." Before the hike on the Inca trail, Hilary had wanted to prove her renaissance intellectual gifts to the other Ivy League hikers, but amid the splendor of the panoramic peaks and the verdant terraces leading to the stone citadel, Hilary felt her insignificance. She thought of her colossal, small-minded, dilettante self, and it made her hang her head in shame.

Together the women formed a grungy, motley group of hikers. Their dimness was balanced by K'antu's golden glow and sparkling emerald eyes, reflecting the Andean rule of duality: darkness and light, love and hate, life and death. Because the floods of days ago had forced the authorities to close the citadel, there were no other hikers anywhere in sight. The lone guard looked astounded when he recognized Taki.

"What has happened to you, *mamita?*" he asked. "Why are you here? How did you get here? They rescued all the hikers."

Koyam pushed past him.

"Nephew, you ask too many questions. Do you want Taki to bless you or not? We're going in past your flimflam turnstile, so don't act like you own the place. Is your name Pachacuti Inca Yupanqui?" She waved at the expanse of Machu Picchu with both arms. "Is all of this your sacred estate? You must be as delusional as Hiram Bingham!"

Taki stepped forward and cupped his head. "You are a guardian angel of this holy place," she said. "Won't you allow us some time to give our thanks to the Huayna Picchu *apus* for bringing us safely to your care?"

Koyam hustled her charges through the turnstile like a know-it-all tour guide, and headed for the Sacred Plaza. Taki followed, leaving the guard shaking his head in disbelief. Since January 29th the authorities had been counting heads of the registered hikers as they made their way through the Sun Gate. The torrential storm had taken the life of an Argentine woman hiker and her guide on the Inca Trail, and thousands of tourists were helicoptered out of Aguas Calientes, where the overfed river had belched bodies downstream days later.

Koyam knew exactly what she had to do, and she led her hikers to the energetic vibrations of the *intihuatana* stone, the vast religious sundial known as the Hitching Post of the Sun that is aligned with the sacred peaks. She studied the reactions of the women as they touched the stone and absorbed the sacred energy, its massive potency. Mercy and Gabby politely acknowledged the importance of the stone to Koyam and Taki, but did not feel any magnetic pull or electrical push. They had regressed to their familiar twenty-first-century spiritual shields and had repelled any insights attained in the new dimension of Machu Picchu.

But Hilary handed K'antu to Gabby and knelt in front of the stone. She wrapped her arms around its curved base, resting her head on her stone pillow. With her condor-sized wing span she hugged the stone in a homecoming embrace, and let her tears fall, free of self-reproach. She was an engineer by training,

"She led the hikers to the energetic vibrations
of the *intihuatana* stone."

a woman who understood the science behind the physical world, but as she knelt there with an open mind and a mute heart, the stone energized her and reaffirmed her new life among these sacred, luminescent peaks.

A cellular ring interrupted the significant silence, and Mercy patted all her pockets to find her phone.

"We must be out of cell-hell now," Mercy announced, holding up her phone to read the text. "She's incorrigible! You won't believe what Tiffany texted me! 'Hey bitches. If you're reading this text then you're alive and I need your help. I hooked up with one of the hunky Swiss guys on the Inca trail and he brought me to the middle of the Amazing River instead of tangoing in Bunos Aires. But whatever.'"

"She lands on her feet every time," chuckled Gabby. "I want her to video-blog for my new site. It's going to target the fearless and adventurous woman."

Mercy raised her eyebrow quizzically. "What was that you said earlier about your personal *transformation* after our brush with death?"

"I was delirious. Read the rest of her text."

"That Tiffany is one in a million. She texted: 'Sucks balls here! Cheap shit left without paying my share of the hotel bill. I need lawyer pronto. Can u pay my bill by credit card? This town is called Man-ass. I swear.'"

"I bet she means Manaus," said Gabby. "That's in the heart of the Amazon River in Brazil. What are you going to do?"

"*We* are going to do the right thing. We will bail her out *once* for the ordeal that we've all gone through.'"

"I'm in. What about you, Hilary?"

Hilary was busy repeating words after her tiny Quechua language teacher. Whenever K'antu shouted *"¡Sumaj k'achitu!"* Hilary agreed wholeheartedly that everything was beautiful.

Through the innocent emerald eyes of this golden child, Hilary understood the profound meaning of life overwhelming her senses.

She tuned out her friends, the women with whom she had shared the most transformative journey thus far in her life, disappointed by their instant return to their old ways. Had they learned nothing from the perilous trek that had brought them to this peaceful Eden, this El Dorado, this Wonder of the World? Shouldn't they extract grains of truth to change their ways? The wounds of their ordeal still oozed from Hilary's face and from her soul, but Gabby and Mercy had put on their professional, Ivy-League armor, the guise that best suited them back home, as though nothing had happened to them on the Inca Trail, as though a madman hadn't shoved his hand in their chests and pulled their hearts out.

Taki's body shook with a final vision: it showed her that Mercy and Gaby needed one final soul-awaking experience, one last fateful event that would demonstrate once and for all that life is tethered to death by a singular thread from a woven shawl, the weak strand from a *mallqui's* hair, the silk spun by the tarantulas of the Andes. Taki whistled faintly and grabbed both women by the hands, just to absorb some of their youthful energy.

Koyam rested with her back against the Hitching Post of the Sun savoring the last swig of her bottle of whiskey. "*Ooyooyooy*," she said. "Wait until we get back to the plaza and tell everyone all the mouthwatering details of this crazy hike."

Taki cupped her hands over Koyam's head. "You bring joy and laughter to everyone around you. Protect the giant and the golden child," she said.

She linked arms with Mercy and Gabby and led them in the direction of the steep, steep steps of Huayna Picchu. The *gringas* were walking to humor her, and because they felt grateful to Taki. They had no idea of Taki's own reasons.

By taking the delicate *mallqui* out of her centuries-old cave, Taki had broken a celestial rule: to protect the ancient *mallquis* at all costs, for they were oracles whose enigmatic prophecies would make perfect sense one day. The young women next to her might or might not broadcast to the world what they witnessed, and her sweet *mallqui* might appear on Gabby's website and go viral, her image becoming as ubiquitous as a Spanish-speaking Chihuahua.

Taki walked slowly to the zenith and the abyss of her life. She had destroyed the precious *mallqui* in exchange for the life of the *gringas*, yet she sensed they had already re-embraced the folly of their old ways; their lack of discernment that had brought them to these peaks in the first place. These two women had not absorbed the ancient messages emanating from the granite truths of her ancestors. This meant that Taki could no longer stall the inevitable. She had to meet her fate.

She led the way, leaning into the side of the cliff, whistling non-stop and pointing to the views she wanted Mercy and Gabby to etch in their brains. But both women had lost their interest in climbing to the top of this peak.

"Let's just humor her and take some photos from halfway up," Gabby muttered. "I'm through with hiking."

"I need to get back to the business center in the hotel and answer my emails," Mercy said. "I don't even want to take any photos. I'm done."

"Wait, wait, wait!" Gabby held up a hand. "I think that Taki's some kind of fortune teller. Let me ask her something important."

"Make it quick."

Gabby tapped Taki's arm. "Taki, can you make some predictions about the future?"

Taki had been thinking those exact thoughts about her world, the world of Machu Picchu, and her beloved Andean peaks.

"*Ooy*, yes child," she said. "After 100 years, Mr. Bingham's people will return most of our ancestors' remains by 2012, but other scientists will come back to take samples of our bloodlines, our DNA, and we must not allow them…they may never return our souls."

Mercy rolled her eyes. "Right—great predictions."

Gabby blushed with embarrassment at her own credulity. She had hoped the old crone would tell her if she was going to finally monetize her website. Gabby planned on telling the world about the ancestral mummy, about its fetal position and its mouth open in an infinite scream. She had seen the mummy in mortal action, and after she sensationalized its curses and enigmatic predictions, Gabby would become the online oracle screaming truths to generation X, Y, and Z—for a fee.

"Why the hell not," Gabby said, half to herself. "Everyone else profited by copying *The Scream* by Edvard Munch. And he based it on the Peruvian mummy he saw at the 1889 Exposition Universelle in Paris."

"You're delirious again—let's get the hell out of here," said Mercy, frowning at her. She tapped Taki on the shoulder. "Thank you for showing us this view, but we're spent. We really have to go back."

They didn't care if the old woman understood them or not. Mercy and Gabby turned around and walked back down the steps with a confidence and vigor they attributed to their fitness program back home, not to the energy freely transmitted to them by the *intihuatana* of Machu Picchu, the only Inca sundial to survive the wrath of the Spaniards. Gabby and Mercy jogged down the slippery hand-hewn steps constructed by those who revered and feared this sacred site, certain that Taki was right behind them since her chipper whistling followed them with love and care.

Hilary carefully tossed K'antu up in the air. They were both laughing. K'antu pointed to the birds and taught Hilary that word; she saw a cloud and also said its Quechua word. Then she pointed to the double rainbow across Huayna Picchu.

"*K'uychi!* Rainbow!" she shouted.

Koyam gazed up toward the peak and noticed that Gabby and Mercy were walking back without Taki. Koyam whistled to Taki, emulating the raucous trills and warbles of the Andean Cock-of-the-Rock, but no reply came, not even a faint chirp. Koyam tried again in her most obnoxious bird cry, the one that Taki always responded to, just to shut her up—but again there was no reply. Hilary stepped up to Koyam's side and instinctively held the shivering old vendor in a warm, protective hug.

K'antu pointed to the sky.

"*¡Sumaj k'achitu! Sumaj k'achitu!*" she shouted. And indeed, the sight in the heavens was breathtakingly beautiful. Taki's kaleidoscopic shawl soared under the radiant rainbow sky, escorted by thousands of butterflies on its ascent to the snowy peaks beyond Machu Picchu.

AFTERWORD

I'm forever grateful for the quirky folk traditions of my South American heritage. While growing up in California, other kids feared their parents when they misbehaved; I on the other hand feared the wrath of the soul of my deceased maternal ancestor, who had been dead for decades. If I didn't earn an A on a spelling test, *"la alma de mamacita,"* my great-great-great-grandmother's soul, would sit close to me—very close—while I studied for next week's test. If I stayed out past the 10 p.m. curfew on a Saturday night, *la alma de mamacita* would be my chaperone the following Saturday. Her soul could also be very helpful in an emergency: if I got a flat tire on a dark road, *la alma de mamacita* was right next to me with the crowbar ready to hit a potential evildoer.

What I didn't know then was that the anthropological background behind the claim that my ancestor's soul was always near me was, in all probability, rooted in the practice of mummification in the Andes Mountains. Despite the fact that my family is of Spanish descent, the venerable Inca ways have permeated deep into the culture and psyche of all Andean people. Now, after decades of travel and study, I realize that what my family alluded to as the ever-present soul of our ancestor—*la alma de mamacita*—referred to the ancient Andean belief in the continuity between the living and the dead. The dead had influence on the actions of the living, and together the living and the dead had an obligation to take care of one another. My late beloved mother used to describe, in poetically morbid detail, the disinterment of her own mother and the gathering of the bones (ossilegium)—after decomposition—for placement in an ossuary, and of the responsibility of the living relatives for polishing the bones of the exhumed relative for their final resting place. "Polishing of the bones" was a macabre fusion between the Roman Catholic practice of exhumation for re-burial in a mausoleum or family crypt in a cathedral, and the Andean belief of paying respect to the ancestral mummies. It was this family event, the gathering of the bones, which provided me with the framework—*the skeleton*—of this novel.

The practice of mummification was prevalent in the Andes region even prior to the Inca civilization. Unlike other cultures that preserve mummies for a future resurrection, the Andean mummies continued to reside among the living and were revered for their advice and protection. Mummies of Inca rulers continued to own estates and were presented with food, drink, and entertainment daily. Marvelous textiles were woven for them, and gold and emerald jewelry adorned their desiccated bodies. Mummies were consulted on all matters, and their skeletal remains were a source of pride and respect. In fact today, it is said that many families in the remote highlands still display the skull of a relative in their home shrines. Because mummies continue to be uncovered by looters and researchers throughout the Andean landscape, the fascination and controversy with Andean mummies continues to the present day.

One such cry of controversy has been the 100-year-old diplomatic and legal battle between Peru and the American institutions responsible for the removal of archaeological and human remains by Hiram Bingham and his expedition of 1911. This is in some ways a very simple case of disrespect, recrimination, and betrayal by all parties. It became a *cause célèbre* that was finally resolved when Peru received a shipment of its artifacts in 2011—a century after they were spirited away. Please consult the bibliography for further reading on this matter.

Another cry of "biopiracy" was heard in May 2011, when the indigenous Q'eros people of the Andes Mountains resisted DNA sampling as part of National Geographic's Genographic Project. They claimed that the organizers failed to obtain informed consent. "We don't need research called genetics to know who we are," their spokesperson said. "We are Incas, always have been and always will be."

The historical figures and events mentioned in this novel are as follows:

The female mummy known as the Ice Maiden of Ampato, who indeed made the rounds of museums internationally in the late 1990's, as did the Peruvian mummy exhibited in the 1889 Exposition Universelle in Paris. The latter is said to have been the model for the iconic painting *The Scream* by Edvard Munch.

Much of my research was done from both Spanish and translated sources of Inca-Spanish, and Spanish chroniclers: Felipe Guamán Poma de Ayala, whose 1615 book and line drawings, *The First New Chronicle and Good Government*, illustrates the injustices of Spanish rule on the indigenous people of Peru. His prized original chronicle remains in the hands of the Royal Danish Library in Copenhagen. I also relied on the commentaries by Inca Garcilaso de la Vega in his 1609 book, *Royal Commentaries of the Incas*. Both chroniclers were descendants of Inca and Spanish nobility. For religion and customs of the Incas, I sourced the work of Father Bernabé Cobo in his 1653 book, *Inca Religion and Custom*. All three chroniclers appear as minor characters in this novel. Please refer to the bibliography for further reading.

The Inca ruler Atahualpa was held captive by the Spanish in 1532 while his subjects filled two rooms full of gold and silver as a ransom payment. Alas, Atahualpa was still garroted. Manco Inca and Tupac Amaru were Inca leaders, Tupac Amaru II was a rebel leader, and Francisco Pizarro was a Spanish conquistador.

Infant trafficking is a heinous crime that persists worldwide. The perils of online dating can be researched through reliable sources.

My most recent visit to Machu Picchu was in June of 2011 where I spent days verifying many of the facts on the trails, peaks, flora and fauna of the region. I accomplished a personal goal to climb to the very top of the famously precipitous Huayna Picchu peak, where I stood transfixed by the luminescent view of the citadel of Machu Picchu. Above all, I loved spending time with the indigenous historians and guides on the long and memorable hikes on the Inca Trail, and I enjoyed interacting with the street vendors in Cusco, whose irreverent humor had me in stitches for days.

A year after my visit to Machu Picchu, and well after the completion of this manuscript, an amazing example of life imitating art occurred: a new Inca Trail was discovered on July 2012. One that parallels the traditional trail; one that has been hidden by the cloud forest for 500 years; one real-life trail eerily similar to the *fictional trail* in this novel.

This novel has also done quite a bit of international traveling along with my editor, Paula Morris, who took the manuscript from Scotland to London to Hong Kong and Auckland—and back. Thank you for your insight and wise editing. I am also very grateful for the time and talent of my editor, Catherine Knepper.

My most sincere appreciation goes out to the International Latino Book Awards organization for selecting my novel *Traces of Bliss* as the First Place Popular Fiction novel in 2012. They also honored my novel *Gathering the Indigo Maidens* as a finalist in four categories. Additionally, I would like to thank the international Las Comadres organization and their leader Nora Comstock, Ph.D., who in partnership with the Association of American Publishers, selected *Traces of Bliss* as a 2012 National Latino Book Club pick.

Many thanks to the local authors' lecture program at Vroman's Bookstore in Pasadena, California, and to their staff: Jennifer Ramos and Connie Kalter, for their welcoming spirit when all of my friends from the Los Angeles area filled the store beyond capacity. Had it not been for my book signing at Vroman's, I would never have reconnected with my childhood friend Lucinda. *Un fuerte abrazo* to all of my friends for their love and encouragement, and for the memories of our international travel escapades.

I was honored to have the support of Nordstrom South Coast Plaza, Donna Karan Collection, and L'Occitane en Provence who hosted the book launch and signings of my novels. A heartfelt thanks to Jayani Clark, Robert Evans, Michelle Guzzetta, Amy Martin, and Brigitte Aguilar. As always, I am so fortunate for the long-term friendship and backing of the members of my book club: the Wild Swans of South Orange County. Thank you all!

✸

Although my attempts to use *"la alma de mamacita"* as a tool of behavior modification on my two Harvard-educated sons failed miserably, they have been great sports, along with my darling husband Peter, in roaming the dark and dank catacombs of the *Catacombe dei Cappuccini* in Palermo, Italy, the Mummy Museum in Guanajuato, Mexico, and countless graveyards in Spain, Italy, and Mexico looking for long-lost dead relatives—which we have found. Perhaps I shouldn't have taken my sons along to such macabre locales at a young age, but they seem well-adjusted and find humor in their mother's cultural eccentricities. However, my sons drew the line at asking for a blessing from *la alma de mamacita*—but she's always done so without them knowing it.

September 29, 2012
Monarch Beach, California

Glossary

KEY:

C - Corsican

F - French

L - Latin

Q - Quechua

S - Spanish

Achachay – (Q): It is so cold.

Acsu – (Q): A long wrap-around dress.

Alalau – (Q): How frightening.

Acllahuasi – (Q): The house of the chosen women.

Apachita – (Q): Huacas in the mountain passes that were marked by piles of stones, each stone contributed by passing travelers.

Amigo – (S): Friend.

Amor – (S): Love.

Apu – (Q): A traditional nature spirit or local mountain god.

Ararihua – (Q): Guardian animal spirits.

Capacocha – (Q): Human sacrifice ritual.

Cave Cave Deus Videt – (L): Beware Beware God Sees.

Chicha – (Q): A fermented beverage made from maize.

Chasquis – (Q): Runner-messanger.

Chumpi – (Q): Hand-woven belt.

Chuta – (Q): Damn it.

Chullo – (Q): Earflapped knitted hat.

Cío chi un tomba ingrassa – (C): What doesn't kill you makes you stronger.

Cumpi – (Q): The finest quality Inca cloth.

Consensus gentium – (L): Arguing that an idea is true on the basis that the majority of people believe it.

Corazón – (S): Heart or sweetheart.

Cucarachas – (S): Cockroaches.

Despacho – (S): An offering to the mountain gods.

Don – (S): Honorific for sir.

Espérame en el cielo corazón – (S): Wait for me in heaven, sweetheart.

Federales – (S): A slang Spanish term for Mexican federal police.

Gringas – (S): Used as a disparaging term for a foreign woman in Latin America, especially an American or European woman.

Huacas – (Q): Animistic spirits embodied in mummies, stones, or mountain peaks. Sacred places or archaeological ruins.

Huaraca – (Q): Sling.

Huayruru – (Q): Seeds of the *Ormosia coccinea* tree used in Andean rituals.

Ignoratio elenchi – (L): Fallacy of irrelevant conclusion.

Intihuatana – (Q): A sacred stone sometimes referred to as: the Hitching Post of the Sun.

Illapa – (Q): The Inca thunder god was believed to control the weather.

Jetés – (F): A leap in ballet in which one leg is extended forward and the other backward.

La bendicíon – (S): The blessing.

Lliclla – (Q): Shawl or mantle.

K'uychi – (Q): Rainbow.

Machayes – (Q): Sacred caves.

Mallqui – (Q): An ancestral mummy.

Mamacona – (Q): An honored matron in charge of the convent of the Brides of the Sun.

Mamacocha – (Q): Mother Sea or ocean.

Mamita – (S): Little mother.

Mascaipacha – (Q): A red fringe worn by the Inca emperor on his forehead that was the symbol of his title.

Misayoq – (Q): Andean spiritual specialist.

Ooyooyooy – (Q)The author's phonetic spelling of the exclamatory words, "Oh, my gosh."

Pachamama – (Q): Earth Mother.

Pago – (S): An offering.

Piccha – (Q): The presence of the spirit of the deceased for five days after death.

Pongo-camayoqs – (Q): Eunuchs.

Pilpintu – (Q): Butterfly.

Puruc raya – (Q): An annual ceremony held in memory of deceased ancestors.

Pute – (F): Prostitute.

Pièce de résistance – (F): Showpiece.

Salaud – (F): Bastard.

Salud – (S): To health. Cheers.

Saucisson – (F): Sausage.

Silencio – (S): Silence.

Soroche – (S): Altitude sickness.

Sumaj k'achitu – (Q): How beautiful.

Sunsu – (Q): Idiot.

Taita – (Q): Father, dad.

Tawantinsuyo (Q): The name used by the Incas for their empire, literally meaning "the land of the four quarters."

Tocto – (Q): The white feathers of this bird were used ceremonially.

Tambos – (Q): A lodging facility on the Inca highways.

Tu quoque – (L): Fallacy of "you also." Presenting evidence that a person's actions are not consistent with that for which she is arguing.

Tumi – (Q): A sacrificial ceremonial knife.

Tupu – (Q): A metal pin used for fastening textiles.

Tu te souviens de moi, n'est-ce pas? Je suis revenue pour te faire souffrir. Tu me comprends? – (F): You remember me, don't you. I've come back to make you suffer. You understand me?

Vite – (F): Quickly.

Wawa – (Q): Child.

Viscacha – (S): Andean rodent related to the chinchilla.

Zampoña – (S): Andean panpipe.

MISSING IN MACHU PICCHU

About This Guide

We hope that these discussion questions will
enhance your reading group's exploration of
Cecilia Velástegui's novel, **Missing in Machu
Picchu.** They are intended to stimulate discussion, offer new viewpoints, and enrich your
enjoyment of the book.

Questions for Discussion

1. The volatile weather conditions create an atmospheric backdrop to the events in the novel. In what ways does the weather foreshadow the events both at the beginning and the end of the story?

2. Taki and Koyam are lifelong friends with a strong, close relationship, yet they seem to bicker constantly. What are the events and life experiences that bind them?

3. Taki and Koyam want to maintain a close bond with their descendants, yet they often feel rebuffed by the younger generation. Discuss the ways that the elderly women try to stay connected with their descendants.

4. The novel addresses many levels of gossip and subversive alternative narratives, from the buzz among the denizens of the Plaza to exploration of the secrets and rumors surrounding the history of Hiram Bingham to the lies told on online dating sites. Is gossip an inescapable fact of life? Can it have positive as well as dangerous consequences?

5. In the novel, the (fictional) online dating sites are skewered for allowing—or even encouraging—participants to misrepresent themselves. What are your thoughts on the ethics of online dating sites? Is it inevitable that users will make exaggerated claims about their personal appearance, achievements, and qualities? If so, how could these misrepresentations affect a romantic relationship?

6. Why do you think that Hilary, Gabby and Mercy are so disappointed with the results of their online dating experiences?

7. Why is the notion of destroying an effigy of their online dating partners so appealing to the female hikers? What do they hope to achieve?

8. By infiltrating Gabby's Ivy League-alumnae blog, Sandra ingratiates her way into a free trip to Peru. In what ways can the anonymity of the Internet facilitate opportunists like Sandra?

9. What are the stereotypes of tourists that arrive by the droves in Cusco and Machu Picchu? Why does Taki show compassion towards them? Why does Koyam disapprove?

10. Many of the historical characters mentioned in the novel rebelled against the domination of the Spanish during Peru's colonial era. Why do you think that the inhabitants of Machu Picchu and its surroundings did not protest Hiram Bingham's excavations at the Inca citadel in 1912 1915?

11. When the novel reveals the unofficial version of Hiram Bingham's exploration of Machu Picchu, what is suggested of his attitude towards the inhabitants, and to the valuable artifacts taken by his expedition?

12. Why does Taki play down her shamanistic/clairvoyant gifts? Would she be so humble if she didn't have Koyam around to keep her down-to-earth?

13. Does Rodrigo's early childhood in any way explain his eventual narcissistic and megalomaniacal disorders?

14. What is symbolic about Taki's colorful *llicllas*-shawls?

15. Does the character of the Corsican swami represent total, premeditated evil? In what ways are his actions different from the cruelty of Rodrigo? In what ways is his approach to revenge different from that of Violette?

16. Choque and the porters are defeated men who put faith in the promises of the volatile Rodrigo. Why do they remain loyal to Rodrigo for so long?

17. In what ways might a return to the authentic Inca ways be beneficial for the indigenous people of the Andes?

18. Why were three highly educated and attractive women so easily seduced by a charlatan like Rodrigo?

19. The novel highlights the contrasts between modern technology and the traditional ways of the Andes. When the torrential rains and floods destroy all communications on the Inca Trail, what are the consequences for the group of hikers? How is their way of thinking and reliance on technology an anachronism in this context?

20. How are all the women on the hike untrue to themselves and to others? How did their insincerity affect their relationships, and the trek itself?

21. Taki gives blessings that are particular to the person in question. What was meant by her blessing to the Corsican swami: "You must accept the fate you've earned?" How could this blessing also apply to the other characters?

22. Many of the characters have pent-up anger and the desire for vengeance. Do any of them get satisfaction by seeking revenge?

23. In what ways does Tiffany represent the modern, self-absorbed, shallow individual? Is her behavior rewarded? Does she ever change her ways?

24. Although Taki tries to keep up with modern technology and trends, she is ultimately bound to the traditions of the Andean highlands. Do you feel some of her beliefs or her way of looking at the world have value in contemporary life?

25. What emotional or spiritual void do some 21st-century tourists hope to fill by visiting a site like Machu Picchu?

26. Taki finally resolves to ask the counsel and assistance of her ancestor mummy. How does the mummy give Taki and Koyam confidence in their fight against Rodrigo?

27. In what ways does the ancestral mummy represent the genuine heartfelt notion of doing what is right?

28. How does the mummy oracle communicate with Taki? Could it be argued that it was Taki's own consciousness—her intuition—that helps her to do the right thing?

29. The ancestral mummy in this novel was revered by Taki. Do you think it's possible to connect with the past in this way? What do you feel about the contention that "a preserved body is a host to the soul?"

30. The charges of infant trafficking against Rodrigo were dropped at the inquest. However, the novel cites several documented incidences of infant trafficking. What do you think are the causes of this heinous illegal activity? What can be done to stop it?

31. Do the women finally realize that cyberspace only offered them illusive romance? Will any of them continue looking for love through online dating sites?

32. How can an 'adventure' vacation in a foreign country offer solutions to problems faced back home? Is it possible for brief trips to be transformative experiences?

Bibliography

Ayala de, Felipe Guamán Poma. Trans. Roland Hamilton. *The First New Chronicle and Good Government: On the History of the World and the Incas up to 1615.* Austin: University of Texas Press, 2009.

Ayala de, Felipe Guamán Poma. Trans. David Frye. *The First New Chronicle and Good Government.* Cambridge: Hackett Publishing Company, 2006.

Bauer, Brian S., and Charles Stanish. *Ritual and Pilgrimage in the Ancient Andes: The Islands Of the Sun and the Moon.* Austin: University of Texas Press, 2001.

Benson, Elizabeth P., and Anita G. Cook. *Ritual Sacrifice in Ancient Peru.* Austin: University of Texas Press, 2001.

Besom, Thomas. *Of Summits and Sacrifice: an Ethnohistoric Study of Inka Religious Practices.* Austin: University of Texas Press, 2009.

Betanzos, Juan de. Trans. Roland Hamilton and Dana Buchanan. *Narrative of the Incas.* Austin: University of Texas Press, 1996.

Bingham, Hiram. *Lost City of the Incas.* London: Phoenix House, 1952.

Bingham, Alfred M. *Explorer of Machu Picchu: Portrait of Hiram Bingham.* Greenwich: Triune Books, 2000.

Buell, Janet. *Ice Maiden of the Andes.* New York: Twenty-First Century Books, 1997.

Burger, Richard L. and Lucy C. Salazar. *Machu Picchu: Unveiling the Mystery of the Incas.* New York: Yale University Press, 2004.

Cieza de León, Pedro. *Segunda Parte de la Cronica del Peru*. Madrid: Imprenta de Manuel Gines Hernandez, 1880.

Cieza de León, Pedro. Trans. Alexandra Parma Cook and Noble David Cook. *The Discovery and Conquest of Peru: Chronicles of the New World Encounter*. Durham: Duke University Press, 1998.

Cieza de León, Pedro. *Cronica del Peru: Que Trata del Señorio de los Incas Yupanquis y de Sus Grandes Hechos y Gobernación*. Madrid: Manuel Ginés Hernandez, 1880.

Cobo, Bernabé. Trans. Roland Hamilton. *History of the Inca Empire*. Austin: University of Texas Press, 1979.

Cobo, Bernabé. Trans. Roland Hamilton. *Inca Religion and Customs*. Austin: University of Texas Press, 1990.

Cortés, Christoval María. *Atahualpa. Tragedia Premiada por la Villa de Madrid*. Madrid: Don Antonio de Sancha, 1784.

Davies, Lucy, and Mo Fini. *Arts and Crafts of South America*. San Francisco: Chronicle Books, 1995.

Garcilaso de la Vega, El Inca. *Comentarios Reales, que Tratan, de le Origen de los Incas, Reies [sic.], wue fueros del Peru, de su Idolatria, Leies [sic.], y Govierno*, Madrid: Oficina Real de Nicolas Rodríguez Franco, 1722.

Heaney, Christopher. *Cradle of Gold: The Story of Hiram Bingham, a Real-Life Indiana Jones, and the Search for Machu Picchu*. New York: Palgrave Macmillan, 2010.

Heckman, Andrea M., *Woven Stories: Andean Textiles and Rituals*. Albuquerque: University of New Mexico Press, 2003.

Kaufmann-Doig. Trans. Eulogio Guzman. *Ancestors of the Incas: The Lost Civilizations of Peru*. Memphis: Wonders, 1998.

Keatinge, Richard W. *Peruvian Prehistory*. Cambridge: Cambridge University Press, 1988.

Kolata, Alan L. *Valley of the Spirits: A Journey into the Lost Realm of the Aymara.* New York: John Wiley & Sons, Inc., 1996.

Kolata, Alan L. *The Tiwanaku: Portrait of an Andean Civilization.* Cambridge: Blackwell, 1993.

MacCormack, Sabine. *Religion in the Andes: Vision and Imagination in Early Colonial Peru.* Princeton: Princeton University Press, 1991.

Meisch, Lynn A. *Andean Entrepreneurs: Otavalo Merchants: Musicians in the Global Arena.* Austin: University of Texas Press, 2003.

Milligan, Max. *Realm of the Incas.* New York: Universe Publishing.

Neruda, Pablo. *The Heights of Machu Picchu.* New York: Farrar, Straus and Giroux, 1966.

Rostworowski, Maria. Trans. Harry B. Iceland. *History of the Inca Realm.* Cambridge: Cambridge University Press, 1999.

Roza, Greg. *Incan Mythology and Other Myths of the Andes.* New York: Rosen Central, 2008.

Reinhard, Johan. *The Ice Maiden.* Washington D.C.: National Geographic, 2005.

Reinhard, Johan, and Maria Constanza Ceruti. *Inca Rituals and Sacred Mountains: A Study of the World's Highest Archaeological Sites.* Los Angeles, Cotsen Institute of Archaeology at UCLA, 2010.

Salomon, Frank, and George L. Urioste Trans. *The Huarochiri Manuscript.* Austin: University of Texas Press, 1991.

Samanez, David J. *Origen Cusqueno de la Lengua Quechua.* Cusco: Municipalidad de Qosqo, 1994.

Sarmiento, Pedro. *History of the Incas.* New York: Dover Publications, 1999.

Silverblatt, Irene. *Moon, Sun, and Witches: Gender Ideologies and Class in Inca and Colonial Peru.* Princeton: Princeton University Press, 1987.

Spalding, Karen. Huarochiri: An Andean Society Under Inca and Spanish Rule. Stanford, Stanford University Press, 1984.

Sullivan, William. *The Secret of the Incas: Myth, Astronomy, and the War Against Time.*New York: Crown Publishing Inc., 1996.

Stone-Miller, Rebecca. *To Weave for the Sun: Ancient Andean Textiles in the Museum of Fine Arts, Boston.* Boston: Thames and Hudson, 1992.

Turkle, Sherry. *Alone Together: Why We Expect More from Technology and Less From Each Other.* New York: Basic Books, 2011.

Urton, Gary. *Signs of the Inka Khipu: Binary Coding in the Andean Knotted String Records.* Austin: University of Texas Press, 2003.

Urton, Gary, Ed. *Animal Myths and Metaphors in South America.* Salt Lake City: University of Utah Press, 1985.

Urton, Gary. *The History of a Myth: Pacariqtambo and the Origin of the Inkas.* Austin: University of Texas Press, 1990.

Urton, Gary. *Inca Myths.* Austin: University of Texas Press, 1999.

Valderrama, Ricardo F. and Carmen Escalante Gutierrez, Ed. Trans. Paul H. Gelles and Gabriela Martinez Escobar. *Andean Lives.* Austin: University of Texas Press, 1996.

Vega de, Garcilaso. *Royal Commentaries of the Incas and General History of Peru.* Trans. Harold V. Livermore. Cambridge: Hackett Publishing Company, Inc., 2006.

Von Hagen, Adriana, and Craig Morris. *The Cities of the Ancient Andes.* New York: Thames and Hudson Inc., 1998.

Whitty, Monica, and Adrian Carr. *Cyberspace Romance: The Psychology of Online Relationships.* New York: Palgrave Macmillan, 2006.

Image Credits

1. Title Page and Section Headings
   Machu Picchu wall and view of Huayna Picchu.
   iStockphoto

2. Title Page, Section Headings, Spine
   View of the 500-year-old mummy of a young Inca girl recently
   found near the summit of Nevado Ampato in Peru.
   Stephen Alvarez, Photographer
   National Geographic Stock

3. Hiram Bingham
   An informal portrait of Hiram Bingham taken by Elwood Erdis at
   camp in Machu Picchu circa 1912.
   National Geographic Stock
   Page 32

4. Atahualpa
   The Inca King Atahualpa being taken prisoner by the Spaniards
   in Cajamarca, 1617, engraving from American History by
   Theodore de Bry, Peru 17th Century.
   Getty Images
   Page 52

5. Inca Mummy
   A Chachapoyan (pre-Incan) mummy at the cultural museum in
   Chachapoyas, Peru.
   Gordon Wiltsie, Photographer
   National Geographic Stock
   Page 81

6. Excavating Machu Picchu
   Lieutenant Sotomayor and men excavate the ground of the Chief
   Temple circa 1912.
   Hiram Bingham, Photographer
   National Geographic Stock
   Page 126

7. A young Inca boy.
    A young local stands in the finest doorway at Machu Picchu circa 1912.
    Hiram Bingham, Photographer
    National Geographic Stock
    Page 145

8. Guamán Poma de Ayala (Inca chronicler circa 1600)
    Llama offering to the huacas.
    Getty Images
    Page 205

9. Ice Maiden
    View of the 500-year-old mummy of a young Inca girl recently found near the summit of Nevado Ampato in Peru.
    Stephen Alvarez, Photographer
    National Geographic Stock
    Page 254

10. Inca mummy
    An archaeologist unwraps the mummy of a sacrificed Inca child.
    Maria Stenzel, Photographer
    National Geographic Stock
    Page 262

11. Guamán Poma de Ayala (Inca chronicler circa 1600)
    Carrying the Ancestral Mummy
    The Royal Library   The National Library of Denmark
    Page 182

12. Inca Intihuatana
    View of an Intihuatana stone, or Inca sun dial circa 1912.
    H.L. Tucker, photographer.
    National Geographic Stock
    Page 316

13. iStockpboto pages 31, 51, 253

ABOUT THE AUTHOR

Cecilia Velástegui is the International Latino Book Award winning author of the psychological thrillers with historical intrigue: **Traces of Bliss** and **Gathering the Indigo Maidens**. She was also selected on the 2012 Las Comadres and Friends National Latino Book Club in partnership with the Association of American Publishers.

Velástegui was born high up in the Andes Mountains in Quito, Ecuador, where she spent her childhood. Although she now lives at sea level in Monarch Beach, California, she still has two friendly pet alpacas. Velástegui was raised in California and France, and has traveled extensively in over 50 countries. She received her graduate degree from the University of Southern California, and speaks four languages. She serves on the board of directors of several cultural and educational institutions.

Velástegui donates a portion of the proceeds of her novels to fight human trafficking, the underlying theme of her novels.

View book video at www.CeciliaVelastegui.com